Wishing on a Star

Mandy Baggot

embla
books

First published in Great Britain in 2022 by

embla books

Bonnier Books UK Limited
4th Floor, Victoria House, Bloomsbury Square, London, WC1B 4DA
Owned by Bonnier Books
Sveavägen 56, Stockholm, Sweden

A CIP catalogue record for this book is available from the British Library.

eBook ISBN: 9781471411939
Print ISBN: 9781471412905

This book is typeset using Atomik ePublisher

Embla Books is an imprint of Bonnier Books UK
www.bonnierbooks.co.uk

For my wonderful nan who I miss so much.
Kathleen Faircloth, née Jones
22 February 1929–17 March 2022

Cincinnati, Ohio, USA

November

'Sam, can you hear me, man?'

'Give him some space. Sam, buddy, it's Tim. Can you hear me?'

'Is his helmet split? I think his helmet is split! Does that mean his head is split?'

Sam Jackman was smiling on the inside, but he wasn't sure the parts in charge were sending that message to his mouth. His teammate Chad was panicking like he was Sam's mother. But this *did* feel weird. This felt . . . well, it hurt. *A lot.* One second he had been sprinting, heading to the touchline, powering towards victory for his NFL team, the Cincinnati Bisons, and the next he had impacted something. Or rather *someone*. Flying through the air, the thousands of people in the bleachers, the floodlights, the cheerleaders, all morphing into rays of bright rainbow light before he crashed down to the turf-covered earth. Headfirst. Seeing stars.

'Is he breathing?' Sam heard Tim ask.

'You don't *know* if he's breathing?!' Chad with more panic.

'Where are the medics?'

'Sam! Wake up, man! Open your eyes!' Chad's volume was hurting him now.

Suddenly, he felt exhausted. The kind of tired you feel when you've been kept awake by sirens all night long, the sort of exhausted that takes over, folds itself around you and smothers. Sam was already lying down so now all he had to do was keep his eyes closed and give in . . .

'Sam! Sam! Don't you sleep on the job!'

'Sam!'

One

Richmond, London, UK

'Pull, Ruthie!'

'I *am* pulling!'

'Well, pull like we're trying to get Mark Ruffalo into the house instead of a very spiky hulk of a Christmas tree. Ow!'

Anna Heath let go of the branches of the fir as its needles poked through the wool of her gloves like sharp pins. The tree was far too big to easily get through the front door of their terraced house in Richmond and it was going to be far too wide not to obstruct the TV and the fireplace if they ever managed to get it over the doorstep and into the living room. But, the second Ruthie had set eyes on this one, towering amid the selection being sold outside their favourite coffee shop in the early December air, Anna had known what was coming next. *This is the one, Mum. This is Malcolm.*

Ruthie had been in this world for thirteen years and still Anna hadn't been able to teach her that sometimes you had to compromise. The problem was, Ruthie fell in love a hundred times a day and, if it was achievable and wasn't going to bankrupt them, Anna never had the heart to say no. *Mum, they do three kinds of hot chocolate here now – we should try them all. Aww, Mum, look at that cute fluffy donkey toy – his name is Larry and you know we can't leave him behind now he has a name.* It wasn't that Ruthie was spoilt. It was that Ruthie was on the autism spectrum. And Anna was still trying to get her head around the diagnosis, which had come only two years ago.

'Malcolm is sorry.' Ruthie's voice came from somewhere ten boughs ahead.

'Malcolm might have to lose a few limbs if he's going to stay,' Anna answered, whipping off her gloves and observing the redness of her hands.

'We can't dismember him! He's *family*.'

Anna couldn't see Ruthie past the thick foliage of 'Malcolm', but she could imagine her expression. Her bright blue eyes would be flitting from side to side the way they always did as she struggled to focus, the dark curls of hair bouncing around, not being tamed by her winter hat as she fettered the fronds, making sure there was no doubt this tree was coming in. She was so intelligent. Always top of her class.

The autism assessment service called it 'high functioning'. But in everyday life, doing the simple things simply, Ruthie struggled and, as her mum, Anna wanted nothing more than to kiss it all better. Except you couldn't kiss away an integral part of your child. A diagnosis of ASD might not have been what Anna and Ed had expected but there it was, three letters that altered futures, wrapped around a bright, extraordinary child who was all the definitions of special.

'OK,' Anna said, puffing out a breath. 'I'm ready to push again, but you tell me if you want me to stop.' She pulled her own hat down over her brunette bob and hoped her jeans wouldn't slip down and expose her arse to the traffic. She really did need to get a new belt.

'OK,' Ruthie called in answer.

'Sure, Ruthie? Because I'm really going to go for it this time,' Anna told her. 'I'm talking . . . the strength of Thor and Thor's hammer and hopefully the precision of Hawkeye.'

'Mum, I know you're strong. But you're not a superhero.'

'You're crushing my dreams now,' Anna answered. 'OK, after three. One, two, three!'

As she pushed with everything she had, the tree shot through the front door and then there ensued a blood-curdling scream that could have been recorded and used for an episode of *American Horror Story*.

'Malcolm! No! Malcolm's on top of me! Malcolm's on top of me!'

When Ruthie yelled, it really could summon Lucifer from the fiery pits of hell and now all Anna could think was that she *really* hoped Ruthie wasn't properly injured. And then, after that, she was already thinking about damage limitation.

She literally threw herself into the tree, brushing branches away from her face, side-stepping the trunk as she fought her way over the threshold. For the briefest of seconds her eyes went to the framed photo of her Nanny Gwen on the sideboard. Would she be up there in heaven looking down and laughing at this scenario or would she be wondering why Anna hadn't 'got a man in'? As independent as Nanny Gwen had been, as self-sufficient as she had made Anna, there had always been that old-fashioned attitude that some jobs weren't meant for certain genders. But times had changed, and as a single mum, the buck and the Malcolms of this world were her responsibility.

'Ruthie, are you OK?' Anna asked, finally getting where she needed to be.

'Malcolm's hurting me!' Ruthie screamed even louder – if that was possible.

'It's OK,' Anna said, grabbing the tree by the outer limbs and trying to twist it away from Ruthie who was only partially visible, flailing like an Elf on the Shelf caught in the roller of the hoover. She had to get this tree shifted and fast!

'Malcolm, stop!'

It was either sacrifice the unit in the hallway (which housed that photo of Nanny Gwen, Anna's favourite lamp with a bright red glass shade that had belonged to Nanny Gwen, and the telephone) or it was Ruthie continuing to panic and a concerned citizen on the street calling the police . . .

Anna pushed the tree over to the left and forged towards her daughter as the bang of the phone handset crashing to the floorboards was rapidly followed by the sound of smashing glass. Lamp or picture of Nanny Gwen, she couldn't tell.

'You're OK,' Anna said as Ruthie attempted to get to her feet without touching anything – no mean feat when you were prostrate on your back. 'Shall I . . . grab your arm and help?'

'Don't touch my hands!' Ruthie barked as she body rolled and then planted her elbows to the wooden floor, hands extended away from anything that might make contact. 'And don't look at me.'

Anna bit her lip and diverted her gaze to her hallway full of bush and shards of glass from the red lamp – the next danger she had to manage. All she wanted to do was make Ruthie's life easier but sometimes there was really nothing she could do except be there to pick up the pieces. Often literally.

'Can I have a shower now?' Ruthie asked, once she was back on her feet. She had pine needles all over her jumper, and she was looking very uncomfortable about having been on the floor, arms held out like a scarecrow.

'Yes,' Anna said. 'Of course. I'll go up and get your towels out for you. Just, don't move because there's some broken glass, OK?'

'OK.'

As Anna headed to the stairs she looked to the Christmas tree, scattering itself all over the wood floor, the telephone, the smashed lampshade, the Christmas cards she had written but not yet sent, all completing a picture of utter destruction. Nanny Gwen observed, unmoved. Happy, happy holidays. And they had only just begun.

Two

Dr Monroe's Office, Cincinnati, Ohio, USA

The coffee here was always good. Which was weird for a hospital. Sam Jackman nursed the paper cup of dark liquid in his hands and enjoyed the warmth as he waited for the doctor to arrive for their appointment. It was freezing outside and set to only warm up long enough for it to think about snowing.

Sam hadn't ever been a fan of the cold, but he was used to it. Growing up, heating had been almost a luxury, turned on only when the outside temperature got below zero. His mom and dad would never have called themselves 'poor'. *We are blessed with a roof over our heads, food in our bellies and God's love.* But, by most people's standards, that's exactly what they had been.

Theirs had been a second-hand life. Second-hand books for school, fifth- or sixth-hand car, and handmade clothes he was verbally ripped apart for by his peers. But his little sister, Tionne, had felt it much worse. How could she do what her friends were doing – mainly emulating P!nk and shopping at the mall – when she was constantly dressed like she harvested sugarcane in her spare time. Not anymore. Now he could provide. And her Insta feed was testament to it. Having once been ridiculed for her fashion, today Tionne was an influencer and Sam couldn't be prouder of her.

He rested the cup in one hand and pulled at the collar of

his wool coat. It was designer, had cost him over a thousand dollars and he knew he could never tell his parents he had spent that much money on one item of clothing. And, he had to admit, he had hesitated before he made the purchase, eyes flitting over to the sales rack, wondering if nylon could be the new wool if it meant making a saving . . . You could take the boy out of Winton Hills but apparently you couldn't take Winton Hills out of the boy. Having money was still new to him. But he needed to get used to it, because if he thought his wealth from being in the Cincinnati Bisons squad was something, then life was about to get real lit when he joined the top football team in the whole country – the Dallas Diggers. The deal was almost done and it was set to make him the highest earning player in history – or so the story went. He left the nuts and bolts of deals to his manager, Frankie, but he knew this move would mean that he, Tionne and his parents would not only never have to go short again, but they could now afford luxury. Unless this appointment was something other than the all-clear from the tests he'd had done. Maybe it wasn't the sign-off he was expecting. Maybe that concussion a couple of weeks ago had been something else? He had been off colour for four or five days, headaches and nausea like you'd expect, but this time Advil hadn't really touched it. And his best friend at the Bisons, Chad, had checked in at least twice a day. Plus, if Sam hadn't answered his phone, Chad had sent food via DoorDash just to check it got delivered.

Sam glanced around the walls of Dr Monroe's office for a second. Amid the posters about cholesterol and diabetes there were framed certificates, strings of tinsel Sellotaped around them. These accolades were the mark of a professional who had studied hard, worked tirelessly to pass exams and now had the experience to work out what was wrong with the human body. Sam always envied that kind of success because it had a firm foundation. People paid *him* money because he could run fast with a ball and take getting thrown to the ground. And the truth was, he was going to earn a whole heap more with this next deal than a doctor who cured the sick and saved lives. And the thought of his good fortune wasn't sitting quite right . . .

The door of the office opened, letting in a few lines of Christmas carols coming from the speaker on the reception desk Sam had passed on his way here, along with a blast of even cooler air. Perhaps this coat had been an investment after all. And here was Dr Monroe, three pens in the top pocket of his jacket, a bow tie with candy canes printed on it around his neck, an ever-creased brow. Perhaps the doctor regretted those long hours of study at college and those accolades. Maybe he even wished he had decided to toss a ball for a living . . .

'Sam,' Dr Monroe said, stretching out a hand as Sam got to his feet to greet him. Then he withdrew his offering and paused. 'Are we shaking these days? Or fist-bumping?'

Sam offered his fist. 'I could teach you the Bisons' hand jive if you wanna give that a go.'

'Let's shake,' Dr Monroe said, offering his hand again.

Sam took it and then, after the formalities, Dr Monroe flopped down into his executive chair like it was something from a kid's soft play area. The doctor closed his eyes and went completely silent.

'Are you OK?' Sam asked him. Perhaps no one ever asked the guy who was meant to have all the answers about health how *he* was travelling.

'Just . . . never like delivering bad news,' the doctor said.

The doctor opened his eyes then and looked directly at Sam like the sentence was somehow connected to him. *Bad news?* No, this was the all-clear, the final sign-off for his medical assessments . . .

'And still,' Dr Monroe continued, 'it's the very worst part of my job.'

'O-K,' Sam said, his throat feeling a little dry now. 'You're talking about the patient before me now, right?'

'So,' Dr Monroe said, sitting forward and beginning to collate papers, at the same time as pulling a file from his stacked tray. 'I'm only going to deal in facts until your agent gets here. Is she going to be long?'

And the doctor hadn't answered Sam's question.

'I . . .' Sam was thrown. He'd told Frankie not to come today. Dr Monroe's secretary had asked him to include her, but Frankie was working hard on the final touches to his deal and, with Christmas coming at the end of the month, he knew how busy things were for her. Not related to festive activities because Frankie could give Ebenezer Scrooge a run for his money in the not-wanting-to-take-a-break stakes, but because *everyone else* stopped working and she needed to make sure contracts were signed, sealed and paid for before offices closed their doors. And in Sam's mind this had been labelled a check-in rather than a check-up . . .

'Frankie can't be here today,' Sam said. 'She has other commitments.'

'Oh,' Dr Monroe said. 'Oh, I see.' He fingered the file in his hands. Was this file relating to Sam? Wasn't everything digital these days? Suddenly he didn't want this file in Dr Monroe's hands to be opened. There was something wrong. He could feel it in the air now and the once cosy ambience of this room with all the tinsel-laced certificates was turning claustrophobic. He had to pre-empt. Take the play to the other team.

'Dr Monroe, whatever you're worried about,' Sam said, sitting up a little straighter, 'you can hit me with it.' He nodded. 'Is it the concussion? I know I came down hard, the helmet was testament to that. Do I have a blood clot or something? Because if you need to take me in or give me some drugs or something, then you know I trust you to do the right thing. And I can deal.'

The doctor put the file down and pulled at one of the drawers of his desk. A bottle of good whisky landed on the surface, then two red solo cups followed. This was worse than a blood clot. Sam swallowed. What could be worse than a blood clot?

The whisky was poured and a red cup offered across the table to him. Why was the doc giving him alcohol before lunchtime when one of the posters on the wall was a picture of a damaged liver? Sam put his coffee cup down and accepted it anyway. Dr Monroe was already putting the beaker to his lips. Sam didn't know what to say now, it felt like he was up in the air again, the crowd letting out a collective gasp, as he flew towards that concussion.

Dr Monroe put his cup down and picked up the file again. 'Sam, you know the Dallas Diggers wanted all manner of testing before your transfer was finalised.'

'Yeah,' Sam answered. 'I started to wonder if they were gonna leave me with any blood at all.' He frowned. 'I passed the fitness tests though, right?' He didn't know why he was asking that question. He *knew* how fit he was. He'd always looked after himself by eating the right stuff and keeping exercise a priority. Fitness was everything to him. He'd built his whole life around it since high school, working hard, gaining that scholarship and then getting through college, only one goal on his mind – the NFL.

'This isn't about the fitness tests,' Dr Monroe told him. 'Of course you passed those. As cleanly as anyone I've ever had under my care.'

But even though the doctor had said that, Sam didn't feel any more comfortable with this situation. It *had* to be something to do with his fall in the game. But it had been two weeks. The headaches and nausea were long gone. What showed up that long after the fact?

'The Dallas Diggers wanted no stone left unturned. And it's pretty standard now when there's this much investment at stake.'

One hundred million dollars. That was the three-year deal. And it still felt like fantasy currency, like he couldn't imagine what that would look like all laid out in one-dollar bills.

'Understandable,' Sam said, nodding. 'So, what test didn't I pass? Because whatever it is, a bit of cutting back or study or whatever I need to do, I'm good for it.'

Dr Monroe dropped his eyes to that plastic cup, looking like he wished it was half full again. The dude didn't look good and the coffee in Sam's gut felt like it was curdling. Something wasn't just wrong. It was *really* wrong.

'Sam,' Dr Monroe began, his tone on the softer edge of professional. 'There's no easy way to say this so I'm just going to come out and say it. OK?'

Sam held his breath.

'It was the genetic testing that threw us a red flag,' Dr Monroe continued. 'Sam . . . I'm afraid, you carry a positive gene for Huntington's disease.'

Three

Richmond, London, UK

'Christ! Anna, I know you said the Christmas tree was in your hallway but shit!'

'Pavinder would freak if this happened in our house. He literally cries like a baby if there is a hair on the kitchen tiles. His mother was way too hygienic. It has ruined my life.'

Anna smiled as she let her friends Lisa and Neeta into her home, Malcolm still residing where she had left him, branches stretching across the full width of the hall with only a tiny gap to reach the door to the lounge and the rest of the house.

'Thanks for coming,' Anna said, leading the way past the fir and into her cosy living room. In the time it had taken for Ruthie to have a shower, Anna had lit the wood burner and some festive-scented candles and, after trying to light the cork, she had picked up the right implement and opened up a bottle of red wine.

'We only came because you said there'd be wine,' Lisa said, plucking a glass from Anna's shelf and holding it out to her.

'*I* only came because one of Pavinder's colleagues was going to drop around a Christmas card. Who drops around a Christmas card to someone who does not celebrate Christmas? Plus, that is what the Post Office is for,' Neeta said shaking her mane of long dark hair, big circular earrings wobbling from side to side.

Anna filled Lisa's glass and took another off the shelf for

Neeta. Here they were, responding to her call for help with the Christmas tree, her two best friends who both lived a few miles away in the same direction on the very edge of Richmond. Anna remembered the day they had all met so incredibly vividly. It was just over thirteen years ago when Ruthie was three weeks old. The midwife had stopped calling at the house and it was Anna's responsibility to take her baby daughter to the clinic every week to be weighed.

What no one had told her was the mother and baby weighing session at the clinic was akin to sitting in a circle naked while everyone else in the room silently judged you on every nuance of your body. And stripping down your baby to be weighed, when you had heartily wrapped her up against every element the British weather could throw at you, was incredibly difficult. Anna smiled now as she remembered how Ruthie's little leg had somehow become tangled in the sleeve of her babygro and, as she sweated with the stress and group scrutiny and Ruthie yelled with the lung power of Pavarotti, Lisa and Neeta had come to her rescue.

Neeta, it turned out, didn't have a baby herself but she had been ordered to take her cousin's baby for this weighing session while the new mother enjoyed getting a henna tattoo on her deflated belly. Neeta still didn't have children, but Anna had long since guessed that as much as Pavinder might say he wanted a family, he really wasn't ready for the kind of full-on, messy chaos that was parenthood. Pavinder did a very clever job with plants that no one really understood except for the fact that mess stayed in the lab and did not extend to the Khatri home. Lisa had twins – Kai and Kelsey, both being weighed that day. And Lisa and Paul were still so happy together. Unlike Anna and Ed.

'Ugh! You really need to get rid of that photo. It cannot be good for the juju of the house to be looking at a picture of your ex-husband when you relax into an episode of *The Bachelor*.'

'Neeta,' Lisa said warningly.

Anna passed Neeta her glass of wine then tipped the edge of the photo so the glass fell flat on the shelf. It was a family snap she kept up for Ruthie. It was her, Ed and Ruthie at the top of Mount Snowdon a few summers ago. Ruthie had hated every single thing about the climb. The bugs. The rocks. The other people. The sun. The wind. Wales in its entirety. But in the photo you wouldn't know any of that. Smiles on faces, painting the family dream, seconds before Ed had accidentally nudged Ruthie's arm and she had melted down and needed sanitiser spread over the limb from fingertips to elbow. 'There. Fixed.'

'Have you heard from him recently?' Lisa asked, flopping down into her favoured chair – a Nanny Gwen classic that Anna had restored and recovered – and crossing one jean-clad leg over the other.

'Sshh! Bad juju! I swear it is the essence of that man that made the Christmas tree fall over!' Neeta stated, sitting down on the sofa and slurping at her wine.

'No,' Anna said. 'Not since he came to raid the loft last week.'

'What?' Lisa exclaimed. 'He did what?'

Anna nodded. 'Laid claim to four large boxes we hadn't ever unpacked since we moved here. It was stuff his mother gave us. I didn't want it. He doesn't want it. And I can guarantee Nicolette doesn't want it either.'

It was a poor attempt at a show of power, Anna knew that, and that was why she had just let Ed get up the loft ladder and take whatever he so sorely needed but they both knew he didn't. They'd been divorced almost a year now, finally both realising, after Ruthie's diagnosis was confirmed, that the pressure cooker of waiting for a piece of paper to tell them what in their hearts they had already known, had been the only thing holding them together. Anna couldn't pinpoint the moment she had realised the love had slipped away from them, but she knew their relationship had shifted gear when things got tough and she had found herself looking to her two friends for moral support much more than she had Ed. That shouldn't have happened if they'd still been the kind of partners they had been at the start of their marriage. Before parenthood it had been 'us against the world', sharing work dramas over a bottle of wine and home-made pasta, brainstorming how to smooth strained colleague relationships or manage client expectations. Weekends had been Sunday lie-ins and lazy lunches mixed with doing up the house and walks in Richmond Park. The heady rush of being new parents – well-wishers-flowers-and-cards-and-removal-of-stitches-from-Anna's-vagina – had been brief. Being a family had ended up being very much more *Outnumbered* than it had been *The Waltons*. And then Ed had an affair. A classic, stereotypical conclusion.

'I still would not have let him have it,' Neeta piped up, moving cushions to get herself more comfortable. 'The divorce is done. He does not live here anymore. Anything he has left behind is no longer his to take, otherwise where does it stop? Will he be asking for the keys to take away your car? Or what about Ruthie's rabbit? Will Ed suddenly come round one day and decide he wants nothing more than a pet for his new girlfriend?'

'No,' Anna said. 'Nicolette is very much a dog person.' Not that she had been stalking Ed's mistress-now-girlfriend. Unlike at the start, it wasn't an obsession anymore, now they were nearly a year down the line of formally ending things. If Ed had apparently found blissful happiness with someone who posted nearly-nude photos of herself in nothing but Hunter wellies and some strategically placed table lamps, so be it. It was still good to keep yourself abreast of things though. Double Es if the lingerie firm tagged on Instagram was accurate.

'Well, how do you know? If you keep letting him in then it will be seen as an open invitation to pick and mix whenever he feels like it.'

'Neeta,' Lisa said. 'Not so loud. Where *is* Ruthie?'

'She's upstairs in her room,' Anna said, taking a swig of wine and straightening a Christmas card on the mantle before she sat down next to Neeta. 'You know she can't come back down once she's had a shower. She . . . thinks being in this space will get her pyjamas dirty.' She swallowed. No one really understood autism's full impact on the inner workings of Ruthie's mind but at least she could talk freely about it with her friends. With strangers, Anna found herself shamefully creating more palatable excuses for the sake of simplicity.

Since the divorce, Ed had decided to be like those strangers. He'd stopped even pretending to understand his daughter's thinking. He dipped in and out of Ruthie's life like she was the lesser liked relish when you had a few to choose from. Except he didn't have any other children to choose from. He had Ruthie. But now Ruthie was officially on the spectrum, Ed's fatherly duties were seemingly more unsanitised-hands-off than ever.

'Paul's coming in an hour to help sort the tree,' Lisa said, changing the subject. 'He's taking Kai to kickboxing but he's going to pop in after. Do not offer him coffee. He's on a caffeine detox before his parents buy him another barista's gift experience.' She shook her head. 'Last year it was like living with a super-charged Keith Lemon for a week afterwards.'

'Thank you,' Anna said, emotion welling up in her chest. 'For dropping everything for me again and coming round.'

She swallowed quickly, her throat dragging the fragility down into her chest. It wasn't talking about Ed that was making her upset and it wasn't Ruthie and her stress about the pine needles infiltrating her skin somehow. It wasn't even Anna's smashed lampshade and that head-shake she was imagining Nanny Gwen doing. It was kind of all of it, plus the deep, everyday thoughts she had about where her life was right now.

She was a thirty-five-year-old mum who was living on a knife edge trying to somehow achieve equilibrium for everyone. It was like being a circus act and keeping all the plates spinning at the same time, knowing exactly which one needed attention before it started to wobble. If it wasn't Ruthie, it was her boss Adam, if it wasn't either of them it was Ruthie's SENCo at school (Janice) and if it wasn't those three, or Ed – four – it was Mr Rocket (Ruthie's rabbit) who, apart from when he was being handled by Ruthie, had turned a bit Hannibal Lecter. Most nights Anna was in bed before ten wondering how all the hours of the day had escaped her yet again. Gone were the times when she could get herself a manicure or luxuriate with a latte while she had her hair cut; if she was able to get five minutes for an uninterrupted shower, it was a novelty.

'You would do the same for us,' Lisa told her. 'You *have* done the same for us.' She smiled then. 'Remember when we tied up that delivery guy who had been deliberately smashing parcels? Where would I have been without your Girl Guide knowledge in knots?'

'And I did not drop everything,' Neeta answered, sipping her wine again. 'It is a pleasure to be here and not to have to put up with boring talk about the structure of soil or people asking "if we plant our Christmas tree into our back garden in January will it do anything other than annoy our neighbours". The way Pavinder's team talk about it, it is as if they think a needleless spruce is going to hit the earth and suddenly create a cure for the Mosaic Virus.'

'To be honest,' Lisa said, smiling, 'all I had lined up was ironing some tiny top Kelsey *has to* wear for non-uniform day at school and watching a sneaky episode of *Chesapeake Shores*.'

'OK,' Anna said, putting her wine glass on the coffee table. 'So, as you're both here and you both need the escape, you can help me create an impressive new business-restructuring plan for the chip shop. Starting with a new name.'

'What?' Neeta asked. 'The place that triples as a Chinese takeaway and a pizzeria?'

And that was the main issue with this job Adam had

given her to focus her efforts on with a deadline of 'before January'. How *did* you restructure one business when it was trying to be three different things at once? Anna knew she got the jobs no one else wanted now she was part-time and working from home. Her role was 'corporate restructuring specialist' inside a firm that handled business set-up, business growth and business excellence. In a nutshell, Anna took a business on the edge of failure or a company not hitting the heights required and she made suggestions for improvement. But this assignment was about as tricky as it got. And with her mind already portioned up into at least sixteen pieces, concentration was at a minimum. Although, as she got paid per campaign these days, the cash was a big incentive, and it meant she hadn't thrown her initial, rather crap, ideas on the wood burner yet.

'Triple Threat?' Lisa suggested, the words lacking any conviction.

'That sounds like a film featuring Sandra Bullock with braids in her hair and a machine gun over her shoulder,' Neeta replied.

Triple Treat. That wasn't bad. Cheesy, but a lot better than anything she had already. Anna was hoping if she hit on the right name – or names – everything else was going to come together like a highly orchestrated celebrity wedding.

'What about . . . Fries, Fried Rice and Fettucine?' Neeta offered.

'They'd never get that on the signage,' Lisa answered.

Anna sat back into the cushions on her sofa as Neeta offered her reasoning and Lisa countered, taking time to drink in her best friends' good-natured bickering. This was a good moment. This was when she felt a little calmer about her life as a single mum, when things didn't feel quite so chaotic, when she felt supported by the love of others.

Four

American Airlines Flight

'Can I get you anything, sir?'

Can I get you anything? How about a rewind button on life? Press that back arrow and watch the last twenty-four or so hours flick by at speed . . .

'Sir?'

Sam came out of his head and looked up at the air hostess who was addressing him. She was maybe forty, attractive in a neat and tidy kind of a way. She had the whole rest of her life ahead of her serving in the skies, maybe with a guy back home and kids . . . He swallowed. 'I'll take a . . .' He paused. He was going to say a Diet Coke but who was he kidding? His season was blown. His whole life was blown. Where had abstaining from alcohol and taking grilled chicken instead of fried chicken got him? *This far.* And 'this far' was all he was going to get.

'I'll take a beer,' Sam told her. 'And a red wine. Please. And do you have any chips? The ones with the ridges?'

Who *was* he right now? His twelve-year-old self counting quarters he'd saved to feed into a vending machine? Salivating about snacks his contemporaries ate in handfuls every day like they were meaningless?

'Sir, you're in first class. We can do a little better than chips. Dinner service will come around soon.'

She placed his drinks on his tray table and moved the trolley along. Cracking the ring pull of the beer, he swigged

20

the liquid down like it was water after a game. He pulled the blind up and looked out the window at the clouds below. Here he was, up above everything, doing *something*. While he still could. He shut the blind down again, taking another swig of the beer and closing his eyes. He had Huntington's.

It sounded like the name of a very expensive bourbon. *I'll take a Huntington's and ice*. Or maybe a restaurant meal. *I'll have the Huntington's with fries, onion rings and a béarnaise sauce*. Except it was neither of those things. It was a disease that, whenever it felt like it, was going to break down the nerve cells in his brain destroying his ability to move and even to think.

He was twenty-five, had been on the verge of the biggest deal of his life, and he was going to degenerate. Go rapidly from one of the fittest to one of the weakest, just like that. The opportunity he had worked towards his whole career thus far, well that was going to be dead the minute the Dallas Diggers got the news. *News*. That's what he was going to be when this broke. The guy with the world at his feet who missed the most vital catch of his career. All the doing the right things – missing parties, skipping the drugs, no DUIs, not getting too romantically involved – and now a big, black, unavoidable void was his to fall right into.

There had been a moment in Dr Monroe's office when it felt like someone had pressed a thick wad of cotton wool into both his ears. Everything sounded muffled apart from the incessant beating of his own heart. Sam didn't know if the rhythm – strong, loud, ever present – was to magnify the intensity of this appointment or to remind him that despite this diagnosis it was still beating hard and showing no signs of giving up yet. But the noise inside had meant what Dr Monroe had been saying fell on his almost deaf ears. His brain had somehow groped around the sentences and worked out the headlines. *More tests. Another session with the genetics counsellor. The average age things could start to go south was between thirty and fifty*. He'd started to sweat in the coat. He'd gone through his session with the genetic counsellor before the series of tests the Dallas Diggers had wanted, thinking this was just a formality. He'd never failed *any* physical before. And that was part of the problem. It was his talent and his fitness that set him apart and made people accept him in a world he always felt he had to fight to get an equal chance in. And now he felt like he was that little boy again, envious of those who had what he didn't, except this time it wasn't about dollar bills, it was about sand in the timer of life.

Sam settled his head back against his seat and closed his eyes. He'd got back to his apartment on autopilot, he'd packed a bag full of something or other and grabbed his passport. Then he'd ordered a cab to the airport. *Far away.* That's all he could think about. Distancing himself from this time, this place and this diagnosis. He'd looked at that departures board and chosen the furthest flight departing within the next hour. While he still could, he was doing what he'd always done best. He was running.

Five

Richmond, London, UK

'Dad!'

That three-letter word shouted at volume had Anna swallowing her strong coffee and two painkillers down so quickly that one scalded her tongue and the other banged against her throat like Emma Raducanu had volleyed it. It wasn't even eight-thirty. It was a Saturday. And had Ruthie opened the front door? Or did Ed still have a key? That last thought had Anna marching from the kitchen and into the hallway, closing the separating door behind her. She had boundaries. They were *divorced*. He might still be Ruthie's father, they might have years and years of shared history, but it was over. And this house might have once been Ed's home but it had never been his to own.

This place was all Anna's and where she had grown up with Nanny Gwen. The floors, walls and ceilings might all have had to be repaired and replaced over the years, but the bones of the place still held a host of memories. The light-filled living room where Nanny Gwen had taught a pint-sized Anna how to dance, the kitchen where Nanny Gwen had attempted to cook her own grandmother's recipes and usually spectacularly failed, and the master bedroom with its high ceilings and Anna's favourite piece of furniture: a walnut wardrobe that still smelled a little of Nanny Gwen's favourite scent, lily of the valley. A side-eye to her nanny's photo in the hall gave Anna the strength and conviction to face the scene.

There was Ed, his Derby-shoe-clad feet on her welcome mat. The irony. He wasn't welcome. Not if he had let himself in. What was in his hand? *Was* that a key? Anna had to look away because she *had* to be imagining it, right? Instead she focused on his hair. He had always had nice hair – almost white-blond, floppy but tameable – and it was still in the same style as it had been when they'd first met when she was twenty-one. He'd been nice back then. A good guy with an undercurrent of sexy so she hadn't got bored like she had with her first few boyfriends. Marriage seemed like the next logical step and then along came Ruthie . . . Looking back, perhaps she should have changed the pace of their relationship or challenged it. Perhaps it had been all too simplistic. So simplistic that when Ed *was* challenged it had been easy to throw it all away.

Anna opened her mouth to say something in greeting and then there was a high-pitched noise.

'What's in the box? What's in the box?'

Anna had been so busy not greeting the man on her newly named 'unwelcome' mat and reminiscing about his bloody hair, she had somehow missed the festively wrapped cardboard box to Ed's left.

'Ruthie,' Anna said, pacing forward now. 'Calm down a little bit. You've only just had your Coco Pops.' Ruthie could sometimes spontaneously throw up if excitement and not-long-ago-eaten were combined.

'Oh, Christ,' Ed said, taking a step back. 'I . . . thought you'd have had breakfast earlier than now.'

Anna crushed her teeth together. The one time she had a bit to drink and been late to bed because of an impromptu game of Cards Against Humanity with her friends after Malcolm had been safely installed in the living room and Ed was here to witness it. The tree was not yet decorated but she knew she wouldn't be able to hold Ruthie off for long. It might even be today if she could get rid of this slight hangover head . . . and Ed.

'Can I open it?' Ruthie asked, eyes wide, already super-excited, fingers peeling at the Sellotape. She was halfway to doing it anyway.

'Not if it's for Christmas,' Anna stated. 'You know the rules. We don't open anything until the 25th of December.'

'Well,' Ed said, still keeping a little distance. 'Going to have to overrule you on that one. Because it's going to need some air way before Christmas Day.'

Air? Was it something inflatable? Anna hoped it wasn't a helium balloon because she had never forgotten the number seven Ruthie and her friends had taken turns to inhale from when her back was turned, forcing the party to take a dramatic path, one that involved her getting a bill for a full valet of a Mercedes S Class.

There was a very distinctive noise now, a definite miaow and pressure was building in Anna's chest. He wouldn't have. He *couldn't* have.

'Oh! It's . . . it's . . .' Ruthie was almost hyperventilating as from the box popped a long-haired and rather large tabby cat, tail high in the hair, green eyes staring like it might be contemplating the demise of all three of them. And it was a reality. Ed had bought Ruthie a cat. Unless . . .

'Is this one of those fostering schemes I've heard about?' Anna asked quickly as the cat leapt from the box and skidded onto the rug.

'Fostering schemes?' Ed asked, looking as blank as he used to look when Anna would question something he had bought from eBay that had no obvious purpose.

'Like . . . when you adopt someone to be your grandma. It's on TV all the time.' And she was losing this conversation somehow. While Ruthie was already losing her heart to something they could *not* keep if this wasn't temporary!

'I'm going to call it—'

'No!' Anna exclaimed, diving forward and scooping the cat up into her arms. Ruthie hadn't actually touched it yet. Emotional investment could not happen if she got this feline back into its packaging and it and Ed were out of the door. Except the cat was squirming now and it was quite a handful with paws the size of human fists . . .

'Mum! Don't hurt *Cheesecake*!' Ruthie wailed.

And now it had a name, it was game over. Even the cat knew it, deciding that was the moment to let out an angelic mew it would probably never utter again. Why had Ed done this? Without asking her! Anna put the cat down and straightened up to face her ex-husband. She had to quickly temper 'furious'.

'Can I have a word?' Anna asked.

'Christmas!' Ed declared. 'There you go. That's a word.'

Was he serious? Anna folded her arms across her chest as Cheesecake's body slammed to the floorboards, before it cocked a straightened leg behind its head and proceeded to lick its bum-hole.

'I want to speak to you,' Anna made clearer. 'In the living room.'

She didn't wait for Ed's reply but opened the door on her right and stepped into the room that was now mostly taken up by Malcolm. Shit, there was an empty wine bottle on the windowsill. She didn't have time to move it now. Anna positioned herself so that it was blocked from Ed's view as he entered, hands in the pockets of his navy-blue trousers, looking annoyingly relaxed. Well, *she* wasn't relaxed. She was seething!

'Have you really bought Ruthie a cat?' Anna asked him.

Ed shrugged. 'That's what she asked for the last time I saw her.'

'Ed! That's what she's asked for since she was able to speak! And we always said no. Because our lives and this road outside are not conducive to cats. Mr Penderghast lost five cats until he couldn't bear the heartbreak anymore and bought a budgie!'

Ed shrugged again. What was this shrugging? Was it something he had picked up from Nicolette? *Apathy*. She needed to make this about the fact that a cat was not a good idea and not about how she still felt ever so slightly aggrieved that Ed was moving his life along nicely while she was getting all the shite jobs from work and had a social life that revolved around well-meaning pity . . .

'Ed, you didn't tell me you were planning this!' Anna said.

'It was a surprise! You don't tell people about surprises.'

'It's not *my* surprise. It's Ruthie's. And you should have told me beforehand so I could have—'

'So, you could have what?' Ed asked, hands coming out of his pockets to gesticulate. 'Told me it wasn't a good idea?'

'Well . . . yes!'

'Like I don't get a say in what might be good for Ruthie?' Ed blasted.

'What?'

'Well, that's what this attitude is all about, isn't it?' Ed continued, starting to move from his position by the door, strolling into Anna's living space as if nothing had changed between them. 'It's about you wanting all the control . . . again.'

What was happening here? Was this really occurring? Or was it part of her hangover? Anna shook her head and then instantly regretted it as it pounded like Tom Stoltman had bludgeoned it with a dumbbell.

'Ed, you've bought Ruthie an animal. A not insignificant animal that will possibly live to eighteen years old and need care and attention every single day.'

'Well, according to you, it's going to be mown down before Christmas so you won't have that long to worry about it. A few packs of Felix and you'll be good!'

'Ed! That's not fair.'

'And neither is this. Telling me I can't get my kid a cat. A cat I know she will adore!'

Ed plucked the wine bottle from the windowsill and looked at it as if it were highly incriminating evidence on a phoning social services level. 'Big night last night, was it?' He tutted. 'And, Anna, honestly, what *is* this tree? It's big enough to go in Trafalgar Square!'

Before Anna could make any comment, the door to the living room burst open and Ruthie was there, hood of her sweatshirt pulled up and over so tight, all that was really visible were her eyes. This was her I-need-to-be-invisible-because-the-situation-is-triggering stance. And in her arms was the cat. Like it was a trained animal actor it was lying back, head hanging off the crook of Ruthie's elbow channelling all the cute.

'Stop shouting!' Ruthie shouted. 'You both know I have sensory issues and closing a door does not really help reduce the volume of the shouting!'

'Sorry, Ruthie,' Anna said immediately.

Ruthie stepped towards Ed then and next she rather unceremoniously tipped the cat into his arms. 'I can't keep her,' Ruthie said. 'If it's a her. I haven't checked yet. I would check if I was keeping her . . . him . . . them . . . but I can't.'

The cat didn't seem at all impressed with its new place to reside and it turned its smile into a snarl as Ed tried to work out quite how to hold it.

'Ruthie, don't be daft. You've always wanted a cat and I got you one,' Ed said as the cat began to climb up his jumper.

'But Mum has always said no,' Ruthie reminded. 'And I don't like to break rules.'

Anna swallowed. This was heart-breaking. She wanted nothing more than to say Ruthie could keep the animal but . . . it wasn't practical. And Ed knew that.

'Come on, Ruthie. Where am I supposed to take it? It has a pedigree and everything. Its name is four words long. I have all the paperwork.'

Of course he did! A show of the wealth he still had while Anna worked hard to maintain the equilibrium Ruthie had come to know. She had the house. That was and always would be the most important thing. Stability provided a long time ago by Nanny Gwen, but electricity wasn't cheap and neither was decent wi-fi and while Ed could work full-time, Anna couldn't. Plus, what Ed had been asked to contribute following the divorce was frankly a laughable sum.

'You can keep it,' Ruthie said, one hand on the door handle. 'Maybe your new baby will like it!'

And as Ruthie left the room again, Anna listed sideways until she fell right into the Christmas tree.

Six

London, UK

There was a quirky sign with a pointing finger that said 'To Putney' one way and 'To Richmond' the other. As Sam looked at the two pathways going in different directions, he realised that although this was another crossroads he had to decide upon, it was perhaps a much smaller one than getting on a plane to the UK.

When the flight had landed at Heathrow, he had found a cab and left it up to the driver to work out where they were going. Less than ten miles had been his only remit. *Richmond is a bit Toffsville, but it's decent. I take the missus there when I've done something wrong. Nice restaurants, or parks for a walk. Christmas decorations look sweet as, but don't buy your presents there unless you're loaded like that guy who makes the pricey hoovers. Putney, that's all about the rowing.* Still undecided, Sam had been dropped off here at this choosing point with nothing but his backpack for company.

He dropped the rucksack to the ground and contemplated getting out his phone. He hadn't turned it on since he had turned it off for the flight. In this scenario, Sam wasn't Dr Monroe's client, the Dallas Diggers were, and as soon as the doctor reported the findings from the gene testing, this news was going to be everywhere. He unzipped the small pocket at the front of his bag and shivered. It was cold here in England, a sheen of frost on the grass even now at – what time was it? – mid-afternoon. He was used to the snowy Ohio winters but perhaps he should have recalled those when he'd packed his bag. He barely remembered throwing in a few shirts, a couple of tees, a pair of jeans, a pair of trackies and one sweater. Apart from that, his laptop, and underwear, he only had what he was currently standing up in.

His fingers found his phone and he looked at the inanimate shiny black surface. With one push of the button he could light it up and face whatever challenges were going to come his way. As a dog-walker moved past him, chasing a scruffy white pet with a bandana around its neck, Sam wondered who the first message would be from. His coach at the Bisons – Tim? Frankie? Chad wanting to suggest one of his low-key gatherings that always turned into a pool party that got reported on TMZ? The Diggers? No, if the Diggers knew already, they would be communicating with Frankie first. They were a multi-billion-dollar business, they weren't going to drop him a text and say 'heard about your issues, we're out of here'.

Tionne. He winced. He called or texted her most days and he took her out for ice cream every second Friday. Without fail. He'd tried to bail once, when the guys had pushed about team drinks and he'd refused one too many times. It hadn't worked. Tionne had told him in no uncertain terms that if he didn't show up he could consider their siblingship severed. He knew she didn't really mean it, but he also knew that no matter how badass she made herself out to be, there was still a part of her that was the little kid who got teased for her braids and needed her big brother. What was he going to say to her about this? He had always been her strength and now he was what? Flawed? Weak? He shuddered, not liking either of those scenarios.

Slipping the phone back into his bag he looked at the signpost again. Then he made his decision.

Seven

Bean Afar, Richmond

The café, despite always being *really* busy, had forever been
a calming place for Ruthie. From the moment she could
walk with reins, Anna had brought her daughter here for
something sweet to eat. It had also been one of Nanny Gwen's
favourite places when it had been called Spooner's and served
all-day breakfasts, meals in baskets, and mugs of tea and
slabs of cake in the afternoons.

Being here gave Anna the chance for a few moments where
Ruthie was happy and content and she could take a breath.
Somehow, the scent of coffee grounds mixed with the heat
and steam rising from the machines, constituted the same
relaxation vibes of a day spa. It was all normal people, going
about their business – getting takeout coffees for the office,
grabbing a juice after a run, meeting a friend – and Aztec
plant pots nestled up to brightly coloured never-been-used
bottles. It was *exotic*.

It wasn't staring at the four walls of the house you loved
while still deeply envying your husband for being able to
escape to work. Despite being exceptionally happy at having
a baby, Anna hadn't taken to it quite the way she thought
she ought to – or how all the parenting books had told her
that she ought to. Motherhood was hard. It was even harder
when your own mother had passed the gauntlet rapidly to
your grandmother and your grandmother then passed away
so wasn't around to impart advice.

Perhaps Anna had inherited her mother's cold, selfish attitude after all, she'd thought. Maybe her mother had once sought solace in a coffee shop rueing the day she decided to stop the contraceptive pill. Back then, when Ruthie was first born, the dark thoughts had got the better of Anna. Sometimes when she'd glanced into the mirror she had seen the willowy, dark-haired slender figure of her own mother staring back. The soulless eyes, her smile somehow commanding, her quiet depths unknown to everyone – exactly how Anna had come to realise her mother liked it. It was a powerplay.

Maybe it was hereditary, she had thought when she was drowning in nappies and wipes that ripped apart in her hands. The inability to be a mother passed down through DNA. During those days, weeks and months of deep-rooted anxiety and depression Anna had even had thoughts that one day she might snap inside and leave Ruthie bundled up on a bench in Richmond Park. She shook her head now, banishing those thoughts. She hadn't done that. She had been pulled through the worst times with the help of Lisa and Neeta. And as for her mother? She had no idea where she was now. They'd had zero contact since she had turned up uninvited and drunk at Anna and Ed's wedding and made herself the centre of attention. Nanny Gwen had got rid of her that night and whatever she had said – or the money she had given her most likely – there had been no repeat performance.

The baby. Ed was having a baby with Nicolette. Would they get married before the birth? Would Nicolette be the new, improved, doesn't swear or sweat, Mrs Heath?

'The gingerbread men aren't even.'

Ruthie's voice cut through Anna's thoughts and the ambient festive music coming from the radio. It was warm here, the windows misted up, and Anna could see the hanging gingerbread men decorations Ruthie was referring to. Anna studied them – two brown arms, two brown legs, three black buttons, a red smile . . .

33

Ruthie sighed. 'There are four on that side and three on the other side. *That* one is holding hands with a snowman. It doesn't look right. Do you think Esther will change it if I ask her?'

'I don't know,' Anna answered, wrapping her fingers around her favourite black Kenyan coffee. 'But she definitely won't mind you asking.' Ruthie's need for order was well known here. It had started with an odd number of doughnuts on the counter and continued with words on the signage behind. Descriptions had to be written in groups of two, four or six otherwise Ruthie fixated on the imbalance.

Ruthie put her mouth to her mug of hot chocolate and sipped. Once. Twice. Three. Four times. She didn't *always* do it like that. The pattern could vary depending on what her mind told her to do in that certain situation. And everything was dependent on Ruthie's stress levels. Her dad having a new baby was something that would unsettle anyone, but it could affect Ruthie in so many different ways. And Anna was currently wondering just how long Ruthie had held in this secret. She gazed at her daughter, swaddled up in her favourite and softest Marvel oversized slanket, and felt that pinch in her gut at the thought of anyone or anything harming her. That feeling she had which her mother certainly hadn't. The maternal notion that told you in no uncertain terms that this person you had created would be protected by you at *any* cost.

'Ruthie,' Anna began softly. 'When did Dad tell you about . . . the baby?'

Ruthie gave an eyeroll. 'We can't make "the baby" said like that a thing.'

'Did I say it a certain way?' Anna asked even though she knew she had indeed said it a certain way. She'd said it like the word 'baby' had been caked in the darkest, smelliest excrement of said baby and the word was dung to her tongue. However awkward this situation was for her, this baby was going to be in Ruthie's life, just as Nicolette was in Ruthie's life.

'Mum,' Ruthie said. 'You said it like "the baby" was really "Voldemort".'

'Sshh!' Anna said. 'Are we allowed to say his name in here?'

'And Dad didn't tell me about the baby,' Ruthie said, eyes studying her drink. 'Nicolette had her friends round and she was waving this stick in the air and they were all cheering and drinking booze. I thought it was a Covid test and they were all saying "positive" so excitedly, I asked her why it was thrilling to have coronavirus, and then she put on the voice she puts on when she's talking about things she shouldn't eat, like . . . carbs. And she said, "You're going to be a big sister".'

Anna closed her eyes. Springing a huge, life-changing scenario like that on a child with autism was not the way to do things. The news should have been delivered quietly, calmly and softly, when Ruthie was somewhere she'd feel comfortable, not amid a screaming gaggle of women high on Blossom Hill. And, exactly like the cat, *why* hadn't Ed said anything to her? He'd been particularly lacking in information when she had hauled herself out of Malcolm's spiky arms.

Vague comments like 'We were waiting for the first scan' and 'We've only told family' had dribbled from tight lips. That last statement had nipped a bit. Especially now Anna knew Ruthie had found out from women who definitely weren't family and had all basically clutched the pee stick.

'It's OK to feel however you want to feel about it,' Anna told Ruthie.

'That's what people say when really they want you to have a black and white opinion one way or another.'

Super-smart as ever. It was really overwhelming how autism could make simple-to-most tasks into a challenging puzzle, yet Ruthie could happily navigate complexities of the mind like it was the first question on *Who Wants to Be a Millionaire*.

Ruthie sighed. 'I'd rather there wasn't a baby coming. But I won't smother it in its sleep.'

Anna nodded. 'That's good to know.' Was there more coming? You could never tell. Sometimes there would be a whole avalanche of information, other times Ruthie would process things internally before sharing even a tiny thought.

'I think Dad wishes there wasn't a baby coming too,' Ruthie continued.

'What makes you say that?' Anna asked.

Another sigh. 'I heard him on the phone to Uncle Jason. He said he was fucked.'

'Ruthie!' Anna said, caught between covering Ruthie's mouth with her hand or perhaps singing along with the music to take the attention away from the expletive her daughter had just let go of with no shortage of volume.

'What?' Ruthie said, looking bemused. 'It's just a word. It's no different to me saying "beetroot". *People* give words power, you know.'

Anna felt obliged to mouth a 'sorry' at one of their near table neighbours, a woman who had 'Brian' written on her takeout cup.

'But I'm worried about how *you* feel about the baby,' Ruthie said.

'Oh,' Anna replied, dragging her body back into the chair a little. 'Well, I don't . . . I mean . . . It's nothing to do with me, is it?'

'Mum, body language gave you away like a flashing neon sign. You hate the baby.'

'Ruthie! I don't!' Anna realised she was being a little too loud now and brought her voice down to a whisper. 'No one hates a baby. Unless there's something very wrong with them. The person, that is. Not the baby.'

'No, but you don't like Nicolette. Or Dad being with Nicolette. And you don't have anybody else yet.'

That just about summed up the current state of affairs – literally. Except Nicolette was no longer the affair. She was a legitimate – now pregnant – partner and Anna was the ex. Extinguished. And she didn't want to project any of her feelings onto Ruthie.

'We should find you someone else!' Ruthie announced as if it was as easy as popping to the supermarket and taking an appropriate partner down from the top shelf next to the prime sirloin. And this was not a path Anna wanted Ruthie to go down and get obsessed with.

'Mr Dandruff is nice. Apart from the dandruff LOL.'

Ruthie didn't say L-O-L. She said LOL like LOL was a fully-fledged word. And who was Mr Dandruff?

'He's my PE teacher,' Ruthie continued. 'The new one you haven't embarrassed me with at parents' evening yet. He looks a bit like that actor you like . . . Richard someone.'

'Richard E. Grant?'

'Ew! You don't!'

Anna leaned forward now, maybe slightly interested. 'Not Richard Armitage.'

'Yes!' Ruthie said excitedly.

Now Anna was imagining a Richard Armitage lookalike dressed in shorts and a vest running around the netball court. Ruthie had to be exaggerating. If Anna had had a PE teacher like that back in the day she might have actually tried at sports. As it was, Lisa had to promise treats of the non-low-cal kind to get her to even entertain a session of circuit training.

'Shall I say that I'm really struggling with . . . my legs and . . . because I have special needs, Mr Dandruff will need to talk to you about some unique, but not too difficult, exercises for me to do.'

'No!' Anna exclaimed immediately. 'No.' She brought her cup to her lips and flew down out of the RA dream cloud. 'Ruthie, I'm fine. I'm really not looking for anyone. I live a very full life. I have you, I have Lisa and Neeta and I have my latest work project that's going *really really* well . . .'

It wasn't going *really really* well. It wasn't even going well. In between the slightly-marred-by-too-much-wine dreams, her mind had been desperately thinking of a word that rhymed with 'saveloy'. She had no idea where to even begin with this revamp and that was so unlike her. Perhaps the brief had been a little too brief. Maybe she needed to go back to Adam and really nail down the client's exact expectations.

'I know I make things harder for you,' Ruthie said softly, her brilliant blue eyes a little dewy. 'And I know I don't adapt to change very well . . .'

'Ruthie—'

'But you could get a boyfriend. If you wanted one. If he never entered my bedroom, even to check if the radiator was working properly, and he made sure to cough into his sleeve not his hands, and if he liked K-pop and Marvel.'

Anna smiled. 'OK, well, I will take that on board.' She wouldn't. She had no desire to complicate her life more right now. And it was December. Who in their right mind thought about dating just before Christmas? There was way too much going on in her life what with work, worrying about Ruthie and all the activities Ruthie's school put on including one that was happening later today – an afternoon festive fayre. She was helping Neeta on the Winter Warmers stand. Basically it was soup, rolls and vegan Bovril.

'And thank you for letting me keep Cheesecake,' Ruthie added, a marshmallow from her drink stuck to her nose.

Yes, and now she had a cat as well as a rabbit to take care of too. How could she not have given in after the baby announcement? That's what mothers did. They dealt with the tough stuff and they chose their battles. And, for today, a long-haired pedigree tabby whose real name was Professor Poe-Cadbury Frost was winning.

Eight

Montague Road, Richmond

This was a nice part of town. This was not like the London Sam had seen on the internet. The news items he caught back home showed tower blocks and busy train stations amid all that history. Sure, he wasn't dumb enough to think that it was all the Houses of Parliament and Buckingham Palace but these houses were *sweet*. A homey, rural vibe to them somehow.

They looked three storeys, some of them four, with big bay windows and white-painted plaster. There were shutters and grand front porches and most of them were decorated for the season. There were wreaths that looked expensive – a lot more silver bells and golden ribbons than ivy and pine cones – and the trees and hedges outside the properties had lights strung around their boughs and branches ready to illuminate the neighbourhood as soon as the light began to fade.

His mom would like it here. She'd admire the neat driveways or gardens and the drapes at some of the windows and then she'd make a remark that this must be where the good people live. When his mom referenced 'good people' it actually only meant 'rich'. From Sam's experience being a good person hardly ever related to how much money you had in your bank account.

Despite his best efforts, his mom had turned down every handout he'd offered her until he realised he had to get a little cute about it. He'd lied. He said he'd won a team competition and he had to donate the prize – half to charity and half to family. He'd been sent a car for free so they could splash his name on their website and billboards . . .

He knew his mom had probably guessed this was his way of paying her back for raising him and not simple coincidental good fortune, but she'd never said. He'd hoped, when the Dallas Diggers deal was done, that he could finally get his parents to move. A better apartment in the same neighbourhood or a house with a garden and a porch swing, somewhere quiet, somewhere peaceful where his mom could take a load off. Maybe his dad would even retire or at least cut down the amount of time he spent at the car lot. Perhaps Sam would get him a classic – a Pontiac Firebird. His dad could take his time to restore it, Sam could even lend a hand . . .

Huntington's disease. That's all there is now. You failing at the only thing you were good at. Time ticking.

Sam could walk around this unfamiliar place all day long comparing the differences to Cincinnati, but it wouldn't stop the chanting in his head for long. The minute there was a pause, his brain taking a break from thinking about the visual in front of him or a memory from back home, there it was like the Bisons fans calling his name when he made a touchdown.

Maybe it was a mistake. That was a thought he wanted to listen to. It happened *all* the time, people given a cancer diagnosis and then it turned out to be something they had swallowed when they were three years old that had grown into their body. Or patients told they had weeks to live who were still around five years later and running New York marathons.

A second opinion. That's what he needed. All this worrying could be for nothing. Why hadn't he thought about that when he was sprinting out of Dr Monroe's office? Another alternative was maybe, by now, there would be a score of messages and voicemails from the doctor himself saying there had been a mix-up with the results. Perhaps there was another guy thinking he had all the time in the world who really should be getting churned up over this diagnosis. *You should turn on your phone.*

He chewed on the inside of his lip as his feet stopped moving along the street and the weight of his backpack hugged his shoulders a little more tightly. *What are you scared of? That if you look at those missed calls and messages you might not be able to keep pretending that the appointment never happened?*

Checking his watch, his stomach gave a rumble. He needed to grab some food, find a hotel and then think about what came next.

Nine

Whittington School, Richmond

'Is it racist that they always give me the soup stand?'

Anna looked up at Neeta, raising her head from the large rolls she was buttering with a spread that was supposed to *taste* like butter but not *be* butter. It was surprisingly warm under this gazebo with the stove going and what seemed like hundreds of multi-coloured fairy lights around the roof, and Anna was considering taking off her woollen hat. She looked over at Ruthie, un-gloved hands tucked into her sleeves, helping her friends set up the 'guess how many candy canes in the jar' stall. Ruthie wasn't going to take her hat off even if the sun came out. It was part of her armour for events such as these. The one good thing about today was most of the stalls were outside. Ruthie coped much better with large groups of people if there was fresh air and space to escape to should it all get a bit much. As long as there were no bugs or bushes in close proximity. And her friends would look out for her, let Ruthie take the tasks she could manage without discomfort, keep wipes and gel at hand. There was never any guarantee the day would go without a hitch but Anna had a bag of all kinds of remedies for almost every eventuality . . .

'It is the lentils and the chickpeas. I'm sure Celia Duke thinks that anyone who has visited India must have this automatic superpower to be able to cook pulses like Madhur Jaffrey. And that if you have *relatives* in India, then that means one of them *is* Madhur Jaffrey.'

'Neeta, I'm sure that's not true,' Anna answered. 'The bit about you being able to cook pulses better than anyone else is definitely true though.'

Anna knew that Neeta being given the soup stand for the last three years was only to do with her absolute prowess in the kitchen. A fact Anna knew the chairwoman of the school committee was a little bit envious of. But Neeta was terrible at taking a compliment – any compliment – and never believed the sincerity behind them, always looking for the double meaning. Anna also knew that Neeta loved working the soup stand and would be mortally offended if anyone else was given the task of running it. Neeta had joined the school committee after the art classes she was studying as a mature student had come to a sudden end when the teacher at the college had been convicted of art forgery. The news had been splashed all over the papers and Neeta had been so devastated at her association with the guy that she had burned all her painting materials and broken her easel with a sledgehammer. Both Anna and Lisa had tried to encourage her that not all artists were 'as evil as Arthur Shelby' and that she didn't have to give up art completely even if she didn't want to continue with lessons. But when Neeta's mind was made up it was made up for good.

'It is obvious. I need a job!' Neeta said suddenly, popping the top on the vat of soup they were selling to bazaar visitors. 'I need to have something for me. Currently I have community-based projects that are all about helping others. That is nice, of course, but sometimes I think it is too nice. And I am worried that Pavinder and I are at the stage of our marriage where it is time for me to show him a different side of me.'

'Wow, Neeta. Where is this coming from?' Anna asked, covering the rolls over with tin foil and giving her friend a look of concern. And did Pavinder not know all the sides of his wife? They had been married more than fourteen years!

Then again, if Anna's scale of measurement was her and Ed, perhaps Neeta had a point.

'Pavinder is talking more and more about people at work.'

'Pavinder has always talked *a lot* about work.' Even Anna knew how to germinate barley.

'About work, yes. About *people* at work, no.' Neeta sighed, her fingers toying with the knot at her hip that tied the apron. 'There is Adil and Nancy and Sarahh with two h's and Monika – I am not sure how that is spelled – but there is also Jessica. Jessica is mentioned much more often. And he tells me that it was Jessica who came to drop off the Christmas card last night. Why does he not just tell Jessica that we do not celebrate Christmas? Because he does not want to hurt her feelings!'

Was this about Neeta wanting a job or was it about Neeta thinking Pavinder was having an affair with almost everybody from a Lou Bega song? Her friend did look worried though.

'Neeta, where is this coming from?' Anna asked, quickly pouring a glass of very strong orange squash and handing it to her friend. The only wine here was on the tombola stand.

'I do not know! Maybe one of those dreadful magazines Lisa gives to me when she has finished with them that I have to hide when Pavinder's mother comes to visit! Completely ridiculous but also strangely addictive.'

Neeta was on the verge of getting a little bit hysterical and she could go from perfectly placid to volcanic in less time than it took Ruthie to combust in a similar way. And Neeta didn't have autism. But Neeta obviously had real concerns about this, and she had possibly been internally macerating longer than the lentils in the soup.

'I am too nice, am I not? Externally,' Neeta exclaimed. 'I say all the right things in polite company, I do all the right things like a good Indian wife and then what? What happens then? I turn into Pavinder's mother and Pavinder goes looking for someone sexier while I keep cooking the best pulses in Richmond thinking that is more of a turn-on than someone who probably spreads their legs like the jaws of a hungry Venus flytrap?'

'Neeta!' Anna said as her friend's volume increased fifty-fold and Bruce and Eliott who were running the stall selling festive wreaths made from beads, feathers and buttons started to pay more than a fleeting interest. 'This isn't like you.'

'No,' Neeta agreed. 'Because "me" is someone who greets her husband from a hard day at work wearing comfy nightwear, not an outfit that could be shackled to a naughty adult playroom!'

Oh God! This had started with chickpeas and lentils, but it was turning into a deep analysis of marriage. Where was Lisa when Anna needed her? They were a team when it came to holding each other up and conversationally working through their issues.

Customers! If Neeta had people to serve soup to then she wouldn't have the time or the headspace to combust. And hard work would give Anna the time to think of something to say to get Neeta out of this internal funk. Neeta was self-critical to a fault and, in Anna's opinion, Pavinder was about as likely to have an affair as Kevin Bacon.

'Come and get your Christmas soup, everybody!' Anna yelled at the top of her voice. 'Lentil and vegetable or spicy chickpea only one pound per cup! Roll up! Roll up!'

Roll up? Her job was making businesses more productive and enticing! She could do a lot better than that!

'What are you doing?' Neeta asked, still looking like she was closer to boiling point than the soup. She'd downed the orange squash.

A little music was what they needed. Something festive to get the crowd going until the Whittington wind band started their slot. Ruthie had been listening to her phone in the car on the way here. Something by Mariah Carey or Michael Bublé would be ideal. Anna hit the play button and out came . . . 'Ice Ice Baby' by Vanilla Ice. Worse still, it had somehow Bluetooth-connected to the outside speaker system all by itself and was blasting at volume. You had to *love* technology. Celia Duke and Jennifer Atkinson, the headmistress, were going to adore the lyrics of this one. *Turn it off!* All Anna had to do was very quickly make it stop . . . although her hands had suddenly seemed to have lost all ability to press a screen, like they were giant useless cartoon versions of themselves. And now the track was starting from the beginning again. Still, she stabbed at the 'x' relentlessly until she decided swiping up might be a better course of action. Or she could run over and pull the plug on the speakers . . .

'What are you doing?' Neeta wanted to know. 'Are you in control of the music this year?'

God, when did the unsavoury lyrics begin? There wasn't time. Suddenly Anna's mouth was moving and she was busting moves that should never be performed in public. She would have to rap, louder than the soundtrack being blasted out across the field. Could this be turned into something about the soup stand for advertising purposes . . .

Nice, spice, gravy
Nice, spice, gravy
OK, come, sa-salivate and get some
Neeta's here with a brand new yum yum
Soup, will warm you up like a duvet
Fill your belly like a Chinese takeaway
Why not buy two, ho, and we'll grow
Let's make the school, some dough
You get the treats and we get the wonga, filling them cups
for a line like conga
Spend! We're getting down with the lentils
To raise the funds, buy the school new pencils
Christmas, that's why we're here
Doing our best with festive cheer
We know you'll love it, try soup today

*Or you can donate, add Giftaid
Any stomach issues, this food will dissolve it
Check out our stall, hunger we resolve it!*

Suddenly the rap music stopped and was replaced by a cheery-sounding Michael Jackson singing 'Rockin' Robin'. Normality restored. Phew! A few people who had, for some reason, gathered to watch Anna moving across the grass of the school playing field doing The Hammer gave a bit of a slow clap before moving off to peruse handmade snow globes, seasonal fluffy toy alpacas and jumpers made entirely from tumble drier lint – yes, really.

'Anna,' Neeta said. 'Is everything OK with you?'

Neeta was looking at her with those large, brown eyes, giving off something between curious and suspicious. It was the expression she wore when she was determined to get to the very bottom of your inner secrets jar – because Neeta thought everybody had one and it was nested right next to the 'people you wished you'd had sex with before you got married' jar. Anna nodded and went back to the rolls she was spreading. Her mind was actually a jumble of a million things more than it usually was. Did pedigree cats eat different things to working-class cats? With a cat in the house now, did she need to increase security on Mr Rocket's cage like she had when that feral badger was running around the neighbourhood? How long was Ruthie's phase of wanting potato salad with every meal going to last?

'Because you just basically called my soup "gravy",' Neeta continued. 'And you rapped it. Loudly. For everyone to hear. When I was already feeling self-conscious that this year's batch is inferior to last season's as it is tinged with the essence of paranoia and envy.'

And it was at that exact moment that everything came rushing to the emotional sector of Anna's mind and before she could shut it down there were tears rushing down her face like someone had scoured her eyeballs with an onion.

She turned away from Neeta and grabbed a piece of kitchen roll to stop anything getting on the bread products.

'Right,' Neeta said, no nonsense. 'Tell me now. What is going on?'

Anna took a deep breath, but the tears didn't seem to want to stop. 'It's Ed,' she told Neeta. 'He's having another baby.'

Ten

'Ed's lost his mind.'

'Ed is going to lose *all* the sleep. For years to come. And then he is going to lose any money he might have hoped to put towards a mid-life crisis motorbike or a 747-simulator course.'

'Neeta!' Lisa exclaimed.

'What? It is true. As soon as Pavinder hits fifty-five, which is the age that his father had his first heart attack, he wants to ride all over America on a Harley-Davidson.'

Anna's hands were shaking as she put the paper cup of deliciously rich hot chocolate to her lips and let the sweetness lift her just a little. Neeta had whizzed into action as Anna's tears had continued to fall and no amount of kitchen towel mopping seemed able to make it stop. She had found new volunteers for their stand, she had texted Lisa to get hot chocolates and then she had guided them here, to a corner of the gazebo set aside for the drinking of hot beverages.

It was far enough away from the midst of the ongoing fayre that they weren't obviously visible, but not so far that Anna couldn't keep an eye on Ruthie. She looked at Ruthie now. Red-cheeked, showing the candy-cane-filled jar to people at the stall while her friend Emily wrote down entrants' guesses on the competition form. There were a lot more people at the bazaar now and Anna was mindful that being three helpers down would not be ideal. She needed to take the sugar kick from this drink, then get her act together.

'Does Ruthie know?' Lisa asked, shifting her chair a little closer to Anna's.

Anna nodded. 'She's known for a while. At least a few weeks, I think.'

'And she didn't say anything earlier?'

Anna had been thinking that it was a little odd that Ruthie hadn't said anything straightaway. Ruthie usually couldn't keep things that were troubling her to herself because she was unable to manage the concerns and they would carry on pushing their way into the forefront of her mind. So why had she kept this in until today, when really it had been provoked out of her?

'Is she OK with it?' Neeta asked. 'I mean it is a shock to me and I am not his daughter.'

'I don't know,' Anna admitted. 'It's sometimes hard to know exactly how Ruthie's feeling deep down.' It wasn't that Ruthie *didn't* feel things deeply, but sometimes keeping things on a superficial level was like a grade of protection for her, Anna had discovered.

'Well, he's a shit,' Lisa stated, slurping at her drink.

'And he will be a very poor, penniless shit when he is ankle-deep in the shit of babies,' Neeta added. 'And speaking of ankles, my cousin says that that is where her pelvic floor is most of the time. Nicolette's Peloton will be no good for her then.'

Anna gave a small smile; the sweetness of the chocolate on her tastebuds and the pure love coming from her best friends was a pick-me-up she hadn't known she needed so badly today.

'Why didn't you tell us this last night?' Lisa asked. 'You know, when we had wine in our hands.'

'Not that the hot chocolate is not good,' Neeta said. 'But there is nothing like fermented grapes when you are tackling the crazy.'

'I didn't know last night. Ed turned up this morning. With a cat.'

And with Cheesecake – she still couldn't remember the pedigree name off by heart – plus the pregnancy news rattling around the living room and bouncing off Malcolm's boughs,

Anna still hadn't addressed the fact that she was sure Ed had a key to her house. She should definitely change the locks. Although the front door was something she had taken pains to keep, including the brass fittings. It had an original stained-glass panel – roses intertwining – Nanny Gwen had made up endless stories about when Anna was little. *The roses grew in the garden of a palace. A girl called Anna used to sell roses at the market.*

'What?! A cat!' Lisa said, nearly losing hold of her cup.

'Cats,' Neeta said with a hiss. 'I do not like them. They pee where they want to. They look at you like they are superior.' She seemed to consider for a second before continuing. 'They are a lot like Pavinder's Auntie Brinda.'

Suddenly, Lisa's hand was on Anna's thigh. 'I know you dismissed it before but . . . what about trying dating again?' She squeezed and Anna knew it was supposed to be reassuringly cajoling but Lisa had really strong hands from practising all kinds of ball sports with Kai. It was like being patted by a rugby prop.

'Did you not hear me when I said I have a cat?' Anna sighed. 'And a work project I'm battling with and . . . Ruthie and . . . Christmas is coming.'

'It would take only one second to reactivate your profile,' Neeta said, reaching into the pocket of her coat for her phone and tapping on the screen.

'Neeta, no,' Anna said, looking around for somewhere to put down her drink so she could get ready to tackle her friend if needed.

'How about this one?' Neeta asked, showing her phone screen to Lisa.

'He looks good,' Lisa remarked, leaning forward. 'His photo isn't a stock image of Tom Cruise and he doesn't look *too* filtered. In fact, he looks almost natural.'

Anna shook her head, remembering the last time she had taken her friends' advice and tried dating. She had told herself she had nothing to lose. It was only a bit of fun and meeting a guy for a drink didn't mean she had to a) see him for a second drink if he wasn't her glass of Shiraz or b) consider where he might fit on a timeline of life events even if she *did* want to see him again. There were no rules when you were thirty-five and divorced. You didn't have to conform to the get married, have babies, slip into watching *Tipping Point* every afternoon, death remit. It was supposed to be a little looser (like her waistline), a little lighter (definitely *not* like her waistline) and not necessarily made to last (possibly like her waistline if she exercised more often). Except it had all felt so awkward, more awkward than if you had that rulebook to follow. The guys she met who were her age didn't want someone with a teenage daughter, some of the older guys were a little *too* keen on her having a teenage daughter and there was one date who had asked her if she liked the feel of jam on her skin . . .

'If "natural" is Paolo Nutini,' Neeta said, still tapping on the screen.

'Ooo, yes, he does have that look about him,' Lisa agreed.

Anna shook her head again. 'I really don't want to date.'

'But you need something for *you*. Like I need something for me,' Neeta insisted. 'You already have a job so you need something else. And what is so wrong with a few man-shaped distractions?'

'Er, new cat, work, Ruthie, Ed—'

She might not be married to Ed anymore but he was Ruthie's father and that came with co-parenting connotations, maxed up because of Ruthie's individual needs. But this news about Nicolette should not be as earthshattering *to her* as she was making it. It was Ruthie it was going to impact on most.

'Oh! Oh, I pressed!' Neeta suddenly announced, getting to her feet and waving the phone in the air.

Neeta's actions drew attention from people getting ready to try to pin the tail on the reindeer. It wasn't a real reindeer, it was a gym horse covered in a couple of blankets with antlers made out of coat hangers and a Pink Lady apple for the nose . . .

'What did you do?' Anna asked, trying to maintain calm. 'I thought you were just on the website! Did you reactivate my account?' She frowned. Could Neeta do that from *her* phone? Had Anna not taken ownership of the passwords in the end? She didn't really remember.

'I think I gave him a hug,' Neeta said.

'That's OK,' Lisa replied, all chill as usual. 'It would have been much worse if you'd virtually spooned him.'

'I hugged someone?' Anna exclaimed. 'From *your* phone? Well, unhug him! Is there an icon for that?' She got to her feet too and apparently their hot chocolate break was more entertaining than watching a blindfolded person stagger towards the arse area of a fake reindeer with a drawing pin.

'Anna,' Lisa said, in that calming way of hers. 'We know you've got a lot on your plate, but you really do need to put yourself first for once.'

Put herself first. Put herself before Ruthie and Adam and the three eateries eating away at the corners of her mind as she tried to juggle everything else life threw at her.

'Imagine it,' Neeta began. 'Getting dressed up, putting on make-up to the tunes of Katy Perry, sipping some of that fizzy wine that tastes like cherries—'

'Lambrini Cherry!' Lisa said. 'I love that. But don't tell Paul. He's trying to get a place on the Rotary Club and thinks we have to appear like steamed-seabass-and-claret kind of people.'

'Lisa, you are breaking into my imagery,' Neeta said, grumpily. 'Anna, stick with me.' She put an arm around Anna's shoulder and drew her back down into sitting. 'You are all dressed up, a little flushed from the cheap alcohol and there he is, at a mid-range restaurant at worst . . . a date, someone new and attractive. Someone who does not yet know every story you have ever told or every memory you have ever made.'

'And he's interesting,' Lisa continued. 'And *interested*. He wants to *listen* to you. He wants to hear everything there is to know about a successful thirty-five-year-old who won awards for her project management, who renovated her home on a shoestring budget and turned it into the most desirable house on the street—'

Anna smiled as their warm, infectious talk began to make her feel a little bit better. Perhaps she did sell herself short. There was more to her than being a mum, she just didn't get the chance to peel off that top, most used, layer very often.

'With the most desirable MILF decorating the bedroom,' Neeta added.

'O-K,' Lisa said. 'I think Anna gets the idea now.'

'If he replies to the hug, I will ask him if he has ever been to the bar near Aldgate where you have to dress up as a western outlaw. I have always wanted to go there.'

Anna had no idea why that bar would be the measure of someone but sometimes Neeta's thinking did go a little off the beaten track. And whether she went back to the dating apps or not, this chat with her best friends had cheered her up. Perspective had been achieved. There were worse things in life than her ex-husband having a baby with his new girlfriend.

She could be having a baby – infinitely worse and never to be revisited no matter how strong anyone's date game got. Although a baby didn't need a litter tray that she would have to clean out like Frosty Pamplemousse or whatever Cheesecake's real name was.

Anna looked through the gazebo, past the latest contestant swaggering towards the hide of the gym horse, wanting to settle herself with another glance at Ruthie trying her best to engage with people at this event. Ruthie loved Christmas and everything that went with it – the music, the decorations, the markets and fayres, carol-singing, the food, the cold weather. She was like a slightly less having-people-sitting-on-your-knee version of Santa himself. Anna craned her neck a little. The stall was getting crowded now. How would Ruthie be coping with that?

'He is called Douglas by the way,' Neeta continued.

'How old?' Lisa asked. 'Because the name Douglas gives me "could be in his sixties vibes".'

'I . . . can't see Ruthie,' Anna said, standing and stepping slowly towards the open side of the gazebo. Panic was starting to expand inside of her but she was trying to keep it in check with a good dose of common sense. This was a safe space. And Ruthie didn't wander off anymore. Unless she was panicked into it . . .

'What?' Neeta said, at Anna's side already and shielding her eyes as she scanned the stalls across the green from their position. 'I will call Pavinder. See if she is in our greenhouse like she was the other time.'

The other time was the only other time Ruthie had been out of Anna's sight like this. Ruthie had been eight and, unbeknown to anyone else, she had headed to Neeta and Pavinder's home thinking their promise for her to see the plant collection had been an *immediate* invitation. She had left the park they'd been picnicking at, having apparently, on some occasion, memorised their address. But surely their home was too far away to be an explanation now. And Ruthie was older, slightly more streetwise, had been told never to put Anna through maternal hell ever again . . .

'Let's not panic,' Lisa said, standing next to them both now. 'Realistically, she's probably gone with one of the other kids to get a hot dog or something. I'll text Kai and Kelsey if we don't find her in a minute.'

Still Anna couldn't put eyes on her daughter. Where was her too-long tie-dye coat you could only just see her trainers peeking out of the bottom of? That bright pink hat with the bobble on top? Her bright eyes and even brighter smile?

'I didn't tell her I was leaving the soup stand,' Anna said, already walking out of the gazebo, boots hitting the frosty grass. 'I thought, because I could see her, it was OK but . . . it's not OK.'

'Anna, wait,' Lisa called as Anna picked up her pace.

She couldn't wait. She needed to find Ruthie now.

Eleven

Sam bit down into the large sausage in a long roll and closed his eyes. OK, so it wasn't his usual order from Eli's BBQ back home, but the meat with the mustard and ketchup squirted on top was enough for his stomach to realise exactly how much it needed filling. God, it was good. And here he was, in England, standing on almost frozen ground, at some kind of Christmas festival.

'Whittington Academy', the sign on the side of the building said. It looked kind of like a school, here in the middle of park land. *His* school hadn't been like that, his had been squashed between a parking lot and a disused factory where the gangs hung out. This was *quaint*. There were tables set out selling all kinds of items – things that sparkled or looked like snow, hats and scarves, animals made out of wood, giant cakes wrapped in clear film . . . His mom would think this place was paradise. His mom had always thought Christmas was a season anyone could enjoy even if you didn't have much. *It's not what you have, Sam. It's what you make of what you have.* Wasn't that the truth?

Sam took another bite of the hot dog and wished he'd bought two. His dad would approve of these ones. His dad always moaned about the hot dogs at the Bisons, saying they were a whole lot of nothing for almost six dollars. Chad on the other hand had once had the Bisons' hot dogs flown in from Cincinnati to their suite in Beverly Hills. One more bite and this food was gone.

'Give it back!'

'You're a freak!'

'I said, give it back!'

'Are you gonna cry like a baby?'

'No, I'm going to turn this into the Battle of Wakanda!'

Sam turned around and saw the group a little way away from him, at the edge of the wrought-iron fence. There were three tall teenage boys and one girl, much shorter, but she was squaring up to them, hands made into shapes as if she might be about to perform Miyagi-Do moves from *Cobra Kai*. One of the boys was holding a pink hat high and out of reach.

'If you can touch the hat, I'll give it back,' the boy told the girl.

The girl looked like she was thinking then, as her stance softened slightly, perhaps weighing up her options. And then she jumped, trying to claw down the hat at full stretch but failing, landing awkwardly, her ass hitting the icy grass. The boys laughed loud and hard and Sam felt that familiar pounding in his gut. *Bullies*. And he did not stand for them.

'Hey!' he called, making his way to the group. 'Is everything OK over here?'

'What's it to you?' the tallest boy questioned.

'What is it to me?' Sam asked. 'Is that what you said?'

'You deaf?' the boy with the hat queried, earning himself a laugh from his two friends.

Sam stepped closer. 'No. But you're dumb. Give the hat back.'

There seemed to be some discussion between the boys that only involved the movement of their eyebrows, a curling of their lips and some noises made through their noses. He took a step nearer still. He didn't need to use his height and width to intimidate, it just happened. The boys weren't quite so certain in their stance now, one of them even shuffled backwards. And his question to them was not up for debate.

'Now!' Sam ordered.

The hat was thrown towards the girl and the boy who'd taken it sneered. 'It sucks anyway.'

Laughing, the three of them sprinted off across the grass

and for a millisecond, Sam considered giving chase. They'd be no match for him, even given a head start. He'd never met anyone who could outsprint him – well, except maybe Usain Bolt. He'd met him once at a fundraiser but it hadn't seemed like the right time to lay down a challenge.

'Wow!'

Sam turned around and the girl was up off the floor, looking at him with the widest blue eyes. In her gloved hands she was holding a stick and on the end of the stick was the pink hat.

'You were like . . . Falcon and . . . Nick Fury rolled into one.'

Sam smiled. He'd been in the UK only a minute and was being compared to kick-ass Marvel characters? He liked that welcome.

'Well,' Sam said, 'wanna know what else I have in common with those guys?'

'You can fly? You have one eye? No, I can't see any wings and you have both your eyes so . . .' The girl gasped. 'Are you an actor?'

Sam shook his head. 'No. It's only that my name is Sam. Like Falcon and like Samuel L. Jackson. Nick Fury.' He had no idea why he had even made this comparison. 'Kind of wish I had wings now.'

'I'm Ruthie. And you're funny,' the girl answered. 'As well as *really* tall. Taller than Samuel L. Jackson I think. And American. Are you from Washington? I don't ever add the DC because I'm Marvel all the way.'

'I'm from . . .' What was he doing? About to spill the guts of his life to a teenager at a Christmas jamboree? He changed tack. 'Is the hat not yours?' He pointed to the pink beanie hooked onto the stick like the girl had caught a prize.

'Oh, no, it *is* mine. But it's dead to me now.' She nodded like that made all the sense in the world. 'Until my mum disinfects it and disinfects anything it touches from here to the car and then in the car and the house, until it gets into the washing machine and then she washes her hands, twice actually, because Acne Aaron, Gross Gregory and Icky Ibrahim breathed on it.'

Wow, that is a lot.

Sam opened his mouth to make comment but another voice beat him to it.

'Who are you? And what are you doing talking to my daughter?'

The voice was mad as hell. But the owner of the voice was heavenly. She had dark hair just visible poking out from underneath her hat, a neat figure in jeans, boots and a not-too-loose sweater. She had blue eyes like the girl, but these weren't so friendly. In fact, the expression was suggesting if he didn't say the right things she might want to put him in a headlock.

'Hi, ma'am, my name is—'

'Has Ed sent you?' the woman continued. 'Are you spying on us? Because I lost my attention for one second, *one*, and Ruthie knows she's not to wander off and . . . and . . .'

The woman stopped talking for a second, her eyes leaving him and going to the girl. 'Ruthie, why is your hat on a stick?'

'Mum, this is Falcon,' Ruthie announced proudly. 'He's American but he's not from Washington. And he's not a spy.' Next, she whispered. 'He's a superhero.'

Now the woman's eyes were definitely all over him and he wished his backpack was big enough for him to crawl up inside. What was he doing here? At a school. Eating hot dogs and getting nostalgic over festive fayre. In the UK . . .

'Listen, I'm just gonna go now,' Sam said, steadying his backpack and turning towards the gate.

'Oh, you're just going to go, are you? Without explaining a single thing about why you're hanging out at the very edge of a school charity Christmas market with a teenage girl!'

'What?' Sam said, turning back to face her.

'Mum!' Ruthie exclaimed. 'Falcon was helping! Acne Aaron, Gross Gregory and Icky Ibrahim took my hat and now it's dirty and my ears are cold, just like you said they would be, and this stick is heavier than it looks.'

Sam watched the woman's expression soften, her eyes warm, her demeanour turn from 'ready to wage war' to 'ready to deliver hugs'. He might have wanted to stick around a little longer to see her smile if it wasn't for the fact she thought his presence here was not the innocent bully interception it had been.

'Anna! What is going on? Is Ruthie OK? Ruthie, why are you holding your hat on a stick?'

And Sam was definitely going to leave now. Reinforcements had arrived in the shape of another woman who, when she had got over the stick situation, was also going to be looking at him like he should be on a watchlist.

'Goodbye, Ruthie,' he said to the girl. 'And, if those kids bother you again, just run at them, real fast. They won't have a defence for that.'

He waved a hand and then began to stride away.

'Mum! Don't let him leave, you haven't said thank you yet. He was really nice and he got them to give my hat back!'

It was time to find a hotel, catch up on some sleep, carry on avoiding turning on his phone, miss out on getting arrested maybe . . .

He headed out of the school grounds onto the street and contemplated which way to go.

'Excuse me!'

He turned around. And there was the woman, looking slightly less confrontational, but not about to hug him any time soon. He wasn't quite sure what to say. *I'm not a paedophile? I'm not a superhero either? Over in the States people might have called 911 over me already, I could do without the heat here?* Instead he said nothing, but he waited because he wanted to look at her a little longer . . . God, what was the matter with him? Jetlag 101.

'I . . . apologise,' the woman said. 'For assuming the worst. I . . . let my driven-by-watching-too-many-real

-life-crime-dramas imagination take over and I should have listened to my daughter before I judged you on that long, could-be-hiding-anything coat you're wearing and the hefty rucksack.'

'You judged me . . . on my jacket and my bag?' Sam queried.

'Not on a . . . *Project Runway* level,' the woman replied. She sighed. 'That sounded weird. Sorry. Let me start again. I apologise, for assuming the worst. And my daughter says I should thank you for helping out with those arsehole boys who ought to still be suspended for the last time they messed with her.'

And now the woman looked like she had the weight of the world on her shoulders. The eyes had lost their sparkle, the fight had waned, the overall vibe was defeated meets deflated.

'I don't like bullies,' Sam told her. 'But you should know, I think she would have tried to beat them up if I hadn't stepped in. She's got fire, that's for sure.'

Her mouth found a smile then and she nodded. 'Yes, she does.'

'OK,' Sam said, firming up his hold on the rucksack. 'I should get going. While I'm still Falcon and not . . .' He paused, thinking of the very worst villain. 'Thanos.'

'Absolutely,' the woman said, nodding again.

Sam took one last look at her before he stepped off the pavement. He definitely didn't even hear the car coming.

Twelve

Anna had never seen someone hit by a car before. And it wasn't some slow-motion, body rolling up the bonnet, suspended in the air and a gentle floating down to the tarmac like was sometimes portrayed on television. This was very hard and very fast and very *very* scary.

Before she even had a chance to process what she'd just seen, her feet were moving and she was rounding a parked car and running onto the street where the prostrate form of this tall, wide, frankly ridiculously good-looking man was lying. He was very still and his backpack was up near the back of his head.

'Is he alright? I didn't see him. He just stepped out right in front of me.'

It was the driver of the car, shaking, pale-faced, phone clutched in her hand. Anna was torn between asking her to call for an ambulance or asking her if she had been texting while she was driving.

There was movement. 'Falcon' was definitely alive. Anna got down on her knees and wondered if she should move anything. Loosen his coat or shift the rucksack? Why didn't she know any of this stuff? There didn't seem to be any blood, but was that bad or good? Sometimes, if injuries were internal, it was worse, wasn't it?

'I'm going to call an ambulance,' Anna decided out loud. She took her phone from the pocket of her jeans and prepared to press the number nine.

'No . . . don't . . . do that.'

It was him. The voice sounded a little weak but coherent. Maybe he'd heard the word 'elephant' instead of 'ambulance'.

62

She shook her head and watched him move a little more, albeit gingerly.

'Does it hurt anywhere?' Anna asked, reaching out to steady his shoulder as he sat up.

'What happened?' he asked. 'Did the . . . asshole kids come back?' He put a hand to his head.

Was that humour? If that was humour then he couldn't be too hurt.

'Was he . . . American before?' the driver asked, seeming caught between stepping forward and backing away. 'This isn't one of those situations where he's going to start talking in different languages or suddenly be able to play the piano, is it?' She sniffed. '*He* stepped out in front of me. You saw it.'

Anna focused back on the injured party. 'You did step out into the road.'

'Yeah,' he answered. 'Forgot which side you guys drive on.' He tried to get up but flailed a little.

'Falcon!'

Anna winced at the sound of Ruthie's voice and then her daughter was on the road too, looking traumatised, not down on her knees, but bending over in full-on protection mode. He was someone she already cared about. So trusting. So naïve.

'Is he going to be OK?' Ruthie asked Anna.

What could she say? She hadn't established the extent of the man's injuries. She hadn't actually done anything at all.

'I have taken photos!' Neeta said, rushing into the scene too. 'Of your position on the ground, sir, and of the position of your car, madam. I also have a laser measurement tool that can accurately work out your speed and trajectory. I do hope you were going within the speed limit.'

There were too many voices, too many opinions, and Anna couldn't catch up. She put a hand on the man's shoulder while Neeta and the driver of the car had a discussion about braking distances.

'I should call an ambulance,' Anna told him.

'No, I'm good. I just . . . need a minute.'

'Well . . . do you think you can make it just down the street? About . . . half a mile?'

'Is . . . that the nearest hotel?' he answered, getting up onto his knees.

'No,' Anna said. 'That's my house. I can . . . make sure you don't need to go to hospital and . . . get you a warm sugary drink and—'

'You can meet my new cat, Cheesecake,' Ruthie chipped in. 'And my rabbit, Mr Rocket.'

Was a warm sugary drink the thing to do when someone had been upended by a car? Or was it nil by mouth? Sweet tea had always been Nanny Gwen's first suggestion for most things. If that didn't work, then it was gin. Well, whatever it was, Anna could check it out on her laptop when she got home and if he collapsed on the way there then she'd call the emergency services anyway. And if there was blame and a claim, Neeta had the photographic evidence.

'I can make it a few blocks,' the man said, almost on his way to standing.

'Are you sure?' Anna asked. What was she doing? A few minutes previous to this she had been thinking he was about to abduct Ruthie and now she was inviting him into her home, when he was hurt and she had not a clue what to do?

'Drive them!' Neeta ordered, pointing at the woman retreating back to her car. 'You will drive them to the house. If you are capable. It is the very least you can do, right?'

Anna looked at her friend, who was nodding enthusiastically in that way she did to ensure compliance was your only option. It seemed like the decision had been made already.

Thirteen

Anna and Ruthie's home, Richmond

Sam's ribs were hurting every time he took a more than shallow breath inwards and he had a black and white rabbit on his lap. His life had apparently turned into a Harlan Coben TV adaptation. There was a mug of hot, sweet tea on the kitchen table that was nothing like the sweet tea he was used to back home. For one, it was hot and secondly because it contained milk. He would have thought that the British were crazy but . . . he actually quite liked the taste.

'Mum's put Cheesecake in the utility room,' Ruthie said, stroking the rabbit carefully. 'They haven't met Mr Rocket yet so they won't know they aren't allowed to eat family members. We only just got them and we haven't got a cat flap yet, or a litter tray, so they've got a baking tray with flour in it to pee in.'

The cat's name. Not a dessert. Sam nodded. 'A wise idea.'

'How are you feeling now?' Ruthie asked.

'Ruthie,' the woman said, turning her attention away from drying up dishes. 'You asked Falcon that about two seconds ago.'

'It wasn't two seconds. It took more than two seconds to tell him about Cheesecake. Do you want to watch *Loki*? We don't have Sky anymore, Dad cancelled that, but we have Netflix and Disney+.'

What was the right answer here? He should call a hotel and get a room as soon as he finished up this drink. He went to reply . . .

65

'Ruthie, why don't you go into the lounge and set *Loki* up and I'm just going to . . . take Falcon's temperature.'

She was going to do what? Sam moved slightly in this kitchen table chair and a pain ripped through him. He gritted his teeth and let nothing show on his face. He was OK. At least this time, he'd been thrown into the air but there weren't points at stake and he wasn't unconscious.

'OK,' Ruthie said. 'But don't be long.'

As soon as Ruthie was out of the kitchen, the woman took the rabbit from Sam's lap and popped it into a small portable cage on the worktop. It started to nibble on a carrot, unperturbed by the change in location. Nothing like Sam, who had changed his location and still felt totally out of whack. How long had it been since he left the US? This time zone difference was going to kill him even if this car collision hadn't.

'I'm sorry about all that. I expect the last thing you need is a rabbit on your lap and endless chatting about Marvel when you're recovering from a road traffic accident.'

'Do you . . . have any . . . Advil?'

The woman's index finger rose into the air like she was thinking hard. 'Give me a second. I know what that is. Heard it on countless American shows. Ibuprofen. Yes, I do.' She turned away and opened a cupboard that seemed to house a lot of medication. He swallowed. Was that going to be his life soon? Was there even medication to help what he had?

'Oh, God, there *is* blood!'

She'd turned back, was looking in his direction with an anxious expression. 'What?' For some reason, Sam looked at the rabbit. The cute-looking thing had taken his finger in his mouth earlier and grazed skin before he'd realised any intent.

'Just . . . take off your jumper. Let me look. I have . . . crepe bandages from circa 2010 and . . . some sort of ointment I put on my hand when I got burned by a Taser. And hopefully something better than all of those.'

'Did you say I was bleeding?' He turned his head, tried to see over the back of his shoulder. The second he twisted he wished he hadn't, because his whole torso cried out. His fingers found the bottom of his sweater and he attempted to pull it up his body.

'Here,' the woman said, taking ownership and wrenching the material upwards and off him in one easy move. 'Like ripping off a plaster.'

'A what?' Sam asked. This whole conversation was confusing to him. Perhaps he had hit his head after all.

'OK,' the woman breathed. 'It's fine. Well, you know, not perfectly unscathed but not gushing liquid like a car wash. It looks like a scrapey, gravelly concretey kind of thing.'

He had no idea what any of that meant. But then he felt fabric being put to his skin and the woman held it there, standing next to him, applying pressure.

She smiled. 'I'm Anna, by the way. Just in case you were wondering the name of this so-not-a-nurse who is panicking while she tries not to panic.'

'Sam,' he replied. 'And what I'm wondering right now is ... did you really get burned by a Taser?'

'Yes,' she answered. 'But I haven't known you long enough to go into any of the details.'

She had amazing eyes and looking into them was taking his mind off the fact he was now naked from the waist up. And he should keep the conversation going ...

'How's it looking back there? Do you think I'm gonna need stitches?' He hoped not. He was so done with hospitals right now.

'I don't think so but I'm no expert. Just focusing on stopping the bleeding. But you have quite a number of bruises back here.'

And apparently Anna needed to study his entire top half from nape to nearly-coccyx. What was she doing? She had a man in her kitchen. In her and Ruthie's home. She had no idea who he was. This whole scenario could be an elaborate plot to get inside her Chromebook and grab all her financial details. Except, as naïve as Ruthie was, her daughter was equally adept at sniffing out badness. And she had taken to Falcon . . . *Sam*. His name was Sam.

'Some of those bruises are old,' Sam said.

'O-K,' Anna answered, lifting the tea towel a little and then gently pressing the wound again. 'Are you . . . on the run from the cops?'

She felt his body lift and a small laugh escaped into the air. 'No.'

'Is this something you do to claim compensation? I mean, did you pretend to get hit? Swan dive onto that woman's bonnet and then play almost dead?'

'Are these questions serious?' he asked. 'Because I'm pretty sure I've cracked a rib and that's never any fun when you need to laugh.'

'You've cracked a rib?! Then we should get you to hospital! You'll need an X-ray and different painkillers to what I have. All the really strong stuff and not out of date.'

'Hey,' he said. 'Relax. It's fine. I've pretty much cracked all of them before. I just need to . . . not get hit by any more cars while I'm here. And to not bleed to death. So, how is that coming on?'

Yes, she was supposed to be taking charge of this flesh wound not interrogating the guy. She lifted the tea towel again.

'I think it's OK. It's quite a deep graze in places but I think it will be OK with just a dressing.'

Sam shook his head. 'No dressing. It's better to let the air get to it. I'll just give it a minute and put my sweater back on.'

'Oh, no, don't do that,' Anna said. 'It's dirty. I can wash it and . . . find you something else to wear.'

'You don't have to do that. I'm taking up your time and I've made you miss the Christmas jamboree and—'

'Jamboree?' She laughed.

'What's so funny?'

'The chairwoman of the committee would literally put you in the festive stocks and pummel you with mince pies if she heard you calling it a "jamboree". When we started the idea, she insisted it was called a "fayre" – f-a-y-r-e – and not a "fete". A "fete" apparently sounds too common.'

'And putting people in stocks and throwing food at them is so Rockefeller, right?'

'Exactly,' Anna said. 'But, you know, make every second stall "artisan crafts", pop some sweet potato chunks in the soup, not to mention having the school band that have appeared on *Blue Peter twice* now. That is definitely so *not* a jamboree.'

It was then she realised she was still holding the tea towel to his broad, muscular back, standing too close with no need to be there. Lifting the cloth and stepping back, Anna's foot met a stray piece of Mr-Rocket-chewed lettuce and her boot slipped away from her.

'Whoa! You OK?'

'Yes. Yes, I'm fine.'

Despite his injuries, he had caught her with one taut strong arm and it was as sexy as it was embarrassing. Who even was she right now? But, much more importantly, who was he?

Anna righted herself and peeled the lettuce off her shoe. 'Kids and pets. Always leaving something somewhere.'

'Add sisters to that list. Whenever my sister comes over to my apartment my place looks like Ru Paul emptied his make-up drawer.'

He had a sister. That was information. Anna rid her hands of the lettuce, then opened up the door of her washing machine and popped in his jumper.

'So, are you here on holiday?' Anna asked, finding a washing tab, adding it to the mix, closing the door and pressing the on button.

'No . . . I . . . that is . . . kinda, I guess.'

OK, that was a little disconcerting. She straightened up and stayed where she was, back to the worktop as the machine began to fill with water. The kitchen knives were readily accessible if things turned ugly . . .

'Sorry,' Sam began. 'That sounded weird. It is kinda like a vacation. But I didn't plan it . . . I mean, I didn't plan it very well. I wanted to . . . I don't know . . . see the sights and pick up some gifts and before I thought about anything else, I was over here.'

'At a school jamboree in Richmond?' Anna raised an eyebrow.

'I can explain that,' Sam told her. 'That was entirely down to the smell of caramelised onions and sausage. I was so hungry. Plane food is . . . plane food.'

'So, where are you staying?' Anna asked.

'Yeah,' he began, picking up his mug of tea. 'Remember the bit about not planning very well? But, you know, it's OK. Any hotel will be fine. Do you, you know, know anywhere good?'

He had nowhere to stay. This was getting more and more suspicious by the second. And currently he was bare-chested in her kitchen. All six-foot-God-knows-how-many-more-inches of him!

The door to the kitchen suddenly banged open again and there was Ruthie, hands on her hips, looking furious. '*Loki* has been ready to watch for ages. Are you coming, Sam? You need to meet Malcolm. He's even taller than you!'

Fourteen

'What is going on? It's been hours. I have left you eight messages!'

Anna crept out of the living room and into the hallway, cringing every time the floorboards creaked under her movement. She remembered doing a similar thing when she'd first started to date Ed and they'd come back to the house for 'coffee'. Not waking Nanny Gwen had been paramount to the 'percolation' of said 'coffee' and they had never ever succeeded. Nanny Gwen had always appeared – from who knew where – and reminded Anna that she had an early start in the morning. Even if her early start was one of those mid-morning breakfasts from Spooner's on a weekend. Ed would respond by kissing Anna goodbye a little zealousy and in full view of Nanny Gwen. Anna's grandmother had never hidden her dislike of Anna's choice in partner but she had still remained supportive and respected it. Anna gently pulled the door to now and gave half a smile to the photo of Nanny Gwen, then she tiptoed towards the kitchen. Once in there she closed the door.

'Anna!' Neeta screamed. 'If I do not see your face instead of the flooring I am calling the police and then I am coming round there because response times are still inadequate.'

Anna lifted the phone up and put a finger to her lips. 'Ruthie's asleep. In the living room.'

'What? But she never sleeps *anywhere* but her bed.'

'I know,' Anna replied. 'But she's watched all six episodes of *Loki* and had three banana milkshakes.' She pulled out a chair and sat down at the table.

'I am very pleased for her but—'

'Tell me how the fayre was,' Anna jumped in. 'I am so sorry I left you shorthanded. Did you have record takings again this year?'

'We did. And there was a bidding war at the silent auction for my basket of sweet treats. It actually was not silent at all at the end. There was full-on shouting in five-pound increments. It was all very undignified. But that is not why I left you eight messages. Did you not read any of them?'

'Some of them were Bitmojis,' Anna answered.

'That is not an answer. What happened with the hot guy? Please, please, please tell me you got his number . . . and obviously tell me that he did not have a car-crash-related aneurysm.'

Anna's gaze went to the radiator on which Sam's sweater was still drying. 'He . . . didn't have an aneurysm.'

'And his number? Because if Douglas does not hug you back on the app then you have another option.'

Anna swallowed, knowing the second the next words were out of her mouth Neeta was going to reply with volume and lots of gasping and would be straight on the phone to Lisa the moment Anna hung up.

'He's still here.'

'What?!' Neeta's face seemed to get all big and puffy like it had morphed into a giant marshmallow. A very happy-looking giant marshmallow.

'It's perfectly innocent. Ruthie insisted he stay to watch *Loki* and then Cheesecake sat on top of him and Ruthie said he wasn't allowed to move Cheesecake and then Sam fell asleep and then Ruthie fell asleep and now you're right up to date.'

'Are you calling yourself Cheesecake now?'

'No,' Anna said quickly. 'That's what Ruthie's called the new cat.'

'So you have a hot guy asleep in your living room.'

'I'm surprised you're leading with that and not giving me the "stranger danger" talk you gave me before all of my dates. What was it? Meet in a very public place. Never,

ever share transport. If he mentions his mother more than once in the first hour I have to leave.'

'*Has* he mentioned his mother more than once?'

'No. But we haven't really had time to say anything to each other. Ruthie's talked the whole screenplay out loud and I've made hot drinks, milkshakes and a flatbread pizza that had to have Christmas cheese on it because I'd run out of the ordinary stuff. Now that packet is open it isn't going to last until the twenty-fifth. I'll be having Emmental on my toast in the morning and a roll of Roule for my lunch.'

'Forget the cheese! This is *progress*. This is you being empowered after the baby disaster news. This is you reclaiming your vagina.'

Anna hadn't known her vagina was lost. OK, so it might not have had third-party attention for a while but it was present and correct and definitely not at the needs-an-industrial-hedge-trimmer stage. However, her vagina had nothing to do with the man asleep in her lounge. She was . . . making sure he was OK. Just that. Like he had done for Ruthie with those arsehole boys.

'Let me see what you are wearing,' Neeta said suddenly.

Anna dipped her camera a little to show. 'Exactly what I had on earlier when we were selling soup together.'

'Oh my God, you need to change! You will smell like my grandmother's kitchen. And believe me, not even my grandfather wanted to have sex with something that smelled the same as what he was putting in his mouth at dinner time.'

'Neeta! I'm not having sex with him!'

Had she said that too loud? She listened for any sounds of Ruthie or Sam or Cheesecake but all she could hear was the faint hum of the golden fairy-lights she had strung around the door frame.

'Is he married?'

'I don't know.'

'Does he live around here?'

'No. He's visiting. Seeing the sights and Christmas

73

shopping. He has a sister.' And that was the extent of what she knew. Except . . .'And he's got a lot of bruises. Not only from the accident.'

Neeta gasped, all wide brown eyes and excitement. 'Cage fighter! Or . . . or . . . a stuntman. A *bad* boy.'

Anna screwed up her face. 'None of those are appealing.'

'None of those are appealing if you are looking for something long term. But all of those are appealing if you just want someone to dirty your Orla Kiely bedding.'

'Neeta!'

'Lisa would think the same. If you want to call her and ask her opinion.' Neeta sniffed. 'It is all this reserved Britishness. It gets in the way of everything for us. Well, my New Year's resolution is going to be all about empowerment. *My* empowerment. No more cooking ridiculous feasts for Pavinder and his colleagues because it makes me look devoted. No longer pretending to be interested in fungicide. I am going to become a goddess of my own destiny.'

'That's really great.' She took a breath, remembering the things Neeta had talked about at the fayre. 'So, are you going to talk to Pavinder? Iron out your worries about this Jessica woman? I mean, I'm sure that if you tell him how you're feeling, be really honest, he's going to put your mind at rest immediately and maybe you can both get back on the same page.'

'Goddesses of their own destiny write their own stories,' Neeta answered shortly.

'I know,' Anna said. 'And I am all for that, but you can't mean you don't want any chapters containing Pavinder.' Could she?

'It depends where his epilogue lies.'

'Well, you won't know that until you speak to him.'

'Exactly,' Neeta concluded. 'And I am not ready to know. Nor am I ready to talk without pretending we are speaking about someone's book. So let me carry on focusing on the fact you have a man in your house who is not Ed nor the man to read your electricity meter.'

'OK,' Anna agreed. 'I'll let it drop for now. But, Neeta, I am always here for you, OK. No matter what.'

'Check his phone,' Neeta said, subject changed.

'What? Why?'

'Because you can find out everything you need to know from someone's phone. You do not even have to dig too deeply, you know.'

Anna did know. Because that was how she had found out about Ed's affair and she hadn't even had to surreptitiously unlock it. The message had been right there, brazen, uncaring for who might discover it. Thank God it hadn't been Ruthie . . .

'If the last thing he searched the internet for was not Wordle, is he even human?' Neeta continued.

'I'm not going to look at his phone,' Anna answered. 'Because he's only here because he got hurt. As soon as he wakes up I'll call him an Uber and then I'll never see him again.'

'Face ID only needs a quick flash of the eyes and it is unlocked. Pavinder did not even wake up.'

'I'm going to go now,' Anna said, standing up.

'Well, call me after he has got in the cab, just so I know he did not turn into one of those crazy woods people from *Yellowjackets*. Perhaps do not let him near the rabbit.'

Anna ended the call before Neeta could go any more cuckoo herself. She put her phone on the table and it was then she saw it. Sam's rucksack on the floor next to the fridge. She shook her head. No, she was not going to let her mad friend into her headspace. She did not invade people's privacy, particularly the privacy of people who had saved her child from bullies and had sat through an entire season of a Marvel spin-off being narrated at them. She turned off the kitchen lights and prepared to head back into the living room and see if Ruthie or their guest had stirred. She absolutely had not noticed that the zip on Sam's bag was a little open . . .

Fifteen

Sam could hear voices.

'What rhymes with "rice"?'

'Nice.'

'Too obvious. Something else.'

'Lice?'

'Eww! No, Ruthie!'

'How about "mice". You'd like that, Cheesecake, wouldn't you?'

The meow that followed sounded like the cat was insulted that something larger hadn't been offered. Sam was properly coming to now.

'I'm pretty sure there was something in the *Richmond Reporter* about one of the local eateries having an issue with rodents. But, you know, I guess they have to mention them when it's the Year of the Rat. Is it the year of the rat? I might be able to do something with that.'

It wasn't a dream. He'd hit a car. Or, rather, a car had hit him. And he was in England. London. God, he felt exhausted. He rubbed his face with his hand. His skin felt like it had a week's worth of stubble peppering his jawline. And how long had he spent sleeping in a chair?

'Sam's awake! Hi, Sam!'

What time was it? What day was it? Why was this girl wearing bright white tinsel-covered trousers and a T-shirt with a picture of . . . was that the owner of Virgin Atlantic on there?

'Hey . . . Ruthie.' He straightened himself up in the chair, his muscles, his bones, all silently weeping inside him.

'I'm going tap-dancing. It's a rehearsal for our Christmas show. Can you guess who I am?'

She spun around and ended the move with her hands on her hips. Sam had absolutely no idea. He shook his head. 'You're gonna have to tell me.'

'I'm Mary! You know, Jesus's mother.' She pulled the T-shirt away from her body a little. 'We're doing alternative costumes. This is Richard Branson. He owns—'

'Maybe Sam would like a coffee before he hears any more.'

It was Anna, moving into the space, a large polka-dot decorated mug in her hands. She was wearing jeans and a bright red jumper that brought out the colour of her eyes. *Sam Jackman, are you blushing right now?*

'Oh, wow, thank you but if I drink all that I'm not gonna sleep tonight,' Sam answered.

Anna frowned. 'It takes you . . . more than twelve hours to get caffeine out of your system?'

Sam's heart punched him. 'What time is it?'

'It's eight o' clock, silly. In the morning. It's Sunday,' Ruthie announced with a kick ball change.

He stood up then, fast, like he was running from the consequences of bad deeds. He had been here *all* night? It was morning. 'I have to go.' He scanned the room for his rucksack and his coat. Then he looked down at his body. He was wearing the long-sleeved top with blue and black hoops that Anna had given him to put on last night. Should he take it off? Should he keep it, have it dry-cleaned and return it later?

'Have some coffee,' Anna said, offering the mug out again.

The coffee *did* smell good. And his stomach was virtually empty again, the hot dog long since digested. Did he eat here last night? He had a vague memory of pizza.

'I just . . . don't wanna take up any more of your time,' Sam told her.

'Mum won't mind,' Ruthie said. 'Especially if you help her with rhyming with the word "rice".'

Sam took the mug as Anna went back to her laptop. There was a small desk in the corner of the living room, half-enveloped by this giant Christmas tree. The desk was covered in notebooks and pens, highlighters, stickers, a framed photo of Ruthie – he guessed – dressed like Spiderman. It was chaotic but the nice kind, the kind that said work was happening here and everything had its role to play.

He stayed standing, taking a sip of the hot black liquid. No milk. How had she known? Had he told her last night?

'Twice?' Sam offered.

Anna turned round in her chair, glasses on her nose now, the thick black framed kind that made women look even more sexy in his opinion.

'No,' Anna said. 'But maybe I could work with "thrice".'

'I'm going to feed Cheesecake,' Ruthie said. 'Will she/he/they be OK with more tuna until we get cat food?'

'Damn,' Anna said. 'I forgot I still haven't got food for it. Yes, Ruthie, tuna will be fine. Be careful with the tin and—'

'I know! And I'll wear my gloves.'

Ruthie left the room, tap-dancing all the way and Sam took a step towards the desk. 'What are you working on?'

'Oh,' Anna said, tapping on the keyboard. 'Highly secretive government work. How to have a party at Number Ten and get away with it.'

'O-K.'

'I'm kidding. Who would want that job? No, I'm in charge of restructuring and re-strategising three eateries, but they're kind of all together and no one seems very clear if they want separate identities or one to cover everything. At the moment, I'm hedging my bets and trying to develop different concepts for both purposes until the owner makes a firm decision.'

'And you're coordinating all this from here?' Sam asked.

Anna turned to face him. 'Are you suggesting this Ikea desk and chair wedged between a Christmas tree and the doorway isn't giving off enough "captain of industry" vibes?'

'I would never dare to suggest anything like that.' He smiled. 'Is that an empty packet of chips just there?' He pointed.

Anna looked back at her desk and then quickly turned

back. 'I can't believe I fell for that. I don't leave empty snack packets on my workspace.'

Sam laughed. 'I got you good.'

'So, what do *you* do for a job?'

'What do *I* do?' Sam wasn't sure why he had repeated the question.

'Do you have a really big office? Nothing like this lounge-strays-are-welcome space I have?'

He smiled. 'I work outdoors mainly . . . on grass.'

Why wasn't he simply telling her? He didn't have to tell her everything. Except perhaps his anonymity here would be compromised if he told her he played football. Would she know who he was? Did he want her to know who the world thought he was?

'Grass,' Anna said, sounding ever more curious.

'Mum!' Ruthie's voice screamed. 'The gloves have split and I have tuna on my fingers! I'm going to die!'

Anna leapt up from her seat, knocking a couple of notebooks to the floor. 'Listen, I can give you a lift into the centre of Richmond if you want me to. It's on the way to Ruthie's class and I know a good mid-range hotel that might have a room.'

'Yeah? That would be cool. Thanks.'

'OK, well, I'll just fix this crisis and we can get ready to go.'

'Sure,' he answered. 'Thanks.'

Except as he was left alone in the room, he started to remember why he was here and why he had fled. Even if the doctor hadn't yet delivered the news to anyone else, the rumour mill would be starting up as soon as he missed his first session of training. He had to make contact with someone today. Even if what he told them wasn't the entire truth, he could buy himself some time before the real reason was out there. But then what? He had no idea.

As he took a deep breath, his eyes were somehow drawn to the radiator under the window. A saucepan was catching drips.

Sixteen

Richmond

'OK, whistlestop tour,' Anna said as they pulled away from the building where Ruthie was going to spend an hour perfecting the festive tap offering. 'I'm going to drive the long way round and point out the most famous sites of Richmond.'

She stopped talking and gave a tiny glance towards the passenger seat. 'Sorry, if you have time for me to do that. I have time because the only things waiting for me at home are a rabbit that needs cleaning out and a cat who seems to want to use the sofa as a scratching post. Maybe I need to buy it a scratching post as well as the other things.'

'It's a cute cat.'

'It's a cute cat we didn't need.'

'I used to con my mom and dad into things all the time when I was her age. Like ice cream when it wasn't my birthday. Being home later than my curfew. Watching movies that were too old for me.'

'I didn't get the cat. That was an early Christmas gift from my ex-husband. Even though we spent most of our marriage telling Ruthie she couldn't have one.'

Anna sighed. And here Ed was again, right in the centre of her thought process by her own volition. She concentrated on the road ahead. They were coming up to traffic. Of course they were. Richmond at its finest. Except she *loved* this place, had always loved it. It was where she had grown up, it was embedded in her. She didn't just know a mid-range hotel, she knew *all* the hotels, the pubs and cafés, the parks, the Thames.

And Nanny Gwen had been such an enthusiastic tour guide, embellishing everything in the best possible ways. *Finest stretch of river in the whole of London. The most handsome ducks living on it.* Your *ducks, Anna.* That was why, when Ed had suggested renting an extortionately priced apartment in the heart of the city with floor-to-ceiling glass and a view of the railway lines – a plus apparently – she had dug her heels in, unable to imagine living anywhere else. Richmond was the kind of place to bring up a family.

What was the point of spending a few wild, carefree years somewhere sharper and edgier with colour-changing lights around the kitchen ceiling when you were going to long for Richmond in the end? And when her nana had passed, it had turned the housing dilemma on its head. Anna had inherited a property she could never have dreamed of affording through hard work alone. But it had been so bittersweet. Her beautiful home, the only family home she had ever known, had come to her at the expense of her beloved grandmother.

'Is it messy?' Sam asked.

'What?' Anna said, distracted by her thoughts as they sat in static traffic.

'With your ex. You said he got the cat and the cat wasn't planned for.'

'Well, actually, the cat not being planned for is the least of his worries right now.'

'Life can hit you like a train, right?' Sam remarked, looking out of the window at the high street.

'Not read that particular note on an inspirational calendar just yet. You should get one going,' she teased.

'Saturday: Life can hit you like a train. Sunday: What rhymes with "rice"?'

Anna laughed out loud. He was funny. Clever funny. The type of funny that exactly matched her wavelength somehow.

'I should be insulted,' she told him. 'I should throw you out of the car right now and not treat you to the delights of Richmond.'

'Please, ma'am. I'm a stranger to these parts and I have ribs that might be broken.'

Anna took her foot off the clutch and pulled forward slowly. 'Check out the wonderful Christmas decorations. You missed the lights being switched on. We had Storm Troopers and music from Radio Jackie plus jugglers and elves and Father Christmas.'

'Hey, you're making it sound like a jamboree.'

'That's my favourite coffee place.' She pointed out of the window. 'Ruthie loves the hot chocolates and if Esther ever tells me who brings her those full, rich, dark beans I might consider getting married again.'

'*That* good?'

'That good.'

'How did you know I didn't take cream with my coffee this morning?' Sam asked.

'Ah, well,' Anna began. 'Obviously I went through your bag while you were asleep.'

Why had she said that? It was supposed to be a joke, but Neeta had suggested exactly that last night. And she hadn't, of course. She needed to backtrack.

'Just kidding,' Anna said a little too loudly. 'I'd never do that. It was meant to be funny and it wasn't and—'

'I was actually impressed,' Sam answered, 'that you could find out I drink black coffee by looking at a few sweaters.'

'Is that really all you brought with you? That one bag?'

The bag that was currently in the footwell, nesting between his very large feet. It was a little bit odd, to come over from the US and to have brought only a backpack. Or perhaps she was overthinking it – wherever she went, a bag that size would soon be filled up with antibacterial wipes, disposable gloves and a few bags of Ruthie's favourite Fox's Glacier Fruits. And she didn't really know he had come from America. He might have the accent but that didn't mean he lived there.

'I came to buy gifts. I figured I'd get a case here and take it back full.'

'Back to where?'

'What?'

'Sorry, I mean, I've been assuming you're American but I'm terrible with accents, you could just as easily be Canadian or . . . Australian.' She had no idea why she had said that. 'Ooo, look, here's a great section of decorations.'

They were still crawling at a snail's pace along the street. 'On this road they wind fairy lights around every tree and actually, because January is usually so miserable, they leave them up until the 1st of February to make people feel a bit brighter when it's all cloudy and gloomy.'

'Classic warm lights. I like those better than the flashing Vegas strip kind.'

And he hadn't told her where he was from. Exactly like he hadn't told her what he did for a job. Who was this man of mystery? Because he didn't immediately strike her as someone who was disingenuous. But perhaps sharing wasn't necessary. They weren't going to see each other again.

'But your tree – Malcolm – he's kinda awesome,' Sam told her.

Anna gasped. 'Are you saying my tree looks like Las Vegas?!'

'Do you leave it there all the year? Like it has a residency?'

'I am appalled at this rudeness!' Anna said. 'Yesterday I practically scraped you off the tarmac, I attempted first aid, I gave you hot, sugary tea and let you use a share of a frankly extortionate monthly fee for Disney+ and—'

'The traffic's moving,' Sam interrupted, a smile on his mouth. His rather striking full-lipped mouth . . .

Anna refocused and let her foot off the clutch to glide the car forward at least a metre.

'I'm from Cincinnati,' Sam said.

'That's a real place?' Anna asked. 'Because it sounds exactly like a troupe of chorus girls from Caesar's Palace.'

'Ouch! I really jabbed you with the tree comment, didn't I?' Sam said, holding his hands in the air in a signal of surrender. 'I apologise. No more jibes.'

She turned the blower on to shift the condensation from the windscreen. The car was almost as old as Ruthie so nothing really worked properly. She had even put some of those little bags of silica gel on the dashboard to rid it of moisture otherwise the inside froze up. 'OK, so, while we wait for the traffic to shift, tell me something cool they have in Cincinnati.'

Something cool about Cincinnati. There were a lot of things cool about Cincinnati but now all that was coming to Sam's mind was the inside of the doctor's office and all the things he wasn't dealing with. And then, before panic could begin to rise, a memory came back to him. Their mom and dad taking Tionne and him to Eden Park. To a nine-year-old Sam it felt like they had left behind the bricks and the alleyways and the smell of the garbage cans and landed on another planet.

'Eden Park is cool,' he told Anna. 'It's right next to the river and there's a couple lakes, an old water tower, the art museum . . . and my favourite thing is this conservatory full of all different kinds of plants. I mean when you're nine years old and you think any kind of scrubland is the purest type of nature, seeing palms and ferns and orchids and bonsai, it blew my mind.'

'We have Kew Gardens, not far from here actually. And on a slightly smaller scale, my friend Pavinder has a rather large greenhouse in his garden full of all kinds of weird stuff that grows.'

'Not a plant fan?' Sam asked her.

'No . . . I mean . . .' She took her eyes off the windscreen for a second. 'I like walking in the park and the different colours when the seasons change but . . .'

'But?'

'I don't know,' she breathed. 'I think maybe I'm a little afraid of nature as a concept.'

'Whoa, what?'

'Before you think I'm completely crazy, hear me out,' Anna said, moving the car a few more feet along the congested road. 'Nature is one of the only things that happens spontaneously, without anyone pushing a button or giving an order. And it could happen *anywhere*. There is a possibility that one day I could wake up being smothered by a full-grown tree that has sprouted in the night.'

Sam laughed hard then. So hard his ribs ached.

'And have you not seen *The Day of the Triffids*? Terrifying.'

'You think a tree is gonna suffocate you in the night?'

'You've seen the size of Malcolm! He may have been cut off at the base but if spiders can grow new legs then who knows what spruces can do.'

'Ow!' Sam said, putting a hand to his chest. 'You're gonna kill me with this laughing.'

She sighed. 'I suppose it's the power of nature that scares me the most. How you can do all the right things to achieve the expected outcome but if "nature" decides it's going to do something completely different there's absolutely nothing you can do to stop it.'

He swallowed. Somehow this was feeling close to the bone now. He had done all the right things. Always. Or as close to always without getting extreme with it. And 'nature' had let him down. Given him this thing that was going to change his life.

'When you're the mother of a child with autism you get a bit defensive about the beauty of something you can't control. Not that I would change who Ruthie is. I suppose she's a bit like my four-leaf clover.'

'Ruthie has autism?' Sam asked. He got that Ruthie was loud and talkative, but he hadn't thought that was anything other than a big personality.

'Her attention to detail didn't hit it home?'

'Hey, attention to detail is good.'

'The sanitiser and the finger-clicking?'

'Quirky, I admit, but who am I to say what's normal? I got hit by a car and I'm wearing someone else's sweater.'

He watched her smile. He liked it when she smiled. And thinking about how he liked it made pinpricks break out on his skin. Damn!

'It's challenging,' Anna said, driving the car forward as the queue seemed to quicken up. 'It's exhausting. But—'

'She's a great kid,' Sam interrupted. 'Still full of energy that hasn't been tackled to the earth by real life.'

'Yes,' Anna answered. 'She's a great kid. Oh . . . oh, here we are, coming up to one of the most well-known places in Richmond.'

'Yeah?'

He looked out the window as the road carried on over an old-looking thick stone bridge, the wide expanse of river flowing under it. Despite the cold, there were rowers on the surface in thin canoes, their oars flicking in and out of the water in rhythm. It wasn't like the Ohio River back home, it was somehow more regal – there were white swans for God's sake – demure, no signs shouting 'look at me' with a hashtag to share with your photo. This was the epitome of understated, smooth Britishness.

'This is Richmond Bridge. It's the oldest surviving bridge on the Thames. And all along here,' Anna said, driving the car super-slow even though the traffic had now disappeared, 'are bars and restaurants. In the summer, the terraced lawns there are filled with people and picnics. It's a really nice spot to lounge out and people-watch.'

'You like to people-watch?'

'Doesn't everyone?'

'Yeah, that's true,' he answered.

But the only person he was watching now was her. She couldn't be more than five-feet-five, but she had strength and sexy curves and those amazing eyes. If this was any other time. If she were in his space in Cincinnati. If he wasn't running away. He might dare to ask her on a date . . .

'It's still nice in winter though, if it's bright and frosty like today rather than raining like it often does here in the UK. Have you thought about where you might like to go in London while you're here?'

'I don't know. All the usual tourist places, I guess. Big Ben. The Queen's house?'

'I'd say Her Majesty's crib is a must. But, getting off the tourist trail is good too. Discover some of the places people miss because they don't know they're even there. Maybe get on the Tube and get off somewhere random . . . just because you like its name.'

'Have you done that?'

'Not for a long time. Ruthie doesn't cope very well with random.'

'Sure.' He nodded.

'Well, as far as Richmond goes, you should definitely make time for Richmond Hill, for the views, and then there's the palace, well, not so much a palace now, just one historic wall and a gatehouse but they're as Tudor as you can get. There's also a museum and a theatre and you should also go to Richmond Park. King Henry's Mound is there and there are deer. Real live deer just eating the grass.'

A few minutes later she pulled the car to a halt. 'Well, this is it.'

He looked up at the sign attached to a building they had stopped at. Crescent Hotel.

'It's a solid three-star and the breakfast is more than a cup of black coffee.' She smiled.

'Anna,' Sam began, his heart beating harder than he would like.

'Yes?'

'Thanks, you know, for being there yesterday and for letting me stay.'

'Thank you for helping with Ruthie. And, for making me laugh. I haven't laughed like that for a while.' She dropped her gaze to her lap and it was cute.

He wanted to see her again. This may have been a chance encounter, but it was one he didn't want to let go of just yet. He couldn't explain it but perhaps he didn't need to.

'Anna, would you—'

The loudest blast of a car horn cut right through his sentence and Anna jumped. The moment was broken.

'Sorry, I'm not meant to stop here unless I'm unloading so . . .' she said apologetically.

'Sure. Right.' *Cool, Sam, cool.*

He opened the door, and gingerly moved himself out of the car. Leaning back in, he picked up his backpack. What was the right thing to say when you had only just met yet somehow there seemed to be a connection there? On his part anyway.

'It was good to meet you,' he said softly.

'Oh, you too,' she answered.

The car behind them blasted his horn again but Sam lingered a few seconds more to imprint this woman into his memories.

'Bye,' he finished.

'Bye, Sam,' she replied.

Seventeen

Anna sighed, looking in her rear-view mirror as she signalled to pull away from the kerb. Except she wasn't as focused as she should have been on the flow of cars, because she was looking at Sam, his back to her, standing at the entrance of the hotel, which was bedecked by festive wreaths. She had enjoyed his company. A lot. It had been a long time since she had felt that way. Felt herself. A grown-up. Not just a mum. A *woman*. She shivered. She was hardly Sylvie from *Emily in Paris*. She was thirty-five! Plus, it had been *one* evening out of necessity, Ruthie had been there the majority of the time *and* he had fallen asleep . . .

And then she couldn't see Sam anymore. Probably because he had gone in out of the cold. She'd never had broken or bruised ribs before but the minus temperatures couldn't be good for them.

Suddenly there was a tapping on her window and it was only the seatbelt that stopped her from full-on leaping from the jump-scare. It was Sam. Had he forgotten something? For some reason he was doing the winding action of an old-fashioned car window in the air with his fist. Bloody nerve! This car wasn't *that* old.

Anna pressed the button to bring the glass down. 'That charade was very retro,' she told him, her breath visible as it met cold air. 'Verging on rude, I'd say.'

He wasn't saying anything, his dark eyes set on her, his breath coming out quick like he was nervous. She had been expecting him to at least crack a smile at her repartee.

'Is everything OK?' Anna asked. 'Is it your ribs? Do you need me to take you to the hospital?'

He shook his head. 'No,' he said. 'Listen, I just wanted to say that . . . I saw your pan this morning.'

'O-K.' This was a bit weird. Which pan was he referring to? The kitchen was the one room she really made an effort to keep on top of every day so if he was insulting her housekeeping right now she wasn't going to be best pleased. Hang on, did "pan" mean the same thing in America? Did this have the possibility of being something dirty?

'So, I wanna fix that for you.'

'O-K.' Was she going to ask him what he was talking about or was she going to keep drawing out this tiny two-syllable word until someone honked her again or called over a traffic warden?

'I'm not a professional, obviously, but my dad always taught me that most things get fixed through logic in the end.'

Anna opened her mouth to say 'O-K' again but stopped herself as finally her brain began to catch up to what Sam was talking about. *The radiator in the living room.* It had been leaking for a few weeks. She had called someone to fix it, but they hadn't turned up. She hadn't had the energy to find another firm yet or tackle it herself.

'Let me do this for you,' Sam carried on. 'To pay back for your help.'

The Brit in her was ready to lead with a 'you don't have to do that' but the other parts of her were practically being thrown around like they were caught in an intoxicating riptide. And she could hear Nanny Gwen loud and clear. *Man's work. Accept the offer.*

And then there was a beep. Probably because she hadn't turned her indicator off. She forced herself back into reality.

'I really have to go,' Anna said. 'I can't afford to get a fine.' She swallowed, hesitant. 'Maybe tomorrow evening?'

'Tomorrow. Great,' Sam said. 'What should I bring?'

'Tools,' Anna answered. 'Literally all I have is a bottle

opener and one of those paperclip mash-ups that opens the SIM card slot on an iPhone.'

He smiled. 'See you, Anna.'

'Bye, Falcon.'

Eighteen

Lisa's home, Richmond

'Mum! The gravy is too thick again!'

'Kai, shut up. You should be grateful we have any food. There are starving people in the world,' Kelsey replied.

'Alright, grandma!'

'Actually,' Ruthie began, 'if you want to narrow it down, the Congo is the place currently most affected by hunger.'

'I bet they wouldn't even eat gravy this thick,' Kai muttered.

Anna took a sip of her non-alcoholic mulled wine and let the griping and the moaning and the banter between the children soak into her. Once a month, Lisa invited her and Ruthie for a Sunday roast and today was the day. Ruthie found it hard to relax if she was out of her routine for long but coming here regularly, *knowing* exactly when she would be coming here, had turned this lunch into part of that routine. Yes, she might have her sleeves over her hands as she picked up the salt and pepper pots but to have her sitting around a table set for six was an achievement. Anna was hoping to encourage a little small audience rehearsal of Ruthie's tap-dancing later too. It was always good to practise, not just the steps, but the performing in front of people in different environments.

'Kai,' Paul said. 'If you're not going to eat any more of that gravy, pass the jug over here. Ruthie and I will scoff it, won't we, Ruthie?'

'I will definitely need more to fill up my Yorkshire pudding,' Ruthie agreed.

'Anna,' Kai said, grinning. 'Your rapping was sick yesterday at the Christmas fayre.'

'Oh, well, I'm not sure I'm going to be headhunted by Drake's record company any time soon but it seemed to stop Neeta's meltdown.' And she still needed to speak properly to Neeta about what was going on with her and Pavinder.

'What's this?' Paul asked. 'You were rapping?'

'Not really very well,' Anna answered.

'Some of my mates got it on video.'

'Well, I very much hope they keep that to themselves.'

'Milo thinks you're fit as.'

'Kai! That's misogyny!' Kelsey yelped. 'Anna is not an object!'

'I think you were fitter when you used to do running, Mum,' Ruthie said, the context going right over her head.

'Have some respect, son,' Paul ordered. 'My advice to you would be to quickly realise that females are always, *always* one step ahead of the male. And probably a few evolutionary grades above Milo.'

'So,' Lisa said, sliding herself into the seat next to Anna. 'I've had a hyperventilating Neeta on my phone every other hour since you spoke to her last night. Where did you drop off your handsome stranger in the end?'

Handsome stranger. She could hear Neeta coining that phrase. But, Anna supposed, it was true. Sam *was* handsome. And only a tiny bit less of a stranger than yesterday.

'Oh, I . . . dropped him at the Crescent Hotel. Got royally beeped for being in the loading bay too long.' She forked some stuffing and sprouts into her mouth.

'If it's not the white van drivers making the roads a misery it's the cyclists as well now,' Paul remarked. 'Since they changed the Highway Code they're all riding two abreast, even in the cycle lane. I mean, it's an accident waiting to happen.'

'So, are you seeing him again?' Lisa asked, ignoring Paul's comment.

Suddenly the table went very, *very* quiet. Even Kai's eating, which usually rivalled a herd of cows simultaneously chewing the cud, couldn't be heard. Immediately, Anna's gaze went over the mountain of roast potatoes in a dish on the dining-room table to Ruthie. Her daughter was looking directly at her, excitement clear to see.

'He . . . might be popping over tomorrow.'

'Is he?!' Ruthie exclaimed, sounding as thrilled as she was when the last Marvel movie release date was announced.

'Is he?' Lisa said too, her expression more on the subtly surprised side.

'Who is this person I know nothing about?' Paul asked, swigging back a mouthful of beer from his bottle.

'Whoa!' Kai said, eyes bulging. 'Are you talking about the big dude who terrified Gross Gregory, Icky Ibrahim and Acne Aaron?'

'You use my names for them,' Ruthie said happily. 'But you have to say them in alphabetical order.'

'The names are so accurate,' Kelsey agreed.

'They said he was seven foot tall and almost as wide. Like The Rock.'

'Is he *that* big?' Lisa asked Anna.

She'd forgotten that Lisa hadn't seen Sam at all, but she was surprised Neeta hadn't given her a full detailed and highly accurate description. 'He's quite tall.' *And more than quite hot.* But she was keeping that thought to herself.

'He watched *Loki* with me. And my rabbit likes him.'

'So, how come he's "popping over"?' Lisa asked, nudging her with an elbow.

Anna lowered her voice so hopefully only Lisa could hear. 'This is nothing like a "hugging" on an app situation. He's just doing me a favour, that's all.'

'Is that what we're calling it these days?' Lisa answered, not quietly in the slightest.

'I think Sam would make a great boyfriend. He's nice to look at. He's kind. He has a very soothing voice that doesn't irritate me. He asks exactly the right amount of questions – enough to show he's interested, not too many that he interrupts all the time—'

'Ruthie, Sam's just coming over to . . . fix the radiator in the living room,' Anna said.

Ruthie gasped then. 'Did you think I meant Sam would make a great boyfriend for *you*?' She laughed then. So much so that her sleeve touched a floret of the broccoli on her plate. Luckily Ruthie didn't notice.

'What's so funny?' Kai asked.

'And if your radiator's bust, why didn't you tell Lisa? I've fixed more radiators in my time than Kai's scored tries for the club,' Paul announced.

'You've *attempted* to fix them,' Lisa remarked. 'We've always ended up calling a professional.'

But Anna was focusing on Ruthie alone, still smiling, still seeming a little aghast. What did Ruthie know about Sam's unsuitability as boyfriend material for her? Not that she wanted a boyfriend, but was there a reason she shouldn't even be window shopping? Ruthie had even suggested it the other day.

'Why wouldn't he make a great boyfriend for your mum?' Kelsey asked Ruthie.

'Because he's so much younger than her, silly! I keep saying she should try Mr Dandruff. He's my teacher.'

Anna had just taken a mouthful of sprout and the ball of green got stuck in her throat as she started to cough. Lisa patted her on the back and passed her drink.

'Ooo, how young is young?' Kelsey asked. 'Like Jason Momoa and Lisa Bonet age gap?'

'They've separated now,' Lisa said. 'But I want to know how young too.'

Anna shook her head. 'I don't know how old he is. But he's . . . you know . . . probably around my age.' He had to be, didn't he? They had shared banter, maybe a tiny bit of flirtation. Or was that in her imagination? All they had really shared was half a minute when the tea towel was pressed to his back and some horn in a loading bay . . .

'If "around" was a very big circle,' Ruthie stated. 'I think he's about twenty.'

'What?!' Kai exploded, bits of food flying from his lips and landing on the table.

'Wipes! Mum! Wipes!' Ruthie shrieked.

'Are you sure you want coffee?' Lisa asked. 'Not something a bit stronger and get a taxi home?'

Anna shook her head. 'I've *got* to get on with some work tomorrow. If I don't give Adam something soon he's going to wonder why he's keeping me on.'

It was only the two of them in the kitchen now; everyone else had decamped to Lisa and Paul's family room that centred around a huge television with all the entertainment you could ever need plus an air hockey machine. Ruthie particularly liked air hockey because she could hold the pushers with her sleeves pulled over her hands. Already you could hear the mainly good-natured banter of Kai, Kelsey and Ruthie as they interacted.

'So,' Lisa said, turning the kettle on. 'Not so keen on Douglas from the dating app but inviting a twenty-year-old to peruse your central heating.'

'Don't!' Anna exclaimed, her hands going to her face. 'I honestly feel a little grubby for even enjoying him topless.'

'He was topless?!'

'It was perfectly innocent. I was tending to his wounds.'

'On his smooth, oh-so-youthful skin,' Lisa said laughing.

'Honestly, Lisa, he can't be twenty. He seems older than twenty.'

'Well, for someone who isn't interested in dating, you seem a little invested in knowing his age.'

'No . . . not at all.'

Except Lisa remarking on smooth skin had given her a rather pleasing flashback of Sam at her kitchen table, bare from the waist up. Despite being a little battered from the collision and whatever else he had recently been through, everything had seemed to be in tip-top condition, from the broad shoulders to the ripped six-pack. And there she was thinking inappropriately about him again when theoretically, if she had started early, he was young enough to be her son.

'Well, if I wasn't happily married I'd be interested in this hunk because he's obviously interested in you. Intervenes when Ruthie's being teased, now he's offering to look at your pipework.'

'Please,' Anna said. 'Can you stop making my leaky radiator sound like an invitation to a pleasure party?'

'Well, I think you should go for it,' Lisa told her, putting coffee in two mugs.

'I'm not "going for" anything. He just wants to say thank you for me taking him home yesterday and patching him up a bit, that's it.'

'And he could have done that with flowers sent to the house or . . . wine sent to the house . . . or an Amazon voucher. No, instead he's putting himself back in the house to see you again.'

'Now it sounds weird.'

'No, it sounds *romantic*,' Lisa insisted, pouring the boiled water into the mugs. 'And you absolutely deserve a bit of romance.'

'Not if he's twenty! Then it would be *ridiculous*.' She tutted and shook her head and felt herself turning into Nanny Gwen when she was disapproving of something on television. *It's not even funny. I've heard more laughs at a funeral.* Or disapproving of Ed. *He doesn't polish the back of his shoes. Never trust a man in a cheap leather coat.*

'Ridiculous to who?' Lisa asked. 'Yes, Kai might have spat vegetables all over the table and yes, Paul might have made the expression he makes when he doesn't approve of how much he thinks I've spent on my hair, but it's none of their business.'

'Ruthie was pretty horrified at the idea.'

'She likes him though,' Lisa said. 'And Ruthie liking someone is a big thing.'

That was true. Ruthie usually took time to form friendships. She needed space to allow herself to accurately get the measure of people before she fully let them in. And, if they let her down after she had let them in, there was usually no going back. But why was she even thinking about this? Sam was saying thank you. Sam was twenty. Sam was not interested in a thirty-five-year-old divorcee whose height of excitement was new episodes of *Selling Sunset*.

'I can hear your brain whirring from here,' Lisa said, passing the coffee.

Anna shook her head. 'It's not. It's just . . . I don't know . . . everyone's moving on and . . . maybe it's time I *did* move on.' Was that what she really thought? Maybe all she really needed was to commit fully to her work project and revel in the fact she was the mistress of her own destiny.

'Concurring over here,' Lisa said, sipping at her coffee. 'And I am expecting a photo of your much younger man, shirtless and inspecting your valves tomorrow night.'

'No, that wasn't what I meant,' Anna corrected, pulling up a chair and sitting down. 'I meant, maybe I might consider . . . trying the dating app again.' She swallowed. Did she really mean that? After everything she'd said about it?

'Wow,' Lisa said, wearing an expression of surprise.

'What?' Anna asked. 'I mean, I know I wasn't keen yesterday when Neeta started cuddling profiles on my behalf but, you know, thinking about it, maybe it does have some merits.' The actual only merit it had was it might give Neeta an outlet she seemed to badly need right now.

'And I think now I know how much you really fancy this Sam. No matter when his birthdate is,' Lisa said with a decided nod.

Anna laughed as her face began to heat up like it was a figgy pudding someone had set light to. 'Hilarious.'

Nineteen

The Crescent Hotel, Richmond

Sam's phone screen was smashed. Probably from the impact of the car or his harsh meeting with the road. And Sam had been staring at it for over an hour now. It was Monday morning. He had showered, he had dressed and now he was sitting in the hotel's dining room waiting to be served a full English breakfast including something called 'black pudding'. And still he hadn't tried to turn his phone on. Because it was broken, right? It had to be. The way the shards of glass were shattered meant certain failure. He took a mouthful of his coffee and it burned a little.

The hotel was good. It was nothing like he had stayed in before. Playing for the Bisons, it was five-star treatment all the way. Every hotel had access to a gym, spa facilities, physios, even if they were only in town for one night. They were rich playgrounds, while this place, this space sang of what he had always imagined quintessential British was. But added to that cuteness was Christmas. And this hotel had gone for it on that front. There was hardly a window ledge, shelf or chair without something covered in glittery white, Santa Claus red, or holly-leaf green and even on his table there were springing snowflakes coming out of the condiments basket.

He picked up his phone. What if there were no messages or missed calls? What if *Frankie* didn't even know anything was amiss? Maybe he could be clear, just while he was here.

Perhaps this was a moment in time where he could be the person he was before he found out that he had this . . . *disease*? Was that really what it was? Because he'd always thought of a disease as something that gets into you and takes over quickly. But he already had it, right? And he was absolutely fine.

Sam inhaled then and without hesitating anymore, he pressed the power button. He held his breath as the screen – under the broken glass – came to life. It was working. *How* was it working? He braced himself a little, ribs reacting to the tensing. It was taking time but . . .

Ping. Ping. Ping. Ping. Ping . . .

It was loud and it was frequent and Sam hadn't realised his silent mode was off and the volume was up. He fumbled with the phone as others in the restaurant gave him attention. He flicked the switch to mute it and tried to catch sight of what some of these notifications were as they fought for room on his home screen.

Frankie: Call me!

Tyrone: Hey homey, where u at? Poker at Mo's tonight?

Frankie: 4 missed calls.

Tim: This is a reminder that evening training will start early all this week as we focus on wellness.

Tyrone: What's up wit you?

Chad: I know this is kinda weird of me to ask but when you were unconscious did you see the light?

Frankie: 10 missed calls.

Dr Monroe's office: 3 missed calls.

Voicemail: 10 new messages.

Tionne: I need your opinion on this guy. Sending a photo. Don't judge the tattoo. He got it done for a dare. x

Tionne: 5 missed calls.

Tionne: Where are you?

Tionne: 17 missed calls.

Chad: Where are you? Did you die?

Finally, Sam exhaled. He couldn't read any more and there were a stack of emails coming in too. The first person he was going to make contact with was his sister.

'Thank God! I thought something had happened to you! I went to your apartment yesterday thinking you might be dead in bed. Are you with that girl who advertised the lingerie that literally disintegrated after one wear? Because if you're somewhere with her you might want to wish you were dead in bed.'

Sam smiled as he walked along the riverside Anna had driven him past yesterday. It was a beautiful spot. It was cold, a sheen of ice on the concrete, white glistening on the grass, mist coming up off the river, but the people of Richmond were coated up, wearing woollen hats – including most of the dogs.

'Hey, Tionne,' he answered. Just hearing her voice comforted him. His little sister behaving like nothing in her world was changed. Because it wasn't. Yet.

'There's something wrong,' Tionne said in response. 'I can hear it in your tone.'

He swallowed. Ever the perceptive one, except when it came to her choice in guys. For some reason, his beautiful, soft-hearted sister never seemed to value her worth and ended up chasing after dudes who didn't treat her the way they should. Almost from the outset Tionne seemed to set herself up to fail by picking an unsuitable match.

'There's nothing wrong. I'm all good,' Sam answered with conviction.

'Chad texted me. He said you didn't answer a couple questions he sent you.'

Sam shook his head. Chad and his superstitions and constant worrying about death. 'Chad texted *you*?'

'He does that sometimes,' Tionne said. 'You're his security blanket. And, if you're not answering whatever it is he's mithering about fast enough then he turns to me.'

'I'm sorry about that.'

'It's OK. He's kinda cute. I might date him if he wasn't always thinking the world is gonna end. Because who wants to eat a Chick-fil-A with someone running through all the ways you could choke on a pickle?'

The analysis of his friend and teammate was enough to draw a laugh. *Ouch*. As good as it was to laugh, it still did hurt.

'So, where are you if you're not with the underwear model?'

'Did I say I wasn't with the underwear model?'

'Sam! There's not one person on Insta who hasn't seen *everything*. I'm all for being liberated and loving yourself but the last post of hers she was serving up the kind of boob realness only a breastfeeding baby should be exposed to.'

'I'm not with Caterina,' Sam replied. And he'd never actually *been* with Caterina. She was simply someone Frankie had told him would be good on his arm for a couple of functions. He was always working on getting more endorsement opportunities. It was lucrative. People wanted physical perfection related to their brands. He wanted to build a solid financial foundation while he had the chance. How fortuitous doing that early had been.

'Good. So, how come you're out of town?'

'I didn't say I was out of town either.'

'Are we playing a game? Because I don't have time. I have to film an ad for some new lashes I got sent yesterday and there are twenty-five different colours.'

He took a deep breath, stopping at the very edge of the river and looking into its murky depths. He felt a bit like this water right now. Nothing unusual at first glance, exactly as it had always been. Yet underneath, deeper, no one knew what was really going on.

'I'm out of town,' he answered. 'For a while. A week or two maybe.'

'A week or two?! What about our ice cream time?!' Tionne

screeched. 'And Tim has sanctioned this? Don't you have one of the biggest games of the season coming up?'

Yeah, they did. 'I know but—'

'And what about your deal with the Dallas Diggers? I thought you said they were gonna parade you on TV with James Corden before Christmas. Weren't they gonna make you do a mix of *Carpool Karaoke* meets Crosswalk Concert?'

'Tionne, you can't tell anyone about the deal, remember?'

'Oh, come on, Sam, it's all over the press. It's one of the biggest deals in history.'

'It's *rumoured* to be. That's real different.'

'Well, Mom's been telling her hairdresser.'

'What?'

'I told her not to. I said, "Mom, if you tell people Sam is gonna be a billionaire they are gonna start charging you double what they charge you now."'

'I'm not gonna be a billionaire.'

'A multi-millionaire then. Rich. Freaking more rich than you are now!'

Sam closed his eyes. This was bad. This was so so bad.

'Tionne, can you do me a favour?'

'Need to know what it is before I agree.'

He sucked in a breath. He could say something now. Here was the opportunity to tell Tionne what he knew. He could start with telling her that he was fine. But where would he stop? He didn't have any answers yet.

'Sam?' Tionne queried. 'Are you sure you're OK?'

'Yeah,' he answered. 'Can you . . . just not date that guy you sent me a photo of?'

'Seriously? He was the best of a pretty shady bunch!'

'For me, Ti. Just, hold off until I get back.'

And what exactly happened when he got back? He told his little sister that he had something wrong with him that was probably going to lose him his career, that was going to change his whole life, that was going to *shorten* his life?

103

And these were only the keywords his brain had absorbed while he was choosing flight over fight at Dr Monroe's office only to end up *on* a flight. On the river a duck flapped its wings as if concurring.

'You're sounding weird again. Do I need to call Frankie to find out what's really going on?'

'No!' Sam said straight off. No one was phoning Frankie. He wasn't even sure he was going to phone Frankie today. The only concern was, if he didn't make contact with her she would likely file a missing persons report. Unless . . .

'She's hard to get things out of but she will eventually tell me who you're dating if I ply her with enough tequila.'

He walked on, past wooden boats that seemed to need a little attention. Some were wrapped up against the elements, others were bare boards and not a great deal else. 'Maybe you could message Frankie. Let her know you talked to me. Tell her I'm fine.'

There was a pause, presumably so Tionne could fully assess what he'd said. He carried on walking, enjoying the icy breeze on his cheeks.

'Has something happened between you two? Have you crossed the client/agent boundaries or something?'

'No!' Sam yelled, loud enough to earn himself a look from a man passing by cradling a coffee. He lowered his voice. 'No, of course not.' He could see that Frankie was an attractive woman, sure, but she had never been attractive to him. Outwardly she was what most men would consider perfection. Inwardly she was harder than rock. In business, her steel often worked miracles, but personally, he didn't think anyone was ever going to get to the bottom of who she was unless she dissolved a bit.

'Then why aren't you talking to her yourself?'

'I will,' Sam answered, with a nod to convince himself.

'When? Because if I'm gonna do this for you she's gonna wanna know a timescale. And it had better be shorter than forty-eight hours.'

'Tomorrow,' Sam breathed. 'Tell her I'll call her tomorrow.'

'Then I will message her. Maybe even before I message Jerome.'

'Ti! If that's that dude then—'

'Promise me you're OK, Sam. Or, that if you're ever not OK you'll tell me.'

Sam closed his eyes, blocking out the river view. He didn't ever want Tionne to carry any worries. He was *her* protector, not the other way around.

'I promise,' he whispered.

Twenty

Mr Wong's restaurants, Richmond

'Which one are we having for tea?' Ruthie asked.

Anna had picked her up from school and decided she needed a work field trip. All that meant was that they were now standing outside the three-in-one-but-still-separate eateries Anna was in charge of revolutionising. It really was a bad look right now, more chip shop than Chinese or Italian, a vague mention of battered chicken balls and noodles and a peeling picture of a pizza slice on one of the windows. There was a slither of tinsel around the door frame and Anna really couldn't make up her mind if this was an effort for this Christmas or something left over from the start of the millennium.

'None of them,' Anna answered. 'We've got spicy beef I took out of the freezer earlier.'

'Can I have Kettle chips instead?'

'No, Ruthie, you can't.'

'Why not?'

'Because that's not a healthy meal, is it?'

'I'll *just* have those and nothing else so it's less calories.'

'It doesn't work like that.'

'Can we get fish and chips then? Or Chinese? Or . . . is that supposed to be a picture of a pizza? It looks like a ham sandwich someone couldn't draw properly.'

Ruthie was not wrong on that account. It was even more terrible than the photos Adam had sent her. How was she supposed to make this better? It was situated on one of the less illustrious streets of the area – far fewer Range Rovers, more ferocious-looking dogs – but it was opposite a piece of land closed off by black-painted iron gates. The grass was cut like someone tended to it and there were mature trees, their bare branches reaching over their boundary a little. Anna couldn't see how far the land stretched back, but just its being there was quirky and unexpected. And nothing like this throwback to Eighties shopping mall décor ahead of her.

'Do you think the pizza actually looks like that? Otherwise, isn't it illegal? If I order something, I like it to look like the picture,' Ruthie continued.

Anna sighed as she made some notes on the pad she was holding. 'Be prepared for a lifetime of disappointment.'

'Maybe we should order a pizza and find out if it looks like a ham sandwich?'

Anna stopped writing and looked at Ruthie. She had her hands in the pockets of her coat and was tapping one foot in and out of a small puddle that had been made in the tarmac.

'You really don't want the spicy beef, do you?' Anna said. 'Don't you like it?'

'I do like it,' she answered.

'Then why don't you want it?'

'I thought Sam might like it.'

'Well, that's a lovely thought, but we don't know if Sam is actually coming, do we?'

'Don't we?' Ruthie asked, looking forlorn.

'He said he might drop round today but, Ruthie, he's here on a sightseeing trip and to do some festive shopping so I hardly think fixing our radiator is going to have more allure than Buckingham Palace.'

'But the Queen doesn't need anything fixing. And I bet she doesn't have spicy beef.'

That was probably true. And as Anna contemplated Her Majesty ever having to worry about what to make for dinner, her mobile began to ring.

Adam.

This probably wasn't good. Adam did all his 'checking in' calls in the morning before any of his staff had a pub lunch. Bad news or enquiries as to why-the-hell-she-hadn't-delivered-any-brilliant-ideas-yet were usually delivered in the afternoons. But, despite not being on top of this project yet, she was here. Actually imbedding herself in the business. Kind of.

'Hello,' Anna answered.

'Anna.'

Eek. Just her name. This sounded serious.

'Yes,' she replied, as if clarification was needed.

'I don't appear to have anything on the Wong account yet.'

Straight to the point. No asking how she was or how Ruthie was.

'No,' she said quickly. 'I know. But I am totally on it. I'm here now actually. Right outside.'

'Oh *really*.'

The way Adam had dragged the word 'really' told her that he *really* didn't believe it. Other than send him a photo, which she would do, her only option now was to hold her own. It was a fairly newly acquired skill she'd got about the time she started minding that Ed was making a mockery of their marriage.

'Have *you* been here, Adam?' Anna asked, taking a few steps nearer to the door of the restaurant/takeaway.

'Have I been there?'

'Here,' Anna repeated. 'Here, where I am right now at Mr Wong's establishment. Outside the awfully titled "Oil of Life"? What is that a play on, do you know? "All of Life"? Or is it simply meant to represent the different kinds of oils their cuisine is deep-fried in? Or maybe someone nicked some of the letters.' She squinted, trying to see. 'Could it have been called "Boil Off Sealife"? Because that's not any better, is it, really?'

'I haven't—' Adam began.

'Well, let me tell you, this place – or *places* should I say, as it's actually trying to be *three* at the moment – these places are not ever going to set the world of cuisine on fire. They're more likely to set fire to the ridiculously cheap-looking packaging I've seen coming out ready for the Deliveroo guys.' She inhaled quickly, not leaving any room for Adam to make comment. 'Before I can really get my teeth into this, Mr Wong needs to decide where he wants to take this business . . . *businesses*. Does he want to make big changes and really elevate them? Or is he happy being the go-to only because he's cheap?'

'Anna,' Adam said. 'Why do I get the feeling you're not relishing this job?'

'Was that a food pun?' Anna asked, turning back to keep her eye on Ruthie.

'Anna, this is the first full project management job I've given you since you started working from home.'

She swallowed, instantly feeling a little regretful that she had been quite brutal in her assessment of the 'restaurants'. But it was all factual. 'I know.'

'And why do you think that is?'

'Because you see me as someone who excels at swooping in when people like Maisie fall down a rabbit hole of fonts and get more caught up in title case and Garamond than she does getting the concept and pleasing the customer.'

'Because you've been missing the mark.'

Oh. Anna hadn't been expecting that. And now she didn't know how to respond. Yes, juggling home-life with work-life had been super-difficult recently, but she was pretty certain all her balls were still in the air. Apart from the ball called Ed that hadn't been dropped but had instead been launched into the stratosphere. But like a boomerang rather than a ball, he always seemed to keep coming back . . . and now she needed to fight her corner.

'I think that's unfair,' Anna began.

'I think we need to have a meeting at the office.'

Oh God. What did that mean? No one who worked from home ever went into the office unless they were going to be officially warned about their conduct. A couple of her colleagues under scrutiny feigned illness for a good two weeks to put off going in for said meeting, allowing them time to get their CVs updated or with an agency.

'No.' Anna found herself saying the word so firmly it could have come from Keir Starmer.

'No?'

She didn't let Adam's irate tone get to her. Instead she plunged on as she strode over to Ruthie to stop her from petting a dog that was tied to the railings. 'No, because I am going to take charge now. That's what I was saying. That's why I'm here! Here outside the premises possibly formerly known as "Boil Off Sealife".' She put her arm through Ruthie's. 'You don't have to do anything. *I* am going to manage the whole project, like you said. *I* am going to fix an appointment with Mr Wong and *I* am going to find out exactly what his business aspirations are.'

'You are?'

'Yes,' Anna answered, latching on to the hint of a reprieve as she cradled her mobile against her shoulder. 'I'm going to go in and set the meeting now. And I'm going to . . . sample the menu. All three of them.'

Ruthie was already jumping for joy like Christmas was coming tomorrow. Maybe Cheesecake Frosted Pom Pom Butt would like spicy beef?

'Right,' Adam said, sounding considerably more level. 'Well, I'm obviously happy for you to take the lead, that's why I gave this job to you. But I know Mr Wong was very keen to relaunch before Christmas and that's a tall order with zero ideas and only a few weeks to go.'

'Yes it is,' Anna agreed. 'But not impossible. However, I might suggest moving any launch to after the festive period to maximise publicity. I mean, I don't know about you, Adam, but I'm craving all the festive fare right the way through December but come January, give me pizza, chips and egg foo young.'

'In that case, perhaps we defer you coming into the office.'

Anna punched the freezing air. This was a result. She and Ruthie might be saying hello to diabetes as a result of having to taste all the cuisines, but she had put off the end of her career for now.

'But I want twice weekly updates from now on. None of this "I've got to take my kid to therapy" or "it's a teacher development day which means we have to watch endless reruns of *Catchphrase* on the Challenge channel".'

God, Adam had really been left scarred by Marta, that one employee they'd had who constantly took the piss, knew it and was also familiar with the workers' rights legislation in its entirety.

'Twice weekly updates. Got it,' Anna said.

'Bye, Anna.'

'Bye, Adam.'

Anna ended the call with a smile on her face until she looked again at the slightly grubby, condensation-covered windows of the takeaway.

'Ooo,' Ruthie said, peering at the peeling menu plastered to the glass. 'Can I have deep fried pickled eggs with cheesy chips . . . a pepperoni and prawn pizza . . . and battered turkey balls with sweet and sour sauce.'

Anna's stomach lurched at the idea of such a combination and she shook her head as she pushed the door. 'I'll tell you what we'll do,' she began. 'We will start with me reining in the saturated fats a little and then we will compromise. Deal?'

'Deal,' Ruthie answered.

Twenty-One

Anna and Ruthie's home, Richmond

Sam had in his hand a bag of tools he had paid a maintenance man at the hotel for. That was who he was right now. Using his money to pay over the odds for something he could have picked up at a hardware store. Except there hadn't seemed to be any within walking distance and he'd spotted the handyman guy by the elevator with a whole host of things that looked capable of taking on repair of a space shuttle, therefore more than able to fix a radiator. Yet here he was, standing outside the house he had left yesterday morning, waiting for something to make him go through with pushing the doorbell.

What was he doing? Escaping his current reality? Trying to find out what it was like to be someone whose life didn't revolve around football? He had tried to call Dr Monroe earlier after listening to his voicemails. The last message had said 'Sam, we need to talk. I cannot hold off on delivering these results much longer. Call me. As soon as you can. And, under no circumstances use the internet to do research until we have spoken.' That final warning shot had hit the hardest. What was he going to find if he googled Huntington's?

Of course, after hearing the voicemail, the very first thing he'd wanted to do was search it. Except he'd only got as far as the letters 'H', 'U' and 'N' before he had stopped himself typing. He needed space. He knew he was on borrowed time before he had no choice but to face whatever was heading

112

his way, but tomorrow he'd have to call Frankie and she was going to have to call Tim, his coach. He didn't know what exactly he was going to tell his agent yet. And he didn't care how she spun whatever he *did* decide to tell her. He simply needed his house in order before he could go back to Dr Monroe.

He held his finger towards the push button. This was a time-out. This was like those moments he gave in to Chad and Tyrone and did something out there just because they could – jet skiing, volleyball on the roof of their team coach, a private plane to New Orleans. This was a chance to be Sam without the usual complications in his life. Without this new bonus complication that might bring everything he was certain of crumbling down.

'You have to push it really hard.'

Sam turned around as someone else arrived on the doorstep. It was a woman with long dark hair, and large gold earrings kind of getting tangled in the hair. She was wearing black jeans and a bright pink coat, and held a large pot in her hands, one she was now transferring under one arm. Something about her was familiar. Maybe her voice? That was weird.

'I haven't pushed it yet,' Sam admitted.

'Well, let me help,' the woman said, bustling past him, pressing her thumb to the bell and holding. Sam could hear it sounding inside the hallway, loud and long. Finally, the woman took her thumb away and turned to face him.

'You do not remember me, do you?'

'I—'

'That is OK. You had been flung metres into the air like a frisbee.'

Then he remembered. She had been there at the accident. Talking even louder than she was now.

'I am Neeta. Anna's best friend. And you are Sam.'

The front door opened then immediately tried to close again. And then there was a scream.

'Cheesecake!'

He saw the cat breaking loose, and he reacted like the furry feline might be a tossed football. Dropping the tool bag fast, he ducked down and grabbed hold of the cat before the four-legged pet could sprint for freedom. It yowled as he cradled it and tried to stop it mauling him.

'Oh my God! I can't believe you caught them! I don't know what I would have done if they'd got out and got lost.'

He could see Anna's eyes were smarting with tears, panic written over the rest of her features. He wanted to reach out and squeeze her shoulder, protect her . . . The cat swung a right hook at him and caught him on the jaw.

'Are you sure the cat is not feral?' Neeta piped up.

'It's a pedigree,' Anna replied.

'In some circles that is one and the same thing. So, are we coming in? Or are we waiting for Mr Penderghast to twitch his netting?'

And Neeta was here. Of course Neeta was here. Because she had probably been camped outside the front door in her car waiting for Sam to turn up. And Cheesecake had almost escaped. It was lucky that Ruthie was nose-deep in trans fats and hadn't noticed. Anna was leading the way into the kitchen and had no idea what she was supposed to do. A virtual stranger was here to fix her radiator, her best friend was carrying a seemingly empty casserole dish and she was eating all kinds of foods that didn't go together no matter how you arranged them on the plate.

'Sam!' Ruthie exclaimed the second they were all through the door. 'Aw, Cheesecake must really like you to let you hold them!'

'Well, I didn't really give them a lot of choice,' Sam answered.

'And let's not dwell on that. Let's put Cheesecake down and I will . . . put the kettle on,' Anna said swiftly.

'Where is your bunting?' Neeta asked, her eyes turned

up towards the ceiling as she padded around the space, still holding the dish.

'Er . . .' Anna began.

The festive bunting in the kitchen was a tradition but it was up in the loft and Anna hadn't been brave enough to go up there yet. She was actually hoping that Ruthie didn't notice so she didn't have to go up there at all, but Ruthie not noticing was like asking the sun not to rise. And now Neeta had pointed it out . . .

'Sam could put it up for us,' Ruthie said.

Ruthie was now drinking the free sweet and sour sauce Mr Wong had given them the moment Anna had told him she was in charge of his project. They hadn't got into details but she had made an appointment to see him later in the week.

'Oh, Ruthie, Sam isn't here to do all these jobs for us,' Anna said turning back from the kettle.

'No?' Neeta asked. 'Then why does he have a tool bag?'

'Oh, man. I left it on the step when I grabbed the cat.'

Sam rushed back out of the kitchen.

'Mum,' Ruthie said, chopsticks holding a battered ball. 'Did Cheesecake get outside?'

'No,' Anna said straightaway. 'No, not really.'

'Could I have coffee?' Neeta asked, pulling up a chair at the kitchen table. 'What is that you are eating, Ruthie?'

'It's Italian mixed with Chinese and fish and chip shop.'

'Neeta, what are you doing here?' Anna wanted to know.

'I came to bring back this long-ago forgotten about dish that I once borrowed. You must have been struggling all these months to cook without it,' Neeta said, passing the pot over to Anna.

'That pot isn't even mine. It's Lisa's. And you know that,' Anna accused.

'Is it? Are you sure?'

'It's not ours, Neeta,' Ruthie piped up. 'Mum has the really old ones that Nanny Gwen left us.'

'Which means,' Anna continued, 'that the only reason you're here is because you knew Sam was coming.'

A look crossed Neeta's face that said she was thinking about whether to continue with this crockery farce or to admit it was an excuse.

'Well, someone has to do something, do they not?' Neeta exclaimed a little too loudly at exactly the same time Sam walked in.

'Black coffee?' Anna offered, desperately trying to maintain some control over what was going on in her house.

'Or wine?' Neeta suggested. With that she pulled a bottle out from inside her coat and plopped it on the table.

'Can I have some wine?' Ruthie asked.

'No,' Anna and Neeta both said at once.

Cheesecake let out a loud miaow and then began to pee on the floor.

'Shall I . . . just go and look at the radiator?' Sam asked the room.

Twenty-Two

'Large black coffee. I'm sorry it took a few minutes. I had to prioritise sanitising the kitchen floor after Cheesecake . . . well, you know . . . they haven't quite got used to the litter box yet.'

Sam was sitting on her living-room floor, his long legs tucked up around one of her chairs as he leaned over the pipe at one end of the radiator. He inched himself out of the space and looked up at her.

'Thanks,' he answered, taking the mug.

'How's it going?' Anna asked. 'Is it safe to take the saucepan away yet?'

'I can't guarantee that yet. I'm gonna tighten everything up a little and see if that solves it but, if not, I'll have to think of something else.' He winced.

'Oh, damn, is that your ribs hurting? Do you want me to move this chair?' Anna stepped forward.

'No, it's cool. The ribs are OK today. Kinda got stuck back together by something called "black pudding".'

Anna laughed. 'You enjoyed breakfast at the hotel?'

'I really did. Feel like I should've run 10k to work it off though.'

'Do you do that often?' Anna asked, leaning against the arm of the chair now.

'Eat until I feel my guts are gonna burst?' He laughed. 'Yeah, pretty much most of my life so far.'

'I meant running.'

'Yeah, I spend a large portion of my life running. Mainly away from other people. I do a lot of sports.'

The door of the living room flew open and there was Neeta,

117

just as the doorbell rang. Why was Anna's home suddenly as busy as Oxford Street this time of year?

'Right, reinforcements have arrived! It is time for you two to get out of here,' Neeta announced.

'Get out of here?' Anna asked.

'I called Pavinder. I asked him about radiators and he gave a very convincing and knowledgeable account of all the things that might be wrong here. And then I phoned Lisa and she said that Paul has fixed—'

'More radiators than Kai has scored tries for the rugby club. He told me,' Anna said. 'But—'

'No buts,' Neeta said. 'You two are going out.'

'Going out?' Anna asked. The words 'going out' hit her insides like 'going out' was a misson to Mars.

'There is a festive tepee bar,' Neeta continued, unabated, it seemed, by Anna's shock. 'In Heron Square. They were setting it up earlier and it opens tonight. Quickly go and put something on that does not make you look like you work in catering. And, Sam, you go and wash your hands. Not in the kitchen because Ruthie will scrutinise the way you do it. Downstairs toilet.'

Sam was standing now, wiping his hands on a cloth. He was most probably wondering what the hell he had walked into. Anna was actually wondering when she'd lost all control of her life in her own home. 'Neeta,' she began.

'Sam,' Neeta addressed, completely ignoring Anna. 'How old are you?'

'Neeta! For God's sake! You can't ask people that,' Anna exclaimed. 'I am so sorry, Sam. You should not have to be part of this utter madness that is my home right now. If I was you I would . . . take your tools and do more of your running.'

'I am going to open the door and let everyone in,' Neeta said, rushing from the room as the doorbell sounded again.

Everyone? Who was everyone? She'd said Pavinder but then she'd mentioned Paul. Was Paul here too? And Lisa? Kai? Kelsey?

'You have a lot of friends,' Sam remarked. He was still smiling for some reason, while she was dying on the inside.

'Yes, and I am rethinking that life decision right now.' She was caught between staying here and rushing to the front door to draw down a virtual portcullis.

'Don't do that,' Sam told her. 'It's good to have friends. People you can count on to—'

'Turn up and order you about and—'

'Offer you a night out?' He sighed. 'I thought the festive tepee sounded kinda cool but—'

'It does,' Anna said quickly. 'It does sound cool but . . .'

'But you'd rather stay here with your friends. I get it. It's OK. And it sounds like you have people with much more experience in fixing stuff than I do, so . . . I should go.'

'No!' Anna said a lot more forcefully than perhaps she meant to. 'No, I mean, you were right. Having friends is good but honestly I see these ones a lot and I mean *a lot*.' She swallowed, nervousness building as her mouth seemed to be working on something her mind hadn't altogether given it clearance for. 'So, we could, if you wanted to, give the festive tepee a go.'

What was she doing? Had she just asked this probably-twenty-year-old on a date? No, no not a date. It was only a drink. Sam was another less crazy friend to add to the others. But it was a chance to go out. To go out without the responsibility of Ruthie. And she felt immediately guilty for feeling a tiny bit excited.

'So, you don't think I should take my tools and run now?' Sam asked, his eyebrow raising.

'No,' Anna answered firmly. 'I think you should wash your hands in the downstairs bathroom and I'll be really quick and change into something that doesn't make me look like I work in catering.' She smiled. 'Neeta can be right sometimes.'

'OK,' Sam said.

The lounge door opened and many faces appeared.

'Hello, I am Pavinder.'

'I'm Lisa.'

'Wow! You really are tall! Do you play rugby?' Kai asked.

'And, more importantly, what's your Instagram?' Kelsey wanted to know.

Twenty-Three

Heron Square, Richmond

The night was cold but clear. A black sky, stars twinkling bright, even though they were surrounded by lights here in this beautiful cobbled square. They had walked here. It had taken a little over twenty minutes and Anna had given him more of an audio tour of the places of interest they'd strolled by. He was finding out that Richmond was quite the gem in London's crown. It was a hot spot for river sports, period houses, independent shops and people-watching. And, apparently, Ruthie was forever hoping to spot Tom Holland who had a home nearby.

The festive tepee bar took up the majority of this space, nestled between two towering Christmas trees and a green decorative fountain. The frontage of the bar was giving off Scandinavian vibes with a wooden hut structure and then the material took over, arching up and reaching a point, golden fairy lights trailing down every canvas-covered pole. Inside looked warm and inviting, fire pits sat in the centre of tables, people already drinking from froth-filled mugs or pint glasses.

'I can see why you like living here,' Sam said, nudging Anna's elbow.

'Oh, it's not all festive tepee bars every day of the week, believe me.'

'No but the cobbles and the old buildings set around this square. It's like it's someone's personal courtyard and any second horses attached to carriages are gonna rock up.'

'What can I say?' Anna asked, shrugging. 'I practically live in *Bridgerton*.' She seemed to catch herself for a minute. 'And you probably have no idea what that is.'

He smiled. 'I have *Netflix* and a sister. I know who the duke is.' He gave a bow, holding out an arm and rolling his hand. 'My lady.'

'Great, a gentleman. You can buy the first drinks. I'll have whatever that red glowing stuff is over there.' Anna pointed through the doors to a pitcher of something that had mist rising from it.

'A lady assuming this will be more than a one goblet night. One is amused.'

She laughed at his impersonation and his body reacted like it had been glitter-bombed from the inside. She was stunning. And he was definitely punching.

'To the fire pit, my liege,' she said, leading the way.

The tepee bar was possibly the best drinking establishment Anna had ever been in. Either that or this Cranberry Cocoon was working its magic on her perception of things. Like her perception of how hot Sam was. As she gazed at him through the orange flames licking up from a neat stack of logs in the trough at the centre of the table, she was getting Michael Culhane from *Dynasty*'s height and build, mixed with the hair of Teddy Soares from *Love Island* and a little bit of *The Weeknd* around the eyes. But none of those celebrities were twenty years old . . . Ruthie had to be wrong about that, right? Because if Ruthie *wasn't* wrong, then she was really worried about it. She could actually hear Neeta's voice in her head purring the word 'cougar' and sounding stupidly happy about it . . .

'Why do you think it's called Cranberry Cocoon?' Sam asked. 'Do you think it's because the ingredients are all wrapped up in this mist? Or is it gonna make us so wasted that tomorrow will need to be a duvet day?'

'I hope it's not the second one,' Anna said, sipping more

of the drink through her straw. 'I have a school run to do and Ruthie's singing at a care home in the evening. It's OK for you, being on holiday.' Anna pointed a finger then, one cocktail down and feeling a teensy bit bold as inebriation took hold.

'Holiday *shopping*,' Sam corrected. 'There's a difference. If I was really on vacation I wouldn't spend it in stores crammed with people, bouncing out onto the sidewalk into musicians playing lame Christmas tunes for cash.'

'Yikes! Did you find Oxford Street already?'

'No, this was the high street right here,' he told her. 'I've heard "Feliz Navidad" at least six times today, varying in degrees of talent. If you push me, I'd say the pan pipe solo was the highlight.'

Anna put her elbow on the table and rested her head on her hand. 'So, where *would* you go on vacation?'

'Everywhere I haven't been. Everywhere's different, right?'

Anna nodded. 'Everywhere is different. But, you know, what would you want to do when you got everywhere? Are you a beach person? A mountain person? Do you have a yearning for Iceland?'

He smiled. 'I like the undiscovered. You know, landing somewhere you've never been before and wondering what might be around the next corner. I haven't had the chance to do enough exploring yet, but, you know, one day.'

Anna swallowed. It was the confidence of youth talking. He had his whole life ahead of him, ready to bloom and blossom. She didn't know if she had ever felt that way. Everything had simply *happened*, almost like it was preordained. Perhaps she just hadn't been born with the gene that hankered after 'adventure' and the 'unknown'. Maybe that was why her mother hadn't stayed. Perhaps somehow her mother had known she was going to be a disappointment in that way. Anna loved Richmond and Nanny Gwen and she had clung tight to them both, was still clinging to the town. Was she giving Ruthie a limited view? Should she be booking them on a few holidays? Yes, going anywhere with Ruthie had its challenges but if you didn't face challenges how did you get to know what you were capable of? Or maybe she should be thinking of a break *without* Ruthie. Girls' time with Lisa and Neeta perhaps? It would almost be respite.

'Anna,' Sam said, waving a hand in front of her eyes. 'You OK? Or are you getting cocooned in your own thoughts over there?'

'Sorry,' she apologised, sitting up straighter on her stool. 'I was just imagining a life that wasn't rigidly planned right down to the last minute.'

'Jeez, I'm so stupid! I'm sorry, I—'

'No, please, don't apologise. It's nice really. To hear about other people's dream destinations.'

'Where would you wanna go, Anna? If you had a limitless budget and no ties.'

She pressed a finger to the rim of her glass and swirled it around. Where would she want to go? Sam had said 'everywhere'. For her it was more a case of 'anywhere'. A buzzy city where the lights were bright and the music was loud and she didn't have to search the depths of her bag for Loop earplugs. Or walking through a lush rainforest, the only sound the wildlife you can't see, humidity making your T-shirt stick, body mixed with adrenaline, fear and excitement, no concerns for rash cream or counting the fronds on plants and hoping they didn't add up to an odd number . . .

'I don't know,' she answered, her mind snapping back into the tepee. This winter night under canvas was unexpected and about as thrilling as any December had got in a long time.

'You don't think about it?'

'I don't have time to think about things like that.'

'Things like . . . you?'

Anna met his eyes then, soulful, dark and deep. *You.* A short three letter word that had sounded so round and thick and visible said by him. She didn't think about herself. How could she? There were too many other things all fighting for space in her life. And everything was prioritised before even the thought of 'me time'. That's just how it was.

'Wow,' Anna said. 'These drinks! Get the conversation going, that's for sure.'

'Hey, I get that your life has to be heavily planned. But, you know, you have a lot of friends and they were there for you tonight – and this wasn't in the plan, was it? Maybe they could be there for you more.'

This was feeling deep. Sam was broaching questions she didn't dare answer out loud. She loathed asking for help. Loathed it. To Anna, if she asked for help, it felt like she was admitting to failure. Mums managed, and they juggled. That was their main role. Yes, sometimes it felt like she had a mixture of flaming torches and machetes she had to keep in the air, but it was what it was.

It hadn't been a great deal different when Ed was still living with them. She was still in charge of keeping things level and highly organised while he told her (sometimes) when they were running low on Actimel . . . She wanted to be the mum that her own mother wasn't. She wanted to be the mother figure Nanny Gwen had been. Solid. Reliable. Her arms always open for Ruthie.

'And . . . it's none of my business, right?' Sam said, sitting back from the flames. 'Sorry, I overstepped. Ignore me.'

'It's OK,' Anna said. 'You have no one to answer to, I'm guessing. You can simply get on a plane and do Christmas shopping in London.'

Sam forced himself to nod. Yeah, that's what this was. A totally non-complicated life. He guessed it had been until that visit to the doctor's office. He'd had a schedule and routine, craved downtime that wasn't beer with the boys, put Tionne before himself. Maybe he and Anna weren't too dissimilar.

'Unless,' Anna began, 'that's *not* why you're really here.'

'Come again?' He shifted on his stool, the fire feeling warmer than ever.

'I'm starting to put you together Mr . . . Mr . . .'

He smiled. 'It's Jackman.'

'And that's a completely fake name!' Anna pointed a finger. 'Sam Jackman. That's not far off Samuel L. Jackson! So *that's* what Ruthie was going on about! Well, I might watch Marvel with her but I don't have the obsession she does. So, what is it really?'

'Anna, that's my name. Really.'

It was OK to tell her, right? She would have no idea who he was. The UK had their soccer celebrities here. His kind of football wasn't spread across the magazines and newspapers on this side of the Atlantic. He wanted the anonymity. Needed it for now maybe.

'O-K. Well, whatever your name is, I see you.'

She pointed her fingers shaped into V's at her eyes and then at his, making a face that earned a laugh from him. Except even when she was being funny she was sexy as hell.

She whispered. 'You're a spy. I've worked it out. That's why you have the bruises, the mysterious air about you—'

'I have a mysterious air?' he asked, sitting forward again. 'I've never been told that before.'

'You're adaptable to all kinds of situations,' she continued.

'Like being hit by a car?'

'Like sweeping in and seeing off Ruthie's bullies.'

'You could have done that,' Sam told her.

'I would have resorted to violence.'

'I'm not a spy,' he whispered.

'That's something a spy would say.'

Sam smiled. 'I give you my word.'

He'd lied the last time he'd said that. It was when his mom had questioned the arrival of that new car, smelling a lack of truth like only a mother could. He was certain she still hadn't believed him and, perhaps worse, his mom now knew his word wasn't always his honour. Albeit for the right reasons.

'Well, in that case . . .' she began.

'Anna?'

Sam turned his head to the owner of the voice. It was a guy dressed a whole lot smarter than him. Grey pants, a long-sleeved navy-blue shirt, a formal jacket. He was looking at Anna almost as if she might be a felon who had absconded from maximum security.

'Oh . . . hello,' she answered.

Sam watched everything that was bright about her suddenly fade and she was tilting her head, trying to get her hair to fall over her face.

'What are you doing here?' the man asked. The question was directed to Anna but the man was now turning his attention to Sam. The way the man was staring seemed to indicate he was on a mission of visual reconnaissance and Sam didn't get the feeling it was about the designer label on his jeans. All his instincts were telling him this person was what his dad would call a 'bent nickel'.

'It's a bar, man,' Sam answered. 'We're having a drink.'

The guy considered him for a second and then he turned his back on Sam, leaning on the table a little and facing towards Anna. *Fuck, I hate him right now.*

'Anna, it's a school night. Where's Ruthie?'

'Oh my God! Where is she? I put her down by that Christmas tree over there!' Anna exclaimed.

'Are you insane?' the man asked.

'No,' Anna responded. 'I was just having a quiet drink. Ruthie is at home with plenty of childcare. Where's Nicolette?'

'Just over there.'

The man pointed and Sam's gaze followed to a table in a nook of the tepee where a woman with long blonde hair was sitting wrapped up in a thick – hopefully fake – fur coat.

'Well, maybe you should go and sit with her instead of annoying us,' Anna suggested.

So, this guy *was* foe not friend.

127

'*Annoying* you?' the man said. He sounded pissed now. 'I was simply saying a hello.'

'No, you weren't,' Anna answered. 'You were actually suggesting that I was a terrible mother being out of the house and drinking alcoholic cranberries on a Monday night.'

Now Sam's senses were overdosing on 'irritated'. This guy had to be Anna's ex. Well, he wasn't about to let him unpick Anna here. Sam knew she had hesitated hard about even taking the night out. But then she had relaxed a little, smiled, laughed . . .

'If that's what you think then . . .' The guy deliberately left the end of the sentence hanging and that was enough for Sam.

Sam stood up, maybe widening his stance just a touch. 'I think you're done here.'

'Sam,' Anna said. 'It's OK.'

'I don't think it *is* OK,' Sam answered her. He was mad now, not uncontrollably so, but enough to feel that pinch, that heightened awareness that came before a confrontation. He got it on the field, a sense that at any moment things could get heated and you needed to be ready.

'I'm sorry,' the man said, not sounding like he was apologetic at all. 'Who *the fuck* are you to tell me when I'm done?'

OK, so this dude was charged. Well, he'd met his match tonight.

'You think that's cool? To use language like that?' Sam asked, the hands that were in his coat pocket bunching into fists. 'You think it makes you the big man? Because, from where I'm standing, I've never seen anyone look smaller. I guess it might match your penis.'

Sam hadn't meant to sound quite so brutal but there it was. He stood his ground, eyeballing, giving off a bit of pre-encounter bravado like he would against any of the Bisons' rivals.

'Honestly!' Anna exclaimed, slipping down off her stool

and putting on her coat. 'This lovely Christmassy tepee bar is now drowning in testosterone, and I am *not* here for it.'

Before Sam could regroup, Anna was walking for the door. Now he had a choice. Give this guy a bigger piece of his mind or catch Anna up?

Twenty-Four

Richmond Riverside

'Anna! Wait up!'

Anna momentarily closed her eyes as she reached the bottom of the steps that led down to the river. Sighing, she opened them again. It was so much colder now, the pavement encrusted with a sheen of white as it began to freeze. The strings connecting festive lights had icicles starting to form. She stopped walking, standing by the water and gazing out over the rippling blackness. Why had Ed had to be there tonight? And why had Sam turned the situation into a high-school locker room man-off? She couldn't even have one evening without drama. She turned to face the person pursuing her.

Sam was already holding his hands up in some kind of apology or show of surrender maybe. All six-foot-God-knows-how-many-inches of him was now slowly walking towards her like she was a swan who might either flee at any moment or attack. Anna didn't think she was going to do either of those things. She was too flipping tired.

'I apologise,' Sam said, close now. 'I shouldn't have acted that way.'

'No, you shouldn't have,' Anna replied. 'Because *I* should have ignored his pathetic jibes and I should have told him where to go. This is 2022, Sam. I know you're only young but—'

'What? I'm *young*? What does that mean?'

'Well, I . . .' She didn't really have an answer. Except perhaps that what had happened tonight had reminded her why this whole thing was a bad idea. But now he wasn't saying anything. He was looking at her with those annoyingly gorgeous eyes waiting for her to dig herself out of this insult-infested hole she'd made.

'Your friend Neeta asked me earlier how old I was. What is with that?' Sam asked.

'I don't know,' Anna replied but she couldn't help dropping her eyes, looking to a duck padding up the river edge whose beak was practically blue with cold.

'And now *you've* called me out for being "young".'

'I shouldn't have said that. And Neeta shouldn't have asked you your age either. I mean . . . what does it matter? It's not like this was a date or anything.'

There it was. Out. Clarification from her side that as fun as it was to flirt a little and find out more about him, this was nothing else and going nowhere. But Sam wasn't saying anything. He was still looking at her, hands in the pockets of his coat, his tall broad frame silhouetted by the moonlight.

'I mean, you were just being nice, offering to help with the radiator because I helped you and . . . you felt sorry for me. Single mum with no clue about DIY. And Neeta and the others hijacked us, right? Practically forced us to go out together.'

'Stop,' Sam said firmly. 'Don't . . . say anything else.'

Now Anna felt upset. *Why* did she feel upset? Why were her eyes welling up with emotion? This was ridiculous. This was nothing. And it was a nothing she had no time or space for.

And then Sam took a step closer to her. With his long stride it meant he was now slightly in her personal space circle.

'I'm gonna level with you now,' he said softly as his eyes met hers. He sighed. 'A little, at least.' He put fingers to the top button on her coat and fastened it. 'I could say that offering to look at your heater was payback for you fixing me up after my road accident. But that wouldn't be the truth.'

He smoothed a hand over her shoulder, then his fingers trailed a path down her arm. Goose bumps were breaking out under the fabric of her coat and Anna knew it wasn't from the cold of the night, it was his touch. It was gentle, caring, yet altogether sensual. She barely remembered 'sensual'.

'Tonight,' Sam began again, 'was always a date for me. It didn't matter if I was holding a wrench sat on your lounge-room floor or drinking cocktails in a tepee bar, I simply wanted to spend more time with you. Because spending time with you, those minutes I wasn't passed out on your couch, I enjoyed them. I enjoyed them a lot.'

He was so close to her now, if she reached out her hands would meet the lower part of his chest. This felt new. This felt *exciting*. It was unplanned. It was something she could never have scheduled in a million years. This man, landing in Richmond, at Ruthie's school fayre, wanted to spend some of his festive break with her. It could be casual. It could be the beginning of getting a tiny piece of her adult life back if she was open to it. She looked up and into his eyes. She knew so little about him. Yet, despite her dismissing it, there was *something*. And it was here now, fizzing between them, by the Thames, under the moon.

'Was I dumb to think you might, I don't know, feel like you wanna hang out with me while I'm here in London?' He smiled. 'I could teach you not to be so freaked out by nature. Unspook the Christmas trees. Although you do have the largest one I've ever seen right in the centre of your home.'

Anna laughed then. It might have broken the spell of sexiness he had somehow been winding around her but he'd jostled her with banter, exactly like he'd been doing since they met.

'You're shaking,' he said, reaching to fasten another one of her buttons. 'It's cold. We should—'

'Keep walking,' Anna interrupted. Something was telling her this evening didn't have to end right here on the riverbank.

Something was telling her she didn't *want* this evening to
end here on the riverbank.

'Yeah?'

'Yes,' Anna answered. 'There's somewhere I want to show
you.'

'Another quick sightseeing tour?'

She smiled. 'Oh, this is a sight to see, I promise.'

He touched her arm then, drawing her back before she
could start walking again. 'Listen, if it helps for you to
know . . . I'm twenty-six on my next birthday.'

'OK,' Anna replied.

'OK?' Sam answered. 'You're sure? You don't wanna give
my mom a call? Check she's down with it? Or . . . ask my
star sign?'

'You are getting way ahead of yourself, Mr "Jackman"
or whatever you're *really* called. It's one date. It's not, you
know . . . Netflix and chill.'

Why had she said that? Her cheeks were practically now
a forest fire!

A wide smile drew across Sam's lips then and he lowered
his brows, dipping his head into her space again. 'I'm too
young to even know what that means.'

Twenty-Five

Mr Wong's restaurants, Richmond

'You're telling me, *this place* is one of *the* sights to see in Richmond?'

Sam was looking at the eateries, steamed-up glass, peeling paintwork, a couple of dogs tied up outside panting hot air into the freezing night.

'I'm telling you that . . . it could be,' Anna answered. 'OK, maybe not one of the top attractions, but a whole lot better than it is now.'

'That was spoken with authority.'

'Was it?'

'*I* believed you.'

'You like me.'

'Oh, I do, do I?'

Warmth was gently moving around inside him. That's what happened when he was with Anna. It was like no matter what else was going on, here was this connection, forward-rolling through everything else, forging on regardless. He liked how he felt when he was around her. He liked who he was when he was around her. This wasn't a pretence. This wasn't going out with someone he'd been told to, to get him Insta attention that was good for his 'brand'. This was *real*.

'This is my job,' Anna said, taking a deep breath. 'I take struggling businesses and plan an almighty shake-up. Or as much of a shake-up as I can do with their budget and their

134

courage. Currently I'm in charge of revamping Mr Wong's pizza Chinese chip shop.'

'Wow,' Sam said. 'I hate to say it, but I think you've got your work cut out if the dude can't even paint his window frames.'

'Ruthie and I had food from here tonight,' Anna continued, watching the door open and customers leave with bags bulging with paper-wrapped goods. 'And, considering we had very low expectations, it was actually nice.'

'Yeah?'

'I mean it wasn't anything they'd ever serve up at The Ivy but not everyone wants that or, more importantly, not everyone can afford that.' She sighed. 'I know Richmond has a bit of a reputation for being all about the high-rollers but we're also diverse and you know, I like that whatever Mr Wong is trying to be right now, he does cater for smaller budgets.'

And all Sam had noticed was the rough paint. Anna had already thought about what this place might mean to the community. Who even was he right now? Perhaps someone who was used to people bringing him high-end everything. A twenty-five-year-old who would do well to remember his days of cheap fries. This place was exactly like one of the places his mom and dad used to save up cash for. An oil-saturated treat to accompany a drive-in movie. He and Tionne would leap into the back of a car borrowed from the lot his father worked at, his mom and dad would be up front trying to make their seats recline a little. Sam and Tionne had always climbed out of the car and sat on the roof, higher than everyone, fries between them, more imitating the actors than paying real attention . . .

'Am I boring you? Sorry, we could have walked to King Henry's Mound. You can see St Paul's Cathedral from there. This was very self-indulgent of me.'

'No,' Sam answered. 'I mean, my very first thought when I got on the plane to come here was . . . I really need to find me a three-cuisine high street takeout spot. London can keep its fancy history. It's all so ostentatious.'

Anna laughed. He liked making her laugh. It took her over, moved her whole body, bled up into her eyes. Made her a million times more attractive to him . . .

'What are you gonna do with it? If you're not gonna suggest turning it into something like The Melting Pot?'

'The Melting Pot?'

'It's a fondue place in the States. I went there once with my guys and you can actually drink melted cheese.'

'Never tell Ruthie that,' Anna said. 'She likes cheese too much already.'

'So, what's the plan to elevate? Apart from getting a paint job and a new sign. What does the sign even say?' He turned his head sideways as if that was going to help him at all. Nope, he was getting nothing.

'I don't know quite yet but, come over here.'

She was walking back onto the sidewalk now, beckoning him. Across the street there were trees in gardens strung with golden lights and 'Santa Stop Here' signs outside porches. But Anna was heading towards iron gates that had no sign of festive adornment and looked less loved than the chip shop.

'Ta da!' Anna said, presenting the gates as if they were a star prize in a game show.

'Wow, Anna, this is . . .' He had no idea what this was. 'Do I need . . . special glasses to see what's here?'

'No,' she said. 'There's nothing here. Not yet anyway. But Mr Wong owns it. His father bought it a million moons ago and he used to park his car on this front bit and had a bit of an allotment behind, but no one's done anything with it since.'

'O-K.'

'Well, I know you have to use tonnes of imagination and then . . . tonnes *more* imagination but I can see tables here amid the trees, if the grass is strimmed *right* down and it was made more appealing. Don't you think?'

Sam put his face up to the fence. 'You can't see how far this land goes back. You can't see much at all.'

'I know but I've got a meeting with Mr Wong and when I find out exactly what he's thinking and hoping for, then I can get him to maybe open up the gates and I'll see if this space could be involved somehow . . . or if I'm thinking so far out of the box I'm flying off near Lapland.'

'You wanna wait?' Sam found himself asking.

'What?'

'Just because the gates are closed, it doesn't mean we can't go in. Wanna scope it out before your meeting?'

'I . . . I'm not sure that we should.'

He laughed. 'You British are so proper.' He took off his coat and handed it to her. 'Let me give you a boost, then put my jacket over the spikes at the top there so you don't get yourself hurt.'

'Are you encouraging me to break and enter?'

'No breaking,' Sam answered. 'I'm done with being bruised.'

'I don't know,' Anna said, still sounding hesitant.

'Too much nature in there for you?'

'I wish I'd never told you about that.'

'Come on, Anna. I'm getting frostbite right now. Step on my hands.'

She was looking over her shoulder, checking the passers-by on the street were only paying interest to their own business before she finally put her foot into his hands and he gave her a push into the air.

'You OK?' he asked, watching her navigate the top of the gate before making her way downwards on the other side.

'Yep. I feel like I'm fifteen years old about to spray-paint graffiti on something, but apart from that.'

Sam laughed and then began hauling himself up the fence. It was no mean feat when his body had been battered around these past few weeks. He whipped over the top, unhooked his coat and dropped down next to Anna who was already walking through the grass and weeds, crisp with frost.

'What are we spray-painting?' he whispered.

'This is so much bigger than I thought,' Anna said, making her way into less dense vegetation. 'It goes quite a way back. Can you picture it in the summer? Lanterns in the trees, the scent of flowers and cut grass, tables and chairs, hammocks even—'

'This is your vision for the takeaway?' Sam asked.

'I don't know yet,' Anna admitted. 'I just . . . saw this piece of land and wondered about the potential.'

'You're an ideas person,' Sam said, nodding.

'Is that a good thing?'

'I think it's a good thing. Ideas people meet challenges head on with several ways to spin themselves out of difficulties. I have a . . . friend who's great at that.'

He thought about Frankie now and wondered if Tionne had messaged her like she said she would. He shouldn't have involved his little sister in covering his ass. He had to step up tomorrow and face things.

'I don't have all the answers. Most of the time lately my head gets filled up with Ruthie and, where I used to be brainstorming for projects, there's now a bank of information about the ingredients of hand gel sanitiser and stuff about how birds aren't really birds but bird robots working for the government.'

'If we see a pigeon should we whisper?' Sam asked in hushed tones.

'They're all hearing and all seeing,' Anna replied. 'And they are *everywhere*. Oh, look at this tree, isn't it lovely?'

She was putting hands on the bark of a silvery trunk, its branches bare, like icy sticks poking out at all angles. Her enthusiasm was infectious. He never thought he would get excited over a patch of overgrown land opposite a cheap takeout joint.

'Steady there with the nature,' he said, moving next to her.

'Imagine this on a warm May day,' she said, closing her eyes and lifting her face like she could suddenly feel the rays of sunlight hitting her skin. 'The branches would be dripping with yellow furry catkins, bees would be buzzing around, children playing tag . . .'

Sam *could* picture it. It was almost exactly how he had planned his life to be. Work hard, play hard, be the best, earn as much money as he could so he was set up for life, so his family was set up for life and then enjoy that hard work, sit back a little, relax, fall in love, have children, watch them grow . . . It had all seemed so simple, so achievable and now he didn't know where he stood or how long he would even be standing for.

'Of course, Ruthie wouldn't like it. Unless she was wearing her hazmat suit and her ear plugs. Not even a joke.'

'Ruthie doesn't like nature either?'

'Mainly bees and wasps and other flying things that make a buzzing sound. We haven't had any close encounters with drones yet.'

'Anna,' Sam said, stepping up alongside her.

'Yes.'

'Wanna come see St Paul's Cathedral with me tomorrow?'

The silence that followed was deafening to him, and the longer it continued the more he felt it in his heart.

Twenty-Six

Outside Anna and Ruthie's home, Richmond

Sam had asked her out and Anna hadn't answered. Instead, she had feigned a cramp in her foot and said that perhaps now she should get back to Ruthie. Why had she done that? She liked Sam. Sam was also an almost respectable twenty-five to her thirty-five. OK, perhaps that wasn't respectable to some people but it was a whole lot better than twenty . . .

Something clicked between them and there was a gorgeously warm undercurrent to their interactions, their personalities blending together like the perfect coffee beans. A sense of familiarity was breeding super-quickly . . . But now Anna was holding back and second guessing. Because of Ruthie? Or because she didn't trust herself to make good decisions?

She let out a shaky breath. The truth was she didn't feel confident enough in herself. Who did she think she was? On a date with a gorgeous twenty-five-year-old man who looked like he'd been specifically carved by God's own hands? This was fantasy. Her thoughts paused for a brief moment and then began flowing like a waterfall. How did she even know Sam was genuine? Maybe this was something like *The Tinder Swindler*. Without the Tinder bit. Perhaps this wasn't actually about her at all. Sam could have thought 'big house, big sums of cash in the bank'. It was all beginning to fit together – the made-up name (Sam Jackman – yeah right!), the appearing out of the blue, maybe even the falling in front of the car to make that connection with her. She should have stuck to her first wary instincts. *That's* why they gelled so well together. Because he was practised at doing this. Maybe she should just tell him the house was inherited. That it was all she had. Then he wouldn't be so keen to take her to St Paul's Cathedral . . .

They'd reached the path that led up to Anna's house and she was still internally imploding, remembering all the times Nanny Gwen had warned her about boys. *They are only after one thing. Don't go for anyone too handsome, they always have a cruel streak.* Nanny Gwen had never trusted men of any shape or form. That's why she had never married and Jane was the product of 'the last time she ever let a man take advantage'. Anna looked up at the house, remembered Nanny Gwen peeping from behind the curtain the first time Ed had brought her home after a date. *Gentlemen don't loiter on a first date. I thought he had shifty eyes.* What would she have thought of Sam? Anna was really missing a bit of grandma intuition more than ever right now.

'Listen,' Sam began. 'I didn't mean to push back there.' He wet his lips, acting nervous. 'You have your work with Mr Wong's project and Ruthie. I should have realised that you can't drop everything to go sightseeing with me.'

'I do own this house,' Anna said, for some reason feeling the need to point at it. 'But I didn't buy it. I inherited it. And I worked my arse off renovating it, I'm talking sanding floors and ripping tiles off walls and restoring the fireplace. And yes, it might be worth a *considerable* amount more than it was when my nan died but it's literally all I have.'

'It's a great house,' Sam answered. 'A really beautiful house, you know, the parts I've seen. And I'm hoping the guys or the girls in there have got to fixing your heater.'

'I have *nothing* else,' Anna continued, trying to drive the point home. 'Please get it. I don't have shares in the next big thing. I don't have hundreds of accounts in far-off places like Marty Byrde. I'm just a single mum with a daughter who has special needs, a rabbit who has to have special feed and a cat with more attitude than Gemma Collins.'

Anna was out of breath, almost panting into the night. And Sam was simply standing there, looking confused, like he'd heard her but he hadn't understood a single thing. Anna didn't know what to say next. Shouldn't he be cutting his losses right about now? Leaving? He would certainly be showing some balls if he tried to continue this now.

'That guy at the bar tonight,' Sam began softly. 'That was Ruthie's dad, right?'

Anna sighed. 'Yes, but he has nothing to do with this. The house is mine. And, you know, I don't care what you try to fabricate to get me to part with equity or whatever, I'm not doing it. So, let's just not waste any more energy on it.'

'Anna,' Sam said. 'I have no idea what you're saying here.'

'You want me to spell it out?'

'Yeah, I think I do. Because I don't know what's happened between us climbing over a fence and imagining summer and this.'

'Well, you know, taking everything into consideration, I've decided that you cannot be who you say you are, Sam! You have to have an ulterior motive. Because otherwise why would you be asking *me* on dates when you could be asking, I don't know, *anyone* else?'

He nodded. 'I get it. I know what this is.'

'It's me saying that nothing has happened yet. You can just walk away and move on to your next mark – or whatever it's called – and I'll go back to being Ruthie's mum and a half-baked ideas person.'

Sam shook his head. 'That isn't all you are. And you're letting other people tell you what to be. I don't know the details but, from what I've seen, you're allowing someone who let you down and moved on, still tell you how to live your life and set your boundaries.'

'Why do you care?' Anna asked. 'Now you know you're not getting any money.'

'Money,' Sam said shaking his head. 'You *really* think I wanted to spend time with you to get money? I *have* money, Anna.'

'Well, you would say that, wouldn't you?'

She watched his face fall and it looked like such a genuine deflation.

'You know what,' Sam said. 'You're right. This really isn't what I thought it was.'

Anna found herself with no answer. He looked a mix of confused, upset and a little bit mad. Had she made an awful mistake? *Was* she still letting Ed govern her somehow? Or was this about her? Going out with Sam for a second time would be moving into a territory she hadn't been in before. Was that what scared her the most? Was the thought that Sam was genuinely interested in her more terrifying than the thought of him embezzling from her?

'Listen,' Sam started. 'I had fun. I enjoyed getting to know you a little. I think Ruthie is an awesome kid and you are a terrific mom to her.' He sighed. 'But, most of all, I liked the way I thought we vibed. I'm . . . in kinda a weird place myself right now and to laugh and to, I don't know, bond over black coffee . . . and cranberries and . . . Falcon, it was pretty cool. To me anyway.' He hit her with as sincere a look as Anna had ever seen. Those deep, dark eyes swept her up and she wished she'd just said yes to that visit to St Paul's. Now he was hurt and she was hurt and Ruthie wasn't going to understand at all . . . But he was visiting. How long was it ever going to last anyway? It was probably for the best.

'So, I'm just gonna say goodbye,' Sam said. He heaved an enormous breath that lengthened and broadened him all at the same time. 'Goodbye, Anna.' He took a step away from her.

She swallowed. 'Goodbye, Sam.'

Twenty-Seven

Bean Afar, Richmond

'Aww, there are more Christmas decorations in here! Look at the snowmen holding hands,' Lisa announced as soon as they were through the door into the warmth of the coffee shop.

Anna didn't want to look. She just wanted to sit at their usual table and get herself the biggest, strongest Kenyan coffee and try to feel better. She felt sad today. Sadder than she had felt for a long time. She could tell herself it was because Mr Rocket had pooped in his food bowl this morning, or that Cheesecake had taken to clawing and hanging off the kitchen units seemingly for fun, or that Ruthie had melted down about her bedroom door not closing properly and it had taken twice as long to get out of the house for the school run. But she knew, despite the craziness of their meeting at all, despite knowing virtually nothing about him, it was because of how things had ended last night with Sam. Sam being around had brightened things. She'd had a spring in her step, a smile on her face, she'd even sung in the shower yesterday . . .

'Dust-collecting tat,' Neeta replied, unfastening her coat as they prepared to sit down.

'Neeta!' Lisa said in protest. 'I know you don't celebrate the season, but you must like all the lights and the baubles. Some of them look like your earrings.'

'Decorations to show respect and love for gods should not be a once-a-year thing.'

'To be fair, we do have Easter as well,' Lisa replied.

'And you tell me how much of that is about religion rather than paying homage to Cadbury's.'

'Anna, help me out here,' Lisa begged.

Anna slumped over the table and put her head in her hands. 'Why am I such an idiot?'

'Well,' Neeta began, 'I thought we were going to have to delicately introduce the conversation about what happened last night, so you coming right out with it is a pleasant surprise.'

'What *did* happen last night?' Lisa asked. 'I know it's only a radiator but Paul was pretty proud of his craftsmanship on those pipes and you—'

'Barely spoke to any of you when I got back.' She sighed. 'I'm so sorry.'

'The usuals, ladies?' Esther called from the counter.

Neeta and Lisa concurred.

'Yes please, Esther,' Anna answered. 'But can mine be twice as big and twice as dark.'

'And that means you are definitely thinking about Sam so whatever happened last night cannot be that bad,' Neeta said.

'It *was* bad,' Anna admitted. 'It was so bad I'm never going to see him again.'

'What?!' Neeta exclaimed.

'That does sound bad,' Lisa replied.

'Start talking,' Neeta ordered. 'Now.'

'Give me one good reason why I shouldn't put super glue inside all the locks of Ed's car? One reason!' Neeta fumed.

Anna couldn't immediately think of anything except that she didn't want to see Neeta in trouble with the police or in any way embroiled with the situation with Ed. But although last night he had been the catalyst, it was her negative thinking and accusations that had escalated the situation.

'It wasn't Ed,' Anna admitted, sipping at the vat of coffee she now had in her hands. 'It was me.'

'Ha!' Neeta exclaimed, hands out in the air, almost swiping a decorative pinecone off the windowsill. 'And there we have it. The way he worms his way into your thinking like a . . . root maggot.'

'Did you really accuse Sam of being one of those people who pretend to be someone else and ask for money for their sick child?' Lisa asked, her stare almost punishing.

Oh God. It was all coming back to her in full gore right now. *Why* had she done that?

'I . . . got scared when he asked me for a second date. I thought "why is someone so gorgeous and kind and . . . gorgeous asking to spend time with me?" And he'd dropped into my lap! Well, not literally, but we weren't meant to meet. He wasn't someone on the dating app, or a new member of the school committee, or Mr Dandruff. He just—'

'Fell in front of a car. Then turned up with tools that have the name "Rodrigo" written on some of the handles,' Neeta said.

'What?' Anna asked. That was suspicious, wasn't it?

'Anna, he has flown here. For a festive shopping trip. Why would he have packed a bag of tools? He has borrowed them from someone called Rodrigo because he wanted to repair your radiator. Because he likes you. And let us not forget that before he fell in front of the car, he was like a superhero, flying to the rescue when Ruthie needed help!'

The last sentence Neeta had bellowed at town crier levels, trouncing Noddy Holder on the radio in the volume stakes. Sam had done that. He had been there for Ruthie, protecting someone he didn't even know because he was a kind, decent person and not someone who wanted her bank details.

'What are you going to do?' Lisa asked, much more calmly than their friend.

'What is there to do? He said goodbye and I don't blame him. He'd spent an evening with Dr Jekyll and Mrs Hyde,' Anna said.

'And he met Frank-Ed-Stein and his diamante-covered little monster,' Neeta added.

'Neeta,' Lisa admonished.

'What?! I wasn't mean about the baby.'

Anna took a much-needed gulp of her coffee while her friends paid attention to each other and not her. The easiest thing would be to do nothing. Her plate was as full as a stacked Christmas dinner serving. Except for all the portions on there, there wasn't anything solely for her. Ruthie. Work. Unplanned-for pets. School committee duties. Anything else had been swallowed up by the rush and tear of life, squeezed until there was no room for things she might want to do, only time for things she *had* to do. Doing nothing would therefore mean life would carry on as it was.

'You could invite him to watch Ruthie sing at the old people's home tonight,' Lisa suggested. 'It's an olive branch gesture, it's about Ruthie, rather than being another date.'

'No, no, no,' Neeta said immediately, hands flying out. 'No more pretending. You think he is hot. He thinks you are hot.'

'We don't know that,' Anna reminded.

'You don't think he is hot? Because I do!' Neeta exclaimed. 'I should get him to come to my house late at night and deliver a Christmas card. See what Pavinder thinks about that!'

'You already know I think he's hot,' Lisa answered.

'OK,' Anna admitted. 'I think he's hot. And I feel a lot better about thinking that when I know he's twenty-five. Almost twenty-six.' Well, she didn't know he was *close* to his birthday but every month helped somehow . . .'But we don't know he thinks I'm hot.'

'You need to say you are sorry and ask him out again,' Neeta said. 'I do not know what all the "let us make it about this" or "let us make it about that" is about. Honesty. That is the only way. Otherwise there is simply too much miscommunication.'

'Honesty, Neeta?' Lisa asked, picking up a wooden stirrer and whisking her coffee with it. 'If you believe what you're trying to sell Anna, then you should just ask Pavinder if he's having an affair with Jessica.'

'No!' Neeta exclaimed straightaway. 'Because that would make me an overly suspicious wife. And overly suspicious wives are not attractive in my culture.'

'Lisa's right, Neeta,' Anna added. 'Pav won't think you're being a suspicious wife if there's nothing going on. Which I am ninety-nine per cent certain there isn't. He's not doing any of the things Ed did, is he?'

'What things?' Neeta asked, leaning a little over the table.

'Hiding his phone. Or stopping the little previews of messages from flashing up. Wearing more Lynx than five normal people. Being really helpful with chores when it means a legitimate reason to leave the house.'

Neeta seemed to consider these points deeply for a moment and then she answered. 'No.'

'Well, then,' Lisa concluded. 'Jessica's obviously a bit OTT and Pav's handling her.'

'What?!' Neeta exclaimed.

'Handling *it*. I meant to say handling *it*.'

Anna took Neeta's hand and gave it a squeeze. 'Pavinder loves you, Neeta. But, you know, if anything ever happens, Lisa and I are always here and we can—'

'Kill all his plants,' Lisa suggested. 'I think that would hurt him more than if we maimed *him*.'

Neeta shook her head. 'I appreciate the solidarity, very much, but, Anna, this coffee session is about you. You need to waterboard all this negative thinking. Stop immediately coming to the conclusion that everyone is as morally corrupt as Frank-Ed-Stein. And I like that nickname. I am going to keep using it,' Neeta concluded.

'OK,' Anna said, nodding. 'I'll try to do that as long as you stop immediately coming to the conclusion that Pavinder must have impure thoughts about someone he works with just because she has . . . what did you say again . . . "an air of Rachel Riley about her".'

'She does,' Neeta answered.

'Neeta!'

'Let's have another coffee and think about it a tiny bit more,' Neeta suggested.

Lisa's groan made the gingerbread men rattle.

Twenty-Eight

King Henry's Mound

'Don't you go anywhere! Give me one second, one second to . . . excuse me, move, I'm taking this table, yeah, not sorry.'

Sam took a sip of his takeout coffee and watched the screen of his laptop on the video call with Frankie. He was sitting on a bench, the computer balanced on his knee, watching his agent elbow her way into the diner, ousting someone from the best table until finally she was breathing a little easier and looking at him with a whole lot of judgement.

'Now, let's get to it,' Frankie started with a smile.

And then her eyes narrowed and her eyebrows formed a harsh V shape and Sam sensed what was coming.

'Where the hell are you, Sam? I'm serious now. Where the hell are you?!'

Sam felt for the other people in the diner having to listen to Frankie like this. This was her in full pissed mode. And he didn't really blame her. He was actually surprised she hadn't at least checked Find My iPhone yet . . .

'I'm safe,' Sam answered.

'I need more than that. I need a hell of a lot more than that.'

'I'm away.'

'Away? Away where? You had a doctor's appointment you gave me no details of and then you what? Head to Tahoe? No, not Tahoe, because when I checked Find My iPhone it had you heading in the other direction. And then nothing!'

He looked out from the bench at the frost-tipped greenery

of Richmond Park. Earlier he had looked through the telescope here and took in the views of the Thames Valley and, in the distance, St Paul's Cathedral. *St Paul's Cathedral*. Before his mind could skip to thinking about Anna and everything that had happened last night, he gave Frankie an answer.

'I'm in the UK.'

'You're *what?!*'

Frankie had jumped up and out of her seat as she screamed, upending both the ketchup and mustard bottles visible on the table in front of her.

Sam said nothing more. Frankie needed to have this freakout before she returned to being the ultimate managerial mastermind that had made her infamous.

'Sam,' Frankie said, a tiny bit less fierce. 'You'd better be kidding me right now.'

'I'm not kidding you,' he answered. 'And, Frankie, for the first time in your life I'm gonna ask you to listen to me. Without jumping in. Without question. OK?'

He watched Frankie lower herself back down onto the banquette seat and tilt her head a little. He knew it was taking all the restraint she had not to make comment. He braced himself too.

'The results of all the tests the Diggers wanted came back and . . . there was an anomaly.'

'What kind of anomaly?'

'Frankie, please.'

She sighed like she was disgruntled but he could see the smallest chink of something in her expression. Something he had never seen her wear before. *Concern*. He took a breath.

'I have a positive gene for a disease. It's called Huntington's disease. Over time . . . it apparently works to . . . kinda stop the brain from doing what it's meant to.'

He was saying the words but, as he did, they felt like they belonged to someone else. Were *about* someone else. He had put everything the doctor had told him into a box and he had sealed it up. Breaking that packing tape now and giving it air was difficult. Because telling someone else made it official.

'I don't know much more than that,' Sam admitted, needing to wet his lips. 'I kinda ran out of Dr Monroe's office and got on a plane.'

'Sam . . .'

That was all his agent said. One word. His name. But Frankie had said it in an unfamiliar tone. It was wobbly around the edges and a bit ragged. And he couldn't allow himself to dwell on that. This was hard. But phoning Dr Monroe for the full details of his condition was going to be infinitely worse.

He ploughed on. 'So, you know, being realistic, the deal with the Diggers . . . it's gonna be off.'

'Well, are you going to get sick? Like soon?'

'I don't know.'

'What's the treatment?'

'I don't know that either. But, Dr Monroe poured me scotch so I don't think it's something you can fix easily.' He swallowed. 'It's definitely gonna . . . I don't know . . . shorten my life.'

It was going to shorten his life. He was no longer in control of his future. Some medical condition had been lying in wait from the moment he was born and that would decide what happened next, not him. He could feel his chest tightening, and his ribs were sore, that urge to end this call and pretend it wasn't happening taking over again.

'Sam, we need to get on top of this. That's what we need to do. We need to get on top of it and crush it, OK? Like we've crushed everything in your career so far.'

'Yeah,' he answered with zero enthusiasm. This wasn't about his career now. It was about his *life*. And he was starting to realise that although those two elements had always been so tightly bound together, going forward there would have to be a degree of separation. Like perhaps there always should have been.

'Sam! Listen to me, OK? This is going to be fine. This is going to turn out being . . . an opportunity. Because that's what I'm a master at. I can turn anything around, OK? *Anything*. I'm the best and that is what you pay me for and . . .'

Frankie carried on talking as Sam began to zone out of their conversation. This was a damage limitation speech. This was Frankie internally firefighting. Her mind was throwing up a million different scenarios to her and while she was telling Sam everything was going to be OK, she was already trying to put together an action plan. Except she was firing a little differently than usual. Sam watched her, without tuning into the dialogue. There was the normal bullish stance, the power suit and red lipstick in place, but then there was the toying with her thumbs, then the sideways look away from the camera. While Frankie carried on saying all the kinds of things that would normally reassure him that whatever issues he had were going to be easily fixed, even sometimes with bonuses, Sam looked deep into her eyes. That's where you held your truth. That was something you couldn't alter no matter how hard you tried. He held his breath as two things were reflected back at him.

Pity.

Fear.

Twenty-Nine

All Seasons Care Home, Richmond

'Why do they always have to dress us as angels when we sing here?' Ruthie moaned loudly as Anna made a tweak to her silver tinsel halo. 'And why do some of us have silver halos and others have gold? Is there a hierarchy in heaven? Because that doesn't fit very well with the fact that God is supposed to love everyone equally.'

'Well,' Anna began, trying to bend the coat hanger wire a little more so it sat neater. 'I think they like you dressed as angels because it's Christmas time.'

'Marissa says that they dress us as angels because they are the very next thing the old people are going to see when they die.'

Ruthie had imparted this nugget of wisdom even more loudly and Anna was glad they were at the very back of the residents' day room waiting for everyone to be settled before the choir were introduced.

'Ruthie, not everyone here is old, remember?'

'*I* remember, but Marissa obviously doesn't. I'll remind her so next time she can say that we're dressed as angels because they are the next thing the old *and young* people are going to see when they die.' Ruthie gave an annoyed sniff. 'Marissa has a gold crown.'

Anna turned Ruthie by the shoulders and realised exactly how grown up she was now. Thirteen going on thirty in some respects, thirteen going on three in others. Sometimes it was a hard mix to handle while trying to come up with the right answers each time.

'Listen, I don't think the colour scheme of the crowns is meant to signify anything but a nice aesthetic against the . . . peach wall-papered walls and the wee-wee coloured carpet. But, if it does, then let me tell you this.' Anna drew a rainbow-shape in the air with a sweep of her hands. 'Sometimes in life, the angels with the golden crowns might seem like they have the better deal. But, with that grander-looking colour comes more responsibility and that usually means having less fun. And fun, well, that's very important.'

Anna sighed. She was now doling out advice that Neeta and Lisa had been telling her long before the divorce became final. *You had fun with Sam. And it scared you. Because you liked it much more than you thought you would. And then you felt guilty about that.*

'Did you remind Dad about tonight?' Ruthie said, beginning a nervous jig from left foot to right and then back again.

'I did,' Anna replied.

Yes, it had half-killed her to make the call, but thankfully it had gone straight to voicemail so she had left a message reminding Ed of the location and start time. She had heard nothing more. But it wasn't unlike Ed to either not bother to come, citing work as an excuse, or to turn up after the beginning, bag a spot near the front and clap the hardest and heartiest and earn admiring looks from all the women over seventy. Ed earning admiring looks had been something Anna had felt smug about at one time. Having this good-looking man by her side knowing they were set forever. How things could change with a good dose of real life and the allure of breast augmentation.

'Do you think he'll come?'

There was a catch to Ruthie's voice. It sounded a combination of wanting Ed to be the dad she deserved with a touch of guilt that she felt that way. Anna didn't want Ruthie to ever feel compromised. Ed should be here. The singing group was important to Ruthie, it had helped give her confidence and it was one of the places she felt most comfortable. Anna remembered when Ruthie had first joined. She had asked for lessons for some time but the cost of private teachers exceeded the price of a decent therapist and Anna knew, like with the dancing, joining a new set of people was going to be testing. But they had taken it slow, introduced Ruthie in short bursts, until the group and their rehearsal space became familiar and part of her regime. It wasn't without its hiccups, particularly when new members joined and didn't at first get Ruthie's need for physical space and her designated place in the line-up, but they worked through it. And it was definitely worth it to see the happiness it brought Ruthie. When she was belting out 'Joy to the World' her autism wasn't on display, just her sweet voice and bucketloads of enthusiasm.

'I don't know, Ruthie. Sorry. But I'm here and I'm going to take videos so we can show Mr Rocket later.'

Ruthie grinned. 'Mr Rocket does like listening to me sing. He puts his ears back and pulls a special face.'

Yes, Anna wasn't quite sure that was the rabbit showing them he was content hearing the recording, but that was what Ruthie thought and that was all that mattered.

'Am I late? Please, tell me I am not late. I hate to be late. This is the beginning, right? I have not missed a first half?'

Anna turned and faced Neeta. Her friend was looking red-faced, her hair plastered to her forehead and cheeks, out of breath like she had been running.

'Neeta, I didn't know you were coming!' Ruthie said excitedly. 'Is Pavinder here too?'

Neeta shook her head. 'No, unfortunately, Pavinder has to work late tonight. *Very* late. So late that he does not want me to cook him a meal. This kind of late lateness has not happened before.'

Every time Neeta said 'lateness' or 'late' she was pulling a face that told Anna there was potentially a lot more to it than overtime. She hated to see her friend so anxious about this. They definitely needed a girls' night to get to the root of the issue. What was the name of that bar near Aldgate?

'Ruthie!' the choir leader called, waving a hand.

Ruthie rolled her eyes at Anna. 'This is when she asks me if I'm quite sure I want to do the solo section in "O Come, All Ye Faithful". Gabby is desperate for that part. I can feel her willing me to go off key. Bye, Mum. Bye, Neeta.'

'Good luck, darling,' Anna said as Ruthie crossed the room to where her group were beginning to get together.

'Neeta, what are you doing here? You hate children singing anything.'

'I do,' Neeta agreed. 'But I wanted to show support to the care home. I thought it might put me in a good position.' She unwound the scarf around her neck and then thought better of it.

'I don't understand.'

'Well, they have vacancies. For workers,' Neeta answered. 'And I told you I need a job. To distract me from thinking about all the things Pavinder might be getting up to when he is being late and "teambuilding".' She made the quote marks in the air.

Anna burst out laughing.

'What?' Neeta asked. 'Why are you laughing and making an extreme expression?'

'Neeta, you can't stand elderly people,' Anna said. 'You dislike them more than children's singing groups.'

'Sshh!' Neeta ordered. 'And that is not true. I do not like the ones who think they know everything and always have a supply of those coins for supermarket trolleys and unbreakable umbrellas and look smug about it.' She lowered her voice. 'These ones . . . they do not say very much. And I love people who do not say very much.'

'Neeta, I'm just not sure it's a good fit for you, that's all. Most of the work here is engaging with people who find it hard to engage anymore. Combing hair and moisturising hands, reading, playing games.'

Anna knew all this because she had watched the staff at a care home not unlike this one spending that time with her Nanny Gwen. When the dementia had really taken over, when Gwen couldn't be left on her own at the house for even a short period of time, a care home had been the only answer. Gwen had started to become a danger to herself, leaving pans boiling over on the stove, going out to the local shop and getting lost. She had been safe at the care home, looked after. Anna had come as often as she could, done some of the caring herself, trying to keep Gwen's mind alive, encouraging her to draw on her memories. It was hard enough seeing the curtains come down, that vacant stare, the days when you weren't recognised by your loved one, when you were a family member, but to do that every day as a job, to watch people ebb away, well Anna wasn't sure she could do it.

'I am caring,' Neeta countered.

'Yes, but—'

'I am sure I can moisturise hands. I once had to inject goo into the stamen of a plant. Yes, I was almost sick but Pavinder said that some of his juniors fainted from the smell . . . oh!'

'What is it?' Anna asked. 'Is it Ed on time for once?'

She turned around and looked to the glazed door of the day room, 'stained glass' reindeers pressed to every inch. The heads of the staff members were definitely turning now. It was Sam.

Anna's cheeks took on the kind of heat you'd need to roast chestnuts. He had come. She had tried to put her invitation out of her mind. Earlier, she had handwritten a short note. Well, it had started out as a short note, but after the ninth attempt at getting it right, it had felt like she'd written a novel. And she had left it at the Crescent Hotel, hoping he was still staying there, wanting him not to have checked out and moved closer to the action in Central London. And he was here.

'You invited him,' Neeta said.

'Maybe.'

'Good. Now, I am really hoping Ed comes.'

Thirty

Sam had an appointment to speak to Dr Monroe tomorrow. He was one night away from finding out exactly how bad this Huntington's disease was. So, tonight, it was about putting that in tomorrow's agenda and forgetting it until then. He had read a book on overthinking once, at a time when his thoughts seemed super-loud all of the time. The crux of it was you had to accept that you could not control everything. Some of the time you could not control *anything*. And accepting that was one of the first steps to a healthier mind. Usually it was easier said than done, but after Anna's note it had been simple to think of putting his health matters on hold for one more evening and come here. He was trying to channel his inner Tyrone. Unlike Chad, Tyrone was that spur-of-the-moment, live-life-as-it-comes-at-you person who you admired and got terrified by all at the same time. Sam wasn't about to opt for the crazy stunts his friend enjoyed so much but taking a chance and coming to a care home to see someone he really gelled with, well, it didn't seem like an unmanageable leap despite his current circumstances.

'Hey,' he said, stepping up to her.

'Hello,' Anna answered.

'Am I late? I didn't wanna be late but there was this Christmas party at the hotel and they were all in the entrance having photos taken and I literally had to go down a service route to get out.'

'Like a real superhero,' Neeta said. 'Hello, Sam.'

'Hi, Neeta.'

'Well, I am going to find someone to talk to about

159

employment opportunities before the terrible screeching noise begins,' Neeta said, leaving them.

'I take it she's not a fan of Christmas carol concerts,' Sam said.

'She doesn't celebrate Christmas and she's not a fan of children singing, period. She likes children but she would prefer them to be quiet book readers than wannabe Ariana's.'

'Ruthie looks excited,' Sam remarked, his gaze finding the girl pulling the sleeves of her angel costume over her hands.

'She's always loved singing. And she's terrific at it. I think it's one of those things where music lends itself to equality. She doesn't feel different here.'

'I get that,' Sam said with a nod. That's all he had ever wanted from his own life when he was small. He may have dreamed of the NFL but all he'd really wanted was to be able to feel he was as worthy as the next person. He didn't want to be looked at as different, but in his case it wasn't autism, it had been poverty. It hadn't been about having the wrong Nikes. It was about having trainers two sizes too big because that was all that had been on sale. Whatever happened next, he had already overachieved. Maybe remembering that would help, going forward.

'So, before the music starts, I just wanted to say that I'm sorry about last night,' Anna began.

Sam smiled at her. 'I thought you did that in the note. How did it go again?' He reached into the pocket of his coat and made like he was going to produce it. "Hey, Sam, it's the crazy lady".'

'You haven't brought it! Don't read it here. Neeta picks up sound like a shark detects blood.'

He laughed. 'Listen, I get it, with your ex and Ruthie and everything. But, just know that, kicking back with someone from across the pond for the holidays doesn't have to be like a legal contract. It can be nothing more than a good time.'

'OK,' Anna said, nodding.

'And . . . maybe you shouldn't assume that everyone you meet wants to take advantage of you. It's good to be wary but, you know, don't shut everyone out.'

'And now I feel like I'm getting a lecture,' Anna said.

'Professor Jackman at your service.' He bowed.

'Is Jackman really your name?'

'Hey, don't hate on it. I can't help that it sounds a little like the name of one of the world's greatest actors. It's a blessing and a curse.'

'Ladies and gentlemen, All Seasons Care Home is proud to present, The Richmond Roof Raisers performing a medley of Christmas favourites for you all. Let's put our hands together!'

'Ooo, it's starting,' Anna said, hands going to her handbag and pulling out her phone.

'Want me to film some?' Sam offered. 'So you can concentrate on watching Ruthie?'

'Would you?'

'Sure.'

Just as the pianist hit the first bars, the door opened, banging against the wall and Sam saw Anna's ex and the woman he had been with at the tepee bar walk in together and start pushing their way to the front. And then a reindeer painting fell off the door and onto the carpet.

Thirty-One

'You were brilliant!' Anna exclaimed, throwing her arms around Ruthie when the concert had come to a close. 'I didn't know you were doing a dance routine too!'

Ruthie beamed. 'Mrs Green said to keep it a secret so all the parents could go "ahh". I've been practising for ages. Luckily I didn't get my tap dance steps mixed up with the steps for this one. It was a bit awkward dancing with a plastic baby in my arms though. One time in practice, his head fell off and rolled under the piano.' She beamed. 'Sam!'

'Hey, Ruthie,' Sam greeted. 'I got you a Coke and one of these great cakes. I think it's meant to be shaped like holly leaves and berries.'

'It looks like a spiky penis,' Ruthie announced.

'Ruthie!' Anna exclaimed.

'What? It does.'

'Well,' Sam said, passing the plate to Ruthie. 'You're not wrong.'

'Ruthie! Come here and give your dad and Nicolette a hug!'

Anna bristled. This overegging in public was nauseating. She was glad he'd come but she wasn't quite as glad that Nicolette was here too. But she had to remember that Ed and Nicolette and the embryo being marinaded were a family now, a package deal.

'Have you showered today?' Ruthie asked Ed.

'Of course I have,' Ed replied, moving closer into their circle. 'What a silly question.' He gave a bit of a fake laugh.

Anna bristled some more. Oh, how little he had learned about Ruthie. It wasn't silly. Not to her.

'No thank you,' Ruthie said. 'But we can air hug if you

162

like.' She formed a half circle with her arms – one hand still holding the paper plate – and made a patting motion with her spare hand. Ed stayed where he was, motionless.

'Sam got me a Coke and a penis cake,' Ruthie announced, biting into one of the red iced berries at the top.

'They're meant to be holly leaves. Made by someone called Reeni,' Sam said.

'Did you like the singing, Dad?' Ruthie continued, happily munching away.

'It was great, kiddo.'

'What about the dancing?'

'The dancing was my favourite part,' Ed answered.

'Really?' Ruthie said, eyes bulging like Ed had announced Putin was getting a Nobel Peace Prize. 'Because you were looking at your phone the whole way through the routine.'

Anna bit her lip. Typical Ed. Typical bloody Ed. He'd turned up, he'd thought that was enough and then he'd favoured his phone screen over his daughter's star part. And Ruthie knew, because Ruthie never missed anything.

Nicolette reached out and touched Ruthie on the arm. '*I* watched, Ruthie.'

Anna held her breath as Ruthie recoiled like she had been bitten by a rattlesnake. Why had Nicolette done that? Which way was Ruthie going to react? Was she going to get angry or sad? Would it be full-on aggressive or sarcastic annoyance to deflect her true feelings? Or utter and complete devastation? Maybe Anna should pre-empt and try to diffuse . . .

Too late. Ruthie was getting very pale very quickly and Anna knew that look all too well.

'You . . . touched me,' Ruthie said, her lips trembling, her pallor whitening even more.

'Ruthie,' Anna said, stepping closer to her daughter. 'Let's go and get some fresh air a second.' It *was* hot in here anyway, presumably so the residents could be kept at an even temperature. Coupling that with excited teenagers, bubbling tea urns and more Christmas lights than on Richmond high street, it was getting up towards stifling and most people were dressed for the outside.

'I don't feel very well,' Ruthie said, her eyes taking on a haunted expression, the arm that Nicolette had squeezed being held out like it was nuclear waste to be kept at a distance.

'She's not going to throw up, is she?' Ed asked with a not insignificant head-shake.

'Ed!' Anna exclaimed.

'Hey, Ruthie, look at me,' Sam said, leaning in close.

Anna watched Ruthie turn her eyes to him.

'Remember what I said about those bullies at your school?'

Ruthie nodded with determination and then, like someone had fired a starting pistol, she was off, barging past her dad and running towards the exit at full pelt, zigzagging past staff with trolleys of Christmas cakes and raffle tickets.

Anna watched her daughter, up the corridor, out of the exit door and then she saw her stop, settling in the car park underneath a security light, taking deep breaths into the cold night.

'You can't just touch Ruthie like that,' Anna said to Nicolette. She tried to keep her voice even but as much hard work as she had to do, there was always someone there to unpick it.

'What do you mean?' Nicolette asked. 'I only squeezed her arm. It was meant to be bonding.'

Sam touched Anna's arm now. 'I'll go watch her.' He didn't wait for a reply, he simply headed out of the room while Anna kept her focus on Ed and Nicolette.

'It's OK,' Ed said, putting an arm around Nicolette's shoulders. 'You weren't to know something as simple as that would set off that reaction.'

'No,' Anna bit back. 'But *you* should have known, Ed. You know Ruthie doesn't like to be touched unless she's made it clear she's comfortable with it.'

'Honestly, Anna, I spoke to a mate at work and his kid

has been under CAMHS for over a year. He's going through exposure therapy now. I mean, not wanting to be touched is kind of a big thing. How's that going to work when she's older? She can't have a meltdown every time she's on the Tube.'

Anna shook her head. Ed was simply unbelievable. It was almost as if she didn't recognise this person as the man she had fallen in love with, married, had a child with. He was colder now, harder, an edge of self-righteousness about him. He wasn't the same guy who had helped her sand old wood floorboards, put Ruthie's cot together and build a bird house for the garden.

'She's autistic, Ed. Remember?' Anna asked. 'It's not something she can be hypnotised out of. It's not a fear or a phobia. And, frankly, I don't know how she's going to manage on a Tube or at college or in a job, but what I do know is people are going to have to be a whole lot more understanding than you are right now.'

'Would you like a piece of Christmas cake, dear?' a care home employee asked, wheeling a trolley into the space.

'No, thank you,' Anna said as politely as she could.

'Oh, so I suppose your new boyfriend is as understanding as they come, is he? Knows all there is to know about special needs and women over thirty,' Ed spat.

Anna was so shocked by that last barbed comment she didn't quite know what to do. Next, there was an audible gasp that hadn't come from her.

'Who are you to say something like that?! You are in a room filled with women over the age of thirty who all have more decorum than you! If you were my ex-husband I would be grabbing that fire extinguisher over there and coating you with foam until you were indistinguishable from Santa Claus and the Michelin man. And then I would put you outside in the car park in the hope that the rats of the neighbourhood would think you were meringue and would gorge themselves on the foam, very, very slowly like it was an appetiser and then treat themselves to a main course of your testicles!' Neeta screamed.

A complete silence had descended and everyone in the day room seemed to be focused on their group. Anna didn't know where to look and longed for the wee-wee carpet to open up like a sinkhole and suck her into its earthy depths. But, as that was never going to happen, she did the next best thing. She ran exactly like Ruthie had.

Thirty-Two

Anna and Ruthie's home, Richmond

'I lit a fire. I hope that's OK. I didn't know how long you were gonna be but it felt a little cold so I—'

'Thank you,' Anna said, coming further into the living room. 'The radiator is fixed now but I try to conserve a bit. And fires are . . . cosy.' She sat down on the sofa and let out a sigh, rolling her shoulders which were absolutely rigid with tension. Cosy was definitely something she needed right now.

'Listen, I didn't mean to overstep back there at the care home,' Sam began.

He was standing in the middle of the room, his right elbow connecting with Malcolm's boughs, shaking the ornaments as he spoke. She should have felt small in comparison to this big, solid man and the equally large Christmas tree, but instead she felt comforted by the solidity of it all. She didn't need protecting, as such, but it felt nice to have the support around her.

'It's just, I saw Ruthie looking like she might pass out and I thought "get her out of that situation the only way I know how",' Sam continued.

'You did the right thing,' Anna agreed, stretching her legs out towards the fire. 'If she hadn't left she would have thrown up, probably all over Nicolette. And as much as that might have been amusing, it would have been mortifying to Ruthie.'

'Is she OK?' Sam asked, putting his hands into the pockets of his coat.

Anna nodded. 'Yeah, she's a little bit up and down still but she's had a shower and she's in bed watching one of the videos that calms her. Ed, he never wanted to acknowledge Ruthie's differences. Even when we began to feel that her behaviours weren't neurotypical, Ed kept thinking she would grow out of it or that it was some kind of phase.' Anna shook her head. 'I always wanted to get to the bottom of it and find help and Ed still even now wants to sweep it under the carpet or pretend it's something other than what it is.'

'D'you think maybe he doesn't acknowledge it because he can't fix it?' Sam suggested. He dropped down onto the sofa next to her and steepled his fingers together. 'You know, like he hates that he can't make things better for her?'

Anna had never really thought about it that way before. While she was searching for a way to live with Ruthie's autism and all the practicalities that went with that, she felt that Ed had just looked for a way out of it. Maybe there was more to it.

'But I don't know him and I don't know the situation real well and it's also none of my business so . . .'

'You're a good person,' Anna said. 'Wanting to see the best in someone who was very rude to you on the two occasions you've both come into contact.'

Sam shrugged. 'People usually need to hurt other people because they're hurting themselves.' He put his hands out towards the wood burner.

'Are you really a professor?' Anna asked, a wry smile on her lips now.

'No,' Sam answered. 'I just have a sister who is always a bitch to me when her latest guy has messed up and broken her heart. He's not around to take it out on so she calls me up. And I take it. Because I don't ever want her hurting.'

'I don't want Ed to keep letting Ruthie down,' Anna told him.

'I know,' Sam said. 'But it's not your job to stop that from happening. You can only pick up the pieces like you did tonight.'

Anna shook her head. 'I just wish he understood.'

'I know,' Sam said. 'I wish that too. For you and for Ruthie.'

Anna sighed. 'Did Ruthie say anything to you when you were outside together? She wouldn't say much about the incident before she went to bed.'

'Well,' Sam said, 'when I first got there she was counting so I just stood and waited for her to finish. And then she asked me how old I was.'

Anna laughed. 'Oh, God, I'm so sorry!'

Sam laughed too. 'It's fine. I told her and she just nodded and then she started telling me about this girl at school who's dyed their hair green and did I think green was a cool colour for hair.'

'Oh no,' Anna said. 'Last summer she wanted to get pink streaks in her hair and when we did it, it turned ginger instead of pink and she wouldn't leave the house for two weeks.'

'Man! I said green was cool. I thought that would be the right answer!'

Anna laughed again. 'It's fine, honestly. I mean, what's the worst that can happen? What will green hair dye mixed with brown hair do?'

'Red? Orange again?'

'It won't be green, will it?' Anna said, laughing harder.

And then, as the laughter died down, she found herself moving towards another emotion as she looked into Sam's dark brown eyes. All of a sudden she felt very warm and it was the kind of warm that started slowly and then quickly gathered pace and it was as soothing as it was sexy. This sofa, where she had spent many nights recently curled up under a blanket wondering what had gone wrong with her marriage, blaming herself for literally everything, it now felt like the happiest of places again. Cosy and safe, holding smiles and laughter, not tears and tragedy.

'You OK?' Sam whispered.

The Christmas tree lights were casting a beautiful glow over his strong jawline, which was peppered with a little stubble. She liked it. She liked him. She nodded and tentatively found his hand with hers and interlaced their fingers. *What are you doing? Think. Don't think. Act. Run.* As Anna's brain fought its way through the conflict, she felt Sam's hand caressing hers from the inside. He had very large hands, smooth on the outside, a little rougher on the inside but gentle, taking care. She shifted a little on the seat, drawing closer to him, her heart beating like a little drummer boy. Whatever this was, she deserved to think about herself for once, right? To be Anna. She leaned in, her body already sensing what it might be like to be up against him, to be kissed by him . . .

And then an almighty yowl transcended everything else. Before Anna could react, Cheesecake had sprinted into the room and had clawed its way up Malcolm, baubles and tinsel and a robin Ruthie had made at primary school scattering like missiles. And next a shout from upstairs, 'Mum!'

Thirty-Three

Neeta and Pavinder's home, Richmond

'You cannot wear this. It makes me look like Nigella Lawson and not in any of the good ways.' Neeta discarded the dress with the plunging neckline onto the plum-coloured cover on her bed. 'Plus you will freeze before you even get to St Paul's Cathedral and perhaps scare the pigeons.'

Anna sighed, checking her phone again. She had moved in to kiss Sam last night and she was still wondering if she would have gone through with it had they not been interrupted by the maniac cat doing its best to wreck the festive display and then Ruthie frantic about what had caused all the crashing noise.

'Ah,' Neeta said, pulling out something thick and woollen that wouldn't have looked out of place on the set of a *Heidi* remake. 'This I wore when Pavinder's mother came to this house for the very first time. It is so long you can barely see my feet. Pavinder's mother has an obsession with people's feet. On my wedding day she told me that I was lucky Pavinder liked plants because my big toes looked like daffodil bulbs.' Neeta tutted. 'I wanted to retaliate and tell her that I had always thought her nose resembled a corn-on-the-cob but I was a dutiful wife and I smiled sweetly and said perhaps she could focus on the rest of me being like a beautiful flower. The witch laughed in my face! On my wedding day! But she is deaf now, so karma does come round in the end.'

Anna nodded, thumbing her phone screen again. She had

texted Sam this morning, to say 'hi' and to ask if twelve o'clock was still OK to meet. There might not have been another almost-kiss moment before he'd said goodbye last night but they had arranged a date. Except now he wasn't responding and it had been a couple of hours.

'Why are you looking at your phone and not at the contents of my wardrobe?' Neeta wanted to know, hands on hips and two very pink outfits over one arm.

'Sam hasn't replied to the text I sent this morning,' Anna said.

'What did you say? Pavinder sometimes tells me I overegg the emojis. Did you send more than ten? I've been told that is the absolute limit.'

Anna shook her head. 'No, I just said good morning and checked that twelve was still a good time to meet. Lisa said she would pick Ruthie up from school today and give her dinner . . . but he hasn't answered.'

'You made this arrangement last night, right?' Neeta asked. 'Well, what can possibly have changed between then and now?'

Anna went to reply as a million and one reasons why she wasn't good enough filtered into her conscience. But that was old, repetitive and something she had to get over. She shook her head. 'I don't know.'

'I will tell you,' Neeta said. 'Nothing. Now put your phone down and start focusing on the potential outfit I am offering to you.' She shook some dungarees that looked like they were covered in candy canes.

'Neeta, why do you have festive dungarees?'

'It was for a fancy dress party. It is a sweet pattern not effigies of the Virgin Mary.'

'I don't think that's the vibe I should go for. It's a bit . . . young-looking. I think Ruthie would like it.'

'I have not worn it,' Neeta exclaimed in horror. 'This is Pavinder's.'

'I don't know,' Anna said, sighing again. 'Maybe I should

just wear something of my own. Be comfortable with who I am. Not dress to impress.'

'Left to your own devices, you would wear jeans and a sweatshirt from Primark.'

'And there's nothing wrong with that.' Except now Anna could hear the voice of Nanny Gwen in her subconscious. It was less a case of 'you're never fully dressed without a smile' and more a case of 'you're never fully dressed without full make-up and a statement necklace'. Gwen would be plucking from Neeta's selections and pairing yellows with browns, not wanting to turn up in trackies and her comfiest pants . . .

'Anna,' Neeta said softly, putting the dungarees back onto the rack and sitting down next to her on the bed. 'This is an excellent opportunity to date again. It is perfect, in fact. Because Sam is here for a limited time. When he goes back to wherever he lives, then it ends. A nice holiday romance like in the films, with someone you actually find attractive. Not someone who has posted an out-of-date photo on the dating app.'

'You're right.' And if she chose a nice outfit and then he ended up cancelling, she could just take Neeta for lunch. She was still lending too much weight to something that was supposed to be simple and fun.

She pointed into Neeta's wardrobe. 'What is the striped thing there?'

'Oh,' Neeta said standing up again. 'I forgot I had that. This I first wore when Pavinder took me to a restaurant that only served desserts. I dropped lemon meringue pie and chocolate brownie on it. But it's been dry-cleaned. Let's get you trying it on.'

Thirty-Four

Richmond and Twickenham Thames Circuit

Sam felt sick. Not the kind of sick you feel when you've eaten too much food, but the type of sick that makes you feel as if your world has been flipped upside down and nothing will ever be the same again. It was a hollowed-out sensation but also so incredibly weighty. And the worst thing was, it was no longer only about him. This thing that was wrong with him. This disease he was carrying didn't start and end here.

His phone rang again. It had been ringing non-stop since he'd ended the Zoom call with Dr Monroe and Frankie. He'd walked almost three miles along the river, trying to pretend he was looking at the water, just on a stroll to walk off his breakfast, a man on holiday with no cares or concerns, smiling at cyclists wrapped up against the cold wind. Except his thoughts were back in Cincinnati, desperately trying to process what was happening.

He took his phone from his pocket and decided to end the monotony of the sound and answer.

'Hey.'

'Why didn't you pick up? I've been ringing for a half hour!' Frankie screamed.

Sam let out a sigh and closed his eyes for a second. 'Because I don't know what to say to you. I don't know what to say to anyone.'

'Sam,' Frankie began. 'I get that this is full-on but—'

'You get that this is full-on?!' Sam exclaimed. 'Do you? Because up until now I was a twenty-five-year-old with literally no complications in my life. And if I had complications then you would fix them. Now I have a disease that is gonna kill me early and turn me into a drooling mess for the latter part of it. And no one can even tell me when that may be. I could be fifty years old or it could start happening today.' He drew in an anxious breath as the real pain hit him. 'And then I find out that . . . that . . .' It was too much. It was so much he couldn't bring himself to repeat what Dr Monroe had explained earlier. The thing that made this so much worse.

'I get it,' Frankie said, softer. 'Well, you know, I don't get it in the same way that you have to get it, but I can understand it's a lot to take in.'

'He said it's . . . hereditary, Frankie,' Sam blasted. 'Did you hear that bit? The part when Dr Monroe said I didn't just develop this on my own, that this was passed down to me.'

'Yeah,' Frankie said.

'So, I have to tell my mom and dad that one of them also has this gene that's gonna make *their* life shorter,' Sam continued. 'And then . . . then . . . there's also a chance that Tionne has it too.'

His parents. His hardworking parents set to enjoy retirement to the full with the spoils he had earned so they never had to worry. *Tionne.* His little sister so full of energy and all the poor decisions that came with youth. He felt so much angrier now than he had felt when he ran out of the doctor's office and onto that plane thinking *his* life was the only thing this was about.

'It's better to know though, right?' Frankie continued. 'I mean, forewarned is *always* forearmed.'

'Yeah? I'm not so sure,' Sam countered. 'I mean, if the Diggers hadn't needed this test . . . I'd never have had it done. Why would I? My parents aren't sick. They can't *know* this is a thing. Did any of *their* parents have it? How many generations does it go through? Someone has to begin the cycle so Dr

Monroe can't know that's not me. Maybe I *am* the beginning.'

'Sam, he said that was almost an impossibility, that it was very *very* rare your body did this on its own. It's more likely that one of your grandparents had it but they were misdiagnosed and—'

'I know, Frankie, I was at the meeting.' Nothing would change for *his* future, but if luck was on his side, if there was even the most remote chance he was somehow the start of a chain, well, he was going to pray for that.

'I think the best thing you can do is get back here and speak to your mom and dad and Tionne and they can all get a test.'

He shook his head even though this was a voice call. He didn't know where to start with that. *Hey, Mom, hey Dad, I found out I have this gene that's gonna make me sick and eventually kill me and I just need you both to have a test to see if you're gonna get sick and die soon too. And, by the way, there's a chance Tionne has it too.* He could visualise how the colour would drain from his mother's face, how his father wouldn't know how to react so he would leave the apartment and go back to the car lot . . .

'What if they don't want a test?' Sam asked her.

'What? Why wouldn't they want to know?'

'Because, sometimes, it's less scary not to know. I mean, if you had the chance to find out how you were gonna die, would you take it?'

'Sure,' Frankie responded.

'Really, Frankie?' he asked, striding upwards onto the bridge ahead of him. 'And what if you found out you didn't have long left and your end was gonna come by choking on one of those scorpion chilli peppers you like to eat? Or you were gonna get hit by a flatbed truck when you step off the kerb from the coffee house?'

'I don't know,' Frankie said. 'Maybe I'd decide to never leave my apartment.'

'And that's my point,' Sam said, pausing on the bridge and inhaling deep. 'If you know, then life becomes different. I know

now. I may not know how long I have left but I am gonna be waiting for my mood to change or the way I walk to alter. When I start slurring, will it be because I've had too much to drink or will it be because the degeneration has started? Maybe my parents won't want that. I don't think Tionne will want that.'

'Well, there are a couple ways we can go forward with this,' Frankie started. 'And I've looked it up. Your career isn't over while you're still well. We can approach the Dallas Diggers ourselves with a suggested scenario as to what happens with the deal. Or we can wait and see what they come to us with. Dr Monroe is going to email them the results today. But you know what the world is like, Sam. This is big news and there's a leak in every establishment ready to make money off of it. I can't guarantee it's not gonna go public, so you need to say something to your family before they hear it on Fox.'

'No,' Sam said, shaking his head. 'You know people, Frankie. I don't care how much it costs, this does not get out until I'm ready.'

'Sam, I may be great but I'm not a miracle worker.'

He put his hands to the railing of the bridge and gripped hard. 'Yeah, OK.'

'Can I make one suggestion without you ripping my head off? Because it's usually me who does that and I don't like this role reversal.'

'Yeah,' Sam answered.

'Think about *you* in all this. Not the deal. Not the football. Not your family, Sam. *You*.'

He hated that Frankie had said that because it made her human. And he knew that Frankie loathed to admit she was human because she thought being human was meek. She was usually cut-throat, all about the dollar . . . except now she wasn't so concerned about her commission on this potential deal, she was talking to him about self-care.

'Do you hear me, Sam?' Frankie asked when he didn't answer.

'Yeah,' he said. 'I hear you. And . . . I'm working on that.'

177

Thirty-Five

St Paul's Cathedral

'Wow!' Sam said. 'I mean, wow! I can't believe I'm really here, looking at this for real.'

Anna smiled at his enthusiasm. The cathedral looked impressive any day of the week but today with a wintry cloud backdrop and the bright lights of Christmas it was picture-postcard special. In front of the building was a large, wide Christmas tree festooned with ice-white and bright blue strings of light and complementing that, the trees that were ever present, now bare of leaves, had spirals of glowing gold wound around their boughs and trunk. Anna almost wished they had come here at night instead of the daytime when the lights would have stood out even stronger.

'This helps you get perspective, right?' Sam said, standing still and seeming awestruck. 'This architecture, big and bold yet quietly beautiful, overseeing everything . . . wow again.'

'I've never had much time to just stand and look at it,' Anna admitted, putting her hands into the pockets of her coat. 'I brought Ruthie here when she was small and she got annoyed by the pigeons.'

'There are a lot of pigeons,' Sam said, nodding. 'But they add to the wow factor.'

'Wow, they're almost pecking at my feet. Wow, they poo a lot.'

He laughed then offered out his hand. 'Come and stand here with me.'

Anna swallowed. Holding hands with someone had always been a big deal to her but Sam seemed to have no problem with that kind of intimacy. She took a few steps forward and drew her hands back out of her pockets. She didn't have to think any further; Sam caught up one of her hands and held it in his.

'I mean it, you know. I never thought I'd ever see this for real,' he told her.

Anna enjoyed the way his big hand practically engulfed hers, warming the skin in an instant. 'You never had plans to come to London before?'

'My life pretty much revolves around my work so most of the year I can't leave the US.'

'You can't leave it? You don't get holidays?'

He shook his head. 'No vacation until the end of the season and then I'm always so tired I let my guys decide where we kick back.'

'The end of the season? Like the holiday season?'

'Kinda.'

'And your guys? Do you mean people who work for you?'

He laughed then. 'My friends. My teammates. Chad always wants to head to Bora Bora and Tyrone votes for Hawaii and I go with the flow.'

'What *do* you do? You said you play a lot of sports but do you do that for a job?'

He sighed and gave her hand a squeeze. 'Yeah. I play football.'

'Really? Ruthie will be impressed. She supports Chelsea, mainly because they wear blue shirts but she could tell you the year they were founded and who all their managers have been. A child with autism never scrimps on the details.'

'It's pretty much all I've ever been able to do. I've been playing since I was five years old.'

'I thought all I could do was stand on my head when I was younger but apparently now I can look after Ruthie, a rabbit, a cat and Mr Wong's desire to be Richmond culinary royalty.'

'I need to find out if I'm good at anything else,' Sam admitted. 'You know, I'm gonna turn twenty-six. My career isn't gonna last forever.'

'Don't most sportsmen go into commentary? Or management? You'll have all the knowledge, just with maybe creaky knees. Over here we barely see Gary Lineker standing up anymore.'

'Yeah, maybe,' Sam said.

His gaze finally drifted away from the sculpted dome of the cathedral and rested on her. Those chocolate irises were questioning now.

'What?' she asked, feeling under a little scrutiny.

'What would you be doing if you weren't working out where Mr Wong should go with his food dreams?'

'Still standing on my head probably,' Anna said laughing. 'Imagine what St Paul's would look like upside down.'

And then she saw his expression change and she really wished she'd thought a bit more carefully about what she'd said.

'No,' she said immediately.

'What?' he asked, laughing.

'I haven't known you very long but I know that look already.'

'Come on,' Sam said, squeezing her hand. 'You said you could do it like it was something you used to do all the time. I don't even know that I can.'

'Sam, we're outside St Paul's Cathedral with . . . people and pigeons and . . . buskers over there doing a grunge version of "Away in a Manger". We can't . . .'

'Can't what?'

'I'm not going to say it.'

'Say it.'

'No!'

'Come on,' Sam said. 'We're gonna stand on our heads.'

'You're crazy! And this pavement is hard and cold and freezing! And I'm sure there's a law against doing this in public.'

'Really? Well, I'll take the blame should the Brit cops come asking.' He pulled her by the hand. '*Carpe diem*.'

'Ah, well, if you don't want to get into commentary you could teach Latin. I hear it's making a comeback.'

Sam stopped them by one of the trees and then he was taking off his coat. 'OK, so cold, hard pavement not so cold and hard now. You're up first because you're gonna have to teach me.'

Anna looked at his coat lying on the ground and the skinny tree that was never going to be as good as the solidity of a wall behind her. She had probably been in secondary school the last time she had done this. But there was something about that that was challenging. Why couldn't she do a headstand in the street? Who said you always had to be completely sane one hundred per cent of the time? It was freeing to even think about it and as her body started to spike with adrenaline, she realised if she walked away from this spur-of-the-moment moment it was going to make a bigger statement than she could ever have given it credit for.

Putting her bag down close to the base of the tree, she didn't hesitate a second longer. Like she was back to being young wearing a school uniform with long socks that had fallen down around her ankles, she drove herself over, head meeting coat, legs coming up and over and her feet gently hitting the trunk of the tree. And all the blood began to rush to her head as she balanced and Sam let out the loudest whistle, one that she knew was going to draw attention she wasn't quite so keen on.

She breathed long and slow and deep as Sam carried on clapping and she focused on St Paul's Cathedral. From upside down it looked more like a film set carved to be that way, made from a perfect template. The pigeons and the people scurried about exactly the same but there was a crazy quality about them from this angle as they moved in lines and circles, up and down and around, perhaps not really getting anywhere at all.

181

'Wow,' Sam said. 'It looks even more beautiful from this position.'

He was upside down too now, his extra-long frame balanced against the tree beside hers, his sweater falling down to reveal a lot of toned abdominals. She needed to refocus or she wasn't going to be able to hold this for long.

'*You* look even more beautiful from this position,' Sam said softly.

'Ha!' Anna answered. 'Because everything going south is such a good look.'

'You shouldn't do that all the time,' Sam said. 'Take the compliment.'

'Because us Brits are so good at that,' she answered. 'And that was sarcasm if you didn't catch it.'

'Oh, I caught it,' Sam answered. 'And I know it's part of your armour.'

Anna swallowed – not so easy when you were balanced on your head – as she realised that the very few men she had dated since the breakdown of her marriage had barely got to know the person she put out there, let alone the person she tucked underneath. But Sam was finding his way inside that top coverlet and getting mighty close to breaking into the rest of the layers she usually kept tied tight.

'You don't need a defence with me, Anna. I promise you that.'

Now her head was starting to swim a bit. With the pressure of the headstand and with Sam's words. She didn't want to keep her guard up all the time. She knew if she did that nothing would ever change and she liked the fact she'd already been brave enough to spend time with Sam. That was progress in itself.

Kicking her way out of the headstand, she came back down to earth the right way up, rubbing her palms together. She picked up her bag.

'I guess that means I win,' Sam said, holding the pose, biceps working hard to keep him upright.

'Win?' Anna said. 'I don't believe we set up any kind of competition.'

'It was pretty obvious the loser was gonna be the one who couldn't stay in hold the longest.'

'And that competitive streak is why you're in sports.'

'I don't think that's a sports thing. I think it's a Sam thing,' he said, effortlessly coming out of the headstand and picking his coat up off the ground. 'Me and my sister used to go to this restaurant back in Cincinnati and challenge each other to eat the most of something.' He smiled, shaking his head. 'It was one of those places that served a bit of everything, you know. Seafood, Indian, Chinese, Creole . . . Every couple months, if my mom had coupons she would take us there and seriously we did not have to eat for a week after.'

'Who won the most challenges?' Anna asked him.

'Me, except when it came to ice cream. I don't know where Tionne puts it but she has no limit when it comes to that.'

'Shall we get ice cream after we've been inside the cathedral?' Anna suggested.

'Freezing temperatures outside,' Sam said. 'It's a great suggestion.'

'Well,' Anna said. 'Is it too cold for you? Or is it more a case of the competition being too hot?'

The second the words were out of her mouth she realised the double-meaning. It would be so easy to retract or give in to the blush that would usually be roasting her cheeks right about now, but something was making her stand still, push her shoulders back a little, meet his gaze . . .

'OK,' Sam whispered. 'Now all my blood is heading to a different part of me than when I was doing the headstand.'

They were standing close together but for the first time since the attraction had started to form, Anna didn't feel the need to quash it or even censor it a little. In the shadow of graceful yet powerful St Paul's she was unabashed.

'Sam,' she said, barely recognising her own tone.

'Yeah.'

'Kiss me. Before the awful buskers start—'

Anna didn't have time to finish her sentence before her mouth was full of his. The passion Sam had swept in with almost took her off her feet but in that same fluid motion he had caught her up in his arms as his lips delivered delicious sensual heat. It was like hot caramel and sweet brown sugar layered on top of thick deep chocolate ice cream, the heat and the cold and all the sprinkles on top. She caressed the close-cropped spirals of his hair, velvety between her fingers and cared less about this public display of affection than she had about the headstand. And, frankly, *this* was the kind of position she could hold a lot longer and was getting a lot more pleasure from . . .

Then Sam broke away and Anna's lips had never felt so cold. She put a finger to them and smiled.

'Wow,' Sam said, smiling too. 'If I had known sightseeing in London was gonna hit me this hard I would have made the trip a while ago.'

Anna shook her head. 'No, you would have been too young a while ago. Your timing is perfect.'

He took her hand in his and gave it a squeeze. 'Let's go inside. I want to thank St Paul personally.'

Thirty-Six

The Globe Theatre

'Now this looks like true historical England,' Sam said, mouth to his ice cream cone as he stopped in front of the large pale painted building with a thatched roof.

'Oh, it is,' Anna agreed. 'This place is Shakespeare's Globe theatre, constructed close to the site of the original theatre which Shakespeare's players built in 1599.'

'Wow,' Sam said. 'You know the history.'

'Ruthie went here on a school trip. Some things you remember when they've been recited a number of times.'

It was evening now, everything dark except for the lights from the boats and the buildings. There were festive hanging baskets below the streetlamps here and a Christmas tree rising up above the gates. This was as grand as St Paul's Cathedral but in a really different way. This was like someone had exported something from the countryside and dropped it right by the river in the city.

'We should go in,' Sam said, turning to face her.

'It's closed,' Anna said, licking her ice cream.

He raised an eyebrow. 'You mean the gates are shut.' He put fingers around the metal. 'You said that about the land opposite Mr Wong's joint.'

'Sam, seriously, we can't go in here. They really will have CCTV or alarms or all of those things.'

'Anna, we're not gonna steal Shakespeare's diamonds. We're just gonna get a closer look, maybe take some photos.'

'No, we shouldn't.'

'I think I remember you saying that about the headstand and what happened after that?'

'We went for ice cream,' she answered him.

But he saw the fire in her eyes. She knew how hot their kiss had been. And for him it hadn't only been about the sexual intensity, it had been about revelation. He'd discovered a corner of himself that wasn't about his career or his status and rank in life. He'd tapped into who Sam was without any of that . . . and he liked what he'd found. There was a calmness there, no expectations or demands, and he liked how that made him with Anna. Anna was getting to know him without the pro-player connotations, without the dollar signs he got reflecting back when he dated back home. For some reason, someone as beautiful and together as her was giving him a chance. Except perhaps all that simplicity was on borrowed time . . . *You could tell her.* Where had that voice come from? He hadn't told his family yet. *You could open up to someone who isn't going to have their future determined by what you say.* Wasn't sharing with a stranger a thing? Honesty without any judgement? Except now they had shared a kiss and Anna was slowly letting her guard down with him . . . He ignored the thoughts and went back to his ice cream.

'It was, without any contest, the best ice cream I've had,' Sam said, biting into his cone.

'Are we still talking about ice cream?' Anna asked him.

'Sorry, were we talking about ice cream?' He grinned and leaned a little weight onto the gate. To his surprise it groaned open. 'Ha! What do you know? Fate wants us to head in.'

'Did you break something to get it to do that?' Anna questioned. 'I'm sure the police will be lenient when you turn on your US traveller charm, but I don't think they will go so easy on me.'

His stomach tightened. Would US traveller charm really cut him some slack here? Back in Cincinnati, he still got a stop-and-frisk every couple months if he wasn't immediately recognised – apparently fame elevated you little as a black man. He looked at Anna. He didn't think she was naïve, but she lacked any similar experience. And how could he blame her for that?

'Come on,' Sam beckoned. 'No forcing any doors, I promise. Just some photos.'

As he stepped through the gates his phone vibrated. *Once. Twice. A third time. Four.* He slipped his fingers into his jeans pocket and without checking the screen he pressed it off. It was going to be Frankie with an update. She'd understand. She'd told him to think about himself. And if she'd forgotten that then he'd blame the time difference . . .

'You are going to get me into trouble and I don't do getting into trouble,' Anna said, shifting past the ironwork as she finished her ice cream.

'Really? Never?' Sam asked as they stepped into the courtyard dwarfed by the plaster and wood construction.

'Never. Unless you count crimes against karaoke.'

'OK. Hit me with it. What's your go-to song?'

Anna laughed, scuffing a fallen leaf with her boot. 'I don't have a go-to song. That would mean there was prior planning involved. Usually, after one or three too many vodka and tonics – because I only get really drunk on vodka – I'll be forced by Lisa to join her on stage, or a table, she's really not fussy.'

'I think I have to see this,' Sam said.

'Well, every December, Neeta has a Not Christmas Christmas party and there's usually singing involved and everyone dresses up and brings food, except turkey, there's no turkey allowed.'

'For religious reasons?' Sam asked.

'No, just because Neeta really doesn't like turkey. She claims it turns her mouth into how it feels when she comes back from the dentist.'

'I hate that feeling.'

'You should come,' Anna said.

She sounded a little hesitant, as if she was unsure what his response might be. Right now, he wanted to spend every minute he could with her. *Every minute*. He wanted to find out exactly how deeply he could fall given more time.

'But . . . I don't know if you'll still be here so . . .'

'What's the date?' Sam asked, linking his arm with hers.

'It's the 17th.'

'OK,' Sam said, nodding.

'OK you can come?' Anna asked.

'OK I'll come if . . . I can still be here.'

'If you can?' Anna said, slowing their walk a little. 'It almost sounds as if how long you stay isn't your decision.'

Yeah, he had made it sound like that. And he shouldn't have.

'I'm . . . kinda meant to be playing football right now.'

'So, this isn't an official vacation?' Anna said. Then she let out a gasp. 'Did you just decide to leave your job and come Christmas shopping in London without it being signed off? Are you in the main team? Or are you a reserve and they won't notice?'

If only you knew. Or rather, right now, thank God she didn't. 'I . . . think I have it covered for a while but, you know, I'm not sure how long until they miss me.'

'Well,' Anna said, taking a breath and looking up to the thatched roof of the theatre. 'At least you have one gift nailed.'

'Yes, I do,' Sam answered.

He had bought Tionne the funkiest ice cream bowl and matching spoon at the ice cream store they'd visited. It was baby pink with a bright blue triangular pattern. Cool *and* classic and he knew she would love it. It had cost more to have it couriered to his hotel than for the actual product but Anna didn't need to know that. He liked her not knowing who he was. Doing simple things that didn't cost a fortune, keeping it easy. Being Sam Jackman NFL star came with complications and if there was one thing Anna and Ruthie didn't need it was complications.

'Come on, we should get a photo of us being a little badass and breaking in here,' Sam said, taking his phone from his pocket. *Damn.* He'd forgotten he'd switched it off to get it to quit. He shoved it back in his jeans then draped an arm around Anna's shoulders.

'Did you say breaking in? Because you told me the gate was open,' Anna said as she got her phone from her bag.

'I may have given it a little help.'

'Sam!'

'Smile,' he encouraged, resting his head against hers as she lined up the selfie.

'What was your favourite flavour?' Anna asked him, taking snap after snap and changing her expression a little each time.

They had tried so many different combinations of ice creams sitting in the cosy and very festive parlour playing Italianate Christmas music. Chocolate, hazelnut, something called 'winter wonderful', cranberry and cookie, mulled wine and caramel – it would give Ben and Jerry a run for their money. But Sam was in no doubt about his answer to Anna's question.

'You,' he told her. 'My favourite flavour was you.'

And before she could laugh or tell him not to be so stupid, he leaned in and kissed her again.

Thirty-Seven

Anna and Ruthie's home, Richmond

It was Sunday, Anna was on her third coffee and she was buzzing. But it wasn't from the caffeine, it was from her work on Mr Wong's takeaway after their meeting the previous day. She was brimming with ideas, overflowing with suggested names for the ventures and thinking that maybe she *should* suggest some kind of promotional event before Christmas to soft sell the changes.

Except, what exact form the establishment or establishments would take still hadn't been finalised. Mr Wong wasn't sure whether three became one or two, or if the whole concept changed. So, for the moment, Anna was trying to cover all bases. For the chip shop side of things Anna had names like I'm a Frier Starter, Totally Battered and The Good Plaice, for the Chinese there was Chow Main, Egg Fried Nice and You Chew and for the Italian she had Piece of Pisa or Pasta La Vista. But nothing felt absolutely there yet. She felt as if there was something just below the surface on this project that she was missing and fishing that out was usually her forte. Still, she had a few days . . .

Cheesecake was yowling from the utility room where it was shut away while Mr Rocket got some indoor attention from Ruthie. The cat seemed to react like it had been committed to pet Death Row, not closed into a rather spacious laundry area with extra food, treats and a snuggle bed Anna had ordered from Amazon that it had yet to even set a paw on.

'Mum!' Ruthie called from the kitchen. 'Can I let Cheesecake out? We don't *know* that they won't like Mr Rocket.'

White-hot fear rolled through Anna then and she leapt from the chair, brushing into Malcolm and scattering three red baubles and a thankfully plastic and very hardy snow globe as she whisked by.

'No, Ruthie,' Anna said rushing into the kitchen. 'Please trust me. They won't get on. You've seen what Cheesecake does to that toy rat we bought them.'

'Did you find its head?' Ruthie asked, Mr Rocket still in her arms like a sleeping newborn with fur and long ears.

'No,' Anna replied. 'And I don't want to be searching for one of Mr Rocket's paws . . . or worse.'

'Cheesecake only wants to play,' Ruthie mithered.

'I know,' Anna said with a sigh. 'But remember we talked about how sometimes people can have good intentions but can still do bad things.'

'Like Lennie from *Of Mice and Men*.'

'Yes, and we don't want Cheesecake liking rabbits *that* much, do we?'

Right on cue there was a very fierce miaow and more scratching at the utility-room door. And then another door banged closed. The front door. Anna ripped open a drawer and grabbed the rolling pin, holding it in the air, ready to act if required. She took a breath and edged the ajar kitchen door open.

'Jesus Christ, Anna!' Ed yelled as Anna swung the rolling pin towards him.

'Ed!' Anna gasped, momentarily relieved. But then, very quickly, she got angry. 'Do you still have a key to *my* house?'

'The door was open,' Ed replied. But it was about as convincing as the time Anna had asked him if he was seeing someone else and he'd sighed before he lied to her again. All Nanny Gwen's reservations about the shifty eyes and the lingering had come to a sad fruition.

191

'Bullshit!' Anna snapped.

'Mum!' Ruthie exclaimed. 'When I said "bullshit" you said if I said it again you would find some actual shit from a bull and wash my mouth with it.'

'Very common, Anna,' Ed said shaking his head.

'Oh, it's common, is it? Well, I don't think it's worse than breaking and entering but let's see what the police think, shall we?' She reached for her phone.

'Don't be ridiculous. I've come to see Ruthie.'

'You didn't tell me you were coming.'

'I texted Ruthie. Didn't I, Ruthie?'

'No,' Ruthie answered, resting Mr Rocket on her shoulder.

And then Anna saw something change in Ed's expression. It was like the wilting of a poinsettia when the central heating was set too warm or that moment when you realised you had eaten far too many Celebrations chocolates and a food coma was creeping up on you. He looked like he was going to cry . . .

'Ruthie, could you put Mr Rocket in his carrier and make me and Dad some coffee?' Anna asked. Somehow, she was shepherding Ed from the kitchen without having to touch him or even make any verbal suggestion. He was simply shrinking out of the room looking ever-more sombre.

'This will be your fourth coffee this morning,' Ruthie reminded.

'Remember we don't count them at weekends,' Anna said.

'We *only* count them at weekends because in the week I'm at school.'

'I'll come and get them in a minute,' Anna said. She paused in the hallway and looked at the photo of Nanny Gwen for some kind of guidance from the ether. Caution. That's all she was getting. And then she stepped into the living room.

'What's going on?' she asked, once Ed had dropped into a chair.

'I don't know,' he admitted, raking his hands through his hair. 'I just . . . I've messed everything up.'

Everything didn't narrow it down at all. Had he had a row with Nicolette? Pregnancy hormones were dreadful when they kicked in and Ed had probably done his usual trick of burying his head in his phone and trying to pretend whatever was going down *wasn't* going down. She shook herself. Whatever it was, unless it was about Ruthie, it wasn't her concern. She had had too many months when she was still in denial about the end of their relationship where she had looked for anything to cling on to. Marriage needed work. She shouldn't give up. She had made special meals, blown the dust off the more-lace-than-substance underwear. She had tried to find time just for the two of them around Ruthie's combusting. And then she had finally realised, with or without the Nicolette factor, it was only *her* putting in the effort. Ed's idea of fixing things had been counting himself out. Now, she said nothing.

'I keep getting it wrong. No matter what I do.' He shook his head. 'God!'

More unspecific ramblings. Anna looked at her watch. She and Ruthie were meeting Sam at Kai's rugby club's Christmas charity match in an hour.

'I don't know how you do it,' Ed continued. 'I've never known how you do it.'

'Do what?' Anna asked him.

'Parent.'

'Oh, Ed, what are you talking about?'

'I'm talking about how you have some kind of diploma in it and I failed at the BTEC.'

'It's not something you fail at unless you give up trying.'

'Like I did with our marriage?'

He met her gaze then and Anna shivered. Apparently, he was passing with distinction at mindreading. This had to mean he'd had a row with Nicolette but Anna shouldn't be the one doling out the sympathy shots.

'It was so hard,' Ed continued, toying with his fingernails. 'Ruthie is . . . hard. Come on, I mean, it is such a difficult situation.'

Anna shook her head. Even before the final ASD diagnosis, when she got five minutes on her own, all she had wanted to do was cry at the unfairness of it all. Why Ruthie? Why *their* family? Had she done anything wrong during pregnancy to make this happen? Was it *her* fault? But then Ruthie would make her laugh doing the most basic of silly things and with her daughter's smile and determination to simply *be*, Anna had realised that Ruthie was the one most affected, not Anna or Ed. And Ruthie, for the most part, navigated her life the only way she knew how: by just getting on with it.

'It's difficult for *Ruthie*, Ed.'

'It's difficult for all of us. Not knowing whether I was able to come into a room. Having to sanitise my hands if I touched something random like . . . my own arm. Listening to the repetitive talk about the most bizarre things . . . do you remember the time she took us through the anatomy of the perfect bagel?'

'I do,' Anna answered.

'I mean . . .'

He left the sentence open and Anna still wasn't quite sure what the point of all this was. Was this Ed wanting some kind of 'there, there' moment? Because none of his talk sounded like an apology for not paying full attention to Ruthie's dance at the care home.

'I don't know what you want me to say,' Anna began. 'Why are you here now, Ed? For Ruthie? Or for you?'

'I'm saying I'm a shit father,' Ed stated.

'But the most important bit of that sentence is not "shit". It's the fact that you *are* a father. There. That's it. And that will never change. Even if you resign from the position.'

'And I'm going to be a father again and . . . I don't know if I can do it.'

Now Anna's hackles began to raise. She should not be the therapist for her ex-husband. The fact that Ed even thought this was OK, well, it was that same selfish attitude that had got them to this place. Where had he been when she needed consolation after Ruthie's latest paediatric assessment? Where was his loving supportive arm around her shoulders when Ruthie had to be picked up from a school trip because the person in the 'living art' display had shouted out and jump-scared her? Boundaries needed to be firmly re-established.

'You can stay to drink Ruthie's coffee,' Anna said, getting to her feet. 'I'll make myself scarce for half an hour and you can chat to her. Ask her about things that are important to her. And then I want you to leave. And I don't want you coming over without making a firm arrangement to collect Ruthie like the court agreed—'

'Anna—'

'No. I can't do this, Ed. We aren't married anymore. You can't come and go as you please. This is *my* house. Mine and Ruthie's home. I don't know what you're expecting from me right now, but I do know that we both gave up on our marriage, long before you found Nicolette, but you gave up first, without any fight to get things back. And Ruthie's issues, they should have pulled us together not pushed us apart. And because they didn't bring us together, well, maybe we were never ever as strong as we thought we were.'

Emotion hit Anna hard now, her bottom lip trembling and her eyes glazing with tears. Ed got to his feet.

'Anna,' he said, reaching out.

'No,' Anna said, taking a step back. 'Just, please, don't see Ruthie as anything other than Ruthie. Because that's who she is. She isn't this disorder, she's just our girl.'

Thirty-Eight

'Oh, look at all the lights and the decorations. Albert! Are you there? Come out of the pantry and look at where Sam is right now. The UK!'

Sam couldn't help but smile at his mom's excitement about seeing the dressed-up high street with its swags of silver and gold, snowmen and Santas, large candy canes swinging from wire strung across the road. As great as the decorations were, the sight of his mom, trademark mustard-yellow headscarf woven around her dreadlocks, make-up perfect with that light pink eyeshadow she always favoured, was what really warmed his heart. He knew Tionne hated the eyeshadow, was forever encouraging her to try a different shade or some fake lashes, but Dolores was insistent. If it wasn't broken, you did not fix it. And if it *was* broken, you absolutely did fix it instead of throwing it away. 'New' was always second best to 'patched up'. That's how Dolores had raised them and that's why he'd sat on most of his fortune instead of blowing it. He was saving for his future. He wasn't blowing thousands of dollars on pool parties and Maseratis. Except where did that leave him now?

'Albert! Come here, I said! Sam is doing time with his face!'

'Mom,' Sam said. 'You're making it sound like I'm in jail.'

'Why are you there anyways? The Bisons lost their last game. The radio said it was your fault because you were not playing. They said you have an injury. Is that why you are there?'

An injury. Well, he didn't care how Frankie achieved quiet over his absence. An injury was just fine. 'I'm OK, Mom.'

'Fine enough to travel to the other side of the world but

196

not fine enough to play?' she asked. 'Is this something to do with the big secret deal?'

"Big secret deal" had been said at volume but no one here was paying attention to his FaceTime call, they were all too busy speed-walking their way to coffee shops carrying large bags stacked with purchases.

'Albert! Will you get in here!' Dolores yelled again. 'I don't know what's wrong with him lately. He shuffles about like he has the body of a one-hundred-year-old, eats like one too, always spilling things over his clothes . . . Albert!'

The chill iced Sam from the inside, stalling his breath, making him stop walking. His dad was lacking energy? *Degenerating.*

'Mom,' Sam said, his voice shaking a little. 'Is Dad sick?'

'Sick?' Dolores queried, her eyebrows raising. 'He's never been sick in his life!'

'But you said he was . . . shuffling and spilling things.'

'Because he is lazy and clumsy. Albert! Get in here!'

His mom might be dismissing this but a seed had been planted with his own diagnosis. What if this was already happening to his father? He swallowed, watching as his dad came into the shot.

'On a vacation, boy?' Albert asked, a stern expression on his face. 'That team pay you too much money.' He laughed then, exposing the row of glistening white teeth his dad had always thought was his best asset and which had charmed Dolores from across a crowded blues bar . . .

He started walking again. 'Yeah, well, they have to keep their best player sweet, right?' Sam answered, all the while watching his dad for any sign. Any involuntary jerks. Slow eye movement. Difficulty with his speech. Mentally ticking off a list Dr Monroe had given him.

'So, tell me, are we allowed to say anything about the secret deal yet?' Dolores asked in a loud whisper.

Sam paused as he got to the bridge, leaning against the railings. 'Tionne told me you've been telling your hairdresser, Mom.'

197

'That sister of yours! She cannot keep a secret. Did she tell you about her latest boyfriend? Drawings all over his neck. I tell her, I say, if God wanted you to have pictures all over your skin he would have inked you himself and done a much better job than some man with needles in a dirty alleyway.'

Sam was still watching his dad. Were his eyes roving away from the screen because he found FaceTime difficult? Or because his concentration was impaired?

'She . . . er . . . told me about that guy and I told her not to make any decisions on him until I got back,' Sam said.

'And since when has Tionne ever listened to anyone?' Dolores asked.

His dad wasn't saying very much at all. Although Dolores did tend to speak for everyone else as well as herself. Was there an absence about him? Or was Sam overthinking it?

'How's the car lot, Dad?' he asked. A direct question that couldn't be taken over by his mom.

'Busy,' Albert answered. 'I sold five vehicles last week. The new guy only did three.' He chuckled. 'And two of those I did the groundwork for. He still has a lot to learn.' He shook his head. 'They ask me when I am going to retire and I tell them, I will leave only when I can no longer dance around the forecourt to John Lee Hooker.'

'You will die there,' Dolores stated. 'You will collapse one day, fall into the trunk of an old Cadillac and get taken to the breakers yard.'

Sam swallowed. It was now all hitting too close to home. His heart was thumping in his chest as he leaned into the solidity of the bridge, trying to ground his body as well as his thoughts.

'When are you coming home?' Dolores asked. 'Because the butcher wants to know. I was thinking about making jerk chicken with a festive marinade – adding cinnamon and star anise to the usual mix – and then my curried goat.'

When was he coming home? And what was home going

to look like after this news got out? When the deal that was going to make him one of the highest-earning players in history was slashed apart? Cameras in his face, reporters outside his door, everyone wanting an exclusive about his demise . . . He knew he needed to tell them. But, in truth, a delay wasn't going to change anything.

This disease had no cure. If his mom or dad or Tionne had this gene too there was nothing anyone could do to stop it from being fact. Did he protect them for a while longer? Have this Christmas without anyone's health being the main conversation piece? Or was Frankie right? Was this news going to break sooner than they could control? He didn't want his mom or Tionne to hear it from someone on the street with a recorder shoved in their faces asking for comment. And what about Anna and Ruthie? That last thought had his stomach clenching tight. If this news did get out while he was here, what then? He might be able to walk down the street without being recognised at the moment, but with huge news like that being delivered, it could be of enough importance to carry a big pay day for reporters even in the UK.

'Sam,' Albert called, moving his face closer to the screen, so close Sam could almost see his nose hairs. 'Is everything OK with you?'

His dad's forehead always had heavy creases but they looked deepened now, thick tramlines weighing heavy as he waited for Sam to answer his question. He couldn't do it. He couldn't tell them. Not now. Not over an internet connection.

'I'm good, Dad,' Sam said, interjecting as much energy into his voice as he possibly could. 'I'm really good.'

Thirty-Nine

Richmond Harriers Rugby Club, Richmond

'Come on, Kai! Give it some, son!' Paul yelled from the side-lines, breath steaming in the air.

'Yes! Come on, Kai!' Lisa joined in clapping her gloved hands together.

'I have no idea what's going on,' Anna admitted. She'd never really understood the rules of rugby. What was a scrum actually achieving? How on earth did you tell what was offside? And once all the players were covered in mud, how did you tell the teams apart?

'I have no idea what is going on either,' Neeta admitted. 'But the coffee here is always great.'

'And some of the players are cute,' Kelsey said. 'Not the ones that are friends with my brother though.'

'Do you understand it?' Anna asked, looking up at Sam standing next to her. She was a little concerned about him. He'd turned up on time, he'd spoken with Ruthie about the latest trailer for the upcoming Marvel film, but, somehow, he seemed a little distant.

'Yeah,' he answered. 'I get it. I think. We play it a little different in the US but—'

'You're gonna play in the parents' game after this though, right?' Paul chirped up.

'Parents' game?' Sam queried.

'After this match,' Anna began to explain. 'The parents

and any other adults stupid enough to want to do it, put two teams together and play each other. And, while that's happening, Lisa, Neeta and I go around with a bucket collecting for charity.'

'This year we are raising funds for the local hospital's appeal to buy another MRI scanner. You never know when you might need one of those,' Neeta remarked. 'Hopefully not tonight. The last time Pavinder played in the "fun" charity game he ended up wearing a neck brace for a week.'

'I don't know,' Sam said. 'I'm not really—'

'Please play,' Ruthie said. 'I think you'd be very good and Jason Burgess's dad, he always picks people who play rugby properly not just for fun, and last year Paul got a black eye.'

Paul pulled a face. 'Got caught with an elbow. Won the ball though.'

'And you broke the advertising stand for Proper Pies,' Ruthie carried on.

'It wasn't completely broken,' Paul said, looking a little red-faced.

'They had to get someone in to redraw the piggy motif,' Ruthie concluded.

'Is everything OK?' Anna asked Sam, moving them a little away from the others. She wondered if bringing him here, putting him in the centre of her friendship group and all the festive goings-on was maybe too much. They might have shared some hotter-than-hot kisses but it was still casual, wasn't it? With his time here in the UK limited it was the only thing it could be. Maybe she had gone from being unsure about starting anything to pushing too hard . . .

'Yeah,' he answered, eyes on the youths battling hard on the grass in front of them. 'Kinda.' He sighed. 'I spoke to my parents today and . . . I'm a little worried about my dad.'

'Oh,' Anna said. 'I'm sorry. Is he not very well?'

Sam shook his head. 'I don't know what it is but, maybe just a feeling that something isn't quite how it should be.'

'Well, in my experience, and I'm talking about my Nanny

Gwen, you should never ignore your gut feeling particularly when it comes down to older people that *you* know better than any doctor. Older people, they're experts at masking what's really going on inside. That stoic attitude that always gets them through can be their own worst enemy when it comes down to it.'

'Yeah,' Sam agreed. 'He'd never admit if he was feeling off.'

'Well,' Anna said with a sigh. 'My nan was exactly the same. It wasn't until she went into the bathroom one day and asked where the oven was that I really knew that something was wrong.'

'What happened to her?' Sam asked.

'She had dementia. Little by little, over months and then years, she got a little bit worse each and every day. There were good days sometimes, but then they were followed by awful days and it would just go through this dreadful never-ending cycle. I was twenty-two, newly married, Ruthie on the way and I had to watch my beautiful, strong, lively grandmother turn into this empty shell of the person she used to be, knowing how much she would hate to be the way she was.' Anna sighed again. 'When she passed away I was devastated but there was also a part of me that felt relief. Not for me, but for her. Because being that way for so long, that wasn't the life she would have wanted and I hated seeing it.'

Sam didn't know what to say. Anna had watched someone she loved slowly change, getting weaker and weaker until there was nothing left. *Degenerating*. Exactly like Huntington's.

'You should encourage your dad to see a doctor. I'm sure everything will be fine but there's nothing better than having your mind put to rest.'

'Yeah,' Sam answered with a nod. He had to end the conversation now. He'd wanted to share how he was feeling, his concerns about his dad, but this wasn't the time or the place. And he saw the sadness in Anna's expression when she talked about her grandmother slowly deteriorating. He turned back to the bigger group. 'Listen, Paul, I can play. You know, if you want me to.'

'Yay!' Ruthie said, bouncing up and down along from him. 'Of course they want you to. Pavinder is the best and he isn't here so if you don't help them they'll be screwed.'

'Ruthie!' Anna exclaimed.

'What?' Ruthie said, looking all innocent. 'Shouldn't you be preparing your charity buckets? There's not long left of this game.'

'Ruthie is right,' Lisa agreed. 'Keep cheering on Kai for me. Come on, Neeta. And, Kelsey, I need you too.'

'You OK with Ruthie while I get set up?' Anna asked him.

Sam watched Ruthie give an eyeroll and then reply, 'I will be teaching him tactics because I know the game play of everyone on both teams.'

'She's gonna keep an eye on *me*,' Sam said to Anna.

As soon as Anna was out of sight, Ruthie turned to Sam. 'Are you my mum's boyfriend now?'

'Whoa, Ruthie, that's not talking tactics!'

'Isn't it though?' Ruthie said, still hitting him with a direct look.

'I don't know how to answer,' Sam admitted.

'You have to tell me the truth. Everyone knows that you have to tell people with autism the truth even if you tell white lies to other people.'

'O-K.'

'So?'

And now this was even harder. Ruthie was an exceptional kid. Who deserved someone exceptional in her life. And she had that in Anna. She was getting on just fine. What could he tell her? She was thirteen but way more astute than that.

'I really like your mom,' Sam said. 'Is it OK to say that?'

'It's OK to say that if it's the truth.'

He nodded. 'It's the absolute truth.'

'Good,' Ruthie said, seeming already satisfied. 'Because

you might be a bit too young but . . . she smiles more now you're here.'

'She does?'

'Definitely.' Ruthie sighed. 'My dad stopped making her smile a long time before they got divorced.'

What did Sam say to that? The poor kid. He went to put a hand out but Ruthie stepped backward.

'We don't have to touch,' she said. 'Remember?'

'Got it,' Sam said, putting his hand back down. 'So, maybe, if me liking your mom is OK with you, you can help me plan where to take your mom on a date.'

'Really?' Ruthie asked, excited.

'Sure,' Sam replied, smiling. 'I'm gonna need all the help I can get, right?'

'You so are,' Ruthie said. 'Because she likes weird stuff. Like candles that smell like lemons . . . and cleaning stuff that smells like almonds and—'

'Anything other than smells she likes?'

'She doesn't like the smell of Mr Rocket's cage at the end of the week.'

'Lemons, almonds and not rabbit poop. Got it.'

Ruthie smiled. 'Now, Falcon, there's something you need to know about this rugby game you're about to play.'

Sam grinned. 'Yeah? You're really gonna give me tactics? Because I'll let you into a secret. I kinda know how to play this game.'

Ruthie waved a finger. 'You might think you do. But the English invented the game of rugby and it isn't like that weird game you have in America which is all cheerleaders and fireworks and someone singing the national anthem off key.' She eyed him seriously. 'Do you even know what a scrum is?'

'Is it not like a huddle? We all get together and talk big about how we're gonna beat the other team?'

'Oh dear,' Ruthie said, shaking her head and looking at her watch. 'Right, start listening, because we don't have long. You cannot, under any circumstances, pass the ball forward.'

'What?'

'But you can kick the ball at the goal at any time.'

'You're kidding me?!'

'And you're going to be playing it in a festive costume. Last year Paul chose "tails" and he won and got the easier Father Christmas outfits. But if he doesn't win the coin toss again it will be the reindeer outfits and they have bells *and* antlers.'

Oh shit.

Forty

This team huddle they were in looked like something out of a Christmas movie. Grown-ass men dressed as reindeers, bells making a noise even if you simply nodded your head, antlers flapping. Sam's outfit was at least four inches too short, the reindeer legs at mid-calf and the arms mid-forearm and the rest of him was squeezed into the fluffy suit, zip straining.

'Right,' Paul said to his players. 'It's meant to be a friendly game but we know what they're like. *Brutal.*'

Paul had said 'brutal' like he was describing a pack of lions tearing at some unlucky zebras near a watering hole. Maybe this wasn't such a good idea. Actually, it was a terrible plan. He'd invalidate any insurance the Bisons had on him by taking part and he was literally only just out of that rib-busting traffic collision. But what was playing by the rules, when you had a ticking clock guiding your life?

'So,' Paul carried on. 'We know what we have to do. Rip their Santa beards off before we worry about what to do with the ball.'

'Wait, what?' Sam asked.

'It might sound like an odd approach,' Paul said. 'But we've accepted over the years that we aren't the most skilful of players. However, what we lack in that department we make up for in elastic-snapping and nylon hair-tugging. Last year we came very close.'

The group all concurred, heads nodding, bells jangling again. These guys really thought they couldn't win. Inside him, Sam felt something begin to stir. It was like he was back to being a kid on Christmas Eve, pretending he was asleep, alive with excitement about what Santa Claus might leave for him. He knew now it was his mom and dad padding around the apartment, Albert with two coconut shells he used to gently bring together to emulate the hooves of reindeer as they landed on their building . . .

'How about we don't do that this year?' Sam suggested to Paul. 'How about you win it a different way?'

'Win it?' Paul queried. 'We've, er, never won it.'

Now Sam felt determination waking up, that 'about to do battle' emotion that started to build up from about a week before a big game and continued until it was a power to be unleashed against the opposition come showtime. He knew he had the speed and the fitness and now Ruthie had given him all the weird basics of rugby – far more complicated than NFL, in his opinion – surely they had to be in with a chance.

He smiled at Paul. 'Well, let's change that.'

'Any donations gratefully accepted,' Neeta said, shaking her bucket at the spectators. 'Preferably notes, but coins will do, if you're happy to have that on your conscience and know categorically that you or a loved one will never need an MRI scan.'

'Look at them,' Lisa said, indicating the teams on the getting-frosty pitch, floodlights illuminating the grass now. 'Some people are wearing those outfits like a second skin. Did they shrink in the wash?'

'I think most of the players have gained inches since last December,' Neeta replied. 'And not from the gym.'

'I tell you who's busting out of his reindeer suit but in all the good ways,' Lisa began. She nudged Anna's arm so hard Anna almost lost control of her charity bucket. Nothing more needed to be said. She was very aware that Sam was overfilling the fancy dress, from his muscular calves to that broad back, it was like a live billboard advertising personal trainers.

'How are things going with you two?' Lisa wanted to know.

'Good,' Anna answered.

'Oh, Anna, "good" is not good enough. We both want to know if you have smeared the pamper party Loose Juice all over him yet.'

'Oh, God! No!' Anna answered, cringing. 'You guys don't still have that stuff do you?'

Neeta hosting pamper parties was another hobby she'd had for a while. It wasn't quite beauty, it wasn't quite Ann Summers, it was something in between and, wanting to help their friend get over the painting debacle, both Lisa and Anna had held parties. Except, somehow, they had both ended up buying copious amounts of glittery massage gel that had the strangest consistency and smelled a bit like weed.

'I had to order more from eBay when the firm went into liquidation. Paul loves it,' Lisa admitted as money dropped into her bucket.

'Pavinder rubbed it into his plants,' Neeta continued. 'He said it gave the leaves a nice lustre.' She sighed. 'That was kind of what I was hoping for for my clitoris.'

'Anyway,' Lisa said. 'Classic Anna avoiding the question.'

'What was the question again?' Anna said, her gaze going to the two teams in festive fancy dress preparing to do battle on the pitch.

'How far have things gone with Sam?' Neeta asked.

'God, not far. Obviously. I have Ruthie, a cat and a rabbit,' Anna reminded. 'And we haven't known each other very long.' But what exactly was the etiquette when the person you were getting along nicely with was only around for a short time? Did it speed up the timeline? What even was the end goal in a Christmas romance?

'Anna, you sound like someone's mum,' Lisa said.

'I *am* someone's mum.'

'Someone's mum when the someone is fifty-five.'

'What are you waiting for? Because if Celia Duke gets her eyes on Sam, I can tell you she will not hesitate to be all in. They call her the Silver Bareback.'

Anna winced. She needed to hear no more about that. Did Sam think they were going too slow? If he did, he hadn't made it clear. She looked at him now, stretching his arms above his head, running on the spot as play got ready to commence. He still looked hot in the awful-fitting reindeer outfit . . .

Anna shook her bucket and earned some more donations from the onlookers. 'I . . . don't know how this is meant to go though. When I was using the app it was one date and all I had to worry about was making sure I didn't drink too much Pinot and could get myself in an Uber afterwards. With Sam I . . . actually really like him.'

'Exactly our point!' Neeta exclaimed. 'So . . .'

'But it's casual, isn't it? It has to be casual.'

'And having sex with someone does not mean anyone has to pay anyone else a dowry.'

'If you need someone to have Ruthie overnight then I will,' Lisa offered.

'And I will. Ruthie likes my superior hand soap. She told me. She also told me not to tell you,' Neeta replied.

'I don't know,' Anna answered.

'You are impossible! What have you got to lose by making the suggestion?' Lisa asked.

'My dignity,' Anna said.

'I'm sorry but anyone who makes up a rap to a Vanilla Ice track to sell soup has already lost so so much,' Neeta replied.

A loud whistle rang out and some cheering and ruckus sounded from the pitch.

'Come on, Paul!' Lisa yelled.

'Come on, reindeers!' Neeta added.

The ball was caught under everyone's feet – or hooves and boots, such were the costumes – until finally someone from the reindeers got it into their hands. And then it was launched into the freezing air. Within a split second, Sam had captured the ball and was tearing for the touchline faster than the speed of light.

'Oh my gods,' Neeta said, dropping her bucket to the ground.

'Almost exactly what I was thinking,' Lisa agreed, sighing.

Anna bit her lip, enjoying the sight of Sam at full pelt, running almost the entire length of the pitch and touching the ball down to score a try. An enormous cheer rose up from the rest of the reindeers and Sam was engulfed in nylon fabric and antlers, bells activating.

'Still not thinking about it?' Neeta asked.

Forty-One

Outside Anna and Ruthie's home, Richmond

'There are more lights since we left for the game!' Ruthie said excitedly, running along the pavement. 'Look! Mr Penderghast has got an animatronic reindeer . . . oh, but its head isn't working properly, it keeps hitting the fence.'

Sam inhaled the sweet cold air and slipped his arm around Anna's shoulders. He felt good. For the first time in a very long time there was something pure inside him, something that didn't need a genetics doctor to fathom. Despite everything going on, this simplicity he was feeling was empowering. It was safe in this bubble. He felt protected.

'You know that's it now, don't you?' Anna said, looking at Ruthie watching the display.

'What? I have to fix the head of the animatronic reindeer?' Sam asked.

'Obviously. But that wasn't what I meant. I meant Paul was serious about starting up a real rugby team with you at the centre of it.'

Sam laughed. 'He lost me the second he said the word "veterans".'

'You were pretty amazing though,' Anna told him.

'Only "pretty" amazing?' Sam asked. 'The reindeers had never won before. The Santas didn't score a point!'

'Well, I don't want you to get all conceited. That's not an attractive look,' Anna said.

'Really?' Sam said. 'So was the reindeer costume an attractive look?'

They were walking in rhythm now, his arm close to her shoulders, just an ordinary couple heading home in the dark . . .

'It might have been,' Anna said. 'If you hadn't looked like you were squeezing into an outfit for a five-year-old.' She laughed.

'I think Neeta dug it,' Sam replied.

'Neeta needs a distraction at the moment seeing as the nursing home turned down her job application.'

'Actually the result going that way was all Ruthie. If she hadn't given me a rundown of the rules before we started, it could have gone very differently.'

'Really? I didn't realise she ever paid that much attention to Kai's games.' Then Anna shook her head. 'Scrub that, she literally picks up everything super-quickly without having to try too hard.'

They stopped outside Anna and Ruthie's gate. Ruthie was still hanging over the fence to next door, talking to the reindeer. She had been so happy when the reindeers had secured victory, even given him a high-five albeit with her jumper sleeves pulled over her hand. He'd told her the win had been down to her and her smile could have powered the festive lights she was looking at right now. And her joy had warmed him from his bare shins in that too-short costume to the tip of his antlers.

'Do you want to come in?' Anna asked, looking up at him.

'More than you know,' he whispered. He smiled. 'I would kill for a coffee.'

'And . . . if I was offering more than coffee?'

Under the streetlamp Anna had never looked more sexy and that played with him hard. Their connection was everything he could have imagined a relationship to be. It was fun, it was equal, it was going to be hard to say goodbye to when the time came and that time would have to come. But, still, in this moment . . .

'I kinda have a plan with Ruthie,' he admitted.

'Please not another Marvel movie marathon.'

He laughed. 'Sshh, she might hear you.' He reached out a hand and touched Anna's hair. It was smooth and silky and it always smelt so damn fine. 'Are you free tomorrow night?'

'Let me think about that for a second . . . yes.' She smiled.

'Then let's leave coffee and maybe more than coffee for tomorrow night. If that's OK,' Sam said, still stroking her hair.

'OK,' she answered.

He indulged himself looking at her, drinking her in, this woman who had slammed into his life and was somehow anchoring him down from the tsunami of chaos all around him.

'Then kiss me,' he said. 'Before I have to mend the head of that reindeer.'

He waited, wanting to watch her lean closer, take time to enjoy that anticipation. And then their lips were intertwined, and he got that same rush of heat tearing through his body he did every time they connected. If only things were different . . . but then simple maybe wouldn't feel as vital.

'Sam! When you've finished kissing my mum can you come and fix the reindeer? He's called Cecil.'

Anna's mouth left his and she did that cute thing she did where she pushed her hair back from her face and looked a little flushed. A cell phone beep hit the air and Anna got her phone from her bag.

'OK?' Sam asked as her expression altered.

'Yeah . . . it's just Neeta.'

'OK,' he answered. Then he faced Ruthie. 'I'm coming for Cecil!'

Forty-Two

Oxford Street, London

This morning Sam had gone to the ultimate festive shopping experience in London, so he had been told by the receptionist at his hotel. He needed to get his gift-buying game on. He couldn't come to London, this mecca of Britishness, and come back without a host of presents to make his family smile.

A new scarf for his mama's hair maybe? A tie for his dad who always dressed in a suit to sell cars whether it was summer or winter. Something weird with the Union Jack on it for Chad. Maybe something chic for Frankie . . . for a ballbuster she had a rather surprising obsession with pink. And then there was Ruthie and Anna.

It was new but he felt he had to get them something. No, not had to, *wanted* to. Was it wrong to feel kind of attached already? When he thought about going back home, trying to make sense of what was going on, it didn't seem to include forgetting about who he had found here. He swallowed. Except no one in his life had the truth right now. Not his mom and dad, not Tionne or his team, not Anna. When was he going to talk about it? When would this brewing illness leap up and define him?

Sam looked up at the rows of sparkling angels strung across the street, black cabs, red buses, cyclists passing underneath oblivious to the beauty. *Moments*. That was what life was. Not the long game. He let that settle on him. *Moments*. Laughter. Smiles. Conversation.

His cell phone started ringing and when he saw it was Frankie he stepped to the edge of the sidewalk and answered.

'Hey.'

'Hey, Sam.'

There was an instant heaviness to her tone, her guard down.

'Tell me,' Sam said, watching a dog dressed in a festive jumper crossing with its owner as the lights changed. 'Whatever it is, tell me straight.'

Frankie sighed, either not liking the fact he had read her, or not liking what news she had to deliver.

'The deal with the Diggers . . . it's off.'

Sam closed his eyes and leaned against the lamp-post. Even though he'd *known* it, hearing it still made this all the more real. He was never going to be the player who made history. There wasn't going to be another handshake photo for his mom to put up on the wall. Tionne wouldn't be putting diamantes on a shirt with his name on and selling it online.

'Sam, are you OK? Did you hear me?'

'Yeah. Yeah, I heard you.' But what came next? What did he want to know? Why? Well, that last one was straightforward. They were spending millions. They wanted the best. And he was flawed now. They'd move on to the next best. He was a commodity, talent in shoulder pads and compression shorts.

'I tried to bargain. I said what Dr Monroe told me he was going to put in his report – about this being a kind of dormant thing right now. That for all we know you are going to be in A1 condition until well after your career as a player is over but . . .'

A full ending to the sentence wasn't needed. He knew it was over. He had known from the second he fled from the doctor's office. It was why the Dallas Diggers had been so insistent on all these kinds of tests. If they'd found out he had high blood pressure or diabetes it would be the same result. Except those things could all be turned around. You got a second chance.

215

He swallowed. 'So, what happens now?'

'Have you spoken to your parents?' Frankie asked.

'Not in the way you mean.'

'Well, I know you haven't spoken to Tionne since our last conversation because she's desperate for information from me, Sam. It's calls and messages and I think she's one step away from turning up at my apartment with tequila. And you know how I can get with tequila.'

'I don't know what to say to them,' Sam admitted, his throat tightening. 'Because the minute I say something the bottom is going to drop out of their world. It won't be about the Diggers. It will be about the fact one of them most likely has it too and there's a fifty per cent chance for my sister.'

There was nothing he wanted more than to take every part of this damn Huntington's and swallow it. His eyes went inside the store he was standing next to. Christmas decorations in boxes – bright green and red balls covered in gold and silvery white, fairies and reindeer on strings to hang up . . .

'Sam, you need to come back,' Frankie told him.

'Yeah, I know.'

'Then why are you still there?'

'Because . . . I just need to be. For a little longer.'

If he told Frankie about Anna she wouldn't get it. Frankie was the opposite of a hopeless romantic. She thought partners were like appliances. You nabbed them and you used them for what they were best at and then you swapped them for a more up-to-date model. If he tried to explain that Anna was like no one he'd ever met before, that they'd met by chance, that she had the most awesome kid, that when he woke up in the morning lately it was her on his mind and not this disease that was ruining his life, Frankie wouldn't get it. But to be fair, if he had told himself any of these things a few weeks ago, he wouldn't have got it either. He had been playing the bachelor, living fast and free, following the crowd for so long he hadn't realised what else was out there. He hadn't known how much he craved someone to really connect with. He had friendships, with Chad and Tyrone and the rest of his teammates, but it was superficial somehow, like there wasn't time to dig deep in between the games and the training and the social media noise. It wasn't on the same level as having someone getting to know the roots of you. That's what he had with Anna.

'Sam, are you in trouble?'

He was. He knew it. His heart was getting lost to Anna. But he was sure that wasn't what Frankie meant.

'Like Chad getting arrested for stealing a cart full of Eggos? That kind of trouble?'

'The official line was he joyrode the cart and had no intention of taking them out of the store,' Frankie reminded. '*Any* kind of trouble.'

'No,' he told her. 'I'm not in trouble.'

'Sam, like I told you before, it only takes one journalist sniffing around to get even a hint of something and this story is gonna blow up. You need to lie low.'

'Yeah, I heard you the last time.' And he hadn't stopped thinking about it since. He'd even started checking over his shoulder on the street, looking twice at anyone with a camera slung around their neck – and there were many innocent tourists undeserving of his attention.

'And I meant it.'

'I get it, Frankie, OK?' He hadn't meant it to come out quite so harsh but there was no good ending to any of this. That was the truth of it.

'OK,' she said. 'But remember I'm your friend as well as your agent, Sam. You aren't in this on your own. And we don't know what the Bisons are going to do, do we? This deal was huge for them too. So, you need to think about what happens next. If you still want to move, I say we contact other clubs. Yes they might not command the kind of fee we were talking about with the Diggers but you are still a prime asset, Sam.'

A prime asset. Still sounding like steak on a plate. He looked into that store again, his eyes drawn to the many different kinds of adornments. And then he saw it. A black and white rabbit with a crystalline carrot between its lips. It looked just like Mr Rocket . . .

'I've told the Diggers no press conference, no comment about the deal until you're back over here and we can work together in making everyone come out of this as unscathed as possible. So, if we get lucky with everyone keeping their silence and not getting paid off by the press then we should be good to move forward.'

Moving forward. Or staying in Cincinnati. If the Bisons still wanted him . . .

'I gotta go, Frankie. Just . . . one more thing.' Sam moved into the store selling decorations.

'Anything.'

'Are you still into pink?' he asked her.

'Only if you keep that information to yourself,' Frankie answered.

Forty-Three

Bean Afar, Richmond

'Damn!'

Lisa had said 'damn' at least five times already since they had each been given this week's special, a cinnamon and caramel coffee covered in squirty cream and sprinkled with chocolate chips. As Christmas crept ever closer, Esther's specials were getting more and more dramatic in the sugary syrup and decoration stakes.

'Are you saying "damn" like an American because Sam is an American?' Neeta wanted to know. 'You sound a little like Dolly Parton.'

'I'm saying "damn" like that because . . . well . . . look at him!' Lisa said, sounding like she was fangirling over Cillian Murphy.

The 'him' they were gawping at on Anna's phone was Sam. Sam Jackman from the Cincinnati Bisons. Not a football team in the sense Anna had meant it, an *American* football team, a team in the NFL. And Sam was pretty much a celebrity in the US. There were zillions of photos of him dressed in those tight bottoms and a top with shoulder pads to rival Joan Collins in the Eighties, plus other pictures – opening school running tracks, in a tuxedo for gala charity events, one laughing with Jimmy Fallon . . . Anna had scrolled through plenty last night after Neeta's text. The text had simply said 'you need to google Sam' and there had been much to find. And Anna still didn't know how she felt about it.

'It was Kai's friend, Scrubs, who knew. He's big into American football and when Kai showed him the video of Sam he knew straightaway who he was. I texted Neeta first because, I don't know, I didn't know if Sam had told you and you were having to keep it secret or if you didn't know, you might be upset . . . OK, I bottled it. I told Neeta and let her make the decision,' Lisa continued. 'Oh, look at him there, leaning over that Hummer.'

'What kind of a name is Scrubs anyway?' Neeta wanted to know. 'Does his mother want him to be a doctor? Ooo, look at that photo with the aftershave. He's all moist.'

'OK, this is getting a bit weird now,' Anna said, taking her phone back.

'*Did* you know?' Neeta asked, slurping up her drink and getting foam all over her top lip.

'Did I know what? That he advertised aftershave with a tiger?' Anna replied.

'The whole thing. Sam being an NFL player. Sam being a celebrity over there. I mean if he hasn't been invited on *Dancing with the Stars* already, it's got to be in the works,' Lisa said.

'No,' Anna said. 'I didn't know.'

'But you must have asked him what he did for a job.' Neeta gasped. 'Oh my gods. Did he *lie*?'

'No,' Anna said quickly. 'He told me he played football. I just misinterpreted it. I thought he meant football as in proper football. Sorry, America.' She sighed. 'And I thought he was more like the US equivalent of a League Two player not . . . on the list to be invited to play Soccer Aid.'

'Sam is hanging out with *very* famous people,' Neeta said, earrings jangling. 'I mean, Ryan Seacrest!'

'And Kai said he's on the brink of a brand-new multi-million-dollar deal. Paul was pissed off. He really thought he'd found someone who could realise his veteran rugby team dreams.'

Anna had read about that last night. Cheesecake had taken

to sleeping in her room, on her bed, in between her legs so it was impossible to move. So, completely pinned under the duvet, she had read a few articles about this 'once in a lifetime' deal, one the NFL world had never seen before. Sam was destined to be some kind of superior being in his field. So why on earth – or whatever planet this near superhero was from – was he in Richmond visiting a confused mid-range restaurant with her and doing headstands in the street outside St Paul's and . . . kissing her the way he did?

'He has dated a supermodel,' Neeta continued. 'Did you see that?'

'Maybe more than one,' Lisa said. 'He's been linked to Donatella Jorden and Misha D'vice too.'

'Misha D'vice. Isn't she the one from your magazine who spent thousands of pounds on a car covered in diamantes and filled it with lollipops?' Neeta asked.

'She did then donate it to a children's charity.'

'The car?'

'No, just the sweets.'

This was all turning into noise, and even the rather sugar-heavy festive coffee wasn't doing anything to quell the unsettled feeling in Anna's stomach. This made things different, didn't it? Now he wasn't just an almost-twenty-six-year-old from the US. He was on some kind of rich list. His life was parties and hanging out at cool places with celebrities just like him. Sam's life was getting expensive products for free, receiving exclusive pre-access to events mere mortals could only dream about. It was luxurious and sleek. It was the opposite of cats and rabbits and OCD and Christmas songs at a care home . . .

'He's meant to be taking me out tonight,' Anna said.

'Ooo where?' Lisa asked. 'Somewhere swish and exclusive?'

'He gave Ruthie his phone number. She was texting an essay last night and didn't want me to see. She's helping him plan something. I don't know.' Anna put her hands in her hair.

'What do you not know?' Neeta asked. 'I am not supposed

to tell you until after 5pm but I am having Ruthie at my house overnight. Pavinder and Ruthie are cooking *me* Bang Bang chicken. Sorry, Lisa, but Ruthie did confirm that I do have the superior hand soap and she also said that she likes my fabric conditioner that makes the towels soft.'

'But this!' Anna said, holding her phone up again. 'The fact that Sam is . . . well, I don't know who he is. But the US press seem to hail him as some kind of American footballing legend as well as being hotter than . . . all the Hemsworths.'

'He is hotter than all the Hemsworths,' Lisa agreed. 'You didn't need any of these articles to tell you that, surely.'

'He is even hotter than Ryan Seacrest.'

Anna dropped her forehead to the table. If they weren't in the midst of this oh-so-festive café with its calm buzz, gentle Bublé coming from the radio, crumpets, croissants and cake being consumed to the percolating sounds of the finest grounds, she would scream.

'Anna, what is the matter?' Neeta wanted to know. 'You knew he was hot before. You have been looking at him a long time now. Why are you thumping your brain on the table because he has money and . . . designers are wanting him to wear their clothes and their scents and . . . supermodels are wanting him to wear them? Ambition. Is this not a good thing?'

Anna shook her head. She didn't know what it was apart from being a complication. He was *someone*. He was a VIP. She'd already had a freakout about Sam being so much younger than her and now he was still so much younger than her and had apparently dated women who didn't look like their skin care routine was a quick swipe with a Simple wipe but involved a team of professional stylists.

'He's dated someone called Misha D'vice. I mean, I'm Anna Heath. I *eat* lollipops, I don't fill expensive cars with them. I don't have money for an expensive car. And I've never even seen a tiger, let alone encouraged one to pose for a photo with me. The last "gala" dinner I went to they had a fish finger and tiny chips in an even tinier cone. Sam's had four kinds of caviar. I didn't even know there *were* four kinds of caviar! And . . . he came here to England with nothing but a rucksack. Why did he come here with nothing but a rucksack?'

'Esther!' Neeta called, putting her hand up in the air like she might have been at school. 'Do you have a particular coffee to aid with hyperventilation?'

Anna lifted her head from the table and inhaled. She wasn't hyperventilating, was she? Perhaps that was Neeta's aim. To announce a predicament to the room in a backwards manifesting move . . .

'She's not hyperventilating,' Lisa said calmly. 'She's overthinking . . . again.'

'I am doing that,' Anna agreed. 'Because why didn't he tell me? Was he *ever* going to tell me?'

'Let us think about that for a second,' Neeta suggested, pouring some more sugar into her coffee. 'You are a very tall, very broad, very attractive young man about to complete on a life-changing multi-million-dollar deal already earning thousands of dollars a week and you meet someone by chance that you really *really* like and they really like you, because you saved their child from bullies, and they saved you from a road traffic accident. Then you get to know them a bit more and they introduce you to their friends and it becomes nice to know that someone likes you for those qualities rather than how many kinds of caviar you can get them for free.'

Neeta did have a definite way with words. And this had the potential to be accurate. It made sense and it wasn't that Sam had been untruthful, he did play football, just not the kind Anna had assumed. She certainly hadn't imagined the 'dripping in dollar bills' kind either.

'Does it matter?' Lisa said suddenly. 'You know, does it really change anything?'

'Exactly!' Neeta said as Esther came over with a glass of water and two paracetamol, presumably for the 'hyperventilation' that wasn't really happening. 'You liked him before you knew he was money-ed up so it is not like you are a gold-digger and like him more now you know about his wealth.'

'No, but, what if it makes me like him less?' Anna said. She couldn't quite believe the words had come out of her mouth, but it was a gut reaction. Sam was hot property, in the limelight and her initial thoughts were that this meant it ended as quickly as it had begun. Because how could it do anything else?

'What?!'

Neeta and Lisa had said the same word at exactly the same time.

Anna picked up her cup of coffee. 'I mean I knew from the beginning he was only here for a visit, but then, you know, I gave it a try and it was nice. And I've started to really like him. Because he just fitted like he'd always belonged.' She gasped, shocked by her own admission. 'And, I don't know, I stopped thinking about how long he was here for and how long it was going to last and I only began thinking about how fun it was and how much like the old me I felt.'

Neeta put the paracetamol in her own mouth and swigged back some water.

'That's brilliant, Anna,' Lisa told her, reaching for her hands and giving them a squeeze.

'It's not though, is it? Because now it doesn't feel right. Now I'm back to thinking that he can't possibly like me. He's been dating models and women who seem to have the secret to youth smoothed all over them. I can't compete with that.'

'That is true,' Neeta said, nodding.

Lisa elbowed Neeta hard. 'It's not true, Anna. And you always look amazing.'

'You do,' Neeta added, rubbing her sore elbow. 'You really do. And, you know, filters have as much to answer for as beauty products these days.'

'This isn't the worst thing in the world, Anna,' Lisa said softly.

'No,' Neeta said. 'This is not finding out Sam is married . . . or finding out that he has been a star of a Netflix true crime documentary and is wanted in four different states, or finding out that he is more interested in someone at work who knows the difference between a petal cell and a stamen cell.'

Anna took a deep breath. 'Perspective. OK. I mean a few weeks ago I didn't even know he existed so this should not be destabilising me like this. Nothing has changed. He's still here on a vacation and I'm still here with Ruthie preparing for Christmas and . . . shit, what's the time?' Anna pulled her sleeve up to look at her watch.

'Getting close to ten o'clock,' Neeta informed. 'Do you have somewhere to be? Unlike the rest of us who rely on charity events and helping at food banks to pass the time.'

'Yes,' Anna said, swigging back her coffee and regretting the speed as the caramel coated her throat. 'I have a call with Adam about Mr Wong and if I miss it there's a very real possibility that he'll fire me.'

'Take a breath,' Lisa encouraged, standing up too.

'It is a call, right? You have your phone here,' Neeta reminded, picking it up off the table.

And now the battery indicator was orange and had a very slim space left. It was all that image searching of Sam!

'I need to get back home. I need my laptop. I need to charge this thing,' Anna said, taking the phone and putting it in her bag. She took that deep breath. 'So, what am I going to do? About Sam being this high-profile person who gets the red-carpet treatment like I get discount codes for meals at Beefeater?'

'What do you *want* to do about it?' Lisa asked.

'In my opinion,' Neeta started, 'you have two choices. You either pretend you have not found out and see if he ever tells you before he goes back to his lavish lifestyle. Or you expose him tonight – lay all his tiger and fragrance photos bare during your date and see what his story for keeping it from you is.'

Neither of those sounded particularly palatable. A bit like this drink now it had really hit her stomach.

'Anna,' Lisa said. 'There might be a very good reason he hasn't told you.' She put a steadying hand on her shoulder. 'I'm just saying, be honest with him. Ask the questions. And, remember, not all men are like Ed.'

Anna nodded. 'I've got to go. But, thanks, you two.'

'Not a problem,' Neeta said as Anna headed for the door. 'And I am really looking forward to the feast Pavinder and Ruthie have in store for me tonight.'

Feast. The word hit Anna's subconscious and her brain suddenly went into overdrive.

Forty-Four

Anna and Ruthie's home, Richmond

'Now, Ruthie, are you absolutely sure you're OK with staying the night at Neeta and Pavinder's?' Anna said, checking her reflection in the mirror on the wall above the wood burner that evening.

The mirror was something else of Nanny Gwen's she had lovingly restored. It wasn't worth anything in money terms, but Anna had always thought it was pretty. Age had blackened it a little, but she had taken time to bring it back to as close to its former glory as was possible. Anna remembered looking into it, standing side by side with her nan and taking time to really gather in their reflections after an afternoon of curlers in their hair or a makeover session.

At the moment, the mirror was ringed with red furry tinsel, something left over from when she had made Ruthie an outfit for a school Christmas show. This particular sensory experience was one Ruthie enjoyed and, before it was hung around the mirror each year, Ruthie would run it between her fingers and take pleasure in the sensation for a few minutes.

Ruthie was currently doing the same thing with Cheesecake's tail, not seeming to be paying attention to Anna, like she had zoned out. She did that sometimes, usually when she was stressed. Maybe this change with Sam *was* the stress, despite apparently helping to coordinate this night.

'Ruthie?' Anna said, turning fully around from the mirror. 'Did you hear me?'

'Do you think Dad will be the same with the new baby as he is with me?' Ruthie asked. 'I mean, if the baby isn't on the spectrum do you think he will love it more?'

Anna's heart ached as Ruthie delivered the out-of-the-blue questions. Such a deep thinker, carrying the weight of all this inside until there it was, laid bare as she gently twirled her cat's tail. Anna sat down next to her daughter and looked at her beautiful face with the wide-set intelligent eyes. She knew it was impossible to stop her from getting hurt by life but if she was ever granted a wish, that's what she would ask for. She smoothed a hand down Ruthie's curls and earned a little resistance and a scowl.

'Everyone's on the spectrum somewhere, Ruthie,' Anna reminded.

'Some of us are more gripping on to the pie chart than others though.'

'The way your dad can sometimes be really isn't down to you, Ruthie. I've told you that so many times before. He finds it hard to understand and he doesn't get things right, I know.'

'But Sam does,' Ruthie stated.

'Ruthie, Sam hasn't been completely immersed in the situation. It's different.'

'He's seen my bullies. He's watched *Loki* with me and didn't tell me I talk too much. He doesn't make any eye contact when I'm having to look at the wallpaper and count the flowers—'

'I know, but . . . Sam is just visiting. Dad was here all the time and these things, they have a habit of starting off small and then slowly, bit by bit they wear away at you and before you know it they're getting bigger and bigger and out of control. Sam hasn't had that yet. He's only had the good bits so far, not so many of the challenges.'

'Is that what I'm doing?' Ruthie asked. 'Wearing away at people?'

'No,' Anna said quickly. 'No, I didn't mean that at all.

Just that sometimes small things become bigger things over time.' And now she could be talking about her and Ed's slow demise until finally he moved towards Nicolette or her nana's illness, little pieces of Gwen fading in brightness until there was nothing left that made Gwen who she had been. Everything started small but, more often than not, it was those first fragments that made the wider, sometimes insurmountable craters form.

'So Sam is OK with me now, but over time and definitely if he moves in, it's going to be something that starts to irritate him?' Ruthie asked.

Moves in! The doorbell rang.

'Ruthie, I like Sam, you know that. But he's only here in Richmond for a very short time.'

In one quick move Ruthie got Cheesecake down from her lap and folded her arms across her chest. It was her go-to move when she was super irritated. 'For now.'

'Ruthie, he lives in America and he has . . . a very important job.' She hadn't mentioned Sam's status to Ruthie, but she wouldn't put it past Kai to spread the news, if not to Ruthie directly, then on Instagram. 'It's nice to spend time with him but . . .' She stopped because she didn't know how to end the sentence.

The doorbell rang again and Anna sensed this was a Neeta blast this time. 'That will be Neeta and Pavinder. Got your bag?'

'It's by the door. Don't touch it,' Ruthie said, getting to her feet.

Anna rushed down the hall to the door and opened it up before the bell could ring again. Except it wasn't Neeta and Pavinder standing there in the cold, it was Sam.

'Hey,' he greeted, with that amazing smile.

'Oh, hi. I wasn't expecting you yet. Neeta and Pavinder aren't here yet so Ruthie's still here.'

'I know,' Sam answered. 'That was the plan.'

'O-K. Now I'm deeply concerned about the depth of

this planning and . . . you're wearing a suit. And now I'm underdressed because I don't know what we're doing!' She slapped her hands to her wool skirt over tights and boots. She'd been going for smart casual and vaguely warm but now she wished she'd gone for casually smart and sexy and who cares about the cold!

Sam grabbed hold of her hand and held it firmly in his. 'That was also the plan. And you look . . . beautiful.'

Anna swallowed. He sounded so sincere but now she couldn't get rid of the thought of all those gorgeous women who had been on his arm . . .

'Sam!' Ruthie greeted, jostling Anna as she came up behind her. 'I really thought it was Neeta here early. I panicked. Neeta's always early.'

'And I came earlier than early, like you said,' Sam answered. He offered his elbow out and Ruthie bumped it with hers.

'Is it here?' Ruthie asked, eyes alive.

'It sure is,' Sam said.

Anna watched the interchange between them and felt her heart dive a little. It was nice. It was *so* nice, but Ruthie was getting really invested. And when Ruthie got invested it wasn't only someone liking something and being a bit disappointed when it stopped being so present, it was more a case of covering something in all the love, time and energy she possessed and then going through the deepest, most sorrowful mourning process complete with dark clothing choices, emo make-up and 'Everybody Hurts' by REM when it ended.

'Mum, come and see!'

Ruthie tugged at her arm and Anna pushed the door wider until she could see what all this secrecy was about. Anna gasped as she saw two pure white shire horses attached to an old-fashioned carriage were standing in the street behind her car. Neighbours were twitching the curtains and parting their Christmas lights in the windows to get a better look. This wasn't real, was it?

'Tell me you like horses,' Sam breathed as Anna stepped forward. 'Or is this a Ruthie thing and not an Anna thing and I've been made.'

'I like horses,' Anna answered, her heart beating hard in her chest. 'And I always wanted to ride in something like this. They have them in Richmond Park and they're just . . . so expensive that we never . . .' She had to stop talking because the horses were simply so beautiful. Muscular bodies with tufts of mane on their necks and huge hooves, leather tack made festive with swags of red and green and golden bells. Ruthie was already on the street, laying palms on the neck of the nearest horse, talking to it.

'I thought it was very *Bridgerton*, my lady.'

'You are correct, Viscount.'

'Hey, I see myself as more of a Duke of Hastings.'

The smouldering was pretty undeniable . . .

'Good surprise?' Sam asked her.

'A great surprise,' Anna answered, looking to him rather than the horses now. 'I . . . don't know what to say.'

'Say you'll come for a ride with me,' Sam said. 'We can just take Ruthie with us, round the block, until Neeta gets here and then we can get the date started.'

How was this suddenly her life? Standing in the street she knew and loved so well, shire horses waiting to transport her, her daughter crazy happy, a gorgeous, funny, kind guy at her side. They could be characters in a starry snow-globe scene, it was so perfect . . .

'I was kinda hoping for a yes,' Sam said when she didn't immediately answer.

'Yes! Sorry, yes. I'll just get the keys and make sure Cheesecake is secure and I'll be right back.'

She turned away from him and headed back to the house. At the door she watched Sam down on the street, giving something to Ruthie to feed to the horses. And she knew before they'd travelled too far tonight she was going to have to tell him she knew exactly who he was.

Forty-Five

Richmond Park

'I don't even know what sloe gin is,' Sam remarked, taking a sip from his glass. 'Is it called that because it's best drunk real slow?'

Anna laughed. 'It's s-l-o-e. It's a berry. And where gin is a spirit, sloe gin is a liqueur.'

'OK, bartender,' Sam answered.

He pulled the blanket over her knees a little, tucking them both in. The night was clear and crisp but the alcohol was going some way to warm him up. Although, for some reason, there was a bubbling trepidation in his stomach. He wanted this night to go well. He wanted to make this date the most spectacular date Anna had ever been on and he really didn't know why he was wearing all that pressure.

'My Nanny Gwen taught me all about drinks. She thought you could tell a lot about people by what they chose to have,' Anna said, shifting closer to him.

'OK, so, I like a lot of different drinks. What does that say about me?' Sam asked, ducking his head a little into her space.

'You're either a connoisseur of the finer things in life or an alcoholic,' Anna answered.

He laughed. 'That sounds like real wisdom right there.'

'My nan was a very wise person. She would have liked you. She would have called you "dishy".'

'Dishy,' Sam said, shaking his head. 'Is that like the old-style version of "hot"?'

'Very much so.'

Sam watched Anna drop her gaze to the purple-coloured liquid in her glass. Something wasn't quite right with her energy tonight. Maybe she was worried about Ruthie. Maybe she was uncertain about this date. Trepidation bit hard.

'Anna, is everything OK?' Sam asked.

She nodded, but when she turned her head away from the glistening boughs of the frost-touched trees in the park, there was a different look in her eyes. He waited for her to speak.

'Everything's OK,' she began. 'But, after the charity rugby game, one of Kai's friends recognised you. And I'm sorry, I went down a rabbit hole of googling you and I see what your life is like in Cincinnati and what it's about to be in Dallas and it's definitely not all tepee bars and jamborees, it's many kinds of caviar and . . . you've met Arnold Schwarzenegger.'

He closed his eyes and felt that weight of responsibility take ownership of his shoulders. He should have told her from the beginning. But then maybe they wouldn't be here now. Here in this comfortable, vibey place they'd put together. He took a second and then put his hands into his spirals of hair and groaned aloud.

'God! You saw the photo with the tiger, right?'

'I did.'

'And the one where they sprayed me in gold and had me holding something like the Olympic torch?'

'Wearing nothing but a thong.'

He groaned again, bringing the blanket up to his face, too scared to look at her. 'This is bad. This is so so bad.' The horses slowed their pace a little, bringing the carriage to a more sedate speed.

'Why didn't you tell me you were this huge sports star?' Anna asked.

'I told you I played football.'

'And you knew I thought that meant you were something like a not-very-good David Beckham.'

'Is that what you thought? That I wasn't great!'

'I don't know how things work in America. It's so . . . big.'

'Yeah,' Sam sighed. 'It is.' He took a deep breath as everything began to feel tightly wound again.

'So?'

'So . . . I don't know, Anna. I guess I didn't come out with "hey there, some people consider me a celebrity over in the States" because it's not what's important to me.'

'O-K.'

'Because when I got here I was getting away from all that. Like . . . I don't know . . . Julia Roberts in *Notting Hill*. I mean, the English dude—'

'Hugh Grant.'

'They just had this connection, and then it was only when his friends got involved and the fame took over, everything went to crap.'

That's exactly what Sam felt like now. That whatever he said here wasn't going to make a difference to Anna. Pure, honest, beautiful Anna. And little did she know that her finding out he played in the NFL and got paid crazy amounts of money for his name and face on brands really wasn't the biggest thing he was holding back.

'Everything isn't going to crap,' she said softly. 'I just feel a bit like there's a big part of you I didn't know about, a huge important part. I mean I know your career isn't exactly rebranding and relaunching a Chinese chip shop pizza house but it seems the good people of America think you're important in some way.'

'Football is what I do, Anna,' Sam told her. 'But it's not who I am. You've been getting to know who I am.'

And as that sentence hit the night Sam realised that might just be the key to everything. He started again. 'It's taken me a while to realise that the two things shouldn't be so tied together. I don't have to be a carbon copy of what America thinks an NFL player should be. I don't have to . . . use my status to hit VIP areas, or feel guilty for turning down a night out with the team if I wanna lie on my couch underneath a blanket and binge *Better Call Saul*. I can be Sam without football. I think.'

'Well,' Anna said, adjusting the blanket over her knees and gripping her glass. 'Maybe it's time I told you about my secret career. I'm actually an artist.' She whispered. 'People call me Banksy.'

'I've heard of him,' Sam answered.

'Her,' Anna said. 'Because that's me.'

'OK, I think the sloe gin is getting to you now,' he said, taking her glass and putting it carefully on the floor of the carriage.

'Is there any more?' she asked.

'Yeah,' he answered. 'But, I thought you might want a taste of something sweeter.'

He drew the blanket up over her, carefully, protectively, he hoped a little seductively, and inched closer as the horses trotted forward. He didn't care that the carriage was attracting the attention of walkers and joggers and cyclists; here in the coach, it was only the two of them. His lips met hers and he felt an initial hesitation. He pulled back and looked into her eyes.

'You're having second thoughts.' He said it as a statement rather than a question and his internal reaction was scaring him.

'Not second thoughts,' Anna replied, taking one of his hands and squeezing it. 'Just thoughts.'

'What can I do?' he asked, heart hammering.

He watched her take a breath then meet his gaze again with those beautiful eyes. Was this going to be the moment it all fell apart here like it was falling apart over the Atlantic?

'I think it's too late,' Anna admitted. 'I think . . . Ruthie's invested and I'm invested and I know that you're not here for long and that's fine but I also think . . . even if you were running for president or . . . endorsing fake tan . . . I'd still be falling as hard as I'm falling right now.'

This was the crossroads. This was where he committed to this moment and all the moments they could have before he went back to the US and faced everything else, or he got out of this carriage and walked away. She might hurt for a while. Ruthie would not think he was superhero material anymore. But they would survive. They would move on. But what if this *could* be more? What if it wasn't only for how long he was here? He gazed at her, knowing how much it meant to her to have told him she was falling. Could this be something else? Did it have a chance to be for *more* than this Christmas? That would be something completely different. That would mean telling Anna everything.

He reached out, smoothing his fingers down her so soft dark hair. 'Fallen,' he whispered. 'I've definitely fallen.'

Forty-Six

Somerset House, London

'Be gentle with me,' Sam ordered. 'If I break a bone the Bisons are gonna want to murder me more than they want to murder me already for not being there.'

'Actual bisons are going to attack me? Or your team?'

He laughed. 'Chad would talk you to death and probably about death too.'

'I would counter with Ruthie on a rant about Harry Potter.'

'Whoa!' Sam said, grabbing Anna's arm.

They were skating. With hordes of others enjoying the rink that took over the courtyard at Somerset House. It was a beautiful neo-classical building, now a working arts centre, that everyone who was anyone wanted to enjoy at this time of year. It claimed to be London's most beautiful ice rink and with its gigantic Christmas tree fully adorned with tinsel, baubles and lights, plus the romanticism of the imposing building surrounding the skating area, it was a pocket of winter wonderful in the heart of the city.

Sam's height and stature seemed to be a real issue for him though. Being tall and heavy wasn't really conducive to staying balanced on two thin metal blades. She held his arm until he gained some control back.

'Do your team know you throw yourself in front of cars too?' Anna asked. 'I mean, that makes ice skating seem like a less risky pursuit.'

'Hey,' he replied. 'We agreed that although I may not have

237

looked the right way before I stepped off the sidewalk, the woman was going too fast and not looking.' He spread out his arms. 'I'm pretty hard to miss if you have your eyes on the road.'

He rocked on his feet again and Anna tried to stop him from falling, but this time he was way too close to going over and she couldn't halt him from hitting the ice.

'Damn!' Sam yelled but he was laughing, already dusting flakes of cold off his coat sleeves.

'How is it skating in a suit?' Anna asked.

'A little more restrictive than I thought,' he admitted, tentatively getting himself up. 'But I really dressed for later, not the skating. And, as I had nothing but sweats in my luggage, I bought this.'

Anna couldn't deny the midnight-blue suit was a great look on him. But practically any look was good on him. And he had fallen for her . . . just when she'd almost given up on feeling like her again. And now here she was, riding in carriages, ice skating and being as enthused over a work project as she had been since the divorce.

She pushed off onto the ice, enjoying the rush of freezing air hitting her cheeks. 'I had an epiphany about Mr Wong's restaurants.'

'You did?' Sam asked.

'I did. And some of it was down to you.'

'It was?' He was next to her now, that stature as solid as it was sexy.

'You told me about the restaurant in Cincinnati. The one that did all kinds of cuisine.'

'Yeah . . .'

'Well, I pitched the idea to Mr Wong and he *loved* it. I mean, he *really* loved it. Now, I know a restaurant being like an all-inclusive holiday buffet isn't exactly ground-breaking but I've come up with a few little twists I think will really make Feast different.'

'Feast,' Sam said. 'Wow, that is a seriously great name.'

'Shit, that was a spoiler. I'm still refining the branding. I'm stuck between having licking flames coming out of the "f" or spices sprinkling down. What do you think?'

'Man, I don't know. I'm not really experienced in that field. I—'

'Not experienced?!' Anna exclaimed, wobbling on her skates. 'You've literally advertised for the biggest brand names in the US.'

'Anna, I sat on velvet seats while photographers wished I was more will.i.am and less Sam.i.am.definitely.not.'

'I've seen the photos,' Anna reminded.

'And I'm sorry for that.' He wobbled and she held on to his arm. 'This is the most difficult thing I've ever done.'

'Skating?' Anna asked. 'Or answering questions about your times as a model?'

He smiled. 'And that's what I love about this. What I love about us . . . you get me.'

She could feel herself blushing on the inside. It was true. There was the easiest rhythm between them. It didn't have to be thought about, it didn't have to be worked at, it was just there, organically growing and seeming to get stronger and hotter and more intense every single day.

'Hey, did I say the wrong thing?' Sam asked, nudging her as they rounded a corner, still seeming to be going much more slowly than anyone else.

'No,' Anna answered quickly. 'No, not at all. It's just . . .' She stopped herself. This was a perfectly planned date with dinner to come. She wasn't going to bring this up now, maybe wasn't ever going to bring it up at all but, like with everything, it was always about protecting Ruthie. Except, in the midst of that mother's instinct, was a part of Anna telling her this was about her too.

'You've made such an impression on Ruthie,' she began, sliding one foot in front of the other. 'A really great impression.'

'Really?'

239

'Sam, Ruthie doesn't usually take to people easily. Most people can't tailor their responses to meet Ruthie's high standards. Not that I'm saying they should. Of course people should be able to live their way and not worry about – I don't know – the way their shoes scrape on the pavement or touching three different apples before deciding to purchase a fourth one. But I don't know, either by chance, or because you see how Ruthie needs things to be, you've slipped into the ebb and flow of our lives effortlessly.' She took a deep breath and drew them both to a halt by the Christmas tree.

'You're making it sound like a bad thing,' Sam told her.

'I know,' Anna breathed. 'And I know it shouldn't be. It's not . . . not really . . . except . . .'

'I'm hanging here, Anna,' Sam answered, his hand on the surround, breath hot in the air.

'Argh! This is so hard.'

'Just talk to me,' he encouraged, putting a hand on her shoulder.

And there it was, that touch she enjoyed so much, craved when he wasn't around – he had gone from someone she thought was too young to think legally about to someone she didn't want to imagine packing up that backpack and leaving again . . .

'Ruthie is always looking for permanent, Sam. Always. She likes to know that we are going to be living in the same house on the same street with the same mug she likes her green tea in and anything out of her routine needs to be formally announced weeks before it happens with reminders every week and then an almost daily countdown until the event occurs. And, even then, there could be something that upsets her balance, something possibly so minute to you or me, that you just can't cater for it and—'

He put his other hand on her other shoulder, leaving a little of his weight there, strong and comforting. 'I keep saying, she's a great kid. I love spending time with her. She thinks about things in the deepest of ways and that makes me think too.'

Anna couldn't shadow box around the situation anymore. 'I've been trying to keep us light for her, Sam. I've told her, soon, before Christmas, you're going to be leaving and that you and I, we're a "now" thing, not a "later too" thing. And she's telling me she understands but I see the look in her eyes and I've seen a T-shirt she's sewing for you with her best beads as embellishment and it's never going to fit you but . . . I told you she's invested. And when I say that I mean she's *really* invested. And I think when you go back home it's going to break her heart no matter what I do or say now.'

The tears were spilling already and she hated herself for being like this. She and Sam were supposed to be a subsidiary to her life as Ruthie's mum. This was her getting back into the dating game, having some fun, feeling like Anna again but the fun her and the mum her were always going to intersect.

'Hey, come here,' Sam beckoned, taking his hands from her shoulders and drawing her in to his body. 'You're shaking. Come on, my skating can't be that terrifying.' He rubbed his hands up and down her arms trying to instil some warmth.

'It is terrifying,' Anna said, her mouth pressed against his coat.

'Wow, you are slaying me now,' he told her, laughing a little. He drew her away from his body and lifted her chin with his finger, looking deep into her eyes.

'I'm sorry,' she whispered. 'I'm having such a lovely time but if I didn't say anything then I wouldn't be being honest.'

'It's OK,' he told her. 'I'm glad you told me. But you should know, I don't intend on breaking Ruthie's heart.'

'I know you don't,' Anna answered quickly. 'In truth, she breaks her own heart every time but that doesn't mean I don't always want to try and avoid it.'

'And I don't remember ever saying that you and me had a fixed time limit,' Sam continued. 'At least on my part. I told you I'd fallen. I wasn't talking about the car accident or this rink.'

What was he saying? Suddenly Anna couldn't breathe, couldn't think ...

'But ... it's not practical,' she found herself blurting out.

Sam laughed hard then. 'Oh my, Anna. Practical?'

Yes. She had sounded like someone's mum. Someone's mum from possibly the 1800s. Olivia Colman could play her in the movie ...

He ran a hand down from her shoulder, then along her arm until he entwined their hands together. 'There's something I want to tell you over dinner.'

'That sounds highly practical,' Anna answered, squeezing his hand.

He nodded. 'Yeah ... it kinda is. So, we should probably get the most out of the fun part here on the ice. Wanna see if I can moonwalk?' He let her go and backed himself into more space.

'Sam, no, don't do that!' Anna said, turning herself away from the glittering tree to face him on the ice.

'Scared?' Sam asked her, moving backwards but looking exceedingly awkward about it. It was less of a moonwalk and more of a moon stagger ...

'Terrified! Sam, Sam, stop!' Anna called, stepping forward as his motion continued to take him backwards. 'Sam! There's people!'

Then his arms were spinning like a windmill as he crashed down onto the ground.

Forty-Seven

River Thames

'Stop laughing,' Sam said as they walked along the riverbank, everything lit up by golden, silver or icy blue lights. The city was alive with people wrapped up for the cold and he was enjoying leaning into the fabric of it.

'You can't tell me to stop laughing when *you're* still laughing,' Anna answered, squeezing his arm as they walked close together.

'It was lucky I didn't end up with that plastic penguin permanently embedded in me.'

'I think it was more lucky the little boy let go of the penguin before you could knock *him* over instead of his skating aid!'

'You know me. I would have taken out the main Christmas tree before I let a kid get hurt,' Sam reminded her.

'I know,' Anna answered.

'So . . .'

'So what?'

'Know where we're going for dinner yet?' he asked, enjoying this air of mystery he'd wrapped around the date. This part of it was mainly on him, with a hint of Ruthie for the details.

'Well, I know that there's the Christmas market on the Southbank that does the most terrific hot dogs,' Anna replied.

'Oh, wow, Anna, you think I'm gonna take you out into the city for a hot dog?' He shook his head.

'Hold on a second – for one, I like hot dogs and I thought

Ruthie might have told you that in those long text messages she's been sending you. And, secondly, you alluded that you're not all about the swagger and the five stars so . . .'

He laughed again. 'The swagger!'

'I admit I watched the video of you modelling on the runway for charity,' Anna said.

'Is there anything you don't know about me now?' he asked.

'Nothing that's been reported but, you know, you can't believe everything you read is the whole story.'

It was a comment in jest, but it hit home. There was stuff she didn't know. Big stuff. Big stuff that could change how she felt about what they were doing together. Another reason for Anna to be fearful about Ruthie's reaction to it. And she was right. The interviews, the articles, they weren't everything. Plus, the more time he spent here doing things he never made time for back in the US, the more he began to realise what little importance those column inches held.

He put an arm around her shoulders and turned her towards the river. 'I was gonna hire a boat, just for us. A little dinner, cruising down the water seeing the sites of the city all lit up.' He put out a hand and emphasised the horizon, the landmarks of London glowing. 'But then I thought about that and I thought about it being close to Christmas and how I'd kind of showed off with the horses and the carriage and how, you were right, showing off isn't really me so . . .'

He turned Anna a little to the right where a large boat was all lit up, festive music drifting on the air, people already aboard, drinks in hands.

'I think the Christmas vibe is as much about watching other people enjoy it as it is about enjoying it yourself. So, I thought, let's see how the rest of London is doing it and do it with them,' Sam said.

'A party boat,' Anna whispered. 'You booked us on a party boat.'

'And I can tell, just from the way you said that I made the right decision.'

'Is there dancing?' Anna asked him, neck craning a little as if she could see right inside and was hoping for a band or a DJ.

'There is dancing,' Sam said. 'But I have to let you know, my dancing is only mildly better than my skating.'

He watched her put her hand to her chest almost as if she was overawed by the prospect of the boat ride. 'Sam, please tell me this is a basket meal kind of a party boat.'

'A basket meal?' He didn't know what that was.

She smiled, her hair moving a little in the cold breeze that was coming off the water. 'When I was younger my Nanny Gwen took me on a boat a bit like this one. There was a jazz band, it was summer, she let me drink Pimm's, and we had these little plastic baskets with our food in. Chicken breasts and chips and salad, all piled up in these baskets. I thought they were the best thing.'

Her enthusiasm and joy for this memory was tugging at him. If there weren't plastic baskets for the food he was damn well gonna find some.

She waved a hand in the air, laughing again. 'Ignore me, it's stupid. I cannot wait to get on board. Can we get on board?'

'We can. Let's go.'

'Maybe they'll have hot dogs . . .'

It wasn't chicken in a basket, but it was turkey breasts and all the trimmings served in individual boxes. There was something to be said for finding your own space at a table and enjoying the mood with others. So far they had chatted to a team of chartered surveyors, a troupe of England cheerleaders and four ladies in their eighties who had taken part in a Christmas cruise every year together since they met at a bereavement group after their husbands passed away. There had been games and dancing to all the festive classics as well as a fine mix of everything from the Seventies, Eighties and Nineties, the dancefloor underneath swathes of foil garlands in gold, red, white and blue and a Christmas tree stuck to the ceiling acting like some kind of spiky mirror-ball. It had been her and Sam, introducing themselves as a couple, being free and easy and relaxed . . .

Despite the plummeting temperatures outside, inside the boat had turned into quite the sauna with all the frivolity and, as perspiration beaded at Anna's hairline, she was glad to take a minute on the deck and leave their fellow partygoers behind for a bit.

She gulped from her bottle of strawberry and lime cider and relished her thirst being quenched. She wasn't sure she'd had this much of a workout since she was pulling and pushing a toddler Ruthie in a buggy. That was worrying . . .

'Good Christmas party?' Sam asked, standing up close to her, leaning against the railings of the boat.

'Great Christmas party!' Anna said, smiling. 'The best Christmas party . . . but don't tell Neeta I said that.' She put her drink down on a table and moved back to the rail.

'But hers is a *not* Christmas party, right?' Sam said.

'Exactly,' Anna agreed.

The water was rippling ink, the current strong as the boat meandered along passing London's landmarks lit up in gold. It was a sight to behold and Anna wondered how it looked to someone who had never seen it before.

'How do you feel about London?' she asked, gazing up at Sam.

'How do I feel about London?' he said, blowing out a breath. 'Wow, that's quite the question.'

She laughed. 'I just meant, what do you think of Tower Bridge and the Gherkin and Big Ben and . . . the wibbly wobbly bridge.'

'The what now?'

'It's what we call the Millennium Bridge because it . . . well, the nickname's kind of self-explanatory.'

'Honestly,' Sam began, 'London's not been like I thought it would be.'

'Oh no! Don't tell the tourist board! What was it? The shopping? Because it can't be the monuments, they've been the same for hundreds of years.'

'No, all that is as awesome as I imagined it would be but . . . Richmond kind of overshadowed the city.'

'Definitely tell *that* to the tourist board,' Anna answered. 'They'll put it on billboards and T-shirts.' She gasped. 'Maybe they'll put it on the side of a bus. Have you been on the side of a bus before?'

'My face was on a subway train once. Does that count?'

Anna nodded. 'That probably does count.'

'Anna,' he said softly, taking her hand in his. 'If I'm real honest with you. It hasn't been Richmond. It's been you.' He squeezed her hand ever so gently. 'The very best thing about my trip here . . . is you.'

'Oh, Sam, I mean, you've seen St Paul's and you told me you went to Buckingham Palace and the Tower of London.'

'I did say that,' he replied. 'And, you know, no doubt those famous sights are gonna be on millions of camera rolls the world over but . . . the photos I'm gonna look at time and time again are the ones of us.'

Anna's heart began to pick up speed and she knew this wasn't a palpitation comedown from the dancing, this was because he was telling her again how he felt about her.

'I'm gonna tell you something now and I'm gonna tell you because I trust you, Anna.'

'Oh God!' Anna exclaimed, letting go of his hand and putting her fingers to her hairline in a panic. 'The last time someone said that to me it involved me keeping a secret for months and it half-killed me because it was one of Neeta's secrets and her mother-in-law was at the centre of it and she is one *really* scary woman.'

He smiled but it was the kind of smile that was hiding something behind it. Whatever he was about to tell her was serious and just like that she started to feel the beginnings of concern.

She watched him take a long slow breath as they passed under Blackfriars Bridge.

'Sam,' she said. 'What is it?'

He shook his head. 'I want to tell you everything but . . . I can't yet. There are other people I have to tell first.'

'You're scaring me,' Anna said, shivering with the cold as they came out from under the bridge.

'Sorry,' he whispered. 'I don't wanna ruin our perfect night.'

'Tell me,' Anna begged. She took his hand in hers then, turning it palm up and tracing circles on his skin.

He met her gaze. 'You read about my big deal with the Dallas Diggers?'

'That news was everywhere,' Anna admitted.

'Well . . . I'm not gonna be joining them.'

'No?'

He shook his head. 'And no one knows that yet except the Diggers and the Bisons. My agent, she's keeping it out of the press because when it hits, there are gonna be so many questions and . . . . I don't have any of the answers yet.'

Anna didn't know what to say but Sam's expression seemed to be warring with itself. There was worry and hurt and something else she couldn't quantify, maybe a touch of relief?

'God, just getting it out there. That was hard,' Sam admitted, taking his hand from hers and putting it to his hair.

'What went wrong?' Anna asked.

He sighed. 'That's what I can't tell you yet.'

'I don't understand,' Anna said.

'I know,' Sam said as the boat continued along past Shakespeare's Globe. 'But, Anna, I promise, if I could give you more now I would. I just . . . need to talk to my family first.'

'That sounds serious,' she said, a lump building in her throat.

'Listen,' he said, holding her arms and capturing her eyes with his. 'I'm telling you this because, you know, I don't know where my future lies right now. I know I'm not gonna be playing in Dallas, I don't know if I'm gonna be playing in Cincinnati . . . for the first time in my life nothing's mapped out and it's not all about the game.'

'What *are* you telling me?'

'I'm saying that . . . for the first time ever I'm realising that football isn't all that I am. And in realising that I've also found out that, you know, life can throw you curve balls you never expected and it's about how you *decide* to react to them that counts.'

She didn't respond but simply carried on looking at him as he held her arms. Anna knew they hadn't known each other long but he was already such a presence in her life and one she was getting altogether too used to.

'I was running away when I got to London, Anna. And then there you were,' Sam said. 'I may have done a little sightseeing and some shopping, but the reason I've been staying is . . . for you.'

'Sam,' she whispered, tears brimming in her eyes as the alcohol, the sentiment and the sounds of festive music spilled from the party room of the boat all crept up on her.

'Don't cry on me,' he begged, looking like he might cry himself. 'Because I'm pretty sure tears on a Christmas party boat are gonna kill the mood.'

She threw her arms around him then and held his muscular frame as tight as she could. 'When this boat docks,' she told him, 'I want you to come home with me. And I want you to stay the night.'

'You're sure?' he asked her.

'Whatever you can't tell me now,' Anna said, holding him away from her and looking deep into his eyes, 'I can wait. Because . . . I trust you. As long as it's not, I don't know . . . that you have Doja Cat on speed dial waiting for a date. Can you just tell me it's not that?'

He smiled, shaking his head. 'It's not that.'

'Then kiss me,' Anna ordered. 'Before we get to London Bridge.'

He leaned in so slowly, she was trembling before his lips touched hers. This time though it felt different to their other kisses, deeper, more poignant somehow. It was a kiss to savour every beat of, to commit to the memory bank so she could pull it out and revisit it whenever she needed to. But hopefully, there was more to come. A night together. Anna was as excited as she was scared to death about that. She shivered and Sam drew away.

'You OK?' he asked, one large palm at her cheek, sweeping her hair away.

She nodded. 'Will you hold me?'

He moved behind her, wrapping her up in his arms and kissing the top of her head as the boat moved under the bridge and out again, sailing past the Shard. She leaned in to him, relishing the solidity of his form. She had meant it when she said she trusted him. After being someone who thought she would never be able to trust anyone again when it came to her heart, she *did* trust Sam. She just hoped whatever he was holding back wasn't going to be something that turned everything on its head.

Forty-Eight

Anna and Ruthie's home, Richmond

Sam opened his eyes and for a second he didn't know where he was. This wasn't his hotel room. This bedroom was homely and full of life. There were necklaces hanging over the corner of a mirror on a dressing table bedecked with tinsel, books and notepads were on one edge, three packets of wipes were next to two hairbrushes, a can of hairspray, a woollen hat and some gloves and an empty mug, the largest chestnut wardrobe . . . He smiled. Anna's bedroom. Turning in the bed as carefully as he could, feet poking over the end, he looked at her next to him. Her eyes were closed and her mouth was slightly open, contented breaths being exhaled. She looked so peaceful, so beautiful. All the memories of their night together began to come flooding back . . .

They had sung all the way home in the cab and even the driver had joined in with a rendition of 'Last Christmas'. Anna had offered coffee, but by the time he had tripped over Cheesecake, knocked a fairy ornament off of Malcolm and Anna had kissed him again, all thoughts of doing anything but holding her were gone.

He closed his eyes, remembering carrying her up the stairs, their mouths interlocked and not having a clue where they were going. They'd ended up in the bathroom and they'd laughed about that for a second before Anna turned on the water in the shower and started to peel off his suit . . .

He didn't remember ever feeling the way he felt then, the water raining down on them, Anna clawing at his skin as he kissed his way across her body. It was almost as if their bodies recognised each other, knew exactly what to do, not in the base way, but those finer details usually learned over time. *Time.* Did someone up there know something? Was this why things with Anna fitted together like they did? Because it *needed* to move fast?

Sam touched her then, as lightly as if she were fragile glass, just craving the feel of her skin beneath his fingertips.

You are going to hurt her. You don't know how she is going to react to what you have. She already has Ruthie to worry about.

He held his breath, not wanting to hear the inner voice. He could lose her. He knew that. When he'd said he'd fallen he had meant it. But he'd also known that when Anna was presented with all the facts it might not be the distance issue or the fame issue that made this fall apart. He wanted to be straight with her, he wanted to see how far they could go together, but was that better for her or for him?

'Tell me you made coffee and I'm going to wake up smelling a strong, black Americano,' Anna suddenly whispered, eyes still closed but a soft smile on her lips.

He inched closer until he could smell her – shower cream, fresh cotton, home. God, she smelled so good! He put a gentle kiss on her lips. 'No coffee yet, but I pretty much cover the rest of that sentence.'

Very slowly her eyelids lifted and there were those knockout eyes looking up at him. He wanted to Polaroid it. No, he didn't want to snapshot it and make it important, he just wanted to picture having more moments like it.

'I slept the whole night,' Anna said, still unmoving. 'That doesn't happen often.'

'Yeah?' Sam asked. 'Maybe it was the fruit-based cider and the dancing.'

'Maybe it was the shower.'

'Or maybe,' he continued, 'it was that pink glitter massage gel.'

She laughed then, pulling the duvet over her face. 'Don't say it was that!' She edged the duvet down again. 'Do you think it smells like weed?'

'To be honest,' Sam said, 'all I had my mind on was where I was massaging it.'

She giggled and he didn't think he had ever seen her look so light, so trouble-free, so pure. Now *that feeling* he might want to bottle.

'What time is it?' she asked.

'I have no idea.'

'You are definitely not a parent.'

Nor will you be. He swallowed. He hadn't addressed the impact of that on his future at all. He was going to develop this disease and that meant, if he had children, they had a fifty per cent chance of carrying the gene too. Who would take those odds? And if there was a future for him and Anna? What then? Sure, she had Ruthie but maybe she'd like a sibling for her someday. He couldn't give her that. There seemed to be so much one gene was going to dictate. But maybe he needed to pace his thinking.

Sam watched Anna pull her arm out from under the cover and check her watch.

'Oh my God! It's eight o'clock!' She pulled the duvet back and almost fell out of bed, scrabbling for items of clothing that they'd left on the floor.

'Well, I'm on vacation,' he reminded.

'But Ruthie has school and I told Neeta they could drop in here before she takes her there so Ruthie could do her routines to settle her and they will be here in minutes.'

The peaceful, worry-free Anna had left the building and he watched her taking a scattergun approach to getting ready. Hairbrush swiped up first, then underwear on, then a grab for a jumper.

'Should I go?' Sam asked, getting out of the bed too. He

pulled on his trunks and picked his shirt up from a chair it had landed on. 'I could make you coffee and leave before Ruthie gets back if that would help.'

'No,' Anna said, turning to face him. 'No . . . I don't want us to sneak around. We're grown-ups. Sneaking around is stuff Ruthie should be doing if she wasn't predominantly invested in talking to her friends online.' She put her hands to her hair. 'I'm overthinking this. It will be fine.' She picked her phone up from the nightstand, knocking a red bauble to the carpet. 'No crazy worried texts from Neeta. Even better, no texts from Ruthie. Oh, hang on, I'd better check my Instagram messages, she sometimes contacts me on there.'

Sam began to button up his shirt and moved to the curtains that were just about keeping daylight out of the room. He liked waking up in Richmond, seeing what the overnight frost had done to the trees and the buildings. He wondered if Anna's neighbour had kept the animatronic reindeer on all night. He parted the fabric to take a peek and then his heart stalled. The street wasn't quiet like he expected. The frosty sidewalk had people on it, a group of people all congregating in one spot, cameras around their necks or video equipment at their shoulders.

'No Insta messages and she posted something about Bucky Barnes an hour ago so everything's fine,' Anna said.

Sam was still looking out of the window, the blinds partially closed, hopefully enough. This was something else, wasn't it? It had to be something else, *someone* else. Maybe it was local press wanting to photograph the reindeer and the other Christmas lights down Anna's street in a heart-warming, super-cute festive article . . .

'Sam? Are you OK? Has someone done something to my car?' Anna asked.

He pulled the curtains closed as he heard her moving across the room towards him. 'No,' he answered quickly. 'The car . . . is all good.' He found his jacket and pulled his phone from the pocket. Even through the shattered screen he could see it was lit with notifications. Whatever was happening outside was definitely about him.

'Thank God,' Anna said, now fully dressed. 'Last Christmas we had a spate of "foamings". People would spray shaving foam in festive faces on windscreens and paintwork. I know it doesn't sound like the worst kind of criminal activity but when that stuff freezes it is so hard to get off.'

What was he going to do? Did he look at his phone? There were missed calls from Frankie and Tionne and it was the early hours of the morning in Ohio. Did he try to call either of them now? Did he check some newsfeeds?

'I'll make some coffee,' Anna said, smiling at him. 'And feed Cheesecake so they don't trip you up again.'

Before he could decide what to do first, Anna was heading out of the room, onto the landing and towards the stairs. He didn't want her to see what was going on outside. He wanted to make sure all the blinds stayed closed, keep them here where nothing could touch them . . .

'Anna,' he called, racing from the bedroom after her, shirt still not fully buttoned up. She was halfway down the stairs when she turned back to look at him.

'Can you . . . call Ruthie . . . or Neeta? I don't think they should come over here right now.'

She smiled, her hand on the tinsel along the banister. 'Oh, I get it. You want more alone time with me.'

If only. He closed his eyes for a second, not wanting to be the one to burst this bubble. But he had to. For Anna. For Ruthie. He had brought this literally to their door.

'Can you stop them coming here?' he asked, padding slowly down the stairs until he was there next to her.

Anna didn't get a chance to make a reply before a blood-curdling scream could be heard from outside.

Forty-Nine

Anna's heart erupted. It was undoubtedly Ruthie's scream and she was bolting for the front door before Sam took her arm and stopped her.

'Don't go out there,' he begged.

'What are you talking about? That's Ruthie! She's out there now in full-on meltdown mode! Something's wrong and Neeta won't know what to do!' She put her hand to the latch.

'Anna, let *me* go,' Sam said, stepping in front of the door.

'What are you doing? Get out of the way!' Suddenly she was feeling panicked. Why was Sam barricading the door? What was making Ruthie scream like that? Then her phone started erupting in her pocket. She was torn between seeing if it was Neeta and finding out what was going on, and wrenching Sam out of her way and getting outside as quickly as possible.

'There are reporters out there,' Sam said. 'On the street, at the bottom of your steps. I don't want you out there in that. I don't want Ruthie out there in that.'

Now her focus was back on Sam and what he was telling her. Reporters? Outside her house? A crowd of people around Ruthie's path to her sanctuary would definitely have tipped her into a very uncomfortable place. Her brain was trying to catch up and process and make decisions all at once and it wasn't really working.

'Is there a safe place near here?' Sam asked her.

'What, like a church?'

'No,' Sam said. 'Somewhere Ruthie feels safe.' He put his hands on Anna's shoulders then. 'Think quick, Anna.'

'I don't . . .' Anna began. And then it came to her. 'The coffee shop. It's not far from your hotel. It's called Bean Afar.'

'OK,' Sam said, breathing long and slow, his vast chest rising and falling. 'So, I'm going out there. And I'm gonna run. I'm gonna scoop up Ruthie and we're not gonna stop until we get to that coffee shop.'

'Sam . . . I . . . no . . . that's mad.'

'Listen, I don't know *exactly* yet why they're out there, but I can kinda guess they're here for me. I shouldn't have brought this to your door, and I need to fix it.'

'Sam, you can't carry Ruthie all the way to the high street and you'll need—'

'Wipes? Antibacterial gel?' he asked. 'Hit me up with them.' He came away from the door then and speedily climbed the stairs.

What was she doing? She dashed to the kitchen – just as Cheesecake decided now was the best time to dart out from under the table and attack – and grabbed wipes and hand gel from the cupboard stacked full of them. When she got back into the hallway, Sam was down again, pulling on his trousers. Anna held out the wipes and the gel and he put one in each pocket.

Suddenly, the doorbell rang and it was the kind of incessant ringing Anna knew could only be from Neeta. Before Anna could do anything else though, the letterbox rattled and a voice called.

'There are many mini Piers Morgans out here and they have terrified Ruthie! I tried to get her back into the car but now she is running down the street! I am going to go after her!'

'Neeta, wait!' Sam called.

Sam wasn't going to hold off a second longer. He didn't want to see more terror build in Anna's expression. He had made this situation and he had to be the one to try to repair it.

'I'll call you,' he said. 'The second we get there.' He bent down to the letterbox and came eye-to-eye with Neeta. 'Step away from the door, Neeta. *I'm* coming out.'

'Sam,' Anna said, reaching for him.

He stood firm, taking a breath, and then he wrenched open the front door, moving quickly. And next his gameplay took over. It was like having that one mission. Get the ball, run, make the touchdown. With laser focus, he sprinted like everything depended on it, not just a league game, not only a Superbowl, this was about Ruthie, this was for Anna. He clocked there were maybe ten photographers, and the second they saw him they began that desperate dance – a hop from one foot to the other, a shuffle this way, cameras swinging from their necks – before they thought about whether to give chase. Was whatever story had broken big enough news in the UK for them to leap into their cars and follow? He sure as hell hoped not.

Sam could see Ruthie, up ahead, running in a zig-zag, great if she were being chased by a crocodile, not so great if she veered off into the road. Traffic was starting to build.

'Ruthie!' he called.

There was no response, like she couldn't hear him. He shouted again.

'Ruthie!'

In a few paces he was going to be alongside her and she was scared and wandering. He couldn't reason with her, not when she seemed shut off. He had to do what he'd suggested to Anna. Make her safe first. Deal with whatever came next after that.

He swooped in and lifted her off her feet and into his arms, still running. She started to scream again, trying to beat her fists on any part of him she could reach.

'Hey, Ruthie. It's Sam. Falcon. It's OK, OK? We're just . . . going on a mission.'

Ruthie went still then, solid like she had turned into concrete. She stared up at him then, eyes wide, frightened but connected. 'There were people . . . outside . . . coming towards me.'

'I know,' he told her, his breath coming fast as he kept up the rapid pace. 'And I bet that was real scary, right?'

'One of the men hung a jacket on Cecil's head,' Ruthie announced with a sob. 'I hope he dies soon.'

'Well, we're going for coffee. Or hot chocolate. Whatever you wanna get. At Bean Afar.'

'I can't do that,' Ruthie told him as they rounded the corner out of Anna's road.

'Why not?'

'Because I'm not clean now. I came home to get clean from Neeta's house and then the people were there.'

'OK,' Sam said. 'Well, I have wipes and gel. Do you think you could get clean enough to have a drink with me?'

His lungs were bursting now. Despite his fitness he wasn't really the long-distance kind of guy. Ruthie looked like she was thinking about what he'd said. He strained to look over his shoulder, to check if anyone was in pursuit. *Nothing*. He slowed his pace a little, breath hot, feet throbbing.

'Hot chocolate,' Ruthie said, voice wobbling. 'With double cream and . . . sprinkles.'

'You got it,' he answered.

'Sam,' Ruthie snivelled. 'Why aren't you wearing any shoes?'

It was only then, when he looked down and slowed into a walk, he realised he was barefoot.

Fifty

Bean Afar, Richmond

They were drawing a few looks from other customers, but Sam was confident it was down to the fact he had his feet up on a chair wrapped in tea-towels to cover the scrapes and bring down the swelling rather than whatever news was circulating. He still didn't know. Was still ignoring his phone. Because Ruthie's wellbeing was paramount, above all else. She hadn't said very much but she had poured the contents of the antibacterial gel into her palms and rubbed over her coat sleeves, hood, school trousers and used half the packet of wipes to make sure no surface got missed. Then, when she was satisfied, she had ordered the grandest hot chocolate he'd ever seen.

'Why would you have coffee?' Ruthie asked suddenly. 'When you could have hot chocolate with pieces of fudge in it?'

'I . . . have no idea,' Sam replied, his hands around his mug. 'Except, sometimes I have to watch my sugar intake.'

'Do you have diabetes?' Ruthie queried, giving the creamy foam a slurp.

'Not yet,' he answered. 'But maybe that's because I cut down on my fudge.'

'Am I going to get diabetes from drinking this?' Ruthie asked, a look of panic coating her features now.

'No, Ruthie,' he said. 'Don't worry. You're good.'

'I will worry,' Ruthie answered. 'Probably every time I have this now.'

'I didn't mean to—'

Ruthie shrugged. 'It's fine. It's just my brain.'

Sam had no answer to that. He also had no answer to reporters being on Ruthie's doorstep. He wanted to be able to take back what had happened. She had been confronted, outside her own home. It was bad enough for someone who wasn't autistic but a whole different level for Ruthie. Ultimately, that lay with him and this was what was going to happen when this whole thing blew up if he stayed here any longer. Bing Crosby was singing about Jack Frost, cinnamon bagels were being ordered, the coffee machine was spurting and gurgling, life was going on here and he wasn't part of it. Perhaps *shouldn't* be part of it . . . He hated that but right now it was fact.

'Were the photographers there because Kai's friend Scrubs tagged you in the video of you playing rugby dressed as the reindeer on Instagram?'

That, coupled with whatever news was leaking about the Diggers deal or, God forbid, his health, could definitely have done it.

'Maybe,' he admitted, taking a drink of his coffee.

'I don't like Scrubs. He picks his nose,' Ruthie announced. 'One time I saw him wipe a bogey on an apple in Lisa's fruit bowl. I don't eat fruit there anymore.'

Sam smiled. 'Good decision.'

'Is my mum coming here?' she asked, picking up the sugar shaker and putting more into her mug.

'I messaged her,' Sam said. 'I'm sure she's gonna be here soon.'

'How did the date go?'

'It went . . .' He didn't know what to say. It had been the best time. The *absolute* best time. The carriage ride, the ice skating, the party boat and then making love with Anna, wrapping her up in his arms and holding her close.

'Did Mum fall over at the ice skating?' Ruthie asked.

'No,' Sam answered. 'Your mom was a lot better than me. I fell over a penguin.'

Ruthie gasped, putting her hands to her mouth and laughing out loud. 'Not the ones the babies use because they can't skate!'

'I really wanted to use one myself,' Sam admitted.

'Did she like the disco on the boat?'

He nodded. 'She loved the disco on the boat.'

'I knew she would. There are photos when she was young. Dancing at parties. Some of the photos are meant to be of other people and you can still see my mum dancing in the background. When I was little she used to dance to music in the kitchen. She said Nanny Gwen taught her. She doesn't dance as much anymore.'

The poignancy hit him square in the chest. What was he doing? Making things better? Or making things harder in the long run?

The door of the café burst open then and Anna was rushing through into the room, Neeta at her heels. She launched herself at Ruthie, covering the girl with her body and holding her close like she might evaporate.

'Esther!' Neeta yelled at the top of her voice, regardless of disturbing others. 'I will have whatever Ruthie has there but bigger. And please get Anna her usual and add all the sugar.' She stared at Sam then. 'What is going on with your feet?'

'Too much dancing last night,' Sam replied.

'Mum! You're squashing me!' Ruthie moaned, wriggling in her seat until Anna retreated a little, dropping down into the seat next to her daughter.

'Sorry,' Anna said. 'I'm just worried about you. Are you OK?' She looked at the large mug Ruthie was drinking from. 'Is that Festive Fudge Delight?'

'Maybe . . .' Ruthie answered. 'I know I'm not usually allowed a large one but—'

'Hey, that's my bad,' Sam said quickly. 'I, you know, can't get my way around sizing over here so . . .'

'It's OK,' Anna said, looking directly at him.

He met her gaze but he didn't agree with her statement. 'Yeah,' he answered. 'Except it's not.'

'I agree,' Neeta stated. 'I do not want to look at your feet under those cloths and imagine what might be there.'

'Sam—' Anna began.

'Listen,' he said, moving in his chair, bringing his feet down towards the ground. 'I'm gonna go. I need to save you guys any more drama.' He winced as his feet hit the floor.

'Go where?' Anna asked. 'We drove past your hotel. There are more photographers outside there.'

'Yeah? OK, well, I guess I'll find another hotel or, I don't know . . . a chiropodist.' His feet really were hurting now but he was going to leave this café and distance his bullshit from the people he cared about even if he had to crawl.

The sound of jangling keys brought Sam's attention back to the table. It was Neeta's hand, in front of his face, metal swaying from her fingers.

'My car is parked right outside using Ruthie's blue badge for the yellow lines. Why not sit in there with Anna until you decide where you need to be and she can drive you. Ruthie and I will sit here with our extra-large drinks and I will let the school know we might be a little late.' Neeta moved the keys up and down. 'I will let you put the heating on the seats and Magic FM if you must. Esther! Can you make Anna's coffee in a to-go cup?'

It seemed like the decision had already been made.

Fifty-One

Outside Bean Afar, Richmond

'What does it say?' Sam asked.

From the radio, Magic FM was playing soft romantic Christmas tunes that really didn't fit the mood of scrolling through the hits on 'news' when you'd typed 'Sam Jackman' into Safari. Anna's finger lifted then moved on to the next article, did the same again, another one then filling the space a read one had vacated. She'd put Neeta's heated seats on too but it was still ice-cold inside the car. Everyone outside was going about their business, starting their day with coffee or walking dogs in festive jumpers and she was in someone else's car with her boyfriend being hounded by the press. *Boyfriend*.

'They all say pretty much the same thing,' Anna told him. 'The Dallas Diggers deal is off.'

'OK,' Sam said, letting a breath go. 'And there are no other details?'

'Some cute photos of you in a helmet,' Anna said. 'Your agent declining to comment. There's one photo of you with a superimposed bug on your head with the caption "fee flicker". What does that mean?'

'*Flea* flicker is a move in football. I guess they thought that headline was cute,' Sam answered with a sigh. 'OK, it could be worse.'

'Could it?' Anna asked, putting her phone down. 'Because what was I really looking for when I was scrolling and why didn't you want me to do it at first?'

'Because . . .'

'Because . . . ?'

'I don't know. I just can't,' Sam said, putting his head in his hands. 'I have to get back there. I have to make this right.'

'I know that,' Anna said. 'We talked about it last night. I trust you, remember?'

'Yeah, I know,' he answered, raising his head. 'But, you know, maybe you shouldn't.'

What? What had he just said? Anna shivered. 'I don't understand.'

'I can't do this to you,' Sam said, desperately. 'I can't do this to Ruthie.' He shook his head. 'I've been going over and over it – don't get too close, it's for the holidays – and then I moved to justifying it, saying I just needed to stay a little longer, but I've always been thinking about it from *my* perspective. Like "you deserve this, Sam", "this is something great, something you've never felt before" but it shouldn't be about me. It should always be about you, Anna, and about Ruthie.'

'You're not making any sense.' And tears were already forming in her eyes.

'Last night was . . . I don't know, there aren't enough words. It made me feel part of something more, something beautiful, something we started and put together against the odds—'

'Are you breaking up with me?' Anna asked bluntly, a tear already falling down her cheek.

'I'm not gonna make you a part of my mess, Anna,' he told her.

'Oh, so you make me fall for you, you spend the night with me and then that's it? Were you just waiting for the invitation to sleep over and then it was time to leave? Did you arrange the photographers this morning to give you a get out?'

'Yeah and I ran all the way to a coffee shop in bare feet

carrying Ruthie because that just authenticated the whole thing.' He shook his head.

'Well, I don't accept it,' Anna challenged, jutting her chin a little. 'You can't just do that. You can't simply crash into our lives, claim a space in them and then run away when things get tough. I've been telling myself not to get attached and then you told me last night that *you* are attached and this could be something more and then what? Some press outside my house is making you do a full three-sixty or . . . a flea flicker or whatever? No.'

She didn't understand and how could she? She didn't know what world he was from. She might have seen a few photos, made some correct assumptions about wealth and influence, but she could never imagine the demands he was under, how people invaded his privacy, both online and in person like today.

He was an ambassador for his sport, he was a role model for young kids all over America. It was his business to show his face and his power. He had put that first, always, turning away jobs that didn't fit that mould. But he was still off-the-scale busy already but with a new spotlight on him, for negative reasons, it was all going to descend into a different kind of chaos no matter how Frankie managed it. He would become the hunted over the next weeks and months until someone else's life was turned upside down and the hyenas had a new prey to follow.

And then there was the thing Anna didn't know about yet. Huntington's. If the press were already going crazy about the Diggers deal being in the dust then what were they gonna say about the reason behind it? And what was Anna gonna think? She was right. He'd swept into her life unannounced as this superhero. *Falcon.* Strong, dependable, robust. But how long was he going to be able to stay that way? She needed more. She needed better. The fallout from this was going to hurt her more down the line than it was now. And the same went for Ruthie. He never wanted

Ruthie to have to run into danger to get away from a scary situation at her home or her school or anywhere she considered a safe space.

Sam reached for her hands then and held them tight. 'If we stay connected, these people are going to dig into everything about you and Ruthie, Anna. And they are going to report anything they like on the internet. They are going to find out that you like to drink coffee here and they are . . . going to turn up outside Mr Wong's restaurants or . . . Neeta's Not Christmas Christmas party—'

'I don't care,' Anna said, tears wetting her cheeks.

'I care,' Sam said softly. 'And it's because I care that I'm doing this. I thought it would be different here in the UK . . . but that was naïve.'

This way was better. Break it now. She'd never have to watch him disintegrate from the person he was now, forgetting who she was, forgetting who he was, unable to speak, unable to think. It could be years down the line, it could be months. And that unknown was always going to be there, hanging over him, making him question every thought process. She'd read about it maybe, but he'd never have to see that pain meet her eyes. She was one person he could save from going through that, like she'd already gone through it with her grandmother. She'd told him how desperately hard that had been. How shattering it had been to see the person she had always loved most, the person she had *known* best turn into a stranger. *She turned into a body in a chair. Like someone had hollowed her out and taken away everything that made Nanny Gwen who she was. And when I was with her, I had to pretend that everything was fine. I talked about the weather, what Elton John had been up to, what I was making for dinner, knowing there would be no response, that I may as well be calling bingo numbers.* That was why he was leaving now. So he would never be empty skin and bone in a chair to her.

'I'm gonna head back to the States. Today.'

'No, Sam. Don't do this.'

She was crying hard now and all he wanted to do was hold her in his arms and tell her everything was going to be OK. He closed his eyes as he held her hands, remembering everything from last night and the overwhelming feeling he had when he was with her. *Home.* Home had definitely been with Anna even if it had only been for a too short time.

'I don't regret getting on that plane,' Sam told her, putting a hand on her head. 'Not for a second. And that cab driver who thought Richmond was a cool place to be . . . well, I owe him everything.'

'Sam, don't do this. I know Ruthie and I might seem fragile but we're not. We are strong and resilient and—'

'I know you are,' Sam said, cupping her face with his hand. 'And more fierce than you give yourself credit for. That's why you're gonna deal with this just fine.'

She shook her head. 'I could deal with whatever *Entertainment Tonight* wants to throw at us but not this.'

'Listen to me,' he urged, turning in the seat a little. 'I have to see my mom and my dad and my sister and I have to tell them something I don't want to tell them. I can't burden you with that too, I can't.' He sighed. 'But, please, whatever you read or see about me, I want you to know that the real Sam was the one who came here to London. He wasn't wearing his body armour, he was a little bit scared and he didn't know if life was ever gonna be the same again.' He smiled. 'And that Sam found out that no, life was never gonna be the same again. But, in the middle of all that fallout, there were these bright, beautiful pieces that had no right to be there, stringing themselves together, winding their way around me like star-shaped beads.' He took a breath as emotion threatened to get the better of him.

She went to say something, but he silenced her with a kiss he knew was going to be their last. He relished the softness of her lips moving with his, her tears on his fingertips as he cradled her face, it was achingly bittersweet, and he was caught between ending the moment before he second-guessed everything he'd just said to her and having a few seconds more.

'Bye, Anna,' he whispered.

And before she could protest, before she could even react at all, Sam whipped open the door of the car, his bare feet hitting the ground again as he took off up the street.

Fifty-Two

Neeta and Pavinder's home, Richmond

'If you are asleep,' Neeta stage-whispered very loudly, 'do not mind me. If you are not asleep then these plants Pavinder says are good for healing.'

Anna opened one eye from her face-down position in bed in Neeta's spare bedroom and almost got a long spiky leaf in her iris. She didn't know how long she had been here, but all her limbs were telling her if she didn't move soon she might never move again. But right now, never moving again suited quite well.

'Good, you are awake,' Neeta said, plumping herself down on the side of the bed. 'Because it will soon be time to collect Ruthie from school.'

It couldn't be the afternoon? Could it? Had she really been lying here for hours? Everything was a bit hazy and her eyes felt like someone had poured salt into them.

'I could do it,' Neeta said. 'If you do not think you are up to it. Or I could call Lisa. She's going to come round anyway once she's sorted Kai and Kelsey.'

Anna went to speak but nothing immediately came out except a hoarse croak.

'You have not drunk any of the drinks I brought up. There is camomile tea – that will be cold. There is Tizer. I have no idea what that is but Pavinder puts it in petri dishes for some of the seedlings. There is coffee – strong and black but—'

Anna groaned. She didn't want anything, but she

270

particularly did not want coffee. It just reminded her of Bean Afar and sitting outside it, being dumped.

'You are being very dramatic by the way,' Neeta said, plumping up cushions around Anna. 'Almost like this is a break-up.'

What had Neeta said? Anna might not remember everything about how she got to Neeta's house but she definitely remembered telling Neeta that Sam was leaving and it was over.

'He has gone back to his home, that is all. You knew he would be going there before Christmas. Yes, the press pack might have sped up the timeline but nothing has changed,' Neeta continued.

'Neeta, everything has changed. He doesn't want to be with me.'

Saying that burned all the way down her throat and into her stomach and it proved that she had got herself too invested. Deeply invested. She should have stuck to meeting an average guy from a dating app for a large glass of wine at The Old Ship. Conversation, maybe a tiny bit of flirtation and then home to Ruthie knowing exactly where she stood. She crawled her way up the bed now, rolling over onto her back and awkwardly shifting into a sitting position.

'Oh, he said those words, did he?' Neeta asked, moving one particular plant closer to Anna's face. 'He turned to you, in the spacious warm bucket seats of my car, and said "Anna, I do not want to be with you".'

'Well, he didn't say those exact words but his intention was clear.'

'*His* intention was clear,' Neeta repeated. 'And what is your intention?'

Anna frowned. 'Well, it was to stay in this bed a bit longer but now with . . . plants and . . . bright orange drinks I think I'd be better off taking my misery somewhere else.'

'Anna, come on! You are not the type of person to take this lying down!' Neeta exclaimed, batting the mattress with an aggressive hand. 'Even on my silk sheets. So, Sam has decided something and you are going to let him have that control, are you?' Neeta paused for a second and then added, 'Like you did with Ed.'

It was a low blow and Anna felt that twinge of disappointment in herself. She *had* let Ed call the shots over literally everything. Because she had been hurt by his deceit and worried about Ruthie's reaction to the break-up, she had been unable to focus on practicalities while he was signing off on the end of their marriage. The house, her lovely Nanny Gwen's house and everything in it was the only thing she had dug her heels in about.

'If someone doesn't want to be with you, Neeta, you can't force them.'

'So, you want to be with him?' Neeta asked. 'But you think he does not want to be with you?'

'He said he didn't want Ruthie and I to deal with all this stuff going on in the media about his football transfer to Dallas being over.'

'So, what I am hearing from that is "I care about you and Ruthie".'

'Yes, but—' Anna began to protest.

'Anna, I see how Sam is with you. How he looks at you when he thinks no one is watching. It is special,' Neeta stated, picking up the glass of Tizer and holding it out to Anna.

She didn't know how to respond, because all Neeta was doing was making her remember Sam's eyes, deep, dark brown, soul-searing. He'd gazed at her in bed last night, lying next to her, quiet, admiring between their kisses. It was his quiet, the peace and comfortable silences that she had loved just as much as all the times he'd made her laugh.

'And no matter what he says about leaving you, he does not mean it. He cannot mean it. No one could be the way Sam has been with you then just throw it away like an over-seasoned *aloo gobi*.'

Anna didn't know what to say. Her heart was heavy,

sagging with the weight of having had something fun and bright and wonderful ripped from under her. But what could she do? There wasn't any other decision to make except trying to somehow accept it, was there?

'You need to fight for him, Anna!' Neeta spelled out.

Anna sighed. 'Fighting isn't really a good look on a thirty-five-year-old mother of one.'

'And there you are labelling yourself again,' Neeta said. 'That is not all you are. You are a *warrior*. Where is the Anna Heath who filled in all those forms for Ruthie's autism assessment and rang up relentlessly chasing for appointments? Where is the woman who once told my mother-in-law that her legendary *moghlai* was a little too lemony because you knew I needed a win that evening? Or the person who rapped in front of a festive soup stall even though it was really *really* terrible?' Neeta inhaled. 'Fighting doesn't mean you have to beat Sam into submission if he really does want to finish things. It means standing up for yourself. Going after what you're passionate about. Saying and doing what you feel in your heart no matter what the consequences might be.'

She had never seen Neeta so emboldened, so alive, eyes flashing with spirit. Had something happened with Pavinder? Had Neeta asked the questions and got the answers she wanted? She opened her mouth to ask . . .

'This doesn't have to be the end,' Neeta carried on. 'You have his phone number, right? You can call him. You can tell him that whatever his reason for breaking things off that he didn't take account of exactly how deeply you feel for him and, feelings of that nature they need to be protected . . . like a . . . ghost orchid.'

Anna had no idea what a ghost orchid was but there was definite germination in her gut now. Did Neeta have a point? Sam might have said it was better for her and Ruthie that he left and they disconnected, but that wasn't one hundred per cent his decision. They'd been in this together, so she was part of this too. Maybe he *thought* he knew what was best, but she wasn't done. Sam had called her fierce and, if she swallowed down this bitter feeling, perhaps that would come to the fore.

She pulled the covers off her body and took the Tizer from Neeta's grasp. 'I'm going to drink this and then I'm going to collect Ruthie from school.'

'Yes, good! And then what?'

Anna took a sip of the drink. 'I'm going to drive us home and if there's any reporters on my doorstep I'm going to threaten them with the police.'

'Yes!' Neeta said, punching the air.

'And in the time it takes Sam to get across the Atlantic, I'm going to nail the presentation for Mr Wong's new and improved restaurant.' She put the drink down. It had lost its fizz.

'And then?'

'And then . . . I'm going to tell Sam that he needs to reconsider his decision because I'm not ready to let him go.'

'That is the spirit. That . . . and the tiny shot of vodka I put in the Tizer. Tiny. You will be fine to drive,' Neeta assured.

Fifty-Three

Cincinnati, Ohio, USA

Sam wasn't sure how Frankie had done it, but a private plane had picked him up from Heathrow and taken him out of the UK and back to Cincinnati. He'd dressed like a nobody – hoodie, track pants, retreating inside the top like he was a snail set to hibernate. But dressing like a nobody only made him look like a somebody *pretending* to be a nobody. He'd made it out of London unscathed but in his home city, despite landing in a dark corner of the airport and getting straight into a car, there were reporters at the exit knowing it was him, wanting any tiny scrap of his current predicament to make their exclusive.

And now he was here, in a suite, at one of the Hiltons, security in the lobby and outside his door, waiting. Frankie was getting his parents and Tionne, whisking them from their homes with as little explanation as possible, and bringing them here. This luxurious but generalised room was filled with festive cheer Sam wasn't feeling. There was a real fir tree, all its decorations aesthetically pleasing and matching the rest of the mainstream décor, with coordinating wrapped 'presents' at its base. He found himself wondering if they were empty boxes. Even though the kind of guests able to afford a suite like this weren't the type to steal gifts.

There was a knock at the door and Sam sprung from his seated position on the edge of the bed. The door clicked, then opened and Frankie came in. She was dressed in jeans and a sweater. Sam didn't think he had ever seen her in jeans and a sweater before.

'How are we doing?' Frankie asked him.

Sam had no answer for that and his eyes moved from his agent back to the open door. Tionne was first, fast, moody, her expression something between scared and looking like she might punch him. His mom came next, her eyes wide, her complexion a little sallow, her usually colourful appearance muted. Finally, his dad shuffled in. He was wearing his suit like he was ready for work, but he looked tired in it.

'Idiot!' Tionne blurted out. 'Whatever you've got mixed up in, I don't appreciate being taken outta my apartment like it's gonna be a meeting with Liam Neeson!' She thumped him in the chest – hard.

'Ti,' he began. 'I didn't wanna do it, but it had to be done.'

'It's not enough that we got cameras pointing at us since yesterday?' Tionne snapped again. 'I'm trying to keep things easy with Jerome and it's like I'm a Kardashian.'

'Tionne,' Frankie said, moving chairs around to make sure everyone had a seat. 'Give your brother a minute.'

Tionne flipped her head around, hair flying. 'Now I know something's wrong. *You're* being nice. You don't do nice. You do efficient and organised and sometimes kooky when you've had tequila but—'

'Stop talking, Tionne.'

It was their mom interrupting and she had used the tone usually reserved for admonishing them when they had both lived at home and were late for dinner or past their night-time curfew. You didn't question that tone or argue with it. And Tionne had stopped talking.

'Shall I get some food or something to drink?' Frankie suggested.

'No,' Sam answered with a sigh. 'Mom, please, sit down.' He took a few strides towards her, hoping to guide her to a chair but she began to flap her arms in a combination of shrugging her shoulders and waving. It was something she did often when she was annoyed by the gossip from her friends at church.

'I don't want to sit down. I want to know what is going on, Sam. The news is saying that you're not going to Dallas anymore. That there is a problem. And now we are put into a car and brought here like Tionne says. I was in the middle of making patties for the church fundraiser.'

'I should go,' Frankie said. 'Give you some space.'

'No,' Sam said to his agent. 'Would you stay? Please.'

Sam looked at his dad who hadn't said a word since he'd gotten into the room. That wasn't so unusual when his mom and Tionne were both talking enough for everyone but there was something telling about his silence now. It was as if he knew a little of what was coming.

Sam steepled his fingers together and leaned against the desk. 'Mom, I'm sorry you were put through that and, all of you, I'm sorry for the circus that's going on right now and that you had to hear this on the news first and not from me but . . .' He took a breath. 'But it's true, the deal with the Dallas Diggers is off.'

'But why?' Tionne jumped in. 'You said it was a sure thing. I've told people . . . I've pre-ordered merchandise!'

'And I told you not to do any of those things,' Sam reminded. 'I told you all that these things are only a certainty when the ink is dry on the contract.'

'Did they pull out?' Tionne carried on, moving in her seat. 'Or did you? Did you get cold feet about the challenge? Did the Bisons offer you an unbelievable amount of money to stay?'

'Tionne,' Albert said. 'Stop thinking about yourself for once and listen to what your brother has to say.' He adjusted his collar a little. 'We wouldn't be here unless we had to be.'

Saying only what needed to be said when the time was right. His dad was usually a man of few words, but what he *did* say always made people sit up and pay attention.

And his father somehow understanding the severity of the situation drove Sam forward.

'The Diggers pulled out,' Sam said. 'I had to have some tests done before they agreed the deal and . . . I didn't pass one of the tests.'

It sounded like he was describing some kind of high school diploma not genetic testing. It wasn't really a case of failing, could do better, repeat the year and try again, there was no retake, no way of changing it.

'What kind of test?' Tionne wanted to know. 'Like the math of NFL or something? Because I know heaps of players who can't even spell NFL and you're so smart—'

'It was a medical test.'

He needed to keep it straightforward. Facts before emotion. One of his parents would be OK. It would be the lowest blow and extremely rare if they *both* carried the gene. Tionne's chances were fifty-fifty. The toss of a coin.

His mother's expression changed first. It was one thing his dad being astute to the severity of this get-together, it was another to see the look in his mom's eyes when the dime started to drop. She knew this was bad simply from the word 'medical'.

'There's something wrong with you?' Tionne gasped. 'Well, what is it? I mean, you're the healthiest person I know. Do you need treatment? What treatment?'

'Tionne,' his mom admonished. Then she looked straight at Sam. 'Whatever it is, Sam. *Whatever* it is. There is no need to be afraid. You tell us.'

Suddenly Sam's throat was drying up and the thought of forming the words, or really that one word, felt too hard, too world-wrecking. The room fell silent and he could hear music somewhere, maybe outside, maybe from another room, Christmas being anticipated or prematurely celebrated. It didn't match this situation at all. But it had to be done.

'I . . . have a positive gene for something called Huntington's disease.' He sighed heavily. 'It's something that's gonna, eventually, no one knows when, make me lose my cognitive function and slowly, again, some time, it's gonna end my life.'

Out of the corner of his eye, Sam saw Tionne put her hands to her face, her beautiful round brown eyes haunted by what he'd just said. He needed to carry on, get it all out and then let his family fully react.

'But, more important than that,' Sam hurriedly continued, 'the way this gene thing works is that . . . it's inherited.' He couldn't meet anyone's gaze then. He dropped his eyes to the floor and tracked the lined pattern from where he was stood to the floor-to-ceiling windows. 'Chances are, either you or Dad have it, Mom. And, Ti . . . there's a fifty-fifty chance it could have been passed to you too.'

With that information imparted, the silence remained unbroken, but in a matter of seconds, his mom was suddenly in his space, drawing him into her, squeezing tight and whispering in his ear that everything was going to be OK.

'Whatever it is, Sam, God will find a way,' she told him. 'Always.'

He closed his eyes and his heart broke to pieces when he heard his little sister start to cry.

Fifty-Four

Anna and Ruthie's home, Richmond

'So, what do you think, Ruthie?' Anna asked. 'Is Mr Wong going to go for it?'

Anna had tied a king-sized white sheet over the wall that wasn't covered in Christmas cards in the living room and had projected her PowerPoint presentation for the restaurant on to it to show Ruthie. She needed the distraction and she knew Ruthie could do with one too. She was waiting for the moment when Ruthie asked her questions about Sam, questions that she didn't have any answers to.

'I don't know,' Ruthie answered. 'Mr Wong has served me pizza. I don't have enough information about him to know what he would go for or not.'

The kind of answer Anna should have expected from an autistic who was going through a stressful period. 'OK,' Anna said. 'But do *you* like it? What do you think of the concept?'

'I think that I like the idea of the takeaway boxes and different sizes, but I still don't know Mr Wong well enough to know if he will go for it.'

OK, Ruthie definitely needed to get things off her chest. Anna sat down next to her on the sofa and put her arm around her shoulder.

'Don't touch my forearm!' Ruthie exclaimed, jumping in her seat.

'I didn't,' Anna said. Then a little calmer. 'I won't.' Anna quietened and waited for Ruthie to fill the space. She didn't have long to wait.

'Is Sam coming back?'

Anna couldn't help the sigh that left her lips. 'I don't know.'

This time it was Ruthie that sighed. 'I was silently praying that you wouldn't say "we'll see". You always say "we'll see" when it's definitely *not* happening.'

Ruthie was spot on as always. But she didn't want to give her any false hope. Sam had left her with no open door. If she wanted to reconnect it was up to her. She hadn't messaged yet. Hadn't called. There was something holding her back from moving quickly on this. She had a feeling that it was better to pick her timing, get it right, give herself the best possible chance. Focusing on the fact that she wanted to prise the door open again was stopping her from dwelling on how much it hurt that he had ended things.

'I think Sam has a lot going on in his life at the moment,' Anna continued.

'The American football deal that was supposed to be the transfer of the century?' Ruthie asked.

'Is that what it said?'

'That's what *Kai* said. He asked me if Sam had left anything at our house that he could put on eBay.'

'What did you say?'

'I told Kai he was a dickhead.'

'Ruthie!'

'Well it's true and I'm not apologising.' She folded her arms across her chest as she did when she was closing off the matter.

'Sam lives in America. He needed to go back there to sort things out to do with the . . . transfer of the century and—'

'And then he's going to come back here?' Ruthie asked.

'I don't know,' Anna said again.

'You're still not saying "we'll see".'

'Ruthie—'

'Do you want Sam to come back?'

Her daughter was looking at her with the most honest

expression on her face now. It was hopeful and expectant and all the things Anna wanted her to be unafraid about feeling.

'I like him very much,' she admitted.

'And he likes you.'

He had liked her. *A lot*. She knew that, despite his leaving. But was it enough to what? Turn his life upside down and be here with them? Was that what she wanted? Something *that* full-on, *that* permanent? Was it even a possibility?

She didn't get to say anything else before the doorbell chimed. It made her jump. Was it going to be a reporter again? She stayed still, wondering if she should just ignore it . . . Except Cheesecake had bolted from its position underneath Malcolm, pawing the baubles like they were its personal playcentre, and rushed to the door in a blur of fur. And when Cheesecake was curious it howled like a ravenous wolf.

'It's Dad,' Ruthie said, getting up and heading towards the door of the living room.

'What?' Anna asked. 'How do you know?' And Ed never rang the bell. He always let himself in with that bloody key he shouldn't have.

Ruthie shrugged. 'I just know.'

When Anna opened the door, with the chain on to be extra-cautious, it *was* Ed standing there and, looking over his shoulder, she could see that thankfully there were no press present on the street, just the flashing festive lights from the homes across the road.

'Hi,' Ed greeted.

'Hi,' Anna replied.

'Could I . . . come in?'

He was asking. This was new. And he wasn't wearing a coat and it was freezing out there.

'I know I didn't call or text to let you know I was coming but I thought if I did that . . . you wouldn't want to see me and I really wanted to see you,' Ed continued.

Anna swallowed. It was horrible timing. She really wasn't up for getting into anything with Ed right now but there was something about his stance – less confident, not assured – that made Anna think this visit was different.

'Coffee?' she asked.

'That would be great,' he answered.

After releasing the chain, she turned to go into the house and then quickly realised Ed wasn't following.

'Come in,' she told him.

Only then did he cross the threshold.

Fifty-Five

'. . . and then we spin around like this and I do two star jumps as high as I can, go down into the splits and then I do step ball changes all around Megan who's dressed as all three of the Wise Men – her mum has had to make two life-size rag doll men and attach them to Megan's costume – and after that I climb up the Christmas tree scaffolding and forward roll down the slide. And that's the end – with jazz hands of course.'

Ruthie shook her hands in time with Cheesecake who was back foot pedalling bells on the tree as Ruthie ended the impromptu performance. Ed clapped his hands together more heartily than Anna had ever seen before.

'Ruthie, that was fantastic. When is the show again?'

'Are you going to come?' Ruthie asked, picking up Cheesecake.

'I'd really like to,' Ed said. 'If that's OK with you.'

'Are you going to turn up late again?' Ruthie asked bluntly.

'I promise I will be on time . . . if you say I can come.'

Anna watched the scene between father and daughter. This was reminiscent of the Ed from when they'd first met, the Ed who waltzed her around the dancefloor to an Aerosmith classic at their wedding, who cried happy tears when Ruthie was born, who had spent hours and hours helping her to restore the Victorian fireplace right here in this living room. Sometimes it was hard to remember those moments, like the pain of the separation and the divorce had wiped out everything that had gone before.

'You can come,' Ruthie said. 'But you should know that Sam will be coming too.'

What? Anna fell out of her reverie pretty quickly. 'Ruthie—'

'Sam is going to be there,' Ruthie said like she was speaking the purest insight. 'I know he will be.'

'I—' Anna started again.

'I'll make more coffee,' Ruthie said, heading out of the room before Anna could say anything else.

Anna picked up her mug and took a sip of the contents – cold and pretty disgusting. She put it down again.

'So, things are a bit difficult for Sam at the moment,' Ed spoke.

Anna didn't know how to respond so she just dealt in facts. 'He's gone back to Cincinnati. There's no plan for him to come back here. I've tried not to let Ruthie get too attached but—'

'You're speaking to the idiot who bought her an inappropriate cat,' Ed stated. 'Something or someone only has to treat her nicely or be in her corner, and she creates a bond. If there's one thing I do know about my daughter then it's that.'

Anna nodded. 'You've seen the news?'

'Nicolette keeps abreast of celebrity snippets. She was the one who told me who Sam is . . . well, his job and status over there.'

Anna shook her head. 'He didn't tell me at first. I just thought he was—'

'A great guy who paid you all the attention you so richly deserve? Someone who accepts and adores Ruthie exactly for who she is?' Ed waited a beat before carrying on. 'A better man than me.'

'Ed—'

'No, honestly, it's true. I hold my hands up to being the worst husband, the worst ex-husband and a pretty piss-poor excuse for a dad.'

'You weren't always the worst husband and I actually haven't had any other husbands to compare you to so . . .'

Ed shook his head. 'Don't make light of it, Anna. I treated you terribly. As soon as Ruthie showed signs of being different

285

I bowed out because I didn't know what to do. I didn't know how to cope with it. I pushed her away and I pushed you away because I was scared and I continued to do it because I was stupid.' He sighed. 'You were there rising to the challenge, virtually knocking on doors demanding solutions and help for her, for us, and all I could do was think "why Ruthie?" or "why us?". "What did we do to deserve this?" I made our beautiful, clever daughter and everything she's made up of into a negative thing and I will never forgive myself for that.'

Anna didn't know what to say. She didn't know how or why this revelation had happened now but, if Ed meant it, it could only be a good thing.

'I want to be better, Anna. I want to be better for Ruthie, better for you and better for this new child I'm going to have. I know Ruthie's unsettled by it – like she is with anything new – but I don't want her to feel unsettled because she thinks I don't care about her or because she thinks I'm going to care more for the baby.'

'I'm not going to lie to you, Ed. She does think that. But only because you—'

'Keep messing things up.' He sighed, putting his hands to his hair and gripping hold. It had always been his signature move when he was stressed, before he got the light flecks of grey in the blond at his temples. 'I know and, worse than that, I keep messing things up and expecting you to sort it out. Sort *me* out even and that's not your job anymore. Well, it shouldn't ever have been your job. I should be able to make the right decisions myself, instinctively, just like you always have. And that's why I'm here now.'

Anna kept still, could hear the kettle boiling from the kitchen keeping Ruthie away from this conversation.

'I'm here because of Sam,' Ed continued. 'And yes, it pains me a little to say that, but it's true.'

'I don't understand,' Anna said.

'I've watched him with you, Anna. That first night at the Christmas tepee bar when I came over and behaved like . . .

I don't know, some possessive Neanderthal. And then at the nursing home.' He sighed again. 'When I wasn't checking my phone and watching Ruthie, I was watching him and you and . . . Sam watching Ruthie and I saw everything that was missing from you and me.'

Anna held her breath, remembering those nights. The first date when she told Sam he was too young for her, being terrified to start something new, then how he somehow became a part of her every day, making her smile, being there for Ruthie, gradually drawing the before parenthood Anna out again . . .

'I saw him being the person I should have been, Anna. And to begin with I was angry at that. Who was this person replacing me? How could someone swoop in so quickly and have this kind of connection with you and Ruthie?' He took a breath. 'But then I thought about me and Nicolette and how quickly that happened. And yes, how I went about things was totally unacceptable, but sometimes the perfect thing doesn't come along at the perfect time. Sometimes making the right choice breaks all the rules you thought you lived your life by.'

Tears were in Anna's eyes now. For how she and Ed had ended up, for what had happened between her and Sam, for Ruthie and all she was going to have to endure in her future . . .

'I'm glad that you have found someone who makes you happy,' Ed told her. 'He seems like a good guy and next time he's around maybe we could, I don't know, have a conversation. Clear the air.'

'Well, I don't think that's going to happen. Like I said, at the moment, he's over there and I'm over here and that's most probably where it's going to stay.'

Ed shook his head. 'Come on, Anna.'

'Come on what?'

'I just told you, quite awkwardly I'll admit, that anyone can see that you two have the start of something special.'

She knew it. She'd felt it. She still felt it now. And she didn't want to give up on it, but as the hours crept by, as Christmas got closer, the distance would grow – both physically and emotionally – and perhaps Sam would go back to the life he knew and she and Ruthie would become people he met once in London. She'd composed a message – it felt like at least fifty times but nothing seemed right. She might have given Neeta all the *Braveheart* bravado, but the reality was a lot harder.

'Hold out your hand,' Ed said, his voice breaking into her thoughts.

'What?'

'It's not a trick. Come on, hold out your hand.'

'Ed, the last time you ever said that to me, we were in Cornwall and you put a crab in my palm and I screamed and Ruthie screamed and the whole county almost migrated to Devon because of the noise pollution.'

Ed reached out and took hold of her hand. Tenderly he unfurled her fingers and dropped something into the well of her hand. It was a key. A front door key.

'I don't know why I held on to it. I know I shouldn't have. I think part of it was because I didn't want to let go of you and Ruthie and I know that makes no sense because I'm the one who put the nail in the coffin of our marriage and I'm the one who has been sporadic about my time spent with Ruthie but . . . anyway, no more turning up unannounced, proper grown-up behaviour from now on.'

'Proper grown-up behaviour,' Anna said, a slight smile on her lips.

'I know. I'm turning into my dad,' Ed replied.

'Thanks, Ed,' Anna said, squeezing the key in her hand.

'You have absolutely nothing to thank me for,' he said quickly. 'All I've done is make your life harder but, I want to be here now, for Ruthie, for . . . the cat maybe.'

The door to the living room opened and there was Ruthie, two steaming mugs of coffee in her hands. 'Can Cheesecake come if I have a sleepover at your house, Dad?'

Anna looked to Ed. Already time to put his intention into action.

'Will Cheesecake claw Nicolette's new faux fur footstool?' Ed asked, eyebrows raised.

Ruthie pondered for half a second. 'Yes, they definitely will.'

'Good,' Ed answered. 'I hate that thing. So Cheesecake is welcome any time. And obviously you too.'

Ruthie nodded. 'OK, well, I have to make sure that Sam is back here with Mum first but after that . . .'

'Ruthie,' Anna said. 'What did I say?'

'Well,' Ruthie said, carefully putting the coffees down on the sideboard as Cheesecake ran in and started to wind around her legs before heading back to the Christmas tree for more bauble action. 'I know one thing you didn't say. You didn't say "we'll see".'

'Does Cheesecake scratch Nanny Gwen's cotton doilies?' Ed asked Ruthie.

Ruthie laughed. 'Yes! All the time!'

'Good,' Ed replied. 'I never liked them either.'

Anna smiled. 'She knew you hated them. I'm surprised she doesn't haunt you.'

'Oh, I think she does,' Ed said, nodding. 'I think she controls my TV. The other week I couldn't get the channel to change from a programme about making a garden rockery. I think she remembered me once saying I was going to get rid of her gnomes.'

'Really!' Ruthie exclaimed.

Anna swallowed as she watched them together, picking up her coffee and putting her hands around the mug and relishing the warmth. As Cheesecake put on a show of bauble banging, Anna realised that either she made contact with Sam soon and dealt with whatever came of it, or Ruthie was going to continue building up her hopes higher than the Shard from now until her Christmas concert.

Fifty-Six

Dr Monroe's Office, Cincinnati, USA

Sam looked at his phone. The cracked screen didn't make light of the notifications that were still coming in every second – Instagram, Twitter, Facebook, email, text, calls. It was on silent but the screen kept flashing like a strobe. He should turn it off but he'd wanted to see her. *Anna*. He had photos, of her, of them, of Ruthie, the fluffy tail of Mr Rocket as it shot off chasing a rolling carrot in the kitchen . . . It was only days since he'd left but, in some ways, it felt like forever. And now here he was, with Tionne, the morning after that full disclaimer of a meeting in the hotel suite, his parents down the hall. The office hadn't changed much since the last time he'd been here. Still those health warnings pinned to the wall, the addition of a cactus wearing a crown of golden tinsel on the desk.

'So, after they scan my brain, what comes next?' Tionne asked suddenly. 'The counsellor? Or the blood test?'

'I don't know,' Sam admitted.

'But you had the tests.'

'Not in the same way.' The Diggers had arranged all the scans and tests, intricate mapping of his entire body, it hadn't been zoned down to one disease or ailment, they had been looking for anything and everything. This was more precise, focused on this one gene.

'What is the counsellor gonna ask me?'

'Maybe if you're sure you want to take the test.'

'So, he must come first. You *do* know.'

'Ti, you don't have to have the tests now,' Sam reminded her. 'You don't even have to take the tests at all. Dr Monroe told you it's not a decision that has to be rushed.'

'Dr Monroe also said that the results might take four weeks.'

'Worst case scenario,' Sam said.

'Four weeks is a long time,' Tionne told him. 'Do you know how many Insta posts that is? It's after Christmas and New Year's. It's actually longer than most of my relationships.'

He looked at his little sister. She looked as young to him now as she had looked when she took her first faltering steps across the living room of their parents' apartment. Her hair might be longer and bolder now – blue streaks today – but she still had that same innocence about her.

'I'm sorry,' Sam whispered, his eyes filling with tears.

'What are you saying sorry for?' Tionne asked him. 'Mom or Dad have this, you said so last night. If anyone's to blame then . . .' She sighed. 'I didn't mean "blame", they didn't do it to themselves either. It was Grandpop or Grandma Jackman or Gramps or Nana Jeffrey and before that, well, I guess we'll never know where it first started.'

Sam nodded. 'I guess.'

'So, what happens with it? When you get sick. Do you stop being able to walk? Do you forget who people are? Does your hair fall out?'

'I don't think your hair falls out,' Sam replied.

'That's good,' Tionne said, nodding.

'Ti, there's a chance you don't have this. A good chance.'

'Sure,' she answered. 'But you have it. So, if I have it too, we can, I don't know, make a bucket list of things to do before we can't do them anymore. Or, I don't know, plan our care homes or . . . decide to set up anonymous accounts on Insta and mess with our exes.'

Sam reached for her hand. 'I don't have any exes I wanna mess with. And if someone is still messing with you then I wanna know.'

'Jerome is an asshole.'

'Yeah?'

'Don't say you told me so.'

'I won't.'

'You're thinking it. I can hear it!'

He rested his head against hers. 'Ti, I don't want you to have this disease. I can miss out on choosing a matching care home. I don't want you *or* Mom *or* Dad to have it.'

She shrugged. 'If I have it, I have it. This testing ain't gonna change things. It's just gonna tell me.'

'Ti, this is serious.'

'I know that. You have it already. That's all I can think about. My big brother *has* this thing. We know that for sure and there's nothing any one of us can do about that.'

She was stifling her emotions, holding herself stiffly, trying to narrow her nostrils the way she did when she was hurt but not wanting to show she was hurt.

'I'm OK right now,' Sam said, looping an arm around her shoulders.

'But the Diggers didn't want you because of it,' Tionne said, sniffing.

'I don't blame them for that. They invest in perfection. I'm not perfect now.'

'But what if, I don't know, they had bought you and in the first game you got a life-changing injury that ended your career? What then? They still would have paid you a billion dollars or whatever.'

'Ti, they have insurance for that kind of stuff. But they can't knowingly buy a player with a health risk like I have because then the insurance wouldn't pay out.' He sighed. 'If I had an injury, an unrelated one, there's always a chance the insurance company could blame it on this gene and the Diggers don't wanna take that chance. It's business.'

'It's not though, is it? It's your life. Football is your life. It always has been.'

'Yeah,' he said. 'But maybe it shouldn't have been. What's

that thing Mom always used to say? About eggs being in one basket?'

'What are you gonna do?'

He closed his eyes expecting to see a grand flash of inspiration or at least the tiniest germ of an idea to expand on but he had nothing . . . except Anna. How sad she had looked when he'd left her, how the emptiness he'd felt as he sprinted away had overridden the pain in his bare feet. Suddenly the phone in his hand dropped out of it and onto the floor. Tionne beat him to scooping it up.

'OK, talk. Who is this?!'

There was the last photo he had been looking at, now in Tionne's hands. Anna, in the horse-drawn carriage, wrapped up in the blanket, making a stupid face at his camera but still pulling off gorgeous . . .

'Sam!' Tionne exclaimed. 'Who is this?' Before Sam could think about what to say, his sister was scrolling through the rest of the pictures on his phone. 'Is this a rabbit? And . . . whoa! How big is that Christmas tree?'

He grabbed back his phone and locked the screen, putting it away in his jacket pocket.

'Just because you've put it away doesn't mean I'm gonna stop the questions. You know that, right?'

'Ti, I can't do this right now. *You* can't do this right now. We're waiting here to—'

'Have my head scanned,' Tionne interrupted. 'I know. So, I need a distraction and these photos tell me that when my brother ran away he didn't hole up in a hotel room with UberEats on speed dial. He got out and he did things and he did those things with someone . . . so, I say again, who is she?'

Sam swallowed as his heart pumped hard thinking about Anna. The first time when she was all feisty and protective over Ruthie, then caring and concerned over his injuries from the car accident, to funny and sexy and warm and deep . . .

'Oh my God,' Tionne said, hands going to her cheeks.

'*This* is the serious thing right here. I have never seen you look like this before.'

'Ti, don't. We need to . . . look again at the information Dr Monroe left us with or . . . maybe I should go and check how Mom and Dad are doing.' He rose from his chair, but Tionne grabbed his arm in a strong wrist lock he himself had taught her and dragged him back down.

'What's her name?' Tionne asked, her tone softer.

'What?'

'This woman you have so many photos of on your totally broken phone screen?'

He took a breath, feeling that if he said her name out loud it would take every bit of energy he had left and leave him physically and emotionally depleted. Committing it to air, telling his sister, that wasn't something he could take back. That wasn't casual, that wasn't forgetting something and moving on. But did he really want to completely deny what had happened between him and Anna? Never tell anyone how happy he had been while this death sentence was hanging over his head?

'Anna,' he said, her name catching a little on his lips.

Tionne didn't say anything, but she was looking at him, studying him, her brown eyes seeking truth out of his pores or something.

'Wow,' Tionne said finally. 'With all this going on with the Diggers and your health . . . you went to London and you fell in love.'

It seemed that, for now, there was nothing else to say.

Fifty-Seven

Kew Christmas Market

'I think Pavinder would like the things in jars,' Neeta announced, picking one up from the stall she, Lisa and Anna were standing next to, and shaking it. 'I have no idea what it is. Can you eat it, do you think? Or is it more for decoration?'

The fact that Neeta was looking at nice gifts for Pavinder was great. As soon as they stopped for drinks, Anna was going to ask how things were going in that respect.

'It says "festive paste",' Lisa said, reading a label. 'That could mean anything. I mean, can you put wallpaper up with it?'

'Why don't you ask?' Anna suggested. 'When the stallholder has finished with that customer.'

'It looks like frogspawn,' Neeta continued. 'Whatever you are meant to do with it, I want to buy it for Pavinder's work Secret Santa and hope that Jessica gets it. She might think it is face cream . . . what does it smell like?' Neeta looked like she was going to unfasten the lid and Anna quickly grabbed it out of her hands and put it back on the stall.

She had thought positive things too soon. 'Have you still not spoken to Pav about this Jessica person?' Anna asked.

Neeta sniffed and tossed her hair back. 'Have you still not made contact with Sam?'

Anna swallowed. Typical Neeta, changing the focus of the narrative. She had had a lot on her plate over the last couple of days. She had pitched the new restaurant concept to Mr Wong, with Adam watching and making notes on his Remarkable tablet like he was giving Anna some kind of appraisal. But Mr Wong had *loved* all her ideas and was keen to make the changes as soon as possible with a pre-Christmas teaser of what was to come in the New Year.

Anna's plan had involved a complete overhaul of the premises and Mr Wong was all for ringing up someone to knock walls down there and then until Anna reminded him exactly how close to Christmas they were. He was now settling for a gardener to strim the piece of land opposite his establishment, some patio heaters, and benches and banners with the new logo. After that was settled, it had been Ruthie with more tap dance rehearsals, Mr Rocket at the vet's to have a bit of embedded hay removed from his inner ear, and today, it was Christmas shopping. When had Anna had time to message someone who, it had been reported, had been seen visiting an ice cream parlour with an Instagram influencer to get over the end of his mega deal . . . ?

'Pav adores you, Neeta. I don't believe he'd ever even look at another woman,' Lisa announced as they moved to another stall, a brass band striking up from the square. 'Paul on the other hand thinks it's fine to comment on the attributes of actresses when we're watching films together. Honestly, my list on Netflix consists of lead females over the age of sixty-five just so we can focus on the plot. But then there's Helen Mirren, isn't there?'

'There is definitely something he is keeping from me,' Neeta said with a determined nod as they moved along to a stall selling crystals some of which had been styled into festive characters.

'But that could be a nice thing,' Anna suggested. 'It could be that . . . he's in line for a promotion at work or . . . that he's planning a big surprise for Christmas.'

'As he is already Head of Plants I do not think there is a promotion unless he turns into David Attenborough and we do not celebrate Christmas, remember? So, if a big surprise is to change religions then, yes, I guess that might explain the tight-lipped replies when I ask him his movements.'

Anna silently cursed herself. Her brain definitely wasn't working properly. And she hated the fact that, most of the time, it was thinking about Sam. And what to do about how she felt about Sam. But as the days went on, the distance between them began to feel more and more insurmountable. Perhaps it was best to let it go. Ruthie's relationship with Ed was starting to repair. Anna knew her daughter had been FaceTiming him quite regularly since he had turned up that night with the front door key and tonight, Ruthie was sleeping over there. Anna was nervous about it, but she knew she had to let it happen. Ed had to re-learn what Ruthie could manage and what she couldn't and how to deal with it. He was her dad. She knew he tried to do the right thing and yes, he might not get it perfectly right but he could learn.

'You need to ask him,' Lisa said. 'Just plain and simple ask him if he's got designs on this Jessica. Then you'll know and then you can stop worrying about it and worrying us about it. This isn't like you, Neeta. You're usually so . . . so . . . confrontational about things.'

'But what do I do if he says he does? Have designs.' Neeta asked, picking up some rose quartz fashioned into a snowman – kind of. 'What does that mean for our marriage? Do I have to have a marriage like my cousin Sita? She found out in the first six weeks that Javi had other women and she did nothing. Nothing. They have been married for nine and a half years now, with three children, and she says Javi has slept with more women than there are Tube stations.' She put the crystal down again.

'Pavinder wouldn't do that to you, Neeta. You're talking about a man who talks to plants like he's lulling them to sleep,' Lisa continued.

'That could be his patter with Jessica. Everyone wants a nice soft podcast voice these days!'

'Stop,' Anna begged. 'Please, just stop.' She put her hand

on the upright of the stall and took a breath. The cold outside was giving her brain freeze and she didn't have a hat.

'Are you OK?' Lisa asked, a steadying hand at her elbow. 'Was it the mulled wine? I told you I thought there were peppercorns in mine.'

'I'm OK,' Anna answered. 'I just . . . don't want to see my best friend feeling this way about her husband when she has been this powerhouse piece of gnarly granite for me to lean on. Neeta, this is chewing you up. All the time.'

'Not all the time,' Neeta answered, hiding her eyes a little. 'I can almost get through an episode of *Homes Under the Hammer* without wondering if any of the purchasers have ever buried a nemesis in the walls of a remodel.'

'Let's both be honest,' Anna suggested, reaching for her friend's hands. She took a long, deep breath then looked deep into Neeta's brown eyes. 'I miss Sam.'

Neeta's lips were quivering a little now, earrings faintly jangling. Until . . . 'I love Pavinder.'

Anna squeezed her friend's hands tight, a little shocked by her own admission and delighted by Neeta's.

'Should I say something heartwarming too?' Lisa asked, looking into the sky like she was searching for inspiration. 'Um, Paul has aged like a fine wine but the Aldi stuff rather than Majestic?'

'Right,' Neeta said. 'That is it. I am taking control now.'

'You're going to ask Pavinder about Jessica?' Lisa said.

Neeta shook her head. 'I am going to contact Sam and I am going to tell him that whatever hideous football-related nonsense he has going on over there he needs to remember that he made a commitment over here.' Neeta started to delve into her bag.

'He didn't though,' Anna said with a sigh. 'He didn't make a commitment. Neither of us did. We both wanted it that way.'

'And now?' Neeta asked. 'Because I do not remember you saying you missed anyone from the dating apps.'

'Well,' Anna began, 'I only had one date with the guys from the apps. And, I got to know Sam a little and . . .' She stopped talking when she finally realised that she was doing herself no favours.

'OK,' Neeta said looking up from her bag. 'I cannot find my phone, but I am going to make a deal with you.' She drew in a long breath and wrinkled up her eyes. 'If you make contact with Sam . . . I will . . . I will . . . ask Pavinder about Jessica.'

'Seriously?' Lisa said.

'Yes,' Neeta answered and then she pointed a finger at Lisa. 'And you . . . you will tell Paul that his misogyny when you're watching TV dramas has to stop. For good.'

Anna looked at her two friends, Neeta all fired up, Lisa wondering how on earth she had suddenly become part of this. They were the best friends anyone could wish for. She was nodding before she even realised it. Was she really going to commit to this?

'OK,' Neeta said. 'Well, my Not Christmas Christmas party this Saturday. We will all do it then. We will all be there. We can make sure none of us back out.'

Now Anna's heart was pumping. Put on the spot, with an audience, there was no chance she could change her mind.

Lisa put her hand in the air like she was a teen about to ask a question at school. 'Can my kids not be in the room when I speak to Paul about it?'

'Absolutely not,' Neeta answered. 'It is an important lesson for Kai and Kelsey to learn.'

Anna went to ask if she could have a little privacy too but Neeta pre-empted.

'No!' Neeta said, pointing a finger in Anna's direction now. 'We need to see Sam on FaceTime or hear him on the phone before you take it from there.' She turned her attention to the stallholder then. 'How much is the crystal that looks like Lionel Richie?'

Fifty-Eight

Every Day's a Sundae, Cincinnati, Ohio, USA

'Can Huntington's change your tastebuds? Because I've never been a fan of raisins in ice cream before, but this past week I can't get enough of them.' Tionne raised her eyes from her tall glass of multiple flavours of ice cream and looked directly at Sam. 'And before you ask, I'm not eating different because I'm pregnant. I had the period from hell last week. And I'm careful. Always.'

Sam regretted asking for a whole heap of the festive special – cranberry syrup – on his ice cream serving now. He shook his head. 'You promised you wouldn't think about it until you got the call for the results.'

'I know,' Tionne answered. 'But weeks is weeks. And I'm not like Mom. I can't bury my head in the ass of a turkey or a goat and buy enough food to feed the entire neighbourhood from Christmas until Easter. And I can't talk to anyone else about it.'

'I know,' Sam said, letting a breath leave him, his eyes going to the door of the ice cream parlour in downtown Cincinnati. There were press outside. Half a dozen of them still. They'd taken photos when he and Tionne had arrived. They had their cameras trained towards their booth now, even though Sam had picked one at a lesser vantage point. Like dogs fighting over a scrappy bone. Somehow, he had no idea how, Frankie had still managed to keep the sinewy details out of the public domain. No one knew about his diagnosis. No one knew about the potential for his family's health to be in jeopardy. But Sam was aware it wouldn't be like that for much longer.

He put his spoon in the glass and watched Tionne eat. A million things must be going through her mind right now. Did she have the gene? If she did, like him, how long did she have before symptoms started? What about children? He winced a little then. He'd always imagined Tionne having kids, could see her in the centre of two or three school-aged children who'd inherited all their mother's street-smarts, Tionne telling them how it was gonna be. What if that couldn't happen? Was there a way it could, even if Tionne was affected?

'You just told me not to think about it.' Tionne had looked up from her sundae glass now and was studying him.

'I know.'

'Stop saying "I know". You don't know. No one knows. We have to wait the rest of the four weeks. And, bro, I don't even know what you're doing here when those journalist dudes are hanging around everywhere we go. Why aren't you back in the UK with Anna?'

His sister saying 'Anna' made his feelings rise to the top like the wafer fighting for supremacy in his glass. He had told Tionne about her while they were waiting for Tionne's turn in the scanner. Tionne had made him start talking and he hadn't been able to stop. But he had taken no action since. And Anna's social media channels were totally silent. There was nothing since a post featuring Ruthie and Malcolm that had been there for as long as he had known her. He wanted to know how she was. He *longed* to know what she was doing. Even though he knew he had no right to feel that way. He had made the break for all the right reasons.

'I can't go back,' he whispered.

'Why not? Did the Diggers demand you compensate them for their trouble and drain your bulging bank accounts? There's nothing you can do here.'

'Mom's getting turkey and a goat,' he reminded, taking a sip of his espresso. 'I can't bail on Christmas. Especially not now.'

'You're gonna choose eating barnyard animals over seeing this woman who has turned you into a mushed-up hero from a romcom movie? That makes perfect sense. And I told you, Mom is gonna end up freezing most of what she's bought. You can have it for New Year's.'

'It's not that easy, Ti.' He took a breath. 'Anna doesn't know about *this*.' He waggled his hands around his head.

'Is that where this gene is? In our brains?'

'No,' Sam said. 'But that's what's gonna be changed.'

'And you haven't told her . . . why?'

'Gee, I dunno, Ti. Maybe because she's met me when I've been able to feed myself and make conversation. When I've been able to run and—'

'Ice skate really badly judging by the photos,' Tionne interjected.

'She has been through so much in her life already. A divorce. Ruthie's autism. Losing the grandmother that raised her. Yeah, I dove in before I knew about all of that but then, when I did know, I kept on going. And I didn't intend to feel as deeply as I feel about her. I didn't mean for *anything* to happen. It just did.'

Tionne nodded. 'It just did.' She put another spoon of ice cream in her mouth and inhaled through her nose while she enjoyed and then swallowed. 'I would literally give all my free products away for life if I met someone and things *just* happened. I've never had a connection like that. I'm starting to think that I will *never* have a connection like that.'

'Ti, you will. You have your whole life to—' He stopped himself from carrying on with the inappropriate sentence. 'You just haven't met the guy who is gonna treat you better than anyone else yet.'

'No,' Tionne agreed. 'But *you've* met someone who has made you happier than I've ever seen you. And she's done that even when you've been going through one of the most difficult times of your life.'

Yeah, she had. He shouldn't have been in a mental place to be open. But somehow he had been. And he could have picked any destination in the world to land but chance had taken him to London and that taxi driver had taken him to Richmond. And there Ruthie had been, being bullied like he had been once upon a time . . .

'How can I tell her about this?' He couldn't even give the disease a name right now, not when his family were currently being subjected to the horror of it too. 'How can I say that if we make things more permanent, I don't know how long I can give her? Her *and* Ruthie.' He stabbed his spoon into the ice cream. 'And, by the way, while we're going through all this, the press are gonna be hanging off lampposts and climbing onto wheelie bins to get photos?' He shuddered, thinking of how Ruthie had been that last day.

'Oh, wow,' Tionne said. 'Wow.'

'Ti, they need someone the world doesn't care about and they need someone reliable. Anna has been let down big time, and yeah, she's a strong, gutsy woman who has handled everything that's been thrown her way, but whoever she decides to share her life with, they've gotta be in it for the long haul.'

'Keep going,' Tionne said, rolling her eyes. 'I just can't wait to see what's gonna come outta your mouth next.'

'I've let her down now, I know. Because I told her one thing and the very next morning I told her the opposite. But she told me about her nana and how she passed away and it was so similar to what I'm going to go through. I figured hurting her then, leaving then, would be better than telling her I have *this*!'

'And now we're moving on to being totally selfish. Wow.'

'I don't know what to say.' Sam sat back in his chair and folded his arms tight across his chest.

'Clearly.'

He shrugged, not knowing how to continue.

'So, don't stop,' Tionne urged. 'Tell me, what's your plan? Are you gonna give up football just because you didn't become the richest player in history? What do the Bisons say about your diagnosis?'

'I don't know yet. Frankie's giving me a little time to get my head straight before we think about that.'

'Right, so, you may still have a team that needs you. A team that, let's be honest, are pretty much horseshit without you.'

'Ti—'

'But instead of *living* you're gonna focus on dying. Hide in your showstopping apartment, stopping no shows at all outside of those four walls, not continuing with the things that make you happy, not spending time with the people that you love, not trying to enhance whatever time you have left with whatever you can cram in?'

Sam went to say more but Tionne continued.

'D'you know what I'm gonna do if I find out I have this?'

'Pick out a care home that does adjoining rooms?'

'No,' Tionne said. 'That was humour. I am gonna prioritise me. I'm gonna look at all the crap I don't wanna do and I'm not gonna do it.'

Sam shook his head. 'That only works when you have a target to aim for. You can't indefinitely avoid doing things. I may have twenty or thirty years left. I may have five or ten. Or less. There's nothing fixed to work to.'

'And now, dear brother, you are getting it. Because *no one* knows when they're gonna die. If we did, imagine it! If we all knew the date we were gonna die, nothing would get done. We would all be, I don't know, sipping on gin and juice. Why would you avoid doing things with Anna? Why wouldn't you want to spend as much time as you can with Anna?'

'That's not fair. We were talking about you.' He finished his espresso.

'Well, no matter how long I have left, I am not about to

watch you begin a demise that may or may not be happening yet. And if that's what you're intending to do then you may as well run out of this store and into traffic and end it all now.'

And now he was getting echoes of a similar conversation he'd had with Frankie, freaking her out about being mown down outside her favourite coffee store . . .

Sam's eyes went to the outside, the press pack being badgered by two Santa Clauses with buckets looking for charity donations. Beyond them was the traffic, a steady flow moving under the festive lights and angels strung up across the street. Some people somewhere were going to have their lives cut short today and not know it. How was that really different to the situation he found himself in? It wasn't like he had been diagnosed with cancer and knew the timeline leading towards the end. Really, he was as much in the dark as any other person. And it had taken his little sister pointing it out to give him clarity.

'First thing on my list of doing things whether or not I have this gene . . . I want to meet Anna,' Tionne continued.

'Ti, I don't know if she will even want to see me again,' Sam admitted.

'But you want to see her. Don't you? You're saying all this stuff but, when you boil it down, you want to be with her, you're just scared when you tell her about *this* that it's gonna change things.'

'Yeah,' he admitted. 'Because it has to, doesn't it?'

'You tell me,' Tionne said, a fierce expression on her face.

Sam didn't have an answer for that. Could he tell Anna? *Should* he tell Anna before she found out via a news agency? That's what he had wanted for his parents and Tionne, surely Anna deserved the same courtesy. At least then, with all his cards on the table, he would have been completely honest. Maybe he had been selfish. Bailing because he didn't want her rejection, knowing it would shatter his heart. No, that wasn't it, he remembered everything he'd thought about that last morning in Neeta's car. It hadn't been about him. It had been about Anna and not wanting her to accept a fate where she watched a person she cared about lose their mind piece by tiny piece. Would she even make it through that again? He certainly wouldn't choose it for her . . .

'You told me once that the very worst thing you can do in football is show your fear. Even if you're terrified because the opposition are good, you come out strong and let self-belief do the rest.' Tionne looked straight at him with those soft brown eyes. 'It's not your timeout yet, Sam. Don't pre-empt it. Look it straight in the face like it's wearing a helmet and you're in a scrimmage. And for God's sake give me a girl I can be besties with and talk about fashion and boba tea and anything but football because I used all my terminology up right there!'

Sam got up from his seat, came around the table and wrapped his arms around Tionne, hugging her hard.

'I have prayed every day since I found out this could happen to you and Mom or Dad,' he whispered in her ear.

'And I gave up God the second I found out it had already happened to you,' Tionne replied, burying her head in his chest.

He held her tight as she began to cry and his thoughts went back to that homely place thousands of miles away and the person he was missing more than he could ever have envisaged.

Fifty-Nine

Feast, Richmond, UK

'So, what do you think?'

It was Saturday, the night of Neeta's Not Christmas Christmas party, but Anna was making a stop on the way. She had got Adam away from the squash court and they were both standing in a transformed garden area opposite Mr Wong's newly titled buffet restaurant, Feast.

It was its opening teaser tonight and although no walls had yet been demolished inside the eateries, there was the new sign above the doors with a 'coming soon' curtain draped alongside it. Mr Wong had really run with this idea since their last meeting and seemed to have bought every aesthetically pleasing lantern as well as enough fairy lights to decorate an entire forest and not just the few trees in this patch of greenery. There were wooden tables and benches, each with a festive floral display in its centre, housing an LED candle and waiters were going around vast groups of people serving bite-sized portions of cuisine from mashed potato to mussels through teppanyaki to tofu with pizza, pasta and plenty of chips too.

'I think this is utter madness if I'm really honest,' Adam told her, reaching out for a tiger prawn. 'How can a man who runs a chip shop, a Chinese takeaway and an average pizzeria, suddenly be in charge of a global fusion of this scale? When I initially talked to him, he was thinking of a change of wallpaper and cutting back on the menu maybe.'

'Ah,' Anna said. 'Well, as always, because I'm a professional, I upsold and I did my homework. Mr Wong has five sons and two daughters. All of them work in the food industry. And when we crunched the numbers and the crunchings and my vision were presented to the family, it seemed that they all thought this could be a profitable collaborative venture.'

'Anna,' Adam said, shaking his head. 'You've basically made Mr Wong a potential contestant for *Gordon Ramsay's Future Food Stars*.'

'I know,' Anna replied. 'I thought, be thorough. Do the best job I can so my boss realises that he can't do without me, because I think my car might need some help getting through its next MOT.'

Adam shook his head. 'Madness. But, equally, it's genius. And you know that too, right?'

Anna beamed, snatching a finger of pizza from another tray. 'Yes, I do.'

'So,' Adam said, holding up the brochure as festive music began to filter into the evening. 'Talk me through it again. So, we have Full Feast.'

'Yes, Full Feast is an inside dining experience. It will replace the pizzeria. Customers get a choice of all the cuisines, buffet style, all you can eat, *plus* you get the chefs cooking in front of you as you fill up your plates, five extra special dishes that no one else has access to.'

'Right. And then there's . . . Fast Feast.'

'That's the takeaway option, so that replaces the chip shop and the Chinese takeaway elements. Customers will get a scaled-down version of Full Feast, some cuisines taken out, no chefs show-cooking and there will be three sizes of completely compostable containers to choose from . . . Mini Feast, Midi Feast and Maxi Feast.'

'And what's Free Feast, because currently that's making no economic sense to me.'

'I am glad you asked,' Anna said, waving at a very

jovial-looking Mr Wong. 'One thing that buffet restaurants usually get slated for is waste. I suggested to Mr Wong that he aims for being a zero-waste company. Anything left over at the end of the night that can't be repurposed will be delivered to a charity that has food vans going out to feed the homeless and others going through a hunger crisis.'

Again, Adam shook his head. Anna swallowed. She knew she had done good work here but a nod every now and then might be nice. She was still a little worried about the enormity of this change for Mr Wong but she had offered up ideas and the owner had lapped them up like a thirsty reindeer.

'I don't know what to say,' Adam admitted. 'This is above and beyond, Anna, and I can't even give you a raise.'

'I know,' she replied. 'But, you know, you were right about me not giving my all over recent months. It wasn't entirely my fault, but I didn't leave a big enough section of my life for me or for my work.' She looked over to Ruthie who was sitting on a blanket on the grass underneath one of the trees devouring deep-fried pork balls. 'But I'm hungry for more now, so if you could perhaps give me a few bigger clients to get my teeth stuck into . . . I think this project has earned me that, hasn't it?'

Finally, Adam gave a nod. 'I think it definitely has. So, tell me about these boxes again. And also tell me that there is no shame if a single man wants to buy the Maxi Feast and not share with anyone.'

'Absolutely no shame at all. I intend to do the same on opening night,' she answered.

A shiver of pride ran down Anna's back as she looked at the greenery, freshly cut, warmed by pyramid patio heaters, the guests she had invited – from the local MP and Jennifer Atkinson, the Head of Ruthie's school, to entrepreneurs who might use Feast to host corporate events. That was what this open space was going to be commandeered for. For now it was somewhere for patrons of Fast Feast to eat their takeaways if they wanted but, with the gates closed for privacy, it could be transformed into a woodland hideaway in the middle of the city for business meetings or team-building lunches or even wedding celebrations. Anna sighed. But to her it would always be the place she and Sam had walked and imagined and where he had first invited her to St Paul's Cathedral.

'Mum!' Ruthie called. 'If I eat any more pork balls I won't have room for Neeta's tarka dhal and she gets really mad if I don't eat enough to fill the stomach of a walrus!'

'OK,' Anna said, waving a hand. It was time to go.

Sixty

Neeta and Pavinder's home, Richmond

'Ruthie, would you like to try some of my plant-based snacks?'

Pavinder – dressed in a very regal-looking and ornate red sherwani – offered out a bowl of crispy-looking things that actually did look like they were made from the leaves of plants. Everyone was dressed up in fancy dress as Christmas characters except Neeta and Pavinder who always dressed in their Indian finery. Neeta had so many beautiful saris there seemed to be a different one at this party every year. The music was Christmas but without lyrics and it lent itself well as a warm-up to the karaoke later. Anna watched Ruthie eyeing the snacks with suspicion. She wasn't opposed to trying new foods – contrary to a lot of autistics – but texture was always something she considered carefully.

'Do they *taste* of plants?' Ruthie asked him, her snowman carrot nose bobbing up and down as she spoke.

'Oh my goodness, no,' Pavinder said, chuckling. 'These ones are meant to have a flavour of—'

'Grain,' Neeta interrupted. 'They all taste of grain. The best thing Pavinder could do is sell them for chicken feed.' She put an arm out, careful not to actually touch Ruthie, and suggested a move to the left. 'Come and have some tarka dahl instead.'

Anna watched Pavinder's smile fade a little and, even though she was more than full from her stop at Feast, she dived her hand into the snacks and took a couple. Popping them in her mouth and crunching them up she realised, sadly, that Neeta was completely correct about the taste and her entire throat was now as dry as the Gobi.

'They are terrible, aren't they?' Pavinder said, obviously accurately reading all Anna's facials.

'Not terrible. Just, I don't know, perhaps lacking in something I can't put my finger on.'

'Flavour?' Pavinder suggested.

'Maybe.'

He sighed, his shoulders sagging. 'These are supposed to make my fortune, mine and Neeta's fortune, so I spend less time at the laboratory and more time with her.'

'Oh,' Anna said. Well, despite the snacks being awful it could answer the question as to what Pavinder had been doing all those long late nights at the lab.

'Jessica told me I should keep my focus on our research project but, I don't know, there are things I want to discover that aren't part of my remit. I find myself wanting to . . . do something wild, you know, bend the rules, create a new future.'

Wow, Pavinder was not usually a 'bending the rules' kind of guy. But this could be good. Because Neeta was craving more excitement too. Maybe this Jessica person did feel something for Pavinder, but if Pavinder was trying to create crisps to get himself out of the botanical research industry to spend more time with his wife, then the feeling clearly wasn't reciprocated. Neeta didn't need to ask him the direct question, all Anna had to do was get them talking to each other.

'It is a shame that Sam is not here. I might have been encouraged to join the veterans rugby team Paul had in mind.'

At the mention of Sam's name Anna's stomach did a dive, taking the snacks with it. She had sworn she was going to make contact with him tonight, she had even gone slightly less pantomime with her ice queen make-up and more, hopefully, radiant frosty hotness. A few drinks to pluck up some courage and then make a call . . . maybe.

'Well,' she said to Pavinder, 'I don't think you need Sam to start the rugby team.'

'He is a professional and he is much younger and fitter than any of us,' Pavinder continued. 'That is inspiring.'

'I think trying to create crisps to make a fortune and spend more time with your wife is inspiring,' Anna told him.

'I just need to make them taste of something other than millet without compromising the nutritional aspects.'

'I like the shapes,' Anna added hopefully.

'What am I missing out on?' Lisa asked, bundling into Anna and almost taking Anna's eye out with the bell on the end of her elf's hat.

Pavinder put the plant snacks down. 'I will find you some Pringles.' He disappeared towards the kitchen.

'Was it something I said?' Lisa asked, dipping her hand into the snacks.

'No,' Anna answered. 'But I don't think you're going to like those.'

It was too late. Lisa had some in her mouth and then she was making the same kind of face Anna knew *she* had made that didn't say 'glowing review'.

'Ugh! God! What are these?'

'Sshh! Pavinder created them. For Neeta. Except they aren't very good, but the lovely intention was there.'

'Neeta won't like these,' Lisa continued. 'There's literally no flavour.'

'I know,' Anna answered. 'But, perhaps, if Neeta knew *why* Pavinder was doing this maybe she could help. She is the queen of spice after all.'

'I like it,' Lisa said with a nod. 'Oh God, here comes Paul with a sour expression on his face. This means one of two things. Either he's suddenly developed some kind of ailment that only Birra Moretti can cure so I'm driving tonight, or he's been called to an emergency job and he has to go. Which means I'm in charge of the kids not drinking too many energy drinks *and* driving him home to get his van.'

'Hi, Paul,' Anna greeted. 'You make a very fetching Grinch.'

'Hi, Anna, yes, well, Lisa said I was born for the role and I haven't entirely worked out whether to be very insulted by that.'

'Aww, sorry darling. But you do look particularly Grinch-like at the moment. What's the matter?' Lisa asked, putting an arm around his waist.

'Nothing, I just . . . need you to see Kai for a second,' Paul answered a little bit awkwardly.

'You need me to see Kai?' Lisa asked, frowning. 'I can see him from here. Five foot eight, eating samosas by the handful, dressed as a giant Christmas cracker.'

'Lisa,' Paul said softly.

Anna caught the flick of Paul's gaze towards her and immediately her guts began to churn. This was something to do with her.

'What's going on?' she forced herself to ask.

'I . . . well . . .' Paul started.

'Paul,' Lisa said. 'What is it?'

'Well, Kai found something on his phone. I wasn't going to say anything to you until later, Anna.'

'Say anything about what?' Anna asked. Now she was really worried.

'Kai!' Paul called. 'Come over here for a second.'

'Are we ready to start some karaoke?' Neeta shouted. 'I have a new mixture of 1980s power ballads I cannot wait for you all to try.'

Anna was holding her breath now, wondering exactly what this was going to be.

'Don't make me sing a duet with Kelsey, Dad,' Kai said, waddling over in a rather snug cracker outfit that he would definitely not want appearing on his Insta account. 'Last time she blackmailed me over the video footage for months.'

'It's not about karaoke, Kai. It's about what you showed me when we got out of the car,' Paul said. 'That news article. About Sam.'

'Oh,' Kai said, his eyes flashing to Anna like he was keeping all MI5's secrets. 'But I thought we weren't mentioning that until later.'

'Yes, well,' Lisa said, taking charge. 'Whatever it is, we're saying it now.'

Kai produced his phone from inside the sleeve of his cracker outfit and pressed icons on his screen. 'It came up earlier when I did a search for him. I was trying to see whether anyone had shared my video of the rugby game anywhere. Here.' He handed his phone to Anna.

She looked at the screen as Lisa leaned in close and looked too.

NFL star Sam Jackman diagnosed with degenerative disease.

Sixty-One

'You cannot sit on the stairs all night. Ruthie is worried about you. And I know she is worried because she does not want to sing Kate Bush and she always loves to sing Kate Bush,' Neeta told Anna. 'No party is complete without "Running Up That Hill" and an encore of "Babooshka".'

Anna held her own phone in her hand now but on the screen was a medical website giving her facts, figures and diagrams about Huntington's disease. Her bottom had been rooted to Neeta's carpet for at least forty minutes while she read and digested and cried a little and thought a lot.

'I . . . don't know what to do,' Anna answered, her voice giving away every ounce of fear she was currently feeling.

'Well,' Neeta said, plumping herself down one stair below. 'You promised me that you were going to contact Sam tonight.'

'I know. And I was, but—'

'But what?' Neeta interrupted. 'If ever you needed a reason to reconnect then surely this is it?'

'Is it?' Anna asked. 'Because this was what he was really worried about the whole time we were together and . . . he didn't tell me.'

'Anna,' Neeta said, shaking her head. 'This is a huge thing. Even from the bare details of this rather mediocre report, having this diagnosis when you are this very attractive, very active sports personality at the centre of a world-changing transfer to another team – I do not know if I got all those words right – it has to be extremely pressurised. Sam will have had all these internal forces at work, trying to figure out what to do about his job, his entire future, while there was also the certainty of all this outside interest and noise the moment it all became public knowledge.'

Anna knew that. She could see how doubly awful that was going to be. He had told her the deal was off and now she knew the reason. He had asked her to trust him and she said she would. But still . . . She was already thinking about Nanny Gwen, the day they had been given the news about her dementia. Despite it having been something she had guessed was coming, it had still been a shock to have it confirmed, her gran's forgetfulness much more than simple old age. And Sam wasn't even twenty-six . . .

'You said yourself, to start with things were casual, a few dates, knowing it was only going to be while Sam was here. Was he really going to tell the first girl he met in the UK that he has this ailment?'

'No, but—'

'But then things changed and you both started to get in deeper with each other.'

'And he should have told me then.'

'Anna, I think you are missing the point.' Neeta screwed her nose up. 'A little like Lisa is missing the top note of this song . . . Sam, the man you are in love with, has this medical problem, something that has obviously taken him by surprise. You need to work out how you feel about that.' Neeta put a hand on her arm. 'From my perspective, he fled back to America so you did not have to deal with this. That is not the action of a man who wants to break up with you because you do not mean enough. That is the action of a man who cared enough to put yours and Ruthie's feelings first. He thinks this will hurt you. He thinks him having this disease will hurt you.'

'It does,' Anna said, tears building up again. 'It really *really* does.'

And she had told him all about Nanny Gwen and how awful that had been. And Sam had let her talk and held her and told her he couldn't imagine how that must have felt to go through. She held her breath, pain beating at her chest.

'So, what are you going to do?' Neeta asked her. 'Before you found this out, you were going to call him.'

'I know.'

'So, has this changed anything?'

'I don't know.' She put her head in her hands, still clutching her phone. 'Will he want me to call him now I know? Will he think it's *because* I know that I'm calling him?'

'Anna,' Neeta said. 'You are doing that thing again. Considering what everyone else wants. What do *you* want?'

Anna didn't need to think too hard about that. Since reading the news article, and everything she could in forty minutes, about Huntington's, there had only been one thing on her mind. Hearing his voice. Feeling his arms around her again. Watching him smile. Bridging the distance, somehow. There was only one answer.

'I want to call him,' Anna told her.

'Of course you do,' Neeta said, nodding.

With shaking hands, she found his number in her contacts. She pressed on the number and put the phone to her ear, closing her eyes and thinking about what she was going to say. 'Hello' would be a good start but after that she didn't really know. She needed to stop overthinking, let instinct guide her maybe.

But then the dial tone changed and a female American voice began to speak.

'What's happening?' Neeta asked. 'Do you have enough signal? I have never made a call on the stairs before but it cannot be an ideal location.'

Anna shook her head, swallowing a lump in her throat, tears on the brink of falling down her face again. 'It's not the network,' she told Neeta. 'It says the number is no longer available.'

'It must be a mistake,' Neeta said, looking like she wanted to grab hold of the phone. 'Try it again. Or video call him on Instagram. That is what I did when Pavinder's second cousin blocked my number.'

Anna came out of her contacts and onto her social accounts, pressing on the pink camera icon. He hadn't posted since he had left, not even a story, but she had taken comfort in/cried over some of his older posts. She poked at the keyboard, beginning to type in his name. Usually it would be first in her list of 'recents' but it wasn't there. She pressed to search and waited a second. Sam Jackman, London. Sam Jackman, a female from Ontario. Where was Sam Jackman with a blue tick from Cincinnati?

'Your make-up looks great by the way,' Neeta said. 'So, video call him. I will stay here for support until he picks up and then I will get Ruthie another plate of biryani and tell her you are coming to listen to her sing Kate Bush.'

'He's not there,' Anna said, shock coating her vocal cords. 'His account is gone.'

'Do not be ridiculous!' Neeta exclaimed. 'Elon Musk does not own Instagram, does he? Accounts do not just disappear like that. Give it to me.'

But, as Anna handed her phone over, already her heart was sinking. How could she contact him now? And then she had a thought. What was his agent's name?

Sixty-Two

Cincinnati, Ohio, USA

'Oh shit! Shit!'

'Tionne! What is that language at my table? And why do you have your phone?'

'Sorry, Mom, but Sam . . . people know.'

The atmosphere stilled around the table in the middle of the Jackmans' small apartment piled high with festive food. The goat had been prepared, as well as jerk turkey, plantains, green beans, spicy potatoes and cornbread. Christmas dining had come early. The decorations were up in force too. The ugly rag dolls in red and green outfits had been placed around the main room like old-style Elfs on the Shelf, pictures had been framed with tinsel and there was their multi-coloured fake tree sitting on the console next to the TV looking like its best days had been around 1982.

From the look on Tionne's face, Sam didn't need any more information to know what it was that people knew. He gripped the fork in his hand and tried to keep his cool. It was inevitable that this was going to happen. Frankie had told him it was only a matter of time before someone sold the information about his diagnosis. Getting a new phone, a new phone number and deactivating his social accounts had stopped the noise a little, but now the reporters were going to be back.

'Maybe you guys should all go stay at the hotel again. Or a different hotel, there were some press there last time,' Sam suggested.

'No.' Albert said the word so firmly and with such utter determination it seemed there was to be no further discussion about it.

'Dad, I don't want you hounded day and night,' Sam told him anyway.

'And I do not want my life to become like yours,' his dad replied, putting down his cutlery. 'That was not my choice. My choice was to live simply. To work at a car lot. To come home and watch western films with a glass of rum. And that is what I will be doing, whether or not there are people with cameras at my front door.'

'I agree,' Dolores answered. 'We need to show people that we are not afraid. That we will go about our lives like we always have. At the moment, I feel like you are some wanted criminal and we are hiding from our shame. I am not ashamed. Of anything.'

'Oh, Mom,' Sam said. 'I don't want you to feel like that.'

'Then no more going to hotels in the dead of night like we are prisoners being taken to the state penitentiary,' his mom said. 'Pass the plantains, please.'

Sam picked up the tray and handed it across the table to his mother. His family were so strong. Stronger than he had given them credit for. They were all sitting here with a life-affecting issue hanging over their heads and they were still achieving a semblance of normality. Perhaps that was at the heart of all of this.

'What's the best car you have on the lot right now, Pop?' Sam asked his dad.

'Why?' his dad answered. 'Are you going to buy it so I get the commission? Like when you bought the car we have now and said you got it free because of a sponsorship deal?'

So his dad had known all along too. He didn't know how to respond.

'We are grateful, Sam,' his mom continued, serving Tionne more green beans she clearly did not want. 'For everything you've done for us since you got your big career break.'

He was sensing a 'but' coming and he had nothing to offer to make the conversation stop before his mom got to it.

'But money is just paper,' Albert told him. 'Not even that these days. It is numbers. Numbers that we pass to other people for things, from numbers that people have passed to us. That's it.' He took a sip of his root beer. 'I might go to work to put food on the table but that is not the only reason. I go there to have purpose. I get up in the morning and I see how I can help someone else have a good day.'

And that's what Sam was missing, from his work, from his life. Sure, he might help his team attain victory but that wasn't the 'help' his father was talking about. His father was talking about raw care, the kind of spirit that came from old-fashioned values, the way he had been brought up by his parents, the way Sam and Tionne had been raised. Sam had thought that coming from a home with very little it was his duty to achieve more, give back, succeed in ways that wouldn't have been possible for his parents. But his dad was telling him that success wasn't measured by trophies and dollar bills, it wasn't even measured by hard work, it was measured by strength of purpose and how you treat others.

'That is why . . . I did not have the test,' Albert informed.

'What?!' Tionne exclaimed. 'What did you just say? You didn't have the test?!'

'Dad, you said you had the test,' Sam said, shocked by this sudden admission.

'No,' Albert stated. 'I did not say I had the test. I said that I *went* for the test. But, when I got there, I decided the test did not matter to me.' He shrugged. 'I am almost sixty already. Why should I care if I have this gene or not? Something is going to kill me one day. It may as well be that.'

'Mom, did you know about this?' Tionne asked, knocking her knife with her elbow and sending it clattering to the floor. 'Did you not have the test either?'

'Yes, I knew,' Dolores admitted. 'It was your father's choice. Just like it was my choice and your choice, Tionne. I had the test because if I have the gene it is likely that your father does not. Isn't that right?'

'No, Mom, it doesn't work exactly like that.' Sam put his hands to his hair and twiddled with the strands there. 'It's more complicated than that. You could both have it. In rarer cases, none of you could have it. I just—'

'I decided that as I would not be booking myself onto an all-inclusive cruise of the Caribbean islands if I was positive for the gene and I would still be getting up every day and going out to sell cars, it did not matter to me one way or the other,' Albert concluded.

Tionne was shaking her head in frustration, but Sam got it. He wouldn't know he had this if it wasn't for the Diggers needing a biopsy of every inch of him. If he could change that course, if he could renege on the idea of this transfer somehow and be in blissful ignorance, would he? For a second, he wondered how that would feel, to not have the weight of it across his shoulders, but then, super-quickly, he realised that finding out, meeting Dr Monroe and having that diagnosis handed to him had made him fly. Literally. December in Richmond would never have been on his calendar. So without knowing he had this, he would never have met Anna. Never have *loved* Anna.

'Sam,' his mother said, eyeballing him from down the table. 'Are you feeling alright?'

He nodded. 'Yeah, I . . . I want to tell you about something. About someone.'

His mom sat a little straighter in her chair and paid closer attention to him instead of the jerk turkey.

'I've met someone,' Sam announced. 'Her name is Anna.'

Sixty-Three

Anna and Ruthie's home, Richmond

'Ruthie, this is impossible. I can't wrap presents and keep an eye on Mr Rocket and Cheesecake. One wants to eat the other and in between that they are kicking my Sellotape all over the room!' It was the 19th of December, school was finished now and all that was left to do before Christmas Day was wrapping gifts and trying to resist cracking open the Baileys. There was one final festive show for Ruthie tomorrow – the tap dance group extravaganza at the chapel – and then it would be time to baste the turkey crown and try not to sob into a selection box about the fact the man she cared for more than any other had blocked her from his life.

Anna looked up from the gift she was wrapping. Ruthie was kick ball changing around the living room, her arms outstretched, her expression completely focused.

'Did you hear me?' Anna asked.

'Yes,' Ruthie replied, continuing the tap dance. 'I'm trying to process who wants to eat the other and who is kicking the sticky tape.'

'Cheesecake!' Anna said. 'For both scenarios!'

'Mum, you sound a bit stressed. Do you want to light some incense? As long as it's not the one that smells like sweat, I don't mind.'

Anna had no idea that she had any incense that smelled like sweat but Ruthie did have a very good nose. And yes, she was stressed. Because the perfect Christmas she had been planning was slipping away from her. Feast had sucked up all the time and energy she'd had when she hadn't been off in some dating dreamland. Did she regret that choice? She mused on it for a second. No, she didn't. She'd loved every second she'd spent with Sam. But, to make himself unreachable, especially with this health diagnosis out in the news, was unfair. And, surely, Frankie must check her messages. OK, after one too many wines and Celine Dion ringing in her ears, it might not have been the finest message Anna had ever left, but no response at all bordered on cruel. Unless the number she had found on the web was out of date . . .

She sighed. 'Ruthie, why don't you have a rest and come and help me with these gifts?' Currently, she was regretting her present choices because every single thing seemed to be an odd shape.

'I can't rest,' Ruthie announced, still powering around in circles that would make even the most competent dancer feel dizzy. 'I want to be perfect for tomorrow.'

'You're always perfect,' Anna reminded her. 'And sometimes if you *over* practise, well that's when things can go wrong.'

Ruthie stopped dancing immediately. 'That's not true, is it?' Her eyes were bulging in shock now and Anna regretted saying it. Now Ruthie was going to worry about that.

'Well, sometimes that can happen. But not often. Maybe. But it won't hurt to have a rest for a minute, will it? Come and hold the Sellotape or hold Cheesecake. He's sniffing around Mr Rocket's carrier again.'

'I think they're finally friends,' Ruthie announced, picking up her cat and then sitting down with them, encasing them a little in her crossed-legged position as she groomed their fur with her fingers. 'They just needed to get used to each other.'

Anna wasn't so sure. She certainly wasn't about to let them curl up by the wood burner together any time soon.

'I sent Sam a message last night,' Ruthie announced.

'Oh, did you?'

'He didn't reply.'

Anna swallowed. 'Oh, sweetheart, maybe . . . he was busy.' She had kept the fact that she couldn't get hold of Sam from Ruthie. What good would it do?

Ruthie shook her head. 'I don't think so. He usually responds in two minutes. I looked back at his other messages and that was the average response time.' She looked up from Cheesecake grooming and hit Anna with a direct gaze. 'Do you think it's because he's sick? With Huntington's disease?'

Now Anna's heart was breaking anew. She hadn't discussed *that* with Ruthie either. She knew Kai might have told her or shown her, but Anna wasn't going to raise it unless Ruthie raised it first. A lot of the time Ruthie dealt with things by vague acknowledgement that they had happened and then quickly moving forward to a mental place where she felt more comfortable. Someone died, you knew that, you accepted it because you couldn't change it, the world kept turning and you clung to your routines . . .

'I don't think he's unwell yet,' Anna said softly. 'But obviously he has a lot going on and—'

'And that's why he's ignoring me?' Ruthie asked.

What could she say? His number wasn't available but what did that really mean? The same with his social media accounts. Were they gone for everyone or just for her and her friends? No, the thought that he had blocked her, cut her and Ruthie off like that, was madness. That wasn't anything like the behaviour of the Sam she had got to know. This had to be about the press attention. Except it meant there was no way for her to reach out to him. And Ruthie was continuing to reach out, expecting a response.

'I don't think he's deliberately ignoring you, Ruthie—'

'Can you ignore people in a non-deliberate way?' Ruthie queried, looking puzzled.

'I don't think he can be getting your messages. His phone . . . remember the screen was broken? I expect he's had to get a new one. I think maybe he's going to get a new phone number but sometimes that takes time to set up.'

She didn't want to tell Ruthie that this could possibly be anything else, not before her Christmas show, something she had worked so hard towards for so long.

'I read about the disease and it says that people can start to be unwell from their thirties but most of them are a lot older. And it takes them quite a long time to actually die. A bit like Nanny Gwen.'

Anna took a breath. Sam was almost twenty-six. Things could start to decline in a few years or, equally, things could remain dormant for much, much longer. She wanted to speak to him so badly, to tell him how she still felt about him, regardless of any diagnosis, but there was one thing having the courage of her convictions, but it was quite another to constantly have brick walls that didn't exist before put up in your path.

'He's really not going to come to my tap dance performance, is he?' Ruthie said in matter-of-fact tones.

Was Anna going to dress this up? Would it be kinder to give her an 'I don't know, maybe' answer or a 'we'll see'? Or was it better to be completely honest, about this at least?

'I don't think so, Ruthie,' Anna admitted. 'But Dad is coming. And Nicolette. And Neeta, Pavinder, Lisa, Paul, Kai and Kelsey will all be there too.'

'They're only coming for the mulled wine and the mince pies,' Ruthie said with an eyeroll. 'Kai said he wants to attempt to break the Guinness World Record for the fastest time to eat three mince pies. At the moment it stands at 52. 21 seconds.'

'They're coming because they want to see how fabulous you and the rest of your group are,' Anna reassured. She knew mostly they were coming for her, the still-single mum in the group who would always be so grateful for her friends.

'Will you take a video and lots of pictures?' Ruthie asked. 'So that when Sam feels better and has a new phone number we can send them to him and he won't have missed the show.'

Anna's heart ached all over again but she managed a nod as her eyes welled up with tears. 'Of course I will.'

'OK,' Ruthie answered. 'That's enough resting now.' She clambered up from the floor much to Cheesecake's chagrin. 'I wonder what Guinness World Records there are for tap dancing.'

Ruthie began to tap all over again and, ignoring the current gift Anna was trying to get wrapped – an AFC Wimbledon calendar and mug for Paul – she picked up her phone. No new notifications. Was this really how it was going to end?

Sixty-Four

Cincinnati, North Kentucky Airport, USA

'Are you out of your mind, Sam? I mean, seriously, I get what you're going through but a *vacation*? Now? When you've just come back?'

Sam knew Frankie was going to explode when he'd asked her to meet him here at the airport. He'd been given a side room, but the press knew he was here. They were still camping outside his apartment and he'd run out of energy to even engage with them. They all had the same damn questions. *Is your career over, Sam? Can we have a comment on – insert old NFL star's name – interview where he said you'll never play pro again? How are your family?*

'Frankie,' Sam said, firm but fatigued. 'You really *don't* get what I'm going through.'

Just that one sentence was enough for the pitbull temperament to chill a little. Frankie's shoulders sagged slightly, her mouth got less taut, she didn't look quite like she wanted to club him over the head with a baseball bat.

'OK, bad choice of words but Sam, now this is in the open we have options. And I know you mightn't be ready to make any decisions yet, but we can look at different ideas . . . and the Bisons want to talk.'

Did they? Chad had come round but he hadn't wanted to see him, hadn't wanted to see anyone from his team yet. But Chad never gave up easily and Sam had heard the roar

329

of reporters outside, baying for a sound bite. Eventually Sam had given in and buzzed Chad up. It turned out Sam had needed that bro hug more than he had realised and before either of them knew it there were tears. A couple of beers later, and Sam began to realise that there was much more than simple comradeship between them. Whatever superficial life he had led being a walking advertisement and touchdown king, Chad's friendship wasn't only about the game and the team. He had always been there for him. But still Sam couldn't help thinking that, no matter what, Chad and all the others were going to see him as different now. Not the same Sam who went to poker games or was club champion at drills. And there was some truth to it. He *was* changed, how could he not be?

'Sam, you are their best player. The world knows that. And what's wrong with you might not be erasable, but it's not . . . I don't know . . . losing an arm or . . . being given weeks to live.'

Sam stared at Frankie then and waited for the businesswoman in her to shrink back even further. Yes, he was her commodity, just like he was a product for the Bisons, but this was his future, not as a player or a celebrity, but as a man.

'Frankie, I'm taking a holiday. I'm going to Bermuda. I need to be away right now. From everything.' He took a breath. 'I'm gonna be spending my time doing all the things I don't get to do when I'm training. I'm gonna drink cocktails and eat all kinds of cuisine and I'm gonna switch off from all this, completely.'

Frankie was assessing him now, in this airport side room with harsh lighting and absolutely no semblance of the season anywhere. Her expression was saying she wasn't sure she believed him.

'When you say "switch off" what exactly do you mean? Because I'm certain the Bisons could do a meeting on Zoom while you drink cocktails and eat all kinds of cuisine.'

'I mean uncontactable, Frankie. Totally. *Only* if there's an emergency with my parents do you contact me. It's Christmas in a couple days. Everything stops for Christmas.'

'Apparently not the cocktails on the sand,' Frankie said through gritted teeth.

Sam didn't wait for her to say anything else. He pulled her into a bear hug and held on like he was tackling someone in the game.

'What are you doing?' came Frankie's muffled voice from inside his embrace. 'I have my iPad inside my jacket. You're crushing it. You're crushing *me*!'

'Enjoy the holidays, Frankie,' Sam said, still holding on. 'Go see your sister and your nephews.'

'Oh, OK, you get Bermuda and relaxation and I get a Christmas straight out of the *Mickey Mouse Clubhouse*.'

Sam smiled at her comment and finally let go. Frankie came out of the huddle a bit crumpled, pulling at her suit jacket.

'You don't really have your iPad in there, do you?' Sam asked her.

'Maybe,' she answered.

'Turn it off,' Sam told her. 'For a few days, for Christmas. Go outside, find some nature and get inside it.'

Nature. He remembered everything Anna had said about her feelings on nature. He wondered if she had read the latest news and knew about *this*. That was exactly the kind of nature that freaked her out. The kind that had happened during Ruthie's creation, the same type that had slowly taken away her grandmother. It was too late to think about that now. He'd made his decision.

'I did a lumberjack weekend once,' Frankie admitted. 'Nothing but trees and saws and . . . more trees.'

'Wow,' Sam replied. 'Did you get an award?'

'I got poison ivy. That's what I got. The rash took weeks to clear.'

'Not ideal,' Sam answered. 'But better than cramp in your fingers from all that double-tapping.'

'OK, so, you're going to Bermuda and I'm going to . . . consider calling my sister. Maybe.'

'Atta girl,' Sam said.

'But do you think we could put a date in the planner to catch up? I've pulled the "exceptional circumstances" clause in your contract so you're not in breach with the Bisons but I'm getting a little itchy like I have that rash back just thinking about letting you go and leaving things open-ended.'

'I'll call you,' Sam said.

'Right . . . but when? Because—'

'*I* will call *you*, Frankie, OK?'

He could see she was straining to keep herself in check. He reached into the pocket of his jacket then and produced a wrapped gift. Wrapped by the store back in London, not him. 'This is for you.'

'Sam! A gift? You know how I feel about gifts.'

'I know. You think no one ever knows you well enough to buy you anything you'd actually like. And you always have to pretend and that's exhausting, yadda, yadda, yadda.'

'And now I'm cut to the quick. And impressed that you do really listen to me.' Frankie took the package and shook it. 'Is it fragile?'

'Yes,' he said. 'But it survived a flight so unless you give it to your nephews to toss around, I'm sure it'll be good.'

'Well, then, thank you,' Frankie said. 'But I haven't gotten you anything.'

'Yes, you have,' Sam said. 'You're not gonna call me until I call you.'

She smiled, shaking her head. 'Well, then, I guess all that's left for me to say is, happy holidays.'

'Happy holidays, Frankie,' Sam replied.

Sixty-Five

Holy Trinity Church, Richmond

'I can't believe it's actually snowing! Real snow. In Richmond! I don't even care if it gets on my Richard Branson T-shirt, it's snow. Snow!'

Ruthie had been excitable from the moment she woke up on tap dance performance day, but when she had drawn the curtains back and seen a fine sheen of white coating the street and the roofs of the houses opposite she had screamed so loudly Anna had at first thought there was a large spider that needed to be removed or there had been some calamity with Ruthie's clean laundry pile. Both usually warranted a similar kind of reaction. But, no, it had been festive weather, bringing a little winter magic to their street and making Cecil and his other animatronic friends in Mr Penderghast's front garden really look like they belonged.

And now they were here, outside this beautiful church, the snow was falling again. Minute flakes, nothing that was going to stop traffic or warrant train cancellations, but it was pretty, perfect to set the mood for this collection of Christmas offerings from local choral and dance groups. This was the exact time in December when Anna felt her most festive. Presents were wrapped – kind of – food was organised – mainly, although Ruthie was now insisting that her pets needed feline and rabbit versions of a Christmas dinner – and her clients were happy.

Mr Wong was *more* than happy actually. He had sent

her – via the office – a bottle of champagne and a ten per cent off voucher for a Full Feast visit. Ruthie was probably going to be more excited about the idea of that than she was about any of her other gifts. But this year didn't feel quite the same and, as the days went by, and there was no response to the message she had left for Sam's agent, Anna was beginning to wonder whether there ever would be. When did she call full-time on it? And would Sam ever know that she had tried to contact him? Would it make any kind of difference?

'Ruthie! Say goodbye to Mum and come through, darling,' the tap dance group leader called from the entrance of the Grade II listed building adorned with holly wreaths and festive flowers.

'Bye, Mum!' Ruthie said, waving and running off before Anna could react. She watched Ruthie ducking away from offered fist bumps but offering out her elbow instead and she realised, perhaps for the first time, that Ruthie was really growing up and getting more independent in thoughts and in actions. Anna couldn't wrap her up and shelter her from the world, Ruthie would have to find her own way through her challenges. Anna could feel now that she really would.

'Morning, Anna.'

It was Ed's voice and she turned around expecting to greet him *and* Nicolette. Except Ed was on his own.

'Hello,' she said. 'You're—'

'"Early" I think the word is,' Ed said, beaming. 'I don't think I've ever been early in my entire life. It feels a bit odd. But in a good way.'

'Is Nicolette not coming?'

'Not this time,' Ed answered. 'She's decided to . . . take her time with Ruthie. Build a relationship slowly . . . with the help of Ruthie's favourite snacks when she stays over next.'

Anna smiled. 'That's a really good idea. And very thoughtful.'

'I have promised to video though. Videos are allowed, aren't they?'

'I hope so,' Anna said. She remembered her promise to film Ruthie's performance to share with Sam. She had to keep that promise for Ruthie's sake even if nothing came from it.

'Right, well, I'll go in and take a pew with a good vantage point. Do you want me to save you a seat?' Ed asked.

'Thanks,' Anna answered. 'But I'm waiting here for everyone.'

'Of course you are. Right, I will see you after the big show,' Ed said, heading towards the archway.

Anna took a breath and drank in her surroundings. She had so much to be thankful for. Living in the area she had always loved, in Nanny Gwen's house she had made into the perfect home, with Ruthie and two annoying pets she really couldn't imagine life without now and there was Ed, really trying and acknowledging his mistakes, stepping in again and hopefully stepping up for his daughter.

The Christmas tree at the entrance was half the size of Malcolm, with baubles that looked older than God, but it was lit up nicely and seemed to be a meeting point for parents and performers alike. Anna checked her watch.

'We are not late,' Neeta said, suddenly at Anna's elbow. 'I made sure of it.'

'And we promise our bodies won't start to hiss and steam when we get inside,' Pavinder added with a grin.

Anna smiled at the well-worn joke. Neeta and Pavinder always came to the Anglican church to see this event, ever since Ruthie started performing in it. They had assured Anna some time ago that watching children dancing wearing tinsel for necklaces and imitating reindeers was not worshipping a god they weren't supposed to.

'Actually—'

'Do not tell Anna yet,' Pavinder said. 'I want it to be a surprise when we get together at New Year.'

Neeta stopped talking and, in fact, stopped moving, her earrings completely motionless. This was new. Neeta usually didn't stop talking for anyone or anything.

'Well,' Anna said. 'I have no idea what you were going to say, so hang on to the excitement. It's always nice to have something to toast on New Year's Eve.'

'But, Pavinder,' Neeta began. 'I could just say—'

'Please,' Pavinder interrupted again. 'Do the best things not come to those who wait?'

'I have no evidence for that yet. And what is waiting? Because theoretically we are all waiting to die and if the best thing coming to those who are waiting is death then I think I am entitled to—'

This time Pavinder silenced her with a kiss. It was a loving moment that Anna hadn't seen from them in quite some time. Even if she didn't know what Neeta wanted to share, this said quite a lot on its own.

'Here come Lisa and Paul and the children,' Pavinder said, taking hold of Neeta's hand. 'Let us find a seat before you feel you need to tell anyone else our plans.'

'One second, Pavinder. Let me have a moment with Anna,' Neeta said, giving his hand a squeeze.

'Not a word,' Pavinder said, letting her go and putting a finger to his lips.

'I promise,' Neeta replied.

Anna pulled her woollen wrap around her closer as a chill wind started to blow the snowflakes in her direction.

'How are you doing?' Neeta asked, her dark eyes scrutinising Anna but in the kindest of ways.

'I'm fine,' Anna answered. 'I've got all my presents wrapped but soz if you find cat hair or rabbit fur on the Sellotape.'

'And now, how about an answer that does not sound like it has come from the mouth of a politician?'

Anna sighed, eyes at the door of the church where the vicar was welcoming more people into the building through the flurry of snowflakes. 'I'm . . . grateful for Ruthie and our health and food on the table and I'm . . . you know . . . I'm . . . trying to keep swimming.' She swallowed a knot of emotion in her throat. 'But it's hard to keep swimming when it's cold outside and you're back on your own when, just for a moment, swimming had become a team event and the water was warm and there were headstands and cocktails and a horse and carriage and falling asleep to a Marvel mini-series.'

'Oh, Anna,' Neeta said, opening her arms and getting ready to hug.

'No, honestly, I'm OK. I get it, you know. Sam's always done what he thinks is right, from the moment we met when he was helping Ruthie with the bullies. And if he's doing what he thinks is right now then I have to respect that.' She sniffed away her tears. 'And, as he's not on Instagram right now it means I can't stalk his feed and ugly cry when I have a down moment.'

'Guess what?' Lisa said, busting into the group.

Neeta gave their friend an eyeroll at her lack of tact.

'What?' Anna asked, putting a finger to the corner of her eye and dashing away a tear.

'I know I may not have kept my end of the bargain at the Not Christmas Christmas party but . . . I did it. I did it this morning!' Lisa exclaimed.

'I have no idea what you are talking about,' Neeta replied.

'Next weekend, and every alternate weekend after that, *I'm* getting the film choice and I can tell you it's going to be high-def Statham, Momoa and Pattinson all the way.' Lisa punched the air like she was a Wimbledon winner.

'So now you are going to be commenting on the physiques of men like Paul was with women. That is not making any kind of stand,' Neeta told her. 'What you needed to do was tell him how his comments about the actresses made you feel. Then you need to find a joint interest where both of you feel valued and respected.'

'God,' Lisa remarked. 'What's happened? Have you got to the bottom of what's going on with Pav and Jessica?'

'Yes,' Neeta replied. 'And there is nothing going on. And

I cannot tell you any more about our new joint interest because Pav wants to get the timing right.'

Anna sighed. Yes, getting the timing right seemed to be crucial in the success of pretty much everything. It was a shame she'd never been able to control that particular clock.

'Can Kelsey and me wait outside?' Kai asked, hands around a Nintendo Switch console as he, Paul and Kelsey arrived.

'No,' Lisa answered. 'You're watching Ruthie.'

'Yeah, I know,' Kai answered. 'But I don't know any of the other million kids dancing and singing, do I?'

'Have some respect, Kai. Your mum, sister and I don't know all the other kids at any of your rugby tournaments but we still turn up for all the games . . . in the pouring rain . . . or wind . . . or snow.' Paul put his hands out signifying the flakes raining from the sky.

'Alright,' Kai said, disgruntled. 'I get it.'

'Come on,' Kelsey said, ruffling her twin's hair.

'Get off!'

'Anna,' Neeta said, touching her arm as everyone else moved off towards the church porch. 'Are you coming in to get a seat?'

Anna's attention was out of the churchyard and focused on the road, cars with their lights on because of the poor visibility, the grass of Twickenham Green opposite speckled with white, people wrapped up in coats walking dogs or toddlers on reins. It was calm, peaceful, it was home.

'Yes,' Anna answered Neeta. 'Let's go inside.'

Sixty-Six

'Do you think Ruthie looks a bit peaky?' Anna asked as Ruthie's tap dance group waited at the side for their turn to perform. They had seen several dance troupes, two small bands and a local primary school reciting festive poems. It really was the perfect start to the winding-down period before Christmas to get people in the spirit.

'I do not know,' Neeta whispered loudly. 'The lighting in this place is very abstract.'

Anna tried to catch Ruthie's eye, but her daughter's head was down, eyes on her feet. Maybe she was running through her steps? Counting the beats and memorising the patterns? Something was definitely off.

'You do not think she will be sick do you?' Neeta asked.

'I really hope not,' Anna said, feeling her breath catch in her chest.

Finally, Ruthie looked up from her shoes and into the congregation. But then, just as quickly, she dropped her eyes back down again. Anna turned in her pew and looked around at the rest of the audience. Was there someone picking their nose or being less than hygienic about a sneeze? That could be enough to unsettle Ruthie. There were a few people with phones taking photos or getting ready to record but that didn't usually bother her daughter. But then . . . Anna saw what it was that was upsetting Ruthie, or rather who.

'It's Acne Aaron and Gross Gregory,' Anna hissed to Neeta. 'What are they doing here?'

Neeta looked over her shoulder too. 'Those horrible bullies? Ugh, they are making faces and rude gestures. Where are their parents? Or why are they not behind a bus station somewhere drinking cheap vodka?'

'What should I do?' Anna asked. 'If they make Ruby feel uncomfortable then she won't be able to concentrate on her performance. And she's worked so, *so* hard on it.' This was the very last thing they needed.

'Do you want me to go and tell them to stop?' Neeta asked. 'It has been a while since I exercised my dealing-with-teenager tones.'

Anna's eyes were back on Ruthie again. But when she looked this time, her daughter was back to smiling, eyes bright, excitement obvious as she gazed out into the audience, body language completely changed. Anna turned in her seat again, wondering if the boys had done something to redeem themselves. But no . . . they had . . . moved seats or . . . disappeared or . . . was she going mad? Had they even been there in the first place?

'Neeta, you saw them, right? Gregory and Aaron, sitting halfway back.'

'Yes, they were pulling facial expressions that resembled gargoyles,' Neeta said.

'Well, where have they gone?' Anna asked. And, more importantly, were they coming back? She didn't want that possibility hanging over proceedings.

'Ruthie's group are coming on,' Neeta said clapping her hands. 'Pavinder, video!'

Anna clapped her hands as hard as she could and waved at Ruthie as her girl sashayed onto the stage with her restored warm smile and showstopping confidence, dark curls bouncing. *OK, breathe. This is going to be great!*

'Oh, Ruthie! You were amazing! Fantastic! Brilliant! Stupendous! Out of this world—'

'Neeta, leave some words for other people to use,' Lisa said. 'Ruthie, you were the star of the show. Wasn't she, Kelsey?'

'Ruthie, you have to teach me that move you did when you bent right over and sprung back up again,' Kelsey said.

Anna watched, letting her friends have this moment. There would be time later for her to wrap her arms around her girl and tell her exactly what a superstar she was. The tap dance troupe's performance had been the routine of the day, although the pyrotechnics seemed to have come as a bit of a surprise to the vicar. All the group had given one hundred per cent and had danced and tapped – and performed magic – to a medley of upbeat festive tunes and then, randomly, Tight Fit's 'The Lion Sleeps Tonight'. . .

'I know we're probably biased but I think Ruthie was the best of them all,' Ed said, arriving at Anna's shoulder.

'We are biased,' Anna agreed. 'But that doesn't mean we're wrong.'

'Absolutely,' Ed agreed.

'I was worried for a minute. Those horrible boys from the school were here and Ruthie was looking like she might throw up but then they . . . just . . . disappeared.'

'Perhaps it was divine intervention,' Ed suggested. 'We are in a church after all. Or maybe they got bored. Church used to bore the pants off me when I was a teenager.'

'Dad,' Ruthie greeted, a combination of glitter and sweat on her shiny forehead as she bounded up to them.

The church was now a hub of parents and children hugging and congratulating, trying not to knock holly and ivy wreaths from the pews, the organist playing a roaring rendition of 'O Little Star of Bethlehem'.

'Ruthie!' Ed said, waiting patiently to see if this was a hug or high-five or neither moment. 'I . . . have showered this morning.'

Ruthie jumped for an embrace and Anna felt her heart lift. This was so heart-warming to see.

'I saw you watching,' Ruthie told him. 'The *whole* time.'

'I couldn't take my eyes off you,' Ed admitted. 'You were swinging your legs one way and then charging over the other

341

side and sprinkling magic over everyone. I liked the storyline of the unicorns being hypnotised and made bad and then everything coming together in the end.'

'A bit like with us,' Ruthie said, finally letting him go. 'Except you weren't hypnotised . . . and you're not a unicorn.'

'And I'd like to think I'm not all bad,' Ed added.

'You were brilliant, Ruthie. I think there might be some ice cream in your very near future,' Anna told her.

'Mint choc chip?' Ruthie asked.

'How did you guess?'

'Well, I wouldn't have been brilliant if Acne Aaron and Gross Gregory had kept making faces and rude signs at me. But luckily Sam got rid of them. Like he did the last time.'

Anna froze. What had Ruthie said? *Sam?* Ruthie did like mentally creating worlds she could feel safe in, but she had never imagined seeing a person before.

'Ruthie,' Anna said. 'What do you mean? Exactly.'

'Sam got hold of Acne Aaron and Gross Gregory, one hood in each hand, and he pulled them out of the pew and took them outside,' Ruthie explained. 'And then he came back in and he sat at the back to watch my performance and—'

'Hello, Anna.'

342

Sixty-Seven

The low rumble of Sam's deep, beautiful voice almost killed Anna. It took a second to stop reacting emotionally and let her brain catch up. She turned around quickly now and there he was. All six-foot-whatever-it-was, dressed smartly in dark trousers and a fawn-coloured jumper. But as she took him in, everything else inside her was stalling as she attempted to put together the pieces.

'I knew you'd come!' Ruthie exclaimed, running at Sam and leaping up at his frame.

Anna watched him catch her, holding her up high for a second before dropping her back down to the ground again.

'And thank you for getting rid of Acne Aaron and Gross Gregory. I was going to follow your advice and run at them, but they were sitting down and I didn't want Mrs Langdown to think I wasn't going to perform so—'

'You were fantastic out there,' Sam told her. 'I totally loved the whole unicorn story if I'm honest.'

'I said that,' Ed answered. He held out his hand to Sam. 'It's good to see you here.'

Sam didn't hesitate to shake Ed's offering. 'It's good to see you here too.'

'Mum, why aren't you saying anything? I told you Sam would be here! I know you didn't believe me but—'

'Ruthie, why don't we see if it's still snowing outside. I'm not sure there will be enough to even make a snowball, but we can give it a go, right?' Ed suggested.

'Will you pick the snow up though?' Ruthie asked. 'Because I can't touch it without my gloves.'

'Of course I can,' Ed answered, virtually steering Ruthie

down the aisle and towards the door. 'Nicolette has also given me this.' He patted his jeans. 'It's a little sanitiser bottle I can clip to my belt.'

'That's really cool.'

Anna watched Ruthie heading out of the church with her dad. The organist had stopped playing and the audience was thinning out now, everyone keen to head to where there was going to be refreshments for performers and watchers alike. And she was stood here, in the aisle, wondering what came next.

'I . . . didn't know you were coming,' Anna said. That sentence was entirely inadequate for this moment, but she really didn't know where to begin.

'No,' he breathed. 'I got a new cell phone. I deactivated all my social media. I just wanted to reset a few things while I have the chance.'

'Ruthie thought you were ignoring her when you didn't respond.' Anna swallowed. She was saying 'Ruthie' but she was really saying 'we'. As time had gone on, she had started to wonder if he was going to permanently cut her out of his life . . .

'I know I promised her, but I didn't know if I was gonna make it here on time. My flight got delayed and this visit my cab driver drove like he had nowhere to get to so . . . I was a little late.'

The silence was loud, almost as loud as Anna's heartbeat in her ears. What did she say? Part of her wanted to simply hold him close, let his strength seep into her, forget everything else they had going on for a bit longer. But the other part of her knew that there were many questions to address.

'Do you . . . know?' Sam asked, his voice scratchy, hesitant.

Anna opened her mouth to answer but found she couldn't. She knew what he meant. He meant about his illness. And she didn't have any words. She offered a nod.

He shook his head. 'I am so sorry, Anna. I . . . should have told you. Maybe right from the very beginning. It wasn't fair to make out that I was . . . normal.'

'Normal?' Anna offered, as the last remaining members of the congregation headed from the building.

'Wrong choice of word. Bad, bad word option.' He shook his head. 'I don't know, I headed over here because I was terrified of the news I'd just found out. I didn't know what I was doing, I didn't know what to think. And then, when I found out more, I had this responsibility of my family weighing on me.' He put a hand to one of the pews. 'That hurts me the most. To think of them getting sick and going through what Huntington's hands out.'

'I read about the disease,' Anna said. 'When I saw the news on the internet.'

'Yeah?' Sam asked.

'I tried to call you,' she admitted. 'And then I tried to find you on Insta and anywhere at all and . . . well.' She shrugged.

'Oh, God, Anna, what a mess.' He shook his head.

'I almost gave up,' she said, leaning against the pew. 'Except Neeta and Ed – believe it or not – told me that it doesn't matter what the circumstances are, if you believe something is right, you should chase it until every last chance is exhausted.' She took a deep breath. 'I left a message with your agent. Frankie. At least, I think it was her . . . I had had quite a lot to drink by that stage.'

'Anna,' Sam said, reaching out and putting a hand on your shoulder. 'I shouldn't have run away from you like I did. I told Ruthie back when we first met that fear is something you can take control of and own. Sometimes there are situations where it's better to run towards that fear rather than away from it.' He paused for a second before carrying on. 'I didn't follow my own advice and . . . that was a mistake.'

'What are you saying, Sam?' Anna asked, her lips trembling.

'I'm saying . . . I should have told you what was going on with me. Because you were upfront and open from the second we met and I disrespected you by not showing you the same courtesy.' He inhaled. 'I know that we said it was casual and tentative, but I think we both know it outgrew that.' He smiled a little. 'Like a force of nature. Like stars colliding.'

Anna didn't know how to respond. Did Sam feel exactly the same way she did? She shook her head. 'It hurt me when you left. More than it had any right to.'

'For me too,' he admitted. 'And for what it's worth, I regretted it the second my ass left the heated seats of Neeta's car and my bare feet hit the pavement.'

'So, why didn't you call? Tell me you felt like that?'

'Because I had to go to my family and tell them about . . . Dallas and about . . . this gene. It felt like this balloon that was starting to get bigger and bigger and bigger and I felt like I had to handle it before it burst on me.'

Sam's breath was starting to get harder to find and he stopped talking for a second and focused on trying to control it. He looked to the large church candles, burning brightly on the altar, flames tall, strong and steady. That's what he had to be now.

'Are you OK?' Anna asked.

He inhaled, long and slow then he gazed at her. Beautiful Anna. She had steadied his ship when he needed a safe haven. And then she had rocked him, the water underneath changing from a still calm to a current keen to swirl things up. There may be a storm ahead but how long the clouds would take to darken was anyone's guess. And, for now, Sam wanted to set sail. That was why he was here. To tell Anna that . . .

'I love you, Anna,' he whispered. That the words had left his lips threw him for a millisecond. But then it felt good, right. 'And it doesn't matter to me if you don't feel the same right now . . . or ever. I just need you to know that something we started such a short time ago . . . it's been more than I've ever felt with anyone before.'

'Sam—'

'Let me finish?' he asked. 'Because I prepared this whole speech on the plane over here . . . and then I realised how bad it was. So, I'm gonna freestyle.' He smiled. 'Now, I know that my circumstances right now are a lot different to how they were when you met me. And I know you're gonna need some time to think about all that, or not, because maybe you're already done with me. But I wanted to tell you exactly how I feel, whether that scares me or not. Because, while I was processing, everything was telling me to run towards you.' He took another breath and took her hands in his. 'I don't wanna make you feel like you felt with your nana. I don't wanna be the person making you cry your heart out because I end up so changed you can hardly remember why you cared for me in the first place.'

'Sam,' Anna said, as the tears started rolling down her cheeks. 'I had so many amazing years with my Nanny Gwen. I wouldn't have given up any of that just because her ending was incredibly sad. It's like . . . think of the things I would have missed out on. All those precious memories. She was part of my every day, every single day until she passed. And she gifted me my incredible house and that's somewhere Ruthie and I can feel safe and secure and happy.' She squeezed his hands. 'I don't want to miss out on a beautiful journey just because the ending might not be perfect.'

'Really?' Sam asked.

'Besides, there's always a chance that this Huntington's is going to be irrelevant. Any day you could be involved in a freak headstand accident.'

'That is true,' he answered with a nod.

'There's a lot to think about,' Anna admitted.

'Agreed.'

'And there's a lot to talk about.'

'Yeah,' he replied, his eyes meeting hers again.

'So, let's keep talking,' Anna told him. 'And thinking. And . . . this.'

'What?' Sam asked.

He was completely blindsided when she got up on tiptoes and pressed her lips to his. He wrapped his arms around her and kissed her back, the sensation of coming home filling his heart. He held her close and let everything quieten. This felt so right. No matter what his ending was destined to be, this felt like the best kind of beginning.

Sixty-Eight

Anna and Ruthie's home, Richmond

Christmas Eve

'I love that Mr Wong brought us food on Christmas Eve!' Ruthie said, waving a tempura prawn in the air.

'I love that too,' Sam admitted, passing her another takeaway box to pick from.

Anna loved that the two people she cared most for in the whole world were sat around her kitchen table laughing, smiling, playfully fighting over the next festive tune to get played.

'I can't believe you nailed his restaurant vision,' Sam told Anna. 'Full Feast and Fast Feast, all the different box sizes. And the food is real, real good.'

'Don't forget Free Feast,' Ruthie added.

'I love that too. You're good, Anna,' Sam said.

'I know,' she answered. 'And my boss has been reminded of that too. I'm going to be getting my teeth stuck into more projects in the New Year.' Currently her teeth were getting stuck into a chicken skewer.

'Are you staying here for New Year?' Ruthie asked Sam.

'I very much hope so,' Sam answered.

'And what about after that?' Ruthie said. 'February? How about Easter? And my birthday in May?'

'Ruthie, slow down or you're going to choke on your seafood,' Anna told her.

The truth was Anna was nervous about Ruthie thinking things were simple. Sam was here for Christmas, that was amazing. But there was still so much to consider. In Ruthie's eyes it was all very easy, Sam just stayed here with them and they all lived happily-ever-after. The end.

Cheesecake let out a whine from the utility room.

'Oh no!' Ruthie remarked. 'That's the "I've done a poo" noise.'

'Want me to go see?' Sam offered.

'No,' Ruthie said. 'I'm going to try. Mum bought me gloves, a scooper and nappy sacks for it to go in.' She stood up. 'But if it goes wrong I'm going to need wipes and sanitiser and a clear route to the bathroom.'

'I believe in you, Ruthie,' Anna told her as Ruthie headed to the door.

'Another rib?' Sam asked, offering up a box.

'No, thank you. I'm getting towards full.'

'And now you have dates running through your mind, am I right?'

Anna sighed. 'I'm sorry about Ruthie. She likes a plan. Not just for the near future, basically the whole of her life.'

'I get that,' Sam answered.

'And I get that you can't say how long you're going to be able to stay yet.'

'Hold that thought.'

Anna was confused. 'What does that mean?'

'It means . . .' He looked at his watch. 'Give me twenty minutes.'

'What? Why? I don't understand.'

'Mum!' Ruthie shouted. 'I need wipes! And Cheesecake has poo all over their face!'

Anna opened the door to a group of carol singers and she laughed when she realised they included Neeta and Lisa. It was one of her all time least favourite tunes – 'Good King Wenceslas' – and they were full-on murdering the melody.

'Did you arrange this?' Anna said to Sam as they listened from the front door.

'Maybe.'

'I have to tell you, I'm really not keen on carol singers,' Anna admitted.

'I have to tell *you*,' Sam answered, 'I know.' He grinned. 'Ruthie told me.'

Suddenly, Ruthie was behind Anna, barrelling out of the door dressed in her tie-dye coat and bright pink hat, heading down the pathway to the group.

'Ruthie, where are you going?' Anna called after her.

'I'm going singing,' Ruthie answered, joining Neeta and Lisa.

'Do not worry,' Neeta called. 'We will have her tucked up in bed before the made-up character in red arrives down the chimney no real person could fit into!'

'Sam,' Anna said, turning to him. 'What's going on?'

He smiled at her. 'We're gonna . . . do some more talking.'

Sixty-Nine

Richmond Terrace Gardens

'My Nanny Gwen used to love walking here,' Anna said, taking a deep breath of the cold night air. There was still a crust of white on everything, although there had been no new snowfall since the day of Ruthie's tap dance performance. Temperatures had plummeted and the snow had turned to a slush that got hard and crunchy at night. Here in the gardens, so full of flower in the summer, plants were naked in their beds. 'And she loved this naughty statue.'

Anna stopped walking by the pond, the water dark, plant life diminished. A large stone sculpture of the most voluptuous woman owned the space.

'I can admire those curves too,' Sam told her.

'It's Aphrodite,' Anna explained. 'A modern take that caused quite the stir back in the day. It was thought a little too realistic and verging on pornographic. The locals call it Bulbous Betty.'

'Is she riding a dolphin?' Sam asked.

'I'm not sure,' Anna replied.

'Well, I think I like her.'

'I like her too.'

Sam squeezed her hand. 'Will you sit down with me?'

'Here in the nature?' Anna asked. 'After the carol singers?'

He gave a half-smile. 'Facing our fears, right?'

They walked over to one of the wooden benches, and bracing her bottom for the cold, Anna sat down and Sam sat down next to her, taking her hand again.

'Christmas Eve,' he breathed.

'It is.'

'What are you wishing on the stars for this Christmas?' Sam asked.

'What I've been wishing for for quite some time now,' Anna said. 'Stability. Peace. No one to bring me any more pets.' She smiled. 'How about you?'

'I have a couple wishes.' He took a breath. 'For my mom and my sister to get negative test results. For my dad to have somehow escaped fate too. And for you . . . to say yes to my next question.'

She looked up at him, waiting for him to carry on.

'Anna, the moment I really realised what was most important in my life was when my pop gave me a talking to. He told me that he spends his life trying to make other people's lives better. That gives him all the purpose he needs to be happy in his own life and, when he told me that, I was kinda envious of him for feeling that way.' He paused for a beat. 'In the past I was motivated by money and success, not always in a "gimme the riches" kind of way, but in a way where I thought my parents not having a lot was something they needed to climb out of with my help. Turns out they like the simple life and my dad thinks money is a social construct. That wasn't his phrase, but that's definitely what he meant.'

'I like that,' Anna said. 'Spending time making other people's lives better and getting all you need from that. That's exactly how my Nanny Gwen was too.'

'My pop made me realise that no matter how long your life, your time in this world isn't all about you,' Sam said. 'It's about the people you touch in the time you're given.'

Anna felt her heart swell. It was such a beautiful sentiment and she knew, without a doubt, that she cared too much about Sam to ever think about turning back now.

'I promise you, Anna, and I promise Ruthie too, that for the time I'm given – be it three or four years or fifty more than that – I will spend those moments making you feel safe, giving you a little peace, loving you as hard as I can . . . and not buying any more pets. Unless Ruthie gives me that look with those big eyes she makes. Then I might not be able to refuse.'

'Oh, Sam,' Anna said squeezing his hand in hers.

'I know I can't give you a bigger family. We talked about the risk in that but—'

They *had* talked about the risk of that, the night he'd arrived back in Richmond and they'd curled up together in bed, touching, kissing, just crazy pleased to be back in each other's arms. He had told her, the way he felt right now, he wouldn't want to risk passing the gene down the line and she had told him that another child had never been on her agenda. Ruthie was it for her as a mother, a beautiful, full-on handful she marvelled at every day. But this was still new; a while down the line, maybe each of them would feel a little different.

They had also talked about how this disease was going to affect things for them both. It may be a waiting game and that *was* frightening, but you couldn't hide away from life waiting for death. Hopefully, depending on the results for Sam's family, Huntington's was going to be something they put away in the attic until it decided it was time to unbox itself.

'I'm waiting for the question you want me to say "yes" to,' Anna told him.

He took a deep breath. 'OK, here goes.' He looked deep into her eyes. 'Anna . . . can I stay? Here with you and Ruthie? I don't know what I'm gonna do for a job, but I have several million dollars in the bank that should tide me over for a while.'

Anna felt her face light up, cheeks stretching with joy as she moved on the bench, throwing her arms around him and holding on tight. And then she drew away, putting her hands on either side of his face, pausing.

'What?' Sam asked her.

'I'm just checking. Was that the question? Or is there another one coming? Like . . . will you break into the Globe with me again? Or, shall we have cocktails at the tepee bar on our way back?'

Sam smiled at her. 'That was the question.'

'Well, the answer's yes to all of them,' Anna answered. 'Yes! Yes! Yes!' And then she gasped delightedly as something caught in her peripheral. 'Oh, Sam, look! It's the deer.'

She clasped his arm and rested her head on his shoulder as three sleek-bodied antlered deer bobbed across the grass ahead of them looking like they might be on their way to pull that festive sleigh tonight.

Sam sighed. 'You know what? I already love living here.'

Seventy

Anna, Ruthie and Sam's home, Richmond

Christmas Day

'Is that the rabbit in your hands? God, the English are crazy weird! Are you gonna eat that instead of turkey?'

Sam saw the look on Ruthie's face change from sunshine day to frosty winter storm as they sat at the kitchen table, his laptop showing Tionne on FaceTime.

'Ti doesn't mean it, Ruthie,' Sam told her. 'This is Mr Rocket, Ti. He's Ruthie's pet rabbit.'

'Well, hey there, Mr Rocket,' Tionne said, her face getting closer to the screen. 'You are so cute . . . and not juicy at all.'

'Tionne!' Sam admonished.

'Do you eat family members in Cincinnati?' Ruthie countered. 'Or just ice cream? Sam says you eat ice cream until it comes out of your ears. I've never seen ice cream come out of anyone's ears before.'

'Ready?' Tionne asked, turning her ear to the screen.

Ruthie covered her eyes with her hands. 'Eww!'

'Let's start over,' Sam encouraged them both. 'Merry Christmas, Ti.'

'Merry Christmas, Sam. Merry Christmas, Ruthie, it's good to meet you. Sam's told me all about you and I saw some super-cool dance stuff going on.'

'Sam got me this baton that shoots rainbow ribbons out

of the top of it and he got me a glittery ornament that looks just like Mr Rocket. And he got me boxing gloves so I can learn to punch my bullies' faces in,' Ruthie announced.

'I did not say that,' Sam replied. 'I said so you can protect yourself.'

'I'm going to go and get them. Give me Mr Rocket. He needs to have a sleep after all those sprouts Mum gave him.' She picked her pet up and rushed from the kitchen.

'Hey, bro, so, how are things there?' Tionne asked.

'Things are . . . I don't know, Ti, how do you explain real happiness when you've never really had it before?' Sam said.

'Have you been on the tequila? What time is it over there?'

'I had something weird called Babycham. It was Anna's grandmother's favourite drink so she has some every Christmas as a tradition. But no, I'm not drunk, just happy. Which is super-crazy seeing as I have no football career, my life is being dissected over the internet and I have a disease no one can cure.'

'And you're nearly twenty-six,' Tionne said.

'Sshh,' Sam said. 'I haven't told Anna when my birthday is yet.'

'Why not?'

'Well, you know, there's a lot going on here.'

'So, don't keep me in suspense! Where *is* Anna? I wanna see the woman who is getting my brother all sick with love.' She made throwing-up noises complete with the actions.

'If I told you she was washing a cat would you believe me?'

'Well, you have a rabbit at your dinner table and he isn't being carved so . . .'

'Hello!' Anna said, putting her hands on Sam's shoulders as she rushed into the room. 'Sorry, Cheesecake hasn't quite got the hang of washing their rear-end yet. So, you're Tionne. And . . . I can clearly see you're the influencer Sam was photographed with that I was totally not grinding my teeth over.'

'Was it a great photo?' Tionne asked.

'It was a great photo,' Anna said, nodding. 'And it's very nice to see you here now. Happy Christmas!'

'Well, Sam said you were beautiful and . . . you really are. I love your hair. I'm always too chicken to have mine cut any way different.'

'Oh, well, thank you. But I love *your* hair! The red streaks are very festive.'

'I was bored with the blue and I thought, hell, why not, I could be diagnosed with a life-threatening condition any day soon so go big or go dead, right?'

Sam watched Anna give his sister a tentative smile.

'That's her humour,' Sam told Anna. 'I got the better kind.'

'Mum! Can you help me strap up my hands?' Ruthie called from the other room.

'I'll be back. Don't drink all the Babycham,' Anna said, heading out of the kitchen again.

'Your house is like CUT,' Tionne said, referring to their local train station back in Cincinnati.

'It gets real crazy when Anna's friends are all here but, it's nice, you know. Different to leading the bachelor life with nothing but buckwheat smoothies for company or Chad telling me buckwheat smoothies are gonna kill me faster than fries. It's . . . so much more.' He took a breath. 'How are Mom and Dad doing? Are you going over there for Christmas lunch?'

'I am, and Mom's invited some friends from church as she's finally realised she has way too much food. I'm a little concerned about someone called Bradley who's coming over though. Mom's mentioned him once too often and the fact he's single. I really don't wanna be hit on on Christmas Day.'

Sam smiled. 'Give the guy a chance.'

'He's from the church!'

'Which could mean he's a nice guy.'

'I know,' Tionne said. 'That's my issue!'

Sam smiled and drank in everything about his sister. Her crazy hair, her wide smile and dark eyes like his, her up-to-the-second clothes. He was going to miss her when he was here and she was back in the US. But that was what air travel was for and he knew she would love visiting Richmond as much as he was sure Anna and Ruthie were going to love visiting Ohio.

'Don't let them dwell on waiting for the results,' Sam said. 'You neither.'

'What results?' Tionne teased.

'I know it's hard waiting but, you know, whatever the outcome, life goes on, right?'

'Right,' Tionne agreed. 'And that's what I told Frankie when she rang me last night.'

'What?' Sam exclaimed. 'But I told her to take time off, go visit her sister. Why was she calling you?'

'She told me she'd had a voicemail message from, in her words, "someone called Anna who said she loves you". She thought that was important to pass on to you in "Bermuda".'

A smiled spread across Sam's face then as Anna and Ruthie came back into the kitchen, Ruthie wearing her new boxing gloves.

'What did you say? Could you say it again?' Sam asked. 'Someone called Anna says she loves me.'

Ruthie started grinning, jabbing her boxing gloves towards Tionne as she got back behind the screen. Sam looked at Anna who was shaking her head and seeming a little bit bashful all of a sudden.

'That's what she said,' Tionne replied. 'Oh and she said thank you for the pink wineglass with "Be More Chill" written on it.'

'She opened it already?'

'One of her nephews sat on it and the paper ripped. It survived though. She said she's gonna fill it with bourbon if she has to watch *Encanto* one more time.'

'Did you like your gift from me?' Sam asked.

'I had ice cream for breakfast out of it. I loved it, Sam. And if I talk to the bowl it's gonna replace you for conversation every second Friday. Ruthie, hit my brother hard on the shoulder. He can take it.'

'Ow!' Sam said as Ruthie punched him. 'Right, we're gonna go, I think I need to give Ruthie some lessons.'

'OK, just, give me a second with Anna, will you?'

Anna sat down in the seat Sam had just vacated and smiled at Tionne. 'Should I be scared? You sounded serious.'

'I am serious,' Tionne replied.

'Oh.'

'You are making my brother stupid happy and I am absolutely here for it all. He's never been like this before and boy does he deserve it. But I also know how much he overthinks. And I don't want him to worry about me or Mom or Dad because we've got this here without him and he needs to know that. Like we all told him when he told us about you, it's his time now, to do what's best for him, to stop second guessing his every move.'

Anna nodded. 'OK.'

'And just confirm that you have a spare bedroom in that glorious-looking house of yours so I can start planning my visit.'

'I have a spare bedroom and please bring the make-up that makes everything glitter because I think Ruthie would love it.'

'She would definitely love it,' Tionne confirmed.

'Great,' Anna said with a smile.

'OK, one last thing, and don't tell Sam I told you,' Tionne said. 'His birthday . . . it's New Year's Day.'

Seventy-One

Anna, Ruthie and Sam's home, Richmond

New Year's Eve

'Quiet everyone!' Neeta ordered. 'This is the world premiere of a new snack experience.' She had a tea towel over a large bowl looking like she was about to whip the cloth away like a seasoned magician.

'How can it be a world premiere when we tasted them at the Not Christmas Christmas party?' Ruthie asked.

'Ruthie,' Anna admonished a little.

'This is a *new* flavour,' Neeta continued. 'Combining the experience of plant reproduction and growth from my husband, Pavinder, and the flavoursome spices from the heart of my grandmother's kitchen honed over the years by me.'

'Are they like poppadoms?' Kai said loudly.

'Sshh, Kai,' Lisa told him.

'Prepare to "feed your need"—'

'What? Feed your what? Did she say "weed"?' Kai asked.

'Try . . . Forest Yump!' Neeta finished. She pulled the cloth from the bowl and the scent of coriander, cumin and other hot spices filled the kitchen air.

'Forest Yump?' Kai queried. 'Is "yump" a word?'

'It actually means to leave the ground when going over a

high ridge,' Neeta answered. 'I thought it was symbolic to mine and Pavinder's marriage taking a new path with this plant crisps enterprise.'

'Wow,' Lisa said. 'And I was about to say I wasn't sure about the branding until then.'

'Please,' Pavinder said, arriving with another bowl of snacks and passing them around to everyone. 'We want honest opinions on what they taste like. But we have worked very hard together to get this seasoning exactly right, so I am confident.'

'It is going to be a new year and a new beginning for us all,' Neeta said.

Anna put her hand into the bowl and took a crisp, popping it into her mouth. An explosion of flavour wriggled over her tastebuds in all the best kinds of ways. These were delicious!

'Oh, Neeta, Pav, these are . . . incredible,' Anna said. 'Seriously, so good. Can I have another one?'

A smiling Pavinder brought more crisps over to her. 'We work so well together,' he told Anna. 'It made me remember all the reasons why I love Neeta so much. And it is giving her an opportunity to realise all the reasons why she prefers me to not be in her kitchen.' He laughed. 'I am halfway joking, of course.'

'What's the plan for the snacks? Because, seriously, I can help you with the branding if you want me to.'

'Our plan is to begin small. Stalls at food festivals and see where that takes us,' Pavinder told her.

'That sounds like a great idea,' Anna answered.

'And who would guess that it all started with some seedlings and an air-fryer?' Pavinder said happily.

Anna touched the necklace at her throat and really let the solid platinum rub against her fingers. This had been her Christmas gift from Sam. It was shaped into a tree of life, stars hanging from the branches, and it couldn't have been more appropriate. It was the story of them. Nature, life, fighting against it, adapting to it, learning to love every second of it, wishes for the future.

'It's nearly midnight,' Sam said, coming up behind her. 'Should we get the champagne ready for everyone to toast?'

'Yes, we should,' Anna agreed. 'You get the glasses and I will . . . get Ruthie.'

'Last time I saw her she was throwing some of her best punches at Kelsey,' Sam said.

'I'll go and get her.'

Anna knew Ruthie wasn't still with Kelsey. Because Ruthie was in her room putting the finishing touches to something she had pulled together in a week after Tionne's info-sharing on FaceTime. It had involved costume-making, a banner and something really special she hoped Sam was going to love. Anna went up the stairs and paused by the door of Ruthie's bedroom.

'It's not perfect,' Ruthie moaned, looking at the drawing and colouring laid out on the floor.

'It *is* perfect, Ruthie. Because you did it for Sam.' She moved into the room and admired her daughter's art.

'Do you really think he will like it?' Ruthie asked.

'I really think he will love it,' Anna assured. 'Now, bring it downstairs, pop it in the cupboard in the hall, we will all say Happy New Year, then sing—'

'Old Lang's Eyes,' Ruthie said.

'Almost,' Anna answered. 'And then we can put on the music and you can start Sam's birthday celebrations.'

'Are you happy now, Mum?' Ruthie asked poignantly. 'Because Dad made you really sad and I thought you might not laugh like you used to again.'

There were tears in Anna's eyes now as she looked at her very grown-up daughter who knew so much but projected it differently to anyone else. She put a hand on Ruthie's shoulder and squeezed. 'I am happy, Ruthie. And you make me laugh all the time.'

'Sam makes you laugh too. And he makes me laugh. And I hope he doesn't die too soon.'

'Me too,' Anna agreed.

'Right, you make sure the coast is clear. I understand that one now. I used to think it meant it was a nice day on the beach!'

'Happy New Year!'

'Happy New Year!'

'Here's to 2023 being the best year ever!'

Sam shook Paul's hand then high-fived Kai and Kelsey before getting smothered by a hug from Lisa. But he was looking for Anna. She had said a quick 'Happy New Year' and then dashed off across the kitchen away from him. And then suddenly the celebratory music was killed and all that could be heard was the popping of fireworks from outside. Until Ruthie appeared at the door . . . dressed as Captain America.

'Where are my lieutenants?' she asked the room, a serious expression on her face.

'We are here!'

Sam laughed. This was good. Neeta was dressed as Thor and Anna was dressed as Black Widow. The costumes were fantastic.

'The news from S.H.I.E.L.D. is that it is someone's birthday here among us. Someone who is turning twenty-six.'

Sam's smile dropped a little and then he knew. This was down to Tionne. He should have known she wouldn't let this birthday go by without mention.

'Would the person who is turning twenty-six please come into the centre of the room?' Ruthie asked.

It definitely hadn't sounded like a request, there was no doubt this was an order. Sam did as he was told, shaking his head at being the focus of all attention.

'Sam Jackman,' Ruthie said, her eyes almost getting lost as her mask slipped down. 'It is my duty to inform you that today you officially become part of a new family.'

Some music started and Ruthie began to move, firstly

robotically and then more balletic and interpretive. And then came the words:-

Anna and Ruthie want to say, a very Happy Big Birthday.
We are so pleased you're spending it here, even though
you now have no career.
You might die soon, no one knows, but you're super
strong and fight all my foes
We are glad that you're staying but want to make it for
real
So please hear this very special appeal

Sam was caught up in the words as Ruthie performed another dance section and the music decreased in volume.

Mr Rocket, Cheesecake, my mum and me, want you to
join us in our family
Will you hereby pledge today, to give up your Earth name
without delay
We don't feel like Heaths when we're here together so let's
create something we can all keep forever
Welcome, the Falcons, Sam, Anna and Ruthie, present,
correct and ready for duty
We are brave, we are strong, I'm the best looking, Mum
I'll admit is best at the cooking
Sam is our hero, he was that from the start and he's also
the one with the largest of hearts.
Arise, Sir Sam Falcon, be part of our troop, and now
everybody give a great big whoop!

When the whoop came Sam didn't really hear it. His heart was drumming in his head and tears were coming thick and fast like never before. And he was coming undone even more when Ruthie unfurled the banner with drawings of them all on it and the words 'The Falcon Family' at its centre. It was too much. It was more than he could ever have imagined would be his.

'Don't you like it?' Ruthie asked, taking off her mask and looking at him with concern.

'Oh, Ruthie, sure I like it! I love it! It's the most awesome thing I've ever seen.' He swallowed a huge lump in his throat. 'Can we hug?'

'As long as you don't touch my right arm,' Ruthie agreed, positioning herself so the rest of her was accessible.

He drew her in and thought about how lucky he was to be sharing time with this exceptional girl. This might have been the complete reverse of how he saw his future panning out – in all the ways – but this wasn't only different, this was *better*.

'Can I steal Sam away for a second?'

It was Black Widow. *His* Black Widow.

'Only if I can have him back for at least three straight hours tomorrow. He needs to keep up his Marvel movie-watching,' Ruthie said.

'Yes, Captain,' Sam answered, putting his hand to his head in a salute.

Anna led the way down the hall and opened the front door. The air was freezing and the sky was dark but occasionally it was lit up by a fizz of New Year fireworks going off across the town in a spritz of gold and silver.

'Wow, it's cold out here,' Sam said, pulling the door to behind him. 'Should I get us some jackets?'

'This won't take long,' Anna told him, turning on the threshold to face him.

'Are you OK?' Sam asked her. 'You're shaking.' He put a palm to her face and rested it there.

'I'm . . . OK,' she answered, the tremble to her voice giving her up. 'I just, hope you didn't feel ambushed back there. Halfway through Ruthie's performance I had this worry that it could be too much too soon.'

Sam smiled. 'Is this an age reference again? Because I'm literally almost twenty-seven now.'

She laughed, the action dissipating her nervousness.

'I love the Falcon Family,' Sam told her. 'More than love it.'

'It, you know, doesn't have to be anything we get changed on our passports or a certificate hanging on the wall . . . it was an idea Ruthie and I put together to put you officially into our family.'

She watched him muse on that for a while.

'I think I'd like a certificate at least,' he told her.

'I am sure that can be arranged.' Anna reached into her back pocket. 'But I do have something else for you.'

'Wait, that slinky catsuit has pockets?' Sam said, waggling his eyebrows.

She unfurled her fingers and showed him the ring she was holding. Somehow, thanks to a very helpful artisan on Etsy, she had managed to get this delivered for tonight. And her palm was shaking now as Sam picked it out of her hand.

'Leaves,' he said shaking his head. 'And stars. This is a nature ring, Anna.'

She smiled. 'It is. It's meant to be a bit like my necklace. Nature is, I don't know, *growing* on me.'

'It's beautiful,' Sam said softly. He was still looking at the etchings on the band, running his finger over the engravings.

'I don't want to be afraid of nature anymore, Sam. We might not be able to control it, but we can make the best of it. We can wonder at its beauty and we can cry at its destructiveness, but in among all of that we can choose how we perceive it, how we respond to it.'

'And if you drill it down,' Sam replied, 'nature brought me to you.'

'Then nature really is my new best friend,' Anna answered.

Sam slipped the ring onto the middle finger of his left hand then drew her into him, holding on tight.

'Happy New Year, Anna Falcon,' Sam whispered in her ear as more fireworks hit the sky.

She reached for his hand and held it in hers. 'Happy birthday, Sam.'

Epilogue

Feast, Richmond

31st January

It was close to a proud mother moment. Anna beamed as Mr Wong in his smart new Feast uniform – all black trousers and black shirt with the orange logo on the left breast – stood at the door of the completely refurbished restaurant ready to open to its first customers. As soon as the seasonal festivities had ended, Mr Wong had got to it with the renovations and the interior of the building was unrecognisable. Gone were the chip shop counter, the cheap red paper lanterns and the faded flags of Italy and in was sleek, minimalist chic where the décor was concerned, and bountiful platters of food kept hot under state-of-the-art warmers and chef's stations where the cooking would wow. The takeaway area was tastefully cordoned off to separate Full Feast from Fast Feast and it already had a five-star hygiene rating from a visit last week.

'. . . and I want to say the biggest thank you to the genius behind the new enterprise, my now very good friend, Anna Heath,' Mr Wong announced. He slapped his hands together in a clap that had no right to be quite that loud and the gathered crowds followed suit.

'Anna Falcon,' Ruthie muttered.

'Mr Wong doesn't know that,' Anna reminded her.

'Well, he should,' Ruthie answered, folding her arms

across his chest. 'I'll tell him when he's finished talking. If he *ever* finishes talking. All his food will get cold if he takes too long.'

'Oh no, Ruthie,' Neeta said. 'I believe Mr Wong has the elite range of warmers, I've researched a great number of them. If our Forest Yump sales go well, Pavinder and I are thinking of looking into horse chestnut bakes and fries incorporating Butcher's Broom. The health benefits are extraordinary.'

'. . . so now, it is the moment we are all waiting for. It is time to cut the ribbon. That is orange, like our logo, and please, as you come into the restaurant, take a mandarin. This is good luck and prosperity for you and for Feast,' Mr Wong said.

Everybody clapped again.

'Please, everyone, put your hands together for the NFL superstar from America – who has eaten here already and given Feast a five-star endorsement – Sam Jackman!'

'Sam Falcon,' Ruthie moaned.

'Clap, Ruthie,' Anna urged.

'And, Paul, do one of your really loud annoying whistles!' Lisa ordered.

Paul didn't need any further encouragement and he put his fingers to his lips and blew hard. Kai cheered and Kelsey put her fingers in her ears a little too late.

Sam smiled for the two local photographers who had been told to only make this about Feast or there would be no photos at all and then Anna watched him put scissors to the ribbon.

'It is a real honour to be here today, opening what is gonna be a magnificent addition to the area. It's fine dining in, it's fine dining to take out and it's leftover fine dining to distribute to the needy. I don't know about all of you but that makes my soul very happy.' He smiled at the crowd. 'So, let's get in there. I declare Feast open for business!' He snipped the ribbon.

A huge roar of approval went up, followed by the sound

of firecrackers and then a giant windsock-style inflatable air dancer sprung up out of nowhere and started wafting floppy arms around the car park, its T-shirt branded with 'Feast'. That might be fun and quirky for today but Anna was going to make sure that wasn't a permanent fixture.

'You know, if we keep eating here, I'm not going to make 2023's sexiest man alive poll,' Sam told Anna, his mouth full of Cajun chicken wings. 'I don't think my abs are still a thing.'

'Oh, they're a thing,' Anna answered. 'Trust me they felt perfectly a thing last night.'

'But I have been thinking about my fitness,' Sam said, digging his fork into the food left in his recyclable container as a queue gathered to get into the takeaway section.

'You have?'

'Well, there's no research that suggests being fit and healthy stops the onset of Huntington's, but there is evidence that it helps with symptoms once you have them so . . .'

'Oh, God,' Anna said. 'I think I know what you're going to say next.'

'Really? Have we got to that stage yet? We've only been living together a month.'

'Paul's going to set up the rugby team, isn't he? You're going to play,' Anna said.

'Anna Falcon, you can read me already,' Sam replied, grinning.

He'd told Frankie he wasn't going back to the Bisons, he wasn't going back to Cincinnati permanently full stop. She didn't understand. Frankie was Frankie, her life was business and organising chaos and, no matter how much anyone might try to advise her otherwise, she liked it that way. For Sam though, American football wasn't going to be at the core of him anymore. Moving forward he was going to have new goals, a family here in Richmond, and he was researching ways to use his skills to do good. There were many charities and youth groups he'd discovered, who were always looking for volunteers with relevant experience to help with fitness, gaining confidence, self-improvement; and Sam couldn't think of anything more rewarding. That's what he wanted now, to make a difference in the time he had, to make his life about benefitting others.

And he could breathe a whole lot easier now both his mom and Tionne had received the news that neither of them carried the positive gene for Huntington's disease. His prayers for a miracle had been answered. There was obviously still a question mark over his pop, who was still adamant that he wasn't going to have the test. It was likely that his dad was the carrier, but at fifty-seven years old and not showing any obvious impairments or warning signs yet, there was a possibility, albeit a slim one, that this did begin and end with Sam. That's what Sam hoped for now. However, Albert had made one concession: that he would attend a regular check-up with Dr Monroe and tell Dolores if he felt at all out of whack.

'You know that Ruthie wants to change her name to Ruthie Heath-Falcon-Jackman now,' Anna said, circling her arms around Sam's waist and looking up at him. 'She's decided she doesn't want to lose any of the names and she wants to have the same name as Ed and her new little brother when he arrives.'

He nodded. 'I like it.'

Anna laughed. 'I know but there is absolutely no way that any company is going to be able to get that on the name tapes I have to sew into her school uniform.'

'How about Ruthie HFJ? Sounds kinda funky,' Sam said, putting his food box down on the wall. 'Like a rapper.'

Anna flinched. 'Oh no, Neeta's told you, hasn't she? About me rapping to sell soup at the school fayre.'

'No, no no. Remember, it was definitely a jamboree,' Sam countered. 'With someone busting rhymes.'

She thumped his chest. 'Stop!'

371

'Never,' he said, catching her hand in his and looking into her eyes.

She kissed him then, long and slow and there was that pure joyful rush of emotion hitting his heart like it did every single time. Richmond and Anna may have started out as his home for the holidays, but this move was most definitely now destination endgame.

A Letter from the Author

Dear Reader,

I'm not crying, you are! But I really hope they are happy tears and you enjoyed Anna, Sam, and Ruthie's story. Did it make you feel warm and fuzzy? Who was your favourite character? I love hearing your thoughts so why not share them with me?

I must admit, this book was a hard one to write. For a lot of the time, I was grieving the loss of two close family members and writing Sam's story was particularly tough going. But I thought it was an important topic to focus on and poignant too – making the most of our lives while we can. Eat the cake! Dance in the rain! Buy ALL the books!

This novel also puts the spotlight on autism, and this is something I'm passionate about raising awareness of. Just like Anna, I am a mum of an autistic teen and a lot of Anna and Ruthie's experiences in the story are based upon things that happen in my home. I spoke to my teen about Ruthie and made sure they were happy with the character and the way I portrayed Ruthie's issues. Autism can be a superpower, but we do still need more understanding in schools, colleges, and workplaces so everyone can feel safe and included, and can get the most out of their individual and unique journeys.

Finally, if you LOVED *Wishing on a Star* why not leave a review on Amazon? It only has to be a few words, but it would mean the world to me and will help other readers make wise reading choices!

Mandy x

Meet Mandy on social media
Twitter: @mandybaggot
Facebook: @mandybaggotauthor
Instagram: @mandybaggot
Website: www.mandybaggot.com

Acknowledgements

My fantastic agent, Tanera, thank you for all your support during the really trying times I had when writing this book. I don't think I've ever had to lean on you so hard and I am so grateful for you propping me up – and for all the flowers and cards.

Huge thanks to my friends Sue Fortin and Rachel Lyndhurst. You both say all the right things at the right times, and I am so lucky to have you both. Sorry I've been so needy!

My Bagg Ladies – thank you for always leaping to promote my books and for being the best team ever.

Thank you to everyone who answered my many questions about Huntington's disease and genetic testing. I hope I've made Sam's diagnosis as true to life as possible and have managed to highlight everything patients and their families must go through in this situation.

My editor, Hannah Smith, thank you for giving me the little bit of extra time I needed to finish this book in difficult circumstances. And thank you for not panicking when I said, 'this is the hardest book I've ever written' and allaying my concerns. You've always been one of my biggest supporters and I appreciate that so much.

About the Author

Mandy Baggot is an international bestselling and award-winning romance writer.

The winner of the Innovation in Romantic Fiction award at the UK's Festival of Romance, her romantic comedy novel *One Wish in Manhattan* was also shortlisted for the Romantic Novelists' Association Romantic Comedy Novel of the Year award in 2016. Mandy's books have so far been translated into German, Italian, Czech and Hungarian.

Mandy loves the Greek island of Corfu where she has a home. Also a singer, she has taken part in ITV1's *Who Dares Sings* and *The X-Factor*. Most recently, Mandy took part in BBC1's Ready Steady Cook with Greek celebrity chef, Akis Petretzikis.

Mandy is a member of the Society of Authors and lives near Salisbury, Wiltshire, UK with her husband and two children. *Wishing on a Star* is Mandy's 25th book.

About Embla Books

Embla Books is a digital-first publisher of standout commercial adult fiction. Passionate about storytelling, the team at Embla publish books that will make you 'laugh, love, look over your shoulder and lose sleep'. Launched by Bonnier Books UK in 2021, the imprint is named after the first woman from the creation myth in Norse mythology, who was carved by the gods from a tree trunk found on the seashore – an image of the kind of creative work and crafting that writers do, and a symbol of how stories shape our lives.

Find out about some of our other books and stay in touch:

Twitter, Facebook, Instagram: @emblabooks
Newsletter: https://bit.ly/emblanewsletter